Praise for *Sacré Bleu*

"Can Moore find the funny in gloomy Van Gogh? If anybody can-can, count on Moore."　　　　　　　　　　　　　　　　　　—*USA Today*

"*Sacré Bleu* is a consistently compelling blend of love story, mystery, and 'what if?' art history lesson."　　　　　　　　　　—*Entertainment Today*

"Mingling comedy and mystery, Moore crafts an intricate story that teases the reader with numerous twists and bawdy humor. . . . [T]his is an imaginative and amusing look at the Impressionist era, and Moore's prose is fresh and engaging."　　　　　　　　　　　　—*Booklist*

"Art history is playfully—and perilously—rewritten in this ambitious novel. . . . Fans of Moore's mix of wit and slapstick will be pleased."

—*Publishers Weekly*

"Moore's humor is, as ever, sweetly juvenile, but his arty comedy also captures the courage and rebellion of the Impressionists with an exultant *joie de vivre*."　　　　　　　　　　　　　　　　—*Kirkus Reviews*

"Moore (*Fool; You Suck*) set out to write a book about the color blue. What he ended up with is a surprisingly complex novel full of love, death, art, and mystery. . . . Don't let Moore's quirky characters and bawdy language fool you. His writing has depth, and his peculiar take on the impressionists will reel you in. One part art history (with images of masterpieces interspersed with the narrative), one part paranormal mystery, and one part love story, this is a worthy read."

—*Library Journal* (starred review)

"The true joy in *Sacré Bleu* stems from Moore's writing. . . . His writing contains the rare combination of poetry and humor; where one moment you find yourself rereading a passage for its sublime imagery, and the next, you are grinning over a well-placed wisecrack. . . . Of course, it wouldn't be a Moore novel without a healthy dose of sex, debauchery and, yes, demons. Those very same traits helped create some of the most beloved art in history, and, in turn, an excellent novel."

—*Dallas News*

"[A]nother exceedingly bizarre, often raucous, and consistently delightful journey into the sweetly demented mind of novelist Christopher Moore." —*Philadelphia Inquirer*

"*Sacré Bleu* is big fun." —*Pioneer Press* (St. Paul)

"[A] delightfully ribald romp." —*Washington Post Book World*

Sacré
Bleu

Sacré Bleu

A Comedy d'Art

CHRISTOPHER MOORE

WILLIAM MORROW
An Imprint of HarperCollins*Publishers*

Art throughout is in the public domain. Images courtesy of the author.

Grateful acknowledgment is made for the source of the epigraphs on pp. 93 and 289. From Wassily Kandinsky, *Concerning the Spiritual in Art*, M. T. Sadler (translator), Dover Publications (1977 paperback edition).

P.S.™ is a trademark of HarperCollins Publishers.

HarperCollins books may be purchased for educational, business, or sales promotional use. For information please write: Special Markets Department, HarperCollins Publishers, 10 East 53rd Street, New York, NY 10022.

A hardcover edition of this book was published in 2012 by William Morrow, an imprint of HarperCollins Publishers.

FIRST WILLIAM MORROW PAPERBACK EDITION PUBLISHED 2012.

Designed by Jamie Lynn Kerner

Library of Congress Cataloging-in-Publication Data has been applied for.

ISBN 978-0-06-177975-6

12 13 14 15 16   OV/RRD   10 9 8 7 6 5 4 3 2 1

Sacré Bleu

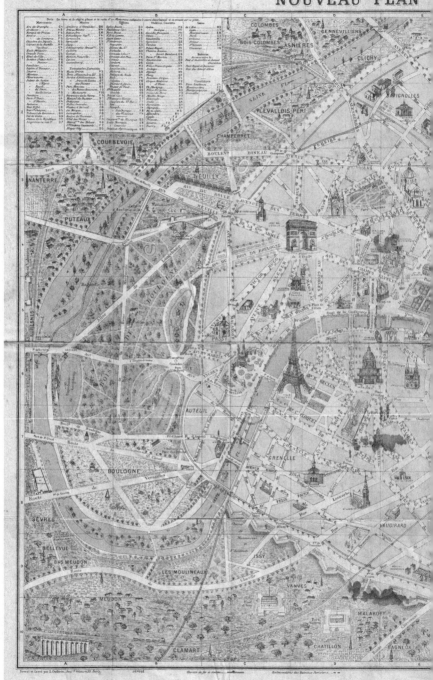

NOUVEAU PLAN

Part I

Sacred Blue

I always feel like a traveler, going somewhere, toward some
destination. If I sense that this destination doesn't in fact
exist, that seems to me quite reasonable and very likely true.
—Vincent van Gogh, July 22, 1888

Well, I have risked my life for my work, and it has cost me
half my reason—
—Vincent van Gogh, July 23, 1890

Prelude in Blue

This is a story about the color blue. It may dodge and weave, hide and deceive, take you down paths of love and history and inspiration, but it's always about blue.

How do you know, when you think *blue*—when you say *blue*—that you are talking about the same blue as anyone else?

You cannot get a grip on blue.

Blue is the sky, the sea, a god's eye, a devil's tail, a birth, a strangulation, a virgin's cloak, a monkey's ass. It's a butterfly, a bird, a spicy joke, the saddest song, the brightest day.

Blue is sly, slick, it slides into the room sideways, a slippery trickster.

This is a story about the color blue, and like blue, there's nothing true about it. Blue is beauty, not truth. "True blue" is a ruse, a rhyme; it's there, then it's not. Blue is a deeply sneaky color.

Even deep blue is shallow.

Blue is glory and power, a wave, a particle, a vibration, a resonance, a spirit, a passion, a memory, a vanity, a metaphor, a dream.

Blue is a simile.

Blue, she is like a woman.

One

WHEAT FIELD WITH CROWS

Auvers, France, July 1890

On the day he was to be murdered, Vincent van Gogh encountered a Gypsy on the cobbles outside the inn where he'd just eaten lunch.

"Big hat," said the Gypsy.

Vincent paused and slung the easel from his shoulder. He tipped his yellow straw hat back. It was, indeed, big.

"Yes, madame," he said. "It serves to keep the sun out of my eyes while I work."

The Gypsy, who was old and broken, but younger and less broken than she played—because no one gives a *centime* to a fresh, unbroken beggar—rolled an umber eye to the sky over the Oise River Valley, where storm clouds boiled above the tile roofs of Pontoise, then spat at the painter's feet.

"There's no sun, Dutchman. It's going to rain."

"Well, it will keep the rain out of my eyes just as well." Vincent studied the Gypsy's scarf, yellow with a border of green vines embroidered upon it. Her shawl and skirts, each a different color, spilled in a tattered rainbow to be muted under a layer of dust at her feet. He should paint her, perhaps. Like Millet's peasants, but with a brighter palette. Have the figure stand out against the field.

"Monsieur Vincent." A young girl's voice. "You should get to your painting before the storm comes." Adeline Ravoux, the innkeeper's daughter, stood in the doorway of the inn, holding a broom poised not for sweeping but for shooing troublesome Gypsies. She was thirteen, blond, and though she would be a beauty one day, now she was gloriously, heartbreakingly plain. Vincent had painted her portrait three times since he'd arrived in May, and the whole time she had flirted with him in the clumsy, awkward manner of a kitten batting at yarn before learning that its claws may actually draw blood. Just practicing, unless poor, tormented painters with one earlobe were suddenly becoming the rage among young girls.

Vincent smiled, nodded to Adeline, picked up his easel and canvas, and walked around the corner, away from the river. The Gypsy fell in beside him as he trudged up the hill past the walled gardens, toward the forest and fields above the village.

"I'm sorry, old mother, but I've not a *sou* to spare," he said to the Gypsy.

"I'll take the hat," said the Gypsy. "And you can go back to your room, out of the storm, and make a picture of a vase of flowers."

"And what will I get for my hat? Will you tell my future?"

"I'm not that kind of Gypsy," said the Gypsy.

"Will you pose for a picture if I give you my hat?"

"I'm not that kind of Gypsy either."

Vincent paused at the base of the steps that had been built into the hillside.

"What kind of Gypsy are you, then?" he asked.

"The kind that needs a big yellow hat," said the Gypsy. She cackled, flashing her three teeth.

Vincent smiled at the notion of anyone wanting anything that he had. He took off his hat and handed it to the old woman. He would buy another at market tomorrow. Theo had enclosed a fifty-*franc* note in his last letter, and there was some left. He wanted—no, *needed* to paint these storm clouds before they dropped their burden.

The Gypsy examined the hat, plucked a strand of Vincent's red hair from the straw, and tucked it away into her skirts. She pulled the hat on right over her scarf and struck a pose, her hunchback suddenly straightening.

"Beautiful, no?" she said.

"Perhaps some flowers in the band," said Vincent, thinking only of color. "Or a blue ribbon."

The Gypsy grinned. No, there was a fourth tooth there that he'd missed before.

"*Au revoir,* Madame." He picked up his canvas and started up the stairs. "I must paint while I can. It is all I have."

"I'm not giving your hat back."

"Go with God, old mother."

"What happened to your ear, Dutchman, a woman bite it off?"

"Something like that," said Vincent. He was halfway up the first of three flights of steps.

"An ear won't be enough for her. Go back to your room and paint a vase of flowers today."

"I thought you didn't tell futures."

"I didn't say I don't *see* futures," said the Gypsy. "I just don't tell them."

"And what will I get for my hat? Will you tell my future?"
Self-Portrait—Vincent van Gogh, 1887

HE SET HIS EASEL AT THE PITCHFORK JUNCTION OF THREE DIRT ROADS. THREE wheat fields lay before him and a cornfield behind. He was nearly finished with the painting, the golden wheat under an angry blue-black sky swirling with storm clouds. He loaded his brush with ivory black and painted a murder of crows rising from the center of the picture into an inverted funnel to the right corner of the canvas. For perspective, so the painting wasn't entirely about color on canvas, although many in Paris were beginning to argue that all painting was just color, nothing more.

He painted a final crow, just four brushstrokes to imply wings, then stepped back. There *were* crows, of course, just not compositionally convenient ones. The few he could see had landed in the field, sheltering against the storm, like the field workers, who had all gone to shelter since Vincent had started to paint.

"Paint only what you see," his hero Millet had admonished.

"Imagination is a burden to a painter," Auguste Renoir had told him. *"Painters are craftsmen, not storytellers. Paint what you see."*

Ah, but what they hadn't said, hadn't warned him about, was *how much* you could see.

There was a rustling behind him, and not just the soft applause of the cornstalks in the breeze. Vincent turned to see a twisted little man stepping out of the corn.

The Colorman.

Vincent stopped breathing and shuddered, feeling in every muscle a vibration, his body betraying him, reacting to the sight of the little man as a recovered addict might convulse with cravings upon the first sight of the drug of his downfall.

"You ran from Saint-Rémy," said the Colorman. His accent was strange, indistinct, the influence of a dozen languages poorly pronounced. He was round-bellied and slope-shouldered, his arms and legs a bit too thin for his torso. With his little cane, he moved along like a damaged spider. His face was wide, flat, and brown; his brow protruded as if to keep the rain out of the black beads of his eyes. His nose was wide, his nostrils flared, reminding Vincent of the Shinto demons in the Japanese prints his brother sold. He wore a bowler hat and a leather vest over a tattered linen shirt and pants.

"I was ill," said Vincent. "I didn't run. Dr. Gachet is treating me here."

"You owe me a picture. You ran and you took my picture."

"I've no need of you. Theo sent me two tubes of lemon yellow just yesterday."

"The picture, Dutchman, or no more blue for you."

"I burned it. I burned the picture. I don't want the blue."

The wind tumbled Vincent's painting off the easel. It landed faceup on grass between the ruts in the road. Vincent turned to pick it up and when he turned back, the Colorman was holding a small revolver.

"You didn't burn it, Dutchman. Now, tell me where the painting is or I'll shoot you and find it myself."

"The church," Vincent said. "There's a painting of the church in my room at the inn. You can see, the church is not blue in life, but I painted it blue. I wanted to commune with God."

"You lie! I have been to the inn and seen your church. She is not in that painting."

The first fat raindrop plopped on the little man's bowler, and when he looked up, Vincent snapped his paintbrush, sending a spray of ivory black into the Colorman's face. The Colorman's gun fired and Vincent felt the wind knocked out of him. He grabbed his chest and watched as the Colorman threw his gun to the ground and ran into the corn, chanting, "No! No! No! No!"

Vincent left the painting and the easel, picked a single, crushed tube of paint from his paint box and put it in his pocket, then, holding his chest, he trudged down the road that ran along the ridge above town a mile to Dr. Gachet's house. He fell as he opened the iron gate at the foot of the stone steps that led through the terraced garden, then crawled to his feet and climbed, pausing at each step, leaning on the cool limestone, trying to catch his breath before taking the next. At the front door he struggled with the latch, and when Madame Gachet opened it, he fell into her arms.

"You're bleeding," said Madame Gachet.

Vincent looked at the red on his hands. Crimson, really. Not red. A bit of brown and violet. There weren't enough words for the colors. Colors needed to be free of the constraint of words.

"Crimson, I think," said Vincent. "This is my doing. This is mine."

VINCENT AWOKE WITH A START, GASPING FOR BREATH. THEO WAS THERE. HE'D arrived from Paris on the first train after word came from Dr. Gachet.

"Calm, Vincent," said Theo in Dutch. "Why this? Why this, brother? I thought you were better."

"The blue!" Vincent grabbed his brother's arm. "You must hide it, Theo. The blue one I sent from Saint-Rémy, the dark one. Hide her. Let no one know you have her. Keep her from him. The little man."

"Her? The painting?" Theo blinked tears out of his eyes. Poor, mad, brilliant Vincent. He would not be consoled. Not ever.

"You can show it to no one, Theo." Vincent convulsed with pain and sat upright in the bed.

"Your paintings will all be shown, Vincent. Of course they will be shown."

Vincent fell back and coughed, a wet, jarring cough. He clawed at his trousers.

"Give it. Give it, please. The tube of blue."

Theo saw a crushed tin tube of paint on the bedside table and placed it in Vincent's hand.

"Here, is this what you want?"

Vincent took the tube and squeezed the last little bit of ultramarine blue out onto his finger.

"Vincent—" Theo tried to take his brother's hand, but Vincent took the blue and smeared it across the white bandages around his chest, then fell back again, letting out a long rattling breath.

"This is how I want to go," Vincent said in a whisper. Then he died.

Interlude in Blue #1: Sacré Bleu

The cloak of the Virgin Mary is blue. Sacred blue. It was not always so, but beginning in the thirteenth century, the Church dictated that in paintings, frescoes, mosaics, stained glass windows, icons, and altarpieces, Mary's cloak was to be colored blue, and not just any blue, but ultramarine blue, the rarest and most expensive color in the medieval painter's palette, the source mineral, more valuable than gold. Strangely enough, in the eleven hundred years prior to the rise of the cult of the Virgin, there is no mention in Church liturgy of the color blue, none, as if it had been deliberately avoided. Prior to the thirteenth century, the Virgin's cloak was to be depicted in red—color of the sacred blood.

Medieval color merchants and dyers, who had been geared up for red since the time of the Roman Empire, but had no established natural source for blue, were hard-pressed to meet the demand that rose from the color's association with the Virgin. They tried to bribe glassmakers at the great cathedrals to portray the Devil in blue in their windows, in hope of changing the mind-set of the faithful, but the Virgin and Sacré Bleu prevailed.

The cult of the Virgin itself may have risen out of an effort of the Church to absorb the last few pagan goddess-worshippers in Europe, some of those the remnants of worshippers of the Roman goddess Venus, and her Greek analogue Aphrodite, and the Norse, Freya. The ancients did not associate the color, blue with their goddesses. To them, blue was not even a real color but a shade of night, a derivative of black.

In the ancient world, blue was a breed of darkness.

Two

THE WOMEN, THEY COME AND GO

Paris, July 1890

L
UCIEN LESSARD WAS HELPING OUT IN THE FAMILY BAKERY ON MONTMAR-
tre when the news came of Vincent's death. A shopgirl who worked near Theo van Gogh's gallery Boussod et Valadon had come into the bakery to put together her lunch and dropped the news as blithely as if commenting on the weather.

"Shot himself. Right there in a cornfield," said the girl. "Oh, one of those lamb pasties, please."

She was surprised when Lucien lost his breath and had to steady himself on the counter.

"I'm sorry, Monsieur Lessard," said the girl. "I didn't know you knew him."

Lucien waved to dismiss her concern and composed himself. He was twenty-seven, thin, clean-shaven, with a shock of dark hair that swept across his forehead and dark eyes so deeply brown that they seemed to draw light from a room. "We studied together. He was a friend."

Lucien forced a smile at the girl, then turned to his sister Régine, six years his senior, a fine, high-cheeked woman with the same dark hair and eyes, who was working down the counter.

"Régine, I must go tell Henri." He was already untying his apron.

Régine nodded and turned away quickly. "You must," she said. "Go, go, go." She waved him off over her shoulder and he could see that she was hiding tears. They weren't tears for Vincent—she had barely known him—but for the death of another mad painter, which was the Lessard legacy.

Lucien squeezed his sister's shoulder as he passed. "Will you be all right?"

"Go, go, go," she said.

Lucien brushed flour from his trousers as he made his way across the square to the edge of the Montmartre, where he looked out over Paris, shining in the noonday sun. Streams of black smoke from the factories in Saint-Denis to the east threw shadows over whole neighborhoods; the river Seine was a silver-blue blade bisecting the city. The boulevards shimmered with heat and activity and the acrid steam of horse piss. Butte Montmartre was above it all, the Mountain of the Martyrs, where St. Denis, Paris's first bishop, was beheaded by the Romans in A.D. 251, and then, performing his final canonical miracle, picked up his severed head and carried it to the very spot where Lucien stood, and looking out over his city for the last time, thought, *You know what would go good right there? A great, skeletal tower of iron. But then, I've lost my head. Ugh.*

They say his head rolled all the way to what is now avenue de Clichy, and now Lucien set off down the two hundred and forty-two steps to that very same boulevard in the neighborhood around Place Pigalle, which was alive with cafés, brothels, cabarets, and on some mornings, the "parade of models" around the fountain in the square.

Lucien went first to Henri's apartment at 21 rue de la Fontaine, where there was no answer. Thinking Henri might be passed out after another late night of absinthe and opium, Lucien asked the concierge to open the door, but alas, the painter was not there.

"I have not seen the little gentleman for two days, Monsieur Lessard," said the concierge, a round, slope-shouldered woman with a bulbous nose and broken veins mapping her cheeks. "That one is out to bite the ass of the devil before he's done."

"If he comes in, please tell him I called," said Lucien. He hoped Madame would not mention to Henri about biting the devil's ass. It would inspire him, and not to art.

Then around the corner to the Moulin Rouge. The cabaret was not open to the public during the day, but sometimes Henri liked to sketch the dancers while they rehearsed. Not today; the dance hall was dark. Lucien asked after his friend at the restaurant Le Rat Mort, where the painter sometimes dined, and several of the cafés on avenue de Clichy before giving up and heading for the brothels. In the salon of the brothel on rue d'Amboise, a girl in a red negligee who had been dozing on a velvet divan when he came in said, "Oh yes, he has been here two days, maybe three, I don't know. Is it dark out? One time he wants to fuck, the next he wants to draw you combing your hair, the next he is making you a cup of tea, and all the time with his absinthe or cognac—a girl needs a personal secretary to keep track of his moods. This work is not supposed to be complicated, monsieur. When I woke yesterday, he was painting my toenails."

"Well, he is an excellent painter," said Lucien, as if that might ease the girl's anxiety. He glanced at her feet, but the whore wore black stockings. "I'm sure they are magnificent."

"Yes, they were as pretty as a Chinese box, but he used oil paint. He told me I had to keep my feet in the air for three days while it dried. He offered to help. A rascal, that one is."

"And where might I find him?" Lucien asked.

"He's upstairs with Mireille. She's his favorite because she's the only one littler than him. Second or third door past the top of the stairs. I'm not sure, listen at the door. The two of them laugh like monkeys when they're together. It's unseemly."

"*Merci,* mademoiselle," said Lucien.

As promised, when he reached the third door from the top of the stairs, Lucien heard laughter punctuated by a woman's rhythmic yipping.

Lucien knocked on the door. "Henri. It's Lucien."

From inside he heard a man's voice: "Go away, I'm riding the green fairy."

Then a woman's voice, still laughing: "He is not!"

"I'm not? I've been lied to! Lucien, it appears that I'm riding the completely wrong imaginary creature. Madame, upon completion of my business, I will expect a full refund."

"Henri, I have news." Lucien didn't think the death of a friend the kind of news one should shout through a whorehouse door.

"As soon as I have completed my—"

"Your business *is* completed," giggled Mireille.

"Ah, so it is," said Henri. "One moment, Lucien."

The door flew open and Lucien jumped back against the railing, nearly tumbling over to the salon below.

"*Bonjour!*" said Count Henri-Marie-Raymond de Toulouse-Lautrec-Monfa, who was quite naked.

"You wear your *pince-nez* when you're shagging?" said Lucien. Indeed, the *pince-nez* was perched on Henri's nose, which abided at the level of Lucien's sternum.

"I am an artist, monsieur, would you have me miss a moment of inspiration due to my poor eyesight?"

"And your hat?" Henri wore his bowler hat.

"It's my favorite hat."

"I will vouch for that," said Mireille, naked but for her stockings, who slid from the bed and padded over to Henri, snatched the cheroot from his lips, then scampered away to the washbasin, puffing like a tiny marshmallow locomotive. "He loves that fucking hat."

"*Bonjour,* mademoiselle," said Lucien, remembering his manners even as he peeked around Toulouse-Lautrec's shoulder to watch the prostitute washing herself at the bureau.

"Ah, lovely, is she not?" asked Henri, following Lucien's gaze.

Lucien suddenly realized that he had stepped into the doorway and was now standing very close to his naked friend.

"Henri, would you put on some trousers, please!"

"Don't shout at me, Lucien. You come here at the crack of dawn—"

"It's noon."

"At the crack of noon, and drag me away from my work—"

"My work," said Mireille.

"Away from my research," said Toulouse-Lautrec. "And then—"

"Vincent van Gogh is dead," said Lucien.

"Oh." Henri dropped the finger he had raised in the air to mark his point. "I had better put on some trousers, then."

"Yes," said Lucien. "That would be better. I'll wait for you downstairs."

He hadn't meant to, but seeing the look on the painter's face, Lucien realized that he had just done to Henri what the shopgirl had done to him: opened a trapdoor in the world through which Vincent had dropped.

LUCIEN WAS ANXIOUS WAITING AMONG THE WHORES. THERE WERE ONLY three in the salon at this time of day (when the house probably supported thirty in the evening), but they all sat together on one of the round divans, and he thought it would be rude not to sit near them.

"*Bonjour,*" he said as he sat down. The girl in the red negligee who had directed him was gone, perhaps entertaining a customer upstairs. These three were new to him, or at least he hoped they were new. Two were older than he, a bit time tattered, and each had hair dyed a different unnatural shade of red. The other was younger, but very round and blond, and looked somewhat clownish, with her hair tied up in a knot on the top of her head, lips large and red, painted into an unlikely pucker of surprise. None of the three looked capable of being surprised anymore.

"I'm waiting for my friend," said Lucien.

"I know you," said the round blond. "You're Monsieur Lessard, the baker."

"The *painter,*" Lucien said, correcting her. *Damn it.* Henri had brought him here two years ago when he was in the throes of an agonizing heartbreak, and although through the mystic haze of brandy, absinthe, opium, and despair Lucien could remember nothing, apparently he had made the acquaintance of this rotund girl-clown.

"Yes, painter," said the blond. "But you make your living as a baker, right?"

"I sold two paintings just last month," said Lucien.

"I sucked off two bankers just last night," said the whore. "I'm a stockbroker now, no?"

One of the older whores elbowed the blond in the shoulder, then shook her head gravely.

"Sorry. You don't want to talk about business. Did you ever get over that girl you were crying about? What was her name? Josephine? Jeanne? You kept wailing it all through the night."

"Juliette," said Lucien. *What is Henri doing? He only had to get dressed, not paint the whole scene.*

"That's right, Juliette. Did you ever get over that slut?"

Another elbow, this one from the other whore, and to the ribs.

"Ouch. Bitch. I was just showing an interest."

"I'm fine," said Lucien. He was not fine. He was even less fine now that he thought he may have tried to find comfort on the body of this rough beast.

"Ladies," called Toulouse-Lautrec from the staircase. "I see you have met my friend Monsieur Lucien Lessard, painter of Montmartre." He was pacing off the steps with his walking stick, stopping on each step. Sometimes his legs hurt him more than others, like when he was coming off a binge.

"He was here before," said round clown.

Henri must have seen the alarm on Lucien's face, because he said, "Relax, my friend. You were entirely too drunk and sad to avail yourself of the ladies' charms. You remain as pure and virginal as the day you were born."

"I'm not—"

"Think nothing of it," Henri said. "I remain your protector. Apologies for the delay, it appears that my shoes escaped during the night and I had to borrow a pair." As he reached the foot of the stairs he lifted his trouser cuffs to reveal a pair of women's high-button shoes, rather larger than one was used to seeing in a women's style, for although Henri was short, only his legs were of small proportion, due to a boyhood injury (and his parents being first cousins); his other parts were man size.

"Those are my shoes," said round blond.

"Ah, so they are. I've made an arrangement with the madame. Lucien, shall we go? I believe lunch is in order. I may have not eaten in days." He tipped his hat to the whores. "*Adieu*, ladies. *Adieu*."

Lucien joined his friend and they walked through the foyer and out the door into the bright sun, Henri a bit wobbly on the high heels.

"You know, Lucien, I find it very difficult to dislike a whore, but that blond, Cheesy Marie, she is called, has managed to provoke my displeasure."

"Is that why you stole her shoes?"

"I did no such thing. A poor creature, trying to make her way—"

"I can see your own tucked in your waistband in the back, under your coat."

"No they aren't. That is my hunchback, an unfortunate consequence of my royal lineage."

As they stepped off the curb to cross the street a shoe dropped out from under Henri's coat and plopped on the cobblestones.

"Well, she was being unkind to you, Lucien. I will not stand for that. Buy me a drink and tell me what has happened to our poor Vincent."

"You said you hadn't eaten in days."

"Well, buy me lunch then."

"Did you ever get over that slut?"
In Rat Mort—Henri Toulouse-Lautrec, 1899

THEY DINED IN THE WINDOW OF THE DEAD RAT AND WATCHED PASSERSBY IN gay summer apparel while Toulouse-Lautrec tried not to vomit again.

"Perhaps a cognac to settle your stomach," said Lucien.

"An excellent idea. But I fear Cheesy Marie's shoes are ruined."

"*C'est la vie,*" said Lucien.

"I think Vincent's passing has upset my constitution."

"Understandably," said Lucien. He thought he, too, might have converted his repast to a spectral roar, if he'd tried to layer his dismay over a dead friend on top of three days and nights of debauchery as had Henri. They had both attended Cormon's studio with Vincent, painted alongside him, drank, laughed, and argued color theory with him in the cafés of Montmartre. Henri had once challenged a man who insulted Vincent's work to a duel, and might have killed him had he not been too drunk to fight.

Lucien continued, "I was in Theo's gallery just last week. Theo said that Vincent was painting like a fiend, that Auvers agreed with him and he was doing good work. Even Dr. Gachet pronounced him recovered from his breakdown in Arles."

"I liked his ideas about color and use of the brush, but his emotions were always so high. Perhaps if he could have afforded to drink more."

"I don't think that would have helped him, Henri. But why, if he was doing good work, and Theo had his expenses covered—"

"A woman," said Toulouse-Lautrec. "When a suitable time has passed, we should call on Theo at the gallery and look at Vincent's last paintings. I'll bet there is a woman. No man kills himself but it is for a broken heart; surely you know that."

Lucien felt a pain in his chest for his own memories and in sympathy for what must have been Vincent's suffering. Yes, he could understand. He sighed and, staring out the window, said, "You know, Renoir always used to say that they were all one woman, all the same. An ideal."

"You are incapable of having a discussion without bringing up your childhood around the Impressionists, aren't you?"

Lucien turned to his friend and grinned. "Like you are incapable of having one without mentioning that you were born a count and grew up in a castle."

"We are all slaves to our histories. I am simply saying that if we scratch van Gogh's history, you will find a woman was at the heart of his disease."

Lucien shuddered, as if he could shake the memory and melancholy off the conversation the way a dog shakes off water. "Look, Henri, van Gogh was an ambitious painter, talented, but he was not a steady man. Did you ever paint with him? He ate the paint. I'm trying to get the color of a *moulin* right and I look over and he has half a tube of rose madder on his teeth."

"Vincent did enjoy a fine red," said Henri with a grin.

"Monsieur," said Lucien. "You are a dreadful person."

"I'm simply agreeing with you—"

Toulouse-Lautrec stopped and stood up, his gaze trained out the window, over Lucien's shoulder.

"You remember when you warned me off of Carmen?" said Henri, putting his hand on Lucien's shoulder. "No matter how I felt, letting her go, it was the best thing for me, you said."

"What?" Lucien twisted in his chair to see what Henri was looking at and caught sight of a skirt—no, a woman, out on the street in a periwinkle dress, matching parasol and hat. A beautiful dark-haired woman with stunningly blue eyes.

"Let her go," said Henri.

In an instant Lucien was out of his chair and running out the door.

"Juliette! Juliette!"

Toulouse-Lautrec watched as his friend ran to the woman, then paused in front of her, as if not knowing what to do. Her face lit up at the sight of him, then she dropped her parasol and threw her arms around his neck, nearly leaping into his arms as she kissed him.

The waiter, who had been drawn out of the kitchen when he heard the door, joined Henri by the window.

"*Oh là là,* your friend has captured himself a prize, monsieur."

"And I fear it's going to soon become very difficult being his friend."

"Ah, perhaps he has some competition, eh?" The waiter pointed across the boulevard, where, straining to see around carriages and pedestrians, a small, twisted man in a brown suit and bowler hat was watching Lucien and the girl with a glint in his eye that looked to Henri like hunger.

Three

THE WRESTLING DOGS OF
MONTMARTRE, PARIS

1873

*"... A delicate thing in a white dress with puffy sleeves
and great ultramarine bows all down its front and at the cuffs."*
The Swing—Pierre-Auguste Renoir, 1876

L UCIEN LESSARD WAS TEN YEARS OLD WHEN HE WAS FIRST ENCHANTED BY the sacred blue. It was a minor enchantment, really, but even the storm that drowns an empire must begin with a single raindrop, and later, one might only remember a spot of moisture on the cheek and having the thought, *Is that a bird?*

"Is that a bird?" Lucien asked his father.

Père Lessard stood over the bread table in the back room of his bakery drawing patterns in the flour with a pastry brush, his forearms dusted white like great snowy hams.

"It's a sailing ship," said Père Lessard.

Lucien tilted his head this way and that. "Oh yes, now I see it." He didn't see it at all.

His father slouched, suddenly looking weary. "No you don't. I'm no artist, Lucien. I am a baker. My father was a baker, and his father before him. Our family has fed the people of the butte for two hundred years. I have smelled of yeast and breathed the dust of flour my whole life. Not one day did our family or friends go hungry, even when there was war. Bread is my life, son, and before I die, I will have made a million loaves."

"Yes, Papa," said Lucien. He had seen his father slide into melancholy like this before, usually, like now, right before dawn when they were waiting for the first loaves to come out of the ovens. He patted his father's arm, knowing that soon the bread would be ready and the bakery would boil with activity that would allow no time to grieve over ships that looked like birds.

"I would trade it all if I could lay down the colors of water like our friend Monet, or move paint like the joy in a young girl's smile like Renoir. Do you know what I am talking about?"

"Yes, Papa," Lucien said. He had no idea what his father was talking about.

"Is he going on about his pets again?" said Mother as she breezed into the room from the front, where she had been arranging the pastries in baskets. She was a stout, wide-bottomed woman who wore her chestnut hair up in a loose *chignon* that trailed tendrils that were either born of weariness or were simply attempting escape. Despite her size, she glided around the bakery as if dancing a waltz, her lips set in a bemused smile and a spark of annoyance in her eyes. Bemused and annoyed was more or less the lens through which Mère Lessard viewed the world. "Well, there are people waiting outside already, and it's for the bread, not that paint stain you are raffling off."

Père Lessard put his arm around Lucien's shoulders. "Promise me, son, that you will become a great painter and that you will not let a spiteful woman ruin your life as I have."

"A *beautiful* and spiteful woman," said Mother.

"Of course, *ma chère*," said Lucien's father, "but I don't need to warn him off of beauty, do I?"

"Warn him off taking in paint-spattered vagabonds as pets, then, would you?"

"We must forgive Madame her ignorance, Lucien. She is a woman and therefore hasn't the capacity to appreciate art, but one day she will realize that my painter friends are great men, and she will repent for her unkind words."

Lucien's parents did this sometimes—talked through him as if he were a hollow tube simply muting the harsh tone and timbre of their words. He had learned that at these times, it was best to stare at a distant and neutral spot on the wall and resist the urge to appear attentive until one of them formulated an exit line sufficiently droll to dismiss the whole exchange.

Mother sniffed the air, which was rich with the smell of baking bread, and harrumphed. "You have a few minutes before the bread is done. Monsieur, why don't you take your son outside to watch the sunrise. Once you turn him into a painter he'll never be up in time to see one again." And then she waltzed past the heavy wooden table and up the stairs to the family apartments.

Lucien and his father slipped out the side door of number 6 rue Norvins and crept down between the buildings and behind the back of the waiting customers, across the Place du Tertre, to look out over all of Paris.

The butte Montmartre rose four hundred feet above the north end of Paris. For hundreds of years Montmartre had been a village unto itself, outside of the city walls, but as the city walls moved out and were torn down to make way for boulevards, Montmartre had become a country village in the midst of one of the biggest cities in the world. If you were an artist in Paris, Montmartre was where you came to starve, and it was Père Lessard who kept you from it.

Père Lessard produced a small pipe from his apron pocket and lit it with a match, then stood with his hand on his son's shoulder, as he did six mornings a week, and smoked as they watched the city turn pink under the dawn.

This was Lucien's favorite part of the day, when most of the work was finished, school was still ahead, and his father spoke to him as if he was the only person in the world. He imagined himself a young Moses, the Chosen, and Father's pipe the Burning Bush, except that he was a short, French, Catholic Moses and didn't understand a word of the Hebrew that the bush was speaking.

"Look there, you can see the Louvre," said Père Lessard. "You know that before Haussmann changed Paris, the courtyard of the Louvre was a shantytown where workmen and their families lived? Monsieur Renoir grew up there."

"Yes," said Lucien, eager to show Father how grown-up he was. "He said he used to play pranks on Queen Amalia's guards when he was a boy." Lucien knew Monsieur Renoir better than Father's other painters, as Renoir had agreed to tutor Lucien in drawing in exchange for bread, coffee, and pastries. Despite their time together, Renoir didn't seem very fond of him. Lucien thought it might be the syphilis.

It had come up during their second lesson, when Lucien was lamenting that he just wasn't smart enough to be an artist.

"Art is not about thinking, Lucien," said Renoir. "It is about the skill in your hands. I am not an intellectual, I have no imagination. I paint what I see. There is more to be said in the look of a man's hands than in his discourse."

"But your hands are tiny, monsieur," said Lucien. Renoir *was* a very slight fellow. Madame Jacob, who owned the *crémerie* across the square, was always trying to convince him to marry one of her two daughters, who she promised would put some meat on his bones and save him from his domestic helplessness.

"What are you trying to say?" asked Renoir.

"Nothing," said Lucien.

"Your hands are tiny too," said Renoir.

"But I am only nine," said Lucien, who was only nine at the time.

"This is why no one likes you, Lucien," said Renoir. "You probably have small hands because you have syphilis."

Lucien didn't know what syphilis was, but he worried it would ruin him as a painter.

"You don't have syphilis," said Father. "Your hands are fine and strong from kneading dough. You will be a great painter."

"I don't think Monsieur Renoir thinks I will be great. He says I'm simple."

"To Renoir, simplicity is a virtue. Hasn't he told you how he loves simple women?"

"I don't think he means virtue simple," said Lucien. "I think he means stupid simple."

Not long after Renoir agreed to tutor Lucien, Père Lessard took the boy down the butte to the color shop of Monsieur Tanguy at Place Pigalle and bought him a drawing pad, pencils, a sanguine crayon, and some drawing charcoal. Then they rode on the top deck of a horse-drawn omnibus to the Louvre to look at paintings, so Lucien would have a reference point from which to start his career as an artist.

"There are many pictures of the Holy Mother," said Lucien. "But each is different."

"The Holy Mother has many faces, but you know it's her from her blue cloak. She is said to be the spirit in all women."

"Look, here she is naked and the baby Jesus has wings," said Lucien.

"That is not the Holy Mother, that's Venus, and that's not Jesus, that is Cupid, the Roman god of love."

"Wouldn't she have the spirit of the Holy Mother as well?"

"No, she is a pagan myth."

"What about Maman? Is the spirit of the Holy Mother in her?"

"No, Lucien, your mother is also a pagan myth. Come, look at these paintings of wrestlers."

Back on the butte, Lucien watched his father watch the sunrise break the horizon, turning the river Seine into a bright, copper-colored ribbon across Paris. A wistful smile shone in his father's eyes.

"Why don't you paint, Papa?" Lucien said. "I can make the bread."

"The racks are too heavy for you. And you are not tall enough to see in the top oven. And I am too old to learn. And if I did, I would have to do it in secret or my painter friends would tease me. And besides, I'm too old to start now, I could never be good."

"If you keep it a secret, why do you have to be good?"

"How do you ever expect to learn anything if you are always arguing, Lucien? Come, the loaves are ready to come out," Father said. He tapped out his pipe on the heel of his shoe, then cuffed Lucien playfully on the head and strode off across the square to work.

The crowd had grown around the bakery, maids and wives, young girls and old men, concierges, café owners, factory workers looking for a loaf to carry for their lunch, the odd whore, dancing girl, and piano player stopping for breakfast on the way home from a late night's labor. All trading *bonjours* and gossip as the smell of freshly baked bread grew tall in the morning air.

At the edge of the group Lucien spotted the painter Camille Pissarro and ran to him.

"Monsieur!" said Lucien, stopping a respectful distance away, resisting the urge to throw his arms out to be swept up for rough kisses from the artist. Pissarro was Lucien's favorite of Father's artist friends. He was a bald, hawk-nosed Jew with a wild, graying beard and fringe; a theorist and anarchist who spoke French with a lilting Caribbean accent, he could argue fiercely in the bakery or café with his artist friends one minute, then give his last *sou* to them for bread, coal, and color the next.

He had a son Lucien's age, who was also named Lucien (but there was no confusion when they played together, for reasons to soon be revealed), and a daughter, Jeanne-Rachel (called Minette), who was a year younger than Lucien. Minette was petite, and pretty, and could throw a rock as well as any boy. She inspired a love in Lucien so profound that it made him nearly breathless with the need to pull her hair and profess her passionate cooties to the world. Lucien was relatively sure that he would one day have to take her as his wife, if only she could be taught to be as spiteful as his mother, so she could properly ruin his life. But she was not with her father today.

"Rat Catcher!" called Pissarro, foiling Lucien's respectable-distance strategy by snatching the boy up by one arm and mercilessly planting a beard-cushioned kiss on each of Lucien's cheeks before dropping him back to his feet.

"Look, monsieur, how they gather to see who will win your painting."

"I think they gather for your father's bread," said Pissarro. He exchanged a warm handshake with Père Lessard, who was about to recite the virtues of his friend's painting and the deep ignorance of the Salon for rejecting his work when there came a tapping on the glass from inside and everyone turned to see Mère Lessard brandishing a *demitasse* spoon like a petite battle-axe, an eloquent and urgent eyebrow raised to convey that the loaves were ready to come out of the oven and Father could dawdle if he wished, and the bread could burn, but at some point he would have to sleep, and it should not surprise him in the least should he wake up dead with a small spoon driven into his brain by way of an ear or nostril.

"In a moment, my friend," said Père Lessard. "The loaves." He shrugged and hurried around the corner.

"I've been drawing," said Lucien. "Monsieur Renoir has been teaching me to draw what I see."

"Show me," said Pissarro.

Lucien was off in an instant, down the alley, in the back door, through the bakery, up the stairs, and back with his sketchbook before Pissarro could get a good ember going in his pipe.

"See?" said Lucien, handing the sketchbook to the painter. "It is two dogs I saw fighting in the Maquis yesterday."

Pissarro looked at the drawing, nodding and turning it in the air, holding it at arm's length while he studied it and stroked his great thundercloud beard, as if he were Jehovah surveying an extracted rib for creative possibilities.

"These dogs are not fighting."

"Yes they are. Like the paintings we saw in the Louvre," said Lucien. "Gecko-Roman wrestling, Father called it."

"Ah, of course," said Pissarro, as if it had become clear. "Yes, Gecko-Roman dog wrestling. Superb! I presume you haven't shown your wrestling dogs to Madame Lessard, then."

"No, monsieur, Mother doesn't appreciate art."

"Ah, well, then I must insist that you give it to me for my collection."

Lucien felt he would nearly burst with pride. "Really, monsieur, you want it?"

"It will hang next to a Cézanne. I believe he has an affinity for wrestling dogs."

"And you will tell Minette that I drew it?"

"Of course."

Lucien started to tear the drawing out of his sketchbook, then paused and looked up. Lucien had dark eyes that often seemed a bit too wide for his face, like those of a hungry kitten, and now they bore distress that bordered on tears. "But, monsieur, I don't want *your* Lucien to feel bad when he sees my wrestling dogs in your house."

Pissarro laughed. "Your friend has his own sketchbook, Rat Catcher, don't you worry about him."

Lucien smiled, tore out the page, and handed it to the painter, who folded it carefully in half and tucked it into his coat pocket.

A murmur rose in the crowd and there was polite maneuvering for position at the door. Mère Lessard pulled up the shade, turned the sign, and opened the door. Madame called out a joyful *bonjour* to the customers and welcomed them into the shop with a breezy flourish and a smile such as one might find on a pre-revolution Marie-Antoinette painted on a teacup, which is to say, sparkling with charm and warm possibility.

"Maman reserves her stormy side for her family," Père Lessard would say, "for the world she has only sunshine and butterflies."

It was then that she smacked young Lucien in the head with a baguette. The crunchy yet tender crust wrapped around his head, bending but not breaking, showing that the oven had been precisely the right temperature, there had been exactly enough moisture, and in fact, by the ancient Lessard test method, it was perfect. Lucien thought this was the way of all French *boulangers,* and he would be a young man before anyone explained to him that other bakers did not have a test boy who was smacked in the head with a loaf of bread every morning.

Madame Lessard held the perfect baguette up to the crowd. *"Voilà,"* she said, pronouncing the day's sales begun.

"May I pick the ticket, Maman? May I pick the ticket?" called Lucien, hopping up and down, crumbs falling from his hair before the customers, who waited four-deep at the counter, most of whom looked quite perplexed at his enthusiasm.

"I already have, Rat Catcher," said Lucien's oldest sister, Régine, who was sixteen and had joined her mother behind the counter. Régine had her father's dark hair and eyes, and stood taller than either of her parents.

Père Lessard said that she would make someone a fine wife someday, and in lieu of that, he could send her to Quebec, where she would be the prettiest lumberjack and Red Indian fighter ever. Régine held the winning ticket in the air. "Number forty-two," she said. "Does anyone have number forty-two?"

As it turned out, no one had number forty-two; in fact, no one in the bakery that morning had bought a ticket at all. An hour later the ticket had been tacked up on the wall under Pissarro's painting, a small landscape looking down from a hill in Auvers-sur-Oise, portraying the red tile roofs and the river below. Pissarro sat at the little café table outside the bakery with Père Lessard. Lucien danced from foot to foot beside the table, his schoolbooks tucked under his arm.

"We can't even give them away," said Pissarro forlornly.

"Nonsense," said Père Lessard. "The winner simply hasn't shown yet. And all the better if they don't. You have the ten *francs* we got for selling the tickets, and your magnificent painting will hang in my bakery where the people may admire it."

"But, Papa—" said Lucien, who was about to correct the arithmetic when Father shoved a buttered roll in his mouth. "Mmmpppf," Lucien continued with a spray of crumbs. After all, the tickets had only sold for a *sou* each, with twenty *sous* to the *franc*, and they'd only sold seventy-eight tickets—why, it was less than four *francs*! And Lucien would have said so if his father hadn't muzzle-loaded him with *un petit pain* while handing a ten-*franc* note across the table to Pissarro.

Across the square a donkey brayed, and they turned to see a bent little brown man in an ill-fitting suit trudging up the street, leading the donkey, but their attention was immediately captured by the girl who walked but ten paces ahead. Lucien's mouth fell open and a ball of half-chewed bread tumbled out of his mouth onto the cobbles. Two pigeons in the square cackled at their good fortune and made a fast walk for the gift from above.

"I'm not too late, am I?" the girl called. She held her raffle ticket before her.

She couldn't have been more than fifteen or sixteen, a delicate thing in a white dress with puffy sleeves and great ultramarine bows all down its front and at the cuffs. Her eyes matched the bows on her dress, too blue, really, and even the painter, a theorist and student of color, found he had to look a bit askew at her to keep from losing his train of thought.

Père Lessard stood and met the girl with a smile. "You are just in time, mademoiselle," he said with a bit of a bow. "May I?"

He plucked the ticket from the girl's hand and checked the number. "And you are the winner! Congratulations! And how lucky it is that the great man himself is here. Mademoiselle . . ."

"Margot," said the girl.

"Mademoiselle Margot, may I present the great painter, Monsieur Camille Pissarro."

Pissarro stood and bowed over the girl's hand. "Enchanted," he said.

Lucien, who was, indeed, enchanted—thought she might be the single most beautiful thing he had ever seen—stared at her, wondering if Minette, in addition to learning to be spiteful, might someday wear a dress with blue bows, and if her voice might take on the sound of a music box like Margot's, and her eyes sparkle with laughter, and if so, he would have her sit on the divan and he would just look at her without blinking, until water came to his eyes. He didn't know that it was strange for the sight of one girl to inspire love to the point of tears for another, because Minette had been his only love, but there was no question that the sight of Mademoiselle Margot had opened his heart for Minette so it felt like it might leap out of his chest with joy.

"Come inside, mademoiselle," said Père Lessard, deftly slipping his hand under Lucien's chin and closing the boy's mouth. "See your painting."

"Oh, I have seen it," Margot said with a laugh. "And I was wondering if instead of the painting, I might have one of your sticky buns as my prize."

The smile with which Pissarro had greeted the girl fell as if he'd been suddenly shot in the face with a paralyzing dart of Pygmy art critics from the darkest Congo. He sat down as if suddenly exhausted.

"I'm teasing," said Margot, touching Pissarro's sleeve coquettishly. "I am honored to have one of your paintings, Monsieur Pissarro."

The girl followed Père Lessard into the bakery, leaving Pissarro and Lucien outside, both a little stunned.

"You, Painter," came a scratchy voice. "Do you need colors? I have the finest hand-ground pigments." The twisted little man and his donkey had moved to the side of the table.

Pissarro looked up to see the little man waving a tin tube of paint in the air, the cap off.

"The finest ultramarine," said the Colorman. "Real color. True color. Cinnabar, madder, and Italian earths. None of that false Prussian shit." The little man spat at the pigeons to show his disdain for Prussians, man-made colors, and, in general, pigeons.

"I get my colors from Père Tanguy," said Pissarro. "He knows my palette. And besides, I have no money."

"Monsieur," said Lucien. He nodded to the ten-*franc* note, which Pissarro still held in his hand.

"Just try some ultramarine," said the Colorman. He capped the tube of paint and set it on the table. "If you like it, you pay. If not, no worry."

Pissarro picked up the tube of paint, uncapped it, and was sniffing it when Margot emerged from the bakery, dancing the small canvas in a great circle in front of her, her skirts swirling around her as she moved. "Oh, it's wonderful, Monsieur Pissarro. I love it." She held the canvas to her breast, bent, and kissed Pissarro on top of his bald head.

Lucien felt his heart leap with the lilt in her voice and he blurted out, "Would you like to see a picture of dogs wrestling?"

Margot turned her attention to Lucien now, and still clutching the painting to her bosom, she caressed his cheek and looked into his eyes. "Look at this one," she said. "Oh, these eyes, so dark, so mysterious. Oh, Monsieur Pissarro, you should paint a portrait of this one and his deep eyes."

"Yes," said Pissarro, who suddenly realized that he was holding a tube of paint and the twisted little man and his donkey were gone.

Lucien didn't remember seeing him leave. He didn't remember the girl leaving, or going on to school, or his lessons from Monsieur Renoir. He didn't remember anything that happened for the next year, and when he did remember again, he was a year older, Monsieur Pissarro had painted his portrait, and Minette, the love of his young life, was dead from fever.

It was a small enchantment, really, Lucien's encounter with the blue.

"These dogs are not fighting, Rat Catcher."
Self-Portrait—Camille Pissarro, 1873

Four

PENTIMENTO

1890

I LIKE A MAN WITH TWO STRONG EARS," SAID JULIETTE. SHE HAD LUCIEN BY the ears and was pumping his head back and forth as if to make sure that his ears had been nailed on properly. "Symmetry, I like symmetry."

"Stop it, Juliette. Let go. People are looking."

They sat on a bench across from the cabaret *Le Lapin Agile*, a small vineyard at their back, the city of Paris spread out before them. They had made their way up the winding rue des Abbesses, looking from each other's eyes only in glances, and although the day was warm and the climb steep, neither was out of breath or sweating, as if a cool pool of afternoon had opened just around the two of them.

"Well, fine then," said Juliette, turning away from him to pout. She popped open her parasol, nearly poking him in the eye with one of its ribs, then slouched and puffed out her lower lip at the city. "I was just loving your ears."

"And I love *your* ears," Lucien heard himself say, wondering, even though it was true, why he was saying it. Yes, he loved her ears; loved her eyes, as crisp and vibrant blue as the virgin's cloak; loved her lips, pert and delicate platform for a perfect kiss. Loved her. Then, since she was looking out over the city and not at him directly, the question that had been circling in his mind all afternoon, only to be chased away by his enchantment with her, finally lit on his tongue.

"Juliette, where in the hell have you been?"

"South," she said, her gaze fixed on Eiffel's new tower. "It's taller than I thought it would be when they started it." The tower had been barely three stories tall when she had disappeared.

"South? South? *South* is not an answer after two and a half years without a word."

"And west," she said. "It makes the cathedrals and palaces look like dollhouses."

"Two and a half years! Nothing but a note saying *'I'll return.'*"

"And I have," she said. "I wonder why they didn't paint it blue. It would be lovely in blue."

"I looked everywhere for you. No one knew where you had gone. They kept your job open at the hat shop for months, waiting for you." She had worked as a milliner, sewing women's fine hats, before she had gone away.

She turned to him now, leaned in close and hid them both behind the parasol, then kissed him, and just when he felt his head start to spin, she broke off the kiss and grinned. He smiled back at her, forgetting for a moment how angry he was. Then it came back to him and his smile waned. She licked his upper lip with the tip of her tongue, then pushed him away and giggled.

"Don't be angry, my sweet. I had things to do. Family things. Private things. I'm back now, and you are my *only* and my *ever*."

"You said that you were an orphan, that you had no family."

"That was a lie, wasn't it?"

"Was it?"

"Perhaps. Lucien, let's go to your studio. I want you to paint me."

"You hurt me," Lucien said. "You broke my heart. The pain was such that I thought I would die. I didn't paint for months, I didn't bathe, I burned the bread."

"Really?" Her eyes lit up the way the children's did when Régine set out the fresh pastries in the bakery.

"Yes, really. Don't sound so gleeful about it."

"Lucien, I want you to paint me."

"No, I can't, a friend has just died. I should look after Henri and talk to Pissarro and Seurat. And I have a cartoon I must do for Willette's *La Vache Enragée* journal." The truth was, he had more pain to vent on her, and he didn't want to leave her side for a moment, but he needed her to suffer. "You can't just pop back into my life from a street corner and expect—and what were you doing on avenue de Clichy in the middle of the day, anyway? Your job—"

"I want you to paint me nude," she said.

"Oh," he said.

"I mean, you can leave your socks on, if you'd like." She grinned. "But other than that, nude."

"Oh," he said. His brain had seized when she'd mentioned painting her nude.

He really wanted to remain angry, but somehow he had come to believe that women were wondrous, mysterious, and magical creatures who should be treated not only with respect but with reverence and even awe. Perhaps it was something that his mother used to say to him. She would say, "Lucien, women are wondrous, mysterious, and magical creatures, who should be treated not only with respect but with reverence, perhaps even awe. Now go sweep the steps."

"Mysterious and magical," his sisters would repeat in chorus, nodding, Marie, usually, holding the broom out to him.

Magical and mysterious. Well, that described Juliette.

But his father had told him that women were also cruel and selfish harpies who would as soon tear out a man's heart and laugh while he suffered as file their nails. "Cruel and selfish," said his sisters, nodding. Régine would snatch the last piece of pie from his plate.

This was also Juliette.

And his teacher Renoir had indeed told him, "All women are the same; a man needs to simply find his ideal and marry her to have all the women in the world."

She was that, Juliette, she was all women to him. He had been with girls before, had even been in love, but she had enveloped him, overwhelmed him like a storm wave.

"But even if you have found the one," Renoir continued, "it doesn't mean you won't want to see them all naked. It is a sick man who is unmoved by the sight of a pretty breast."

"I don't have colors, I don't have canvas for a picture that size," Lucien said.

"What size, *cher*?" She smiled coyly.

"Well it will have to be a large canvas, I think."

"Because I am a large woman? Is that what you're saying?" She pretended to be offended.

"No, because it must contain my feelings for you," said the painter.

"Oh, Lucien, that was the right answer." And she kissed him swiftly, then snapped the parasol shut and was on her feet like a soldier called to attention. "Come, we'll find you color. I know a dealer."

How had that happened? Lucien stood and stumbled after her. "I still have questions for you, Juliette. I'm still angry, you know."

"I know you are. Perhaps I will show you a satisfying way to vent your anger, no?"

"I don't know what that means," said Lucien.

"You will," she said. *Yes, he's the one,* she thought.

BACK ON AVENUE DE CLICHY, TOULOUSE-LAUTREC HAD APPROACHED THE Colorman.

"*Bonjour,* monsieur," said the Colorman. "You are a painter, no?"

"I am," said Toulouse-Lautrec.

When he was twelve, Henri's mother took him to Italy, and in the Uffizi Gallery in Florence, he saw a Tintoretto painting of the Blessed Virgin, in which there appeared to be the ghosts of dark faces in the sky, barely detectable, but the eager young artist couldn't help but notice.

"The effect is called pentimento," said the guide his mother had hired. "The master has painted over another painting, and over the years, the old image is beginning to show through. It is not clear, but you can see that something has come before and does not belong."

Henri had, upon seeing the Colorman, felt a dark pentimento rising in his mind, and somehow it had drawn him across the street.

"You need color, perhaps?" said the Colorman. He tapped the wooden case he carried, big enough, Henri noted, that the Colorman himself might have fit inside with only minor contortionism or dismemberment.

He was shorter than Henri, and twisted in a way that made the painter think that someone may have once packed him into his case with a cannon ramrod, with no concern for comfort or integrity of limb. The painter felt a sad affinity for the Colorman, even as the revulsion of something past and forgotten made the hair on the back of his neck rise.

"Don't I know you?" asked Henri. "Have we traded before, perhaps?"

"Could be," said the Colorman. "I travel."

"Don't you normally have a donkey to carry your wares?"

"Oh, Étienne? He's on holiday. Do you need color, monsieur? I have the finest earths and minerals, nothing false. I have the syrup from which masterpieces are poured, monsieur." The Colorman popped the latches on his case and opened it on the curb, displaying rows of tin tubes, held in place by bronze wires. He snatched one up, unscrewed the cap, and squeezed a dab of dark, bloodred paint onto his fingertip. "Crimson, made from the blood of Romanian virgins."

"Really?" said Henri. His head was spinning and he had to lean on his cane to steady himself.

"No, not really. But it is Romanian. Made from beetles handpicked from the roots of weeds near Bucharest. But they are ugly beetles. They might be virgins. I wouldn't fuck them. You want some?"

"I'm afraid I have all the paint I need. I have a lithograph to put on the stones today, a poster for the Moulin Rouge. And I appear to have some nausea which needs attending as well. My printer will have inks."

"Ach, lithography." The Colorman spat to show his disdain for all things to do with limestone and ink. "A fad. Once the newness wears off no one will do it. Perhaps some vermilion? Made from the finest cinnabar—I grind it myself—you know, to paint the redheads you love."

Henri stepped back and stumbled off the curb, barely catching himself before he fell. "No, monsieur, I must be going." He hurried away, as quickly as his hangover and the pain in his legs would allow, chased by a redheaded ghost he thought he had long left behind.

"I will call on you at your studio, monsieur," the Colorman shouted after him.

"THIS WON'T DO," SAID JULIETTE. SHE STOOD IN THE STUDIO THAT LUCIEN shared with Henri on rue Caulaincourt at the base of Montmartre. They had rented the rear flat on the first floor, so Henri didn't have to endure stairs when moving his canvases, but as artist's studios went, being on the rear bottom floor of a five-story building that was attached to other buildings on both sides and only had a narrow courtyard behind, it had a rather distinct flaw.

"There are no windows," Juliette said. "How can you work with no windows?"

"Look at all the gas lamps. And there's a changing screen for the models. And a water closet. And a stove for making tea. And a café table, and a bar, with everything you could want. And there's a window in the door." There was, indeed, a window in the door, oval, stained glass, and about the size of a modest fedora. It provided just enough light from the foyer to allow Lucien to light the gas lamps without tripping on the clutter and killing himself.

"No," Juliette said. She held her folded parasol as if she might have to use it as a weapon to fend off the canvases that were leaned against walls all around the studio in various states of drying. She took a swipe at an easel that stood empty in the center of the room, as if warning it to stay back. "I will look like a corpse in here. We need sunlight."

"But I mostly work here at night, anyway, when Henri is at the Moulin Rouge or one of his other, uh, workplaces. I have to work most days in the bakery until noon, and . . ." He slumped, unable to think of anything else positive to say.

"There must be another studio," she said, stepping close to him, pushing out her lower lip, and speaking in a pouty, baby-talk voice. "Somewhere where you can paint the warm, golden sunshine on my body." She made as if to kiss him, then pirouetted, her bustle nearly bumping him aside, and headed to the door. "Or not."

"Henri pays most of the rent," Lucien added weakly. "It's his studio, really."

"I can see that—the little troll in his cave, eh?"

She had stopped to look at a stack of canvases leaning against the wall by the door.

"Don't say that. Henri is a good friend to me. I couldn't afford a studio if not for him."

"This is one of Henri's paintings?" She bent down and held the top of the canvas at arm's length. It was the painting of a redheaded woman in a plain white blouse and black skirt, looking out a window.

"That's Henri's laundress, Carmen."

"She looks sad."

"I didn't know her well. Henri said he wanted to show how strong she was. Exhausted, yet still strong."

"Is she not around anymore?"

"Henri sent her away. Well, we persuaded him, along with his mother, to leave her. Then she went away."

"Sad," said Juliette. "But at least she had a window to look out of."

Take her home, eat with her, and sip wine, laugh softly at sad things,
make love to her and fall asleep in her arms; that's what he wanted to do.
The Laundress—Henri Toulouse-Lautrec, 1884

HENRI MADE HIS WAY TO THE SECOND FLOOR AND HIS APARTMENT. THE MAID had been there and there were fresh flowers on the table. He hung his coat and hat on the rack by the door and went immediately to the writing desk. His hand was shaking, whether from drink, or from seeing the Colorman, or both. Either way, a cognac could only help, so he poured himself one from the decanter, then sat down and took the last letter he had received from Vincent from the drawer.

> *My dear Henri:*
>
> *As you advised, the climate in the South is very conducive to painting out of doors, and capturing the colors in the hills not only challenges my abilities, but inspires me to work harder. It is the colors, however, that seem to slow my progress, and my spells have become even worse since coming here. What I thought would be escape from the mad pace of Paris, and from the other influences that threatened my health, has been no escape at all. He is here, Henri. The little brown Colorman is here in Arles. And even when I tell him to go away, I still find myself using his color, and my spells become worse. I lose whole days, only to find pictures in my room that I don't remember painting.*
>
> *People at the inn where I sometimes have my supper tell me I have been there, raging drunk in the middle of the day, but I swear it is not the loss of time that comes from too much drink.*
>
> *Theo has written me that I should not use colors at all, put them down and work on my drawings. I haven't told him about the Colorman, or the girl, as I don't want him to worry. You, my friend, are the only one I have confided in, and for not calling me mad, I thank you. I hope that you are no longer vexed by your own troubles in that regard and that your work is going well. Theo tells*

*me that he has sold two of your paintings, and I am happy for you.
Perhaps, by coming here, I have drawn the sickness away from
Paris, and you can work in peace.*

*I still hope to be able to start a studio of like-minded painters
here in the South. Theo is trying to persuade Gauguin to join me,
and it looks as if he will come. Perhaps it is only my imagination,
a symptom of my illness, that makes me think the little Colorman
is dangerous. After all, his paints are very fine and fairly priced.
I think too much, maybe. I will try to persevere. Strangely, I find I
am better if I paint at night. I have finished a picture of the outdoor
café here, and the inside of a bar where I sometimes pass the time,
both of which I like very much, and I felt no ill effects while
painting them or upon finishing them. I hope to send them to Theo
as soon as they dry.*

*Thank you again for your advice, Henri. I hope to do justice to
your beloved South. Until I see you again,*

I shake your hand,
Vincent

*PS: If you see the Colorman, run. Run. You are too talented
and too delicate of constitution to endure, I think. I am not mad. I
promise.*

Poor Vincent. Perhaps he wasn't mad. If the Colorman had followed
him to Arles, then north to Auvers, was it coincidence that he showed
up in Paris just days after Vincent's death? Until Toulouse-Lautrec had
seen him outside the Rat Mort, he'd forgotten about the strange letter
from Vincent, and indeed that he had ever heard of the Colorman before.
But somehow, he had known him. Perhaps from Vincent's descriptions.
Henri downed his cognac, then poured himself another. He folded the
letter and tucked it back into the drawer, then picked up his pen and put
it to paper.

My dear Mama,

Circumstances have changed, and it turns out that I will be able to join you at Château Malromé after all. Although I have finally been able to find some models, which is peace of mind to a painter, and all very proper young ladies at that, I am over-wrought, not by my work, but by my personal circumstances.

I have recently lost a friend, a Monsieur Vincent van Gogh, a Dutchman who was one of our group of painters. Perhaps you remember me speaking of him. His brother hangs my paintings in his gallery and has done very well by me. Vincent succumbed to a long illness and his loss weighs heavily on my heart, and, I fear, my constitution.

It is not so much a break from my work I need, for it goes well, but a break from the city, from routine. I shouldn't be staying more than a month, as I need to be back in the city in the fall to prepare to show my paintings with the Twenty, in Brussels. I look forward to breathing the fresh air and spending the afternoons with you and Aunt Cécile. Give her my kisses, and to you, always, many loving kisses.

Yours,

Henri

Perhaps a month would do it. However long, he could not be in Paris now. He began to see the image that rose in him, the pentimento in his heart, upon seeing first Lucien's Juliette, then the little Colorman. It was Carmen; not her sweetness, her soft voice and touch, it was something different, and dark, and he did not want to see it fully again, or he knew he would never be able to send it away.

Now a bath, then back to the Moulin Rouge, watch Jane Avril dance, La Goulue the female clown sing and can-can, and then he would ride the green fairy into one of his friendly brothels and stay there in a haze until his train left for Mother's castle in the country.

Henri had found her five years before, on his way to a late lunch with Lucien, Émile Bernard, and Lucien Pissarro, the son of Camille. They were all young artists, full of themselves, their talent, and the infinite possibilities of the results of mixing imagination and craft. They had spent the day at Cormon's studio, listening to the master prattle on about the academic tradition and techniques of the masters. In the midst of the lecture on the atmosphere of the room, of creating the chiaroscuro play of shadow and light like the Italian master Caravaggio, Émile Bernard had painted the backdrop of his painting with bold red stripes. His friends had laughed, and they were all ejected from the class.

They decided to adjourn to the Café Nouvelle Athènes on rue Pigalle. Toulouse-Lautrec paid for a cab to bring them down the hill and they tumbled out of it in front of the café, laughing. Just down the block, a young, redheaded woman was leaving her job at the laundry, her hair in a bun that was unraveling, her hands and forearms were pink from her work.

"Look at her," said Toulouse-Lautrec. "She's magnificently raw." He held his arms out to push his friends back. "Stay back. She's mine. I must paint her."

"She's yours," said Bernard, the baby-face, barely a beard pushing through on his chin. *"Like new mold on cheese,"* Henri had teased him. "We'll wait for you inside."

Toulouse-Lautrec waved them off and called to the redhead, who was trudging down toward the butte. "Pardon! Mademoiselle? Pardon!"

She stopped, turned, seemed surprised that anyone could be calling to her.

Henri approached her with his walking stick held before him with both hands, as if in supplication. "Pardon me, mademoiselle. I don't mean to bother you, but I am a painter. Henri Toulouse-Lautrec is my name. And I—I . . ."

"Yes?" she said, looking down, not making eye contact.

"Pardon, mademoiselle, but you are—you are *extraordinary.* Your look, I mean . . . I must paint you. I will pay for you to model."

"Monsieur, I am not a model." A quiet voice, shy.

"Please, mademoiselle. I assure you, this is not a ruse, I am an artist by profession. I can pay you well. More than you make at the laundry. And even then, I will accommodate your other work."

She smiled then, flattered perhaps. "I've never been painted. What would I have to do?"

"You'll pose for me then? Splendid! Simply splendid! Here is my card." He handed her his calling card with the address of his studio, as well as his full name and title embossed with the family crest.

"Oh my," she said. "A count?"

"It is nothing," said Henri. "Come to my studio tomorrow afternoon, after you finish work. Don't worry about dinner. I'll have food for you. Just come as you are."

"But, monsieur—" She gestured to her work clothes, plain, black and white. "I have a nice dress. A blue dress. I can—"

"No, my dear. Come just as you are now. Please."

She tucked his card into her skirt. "I will come. After four."

"Thank you, mademoiselle. I'll see you then. Now, if you'll excuse me, I must get back to my friends. Good day."

"Good day," said the girl.

Toulouse-Lautrec turned but then remembered. "Oh, mademoiselle, I apologize, what is your name?"

"Carmen," she said. "Carmen Gaudin."

"Tomorrow then, Mademoiselle Gaudin." And he was through the café doors.

Carmen trudged across the Place Pigalle toward Montmartre, then cut down one of the narrow alleys that would lead her to rue des Abbesses and up the hill. Halfway down the alley a pimp, just out for the evening, smoked a cigarette and leaned against a ramshackle shed. There was grunting coming from behind the shed, one of the pimp's whores, perhaps, performing an early stand-up with a customer.

The pimp stepped into Carmen's path. "Ah, look how sweet you are," he said. "You looking for work, my little cabbage?"

"I'm going home," she said, not looking up.

The pimp reached down and took her by the chin, blowing smoke in her face as he appraised her. "You're pretty, but not for much longer, eh? Maybe you should take the work while you can get it?" He tightened his grip, pinched her cheeks roughly to make his point.

"Are you a painter?" she said, a quiet voice, shy.

"No, not a painter. What I am is your new boss," said the pimp.

"Oh, then I have no use for you," she said.

She knocked his hand away and grabbed him by the throat, her fingers sinking into the flesh around his windpipe, then slammed him against the brick wall as if he were a rag doll, crushing his skull. As he bounced off the wall she yanked him backward over her bent knee and his spine snapped like kindling. It had taken a second. She dropped him to the bricks and a last breath sputtered out of him like a wet, lifeless fart.

"No use at all," she said, a quiet voice, demure. She trudged down the alley and was making her way up the butte when she heard the whore begin to scream.

RÉGINE SAW HER YOUNGER BROTHER OPEN THE DOOR TO THE BAKERY FOR A very pretty dark-haired girl in a blue dress. *Strange,* she thought, *Lucien never brings his girls to the bakery.*

"Juliette, this is my sister Régine," said Lucien. "Régine, this is Juliette. She's going to model for me."

"*Enchanté*," said Juliette with a slight curtsy.

Lucien led Juliette around the counter and into the back room. "We're going to take a look at the storage shed in the back."

Régine said nothing. She watched her brother grab the ring of keys from the wall, then lead the pretty girl out the back door of the bakery and into the little, weed-choked courtyard behind. A pentimento rose in her heart now, too, of another pretty girl being led to the storage shed, one she'd barely gotten a glimpse of. She backed to the stairs and took them two at a time up to the apartment.

LUCIEN THREW OPEN THE WORN PLANK DOOR, REVEALING A LONG, OPEN, whitewashed interior filled with sunlight from a large skylight. Particles of dust, or perhaps flour, chased one another through the sunbeams in faerie maelstroms. Bags of flour and sugar were stacked near the door. An old, disused easel covered in dust stood at the far end of the room.

"My father put in a skylight," said Lucien. "And look, there's plenty of room for you to pose."

Juliette joined in his enthusiasm, squeezed his arm and kissed his ear. "It's perfect. Private, and with plenty of sunlight. You can pose me like that Manet you took me to see."

"*Olympia*," said Lucien. "A masterpiece, but you are much prettier than Manet's model, Victorine. He painted her for *Luncheon on the Grass*, too. Both masterpieces. Monet and Degas are trying to get the State to buy them from Madame Manet for the Louvre. If Manet had a model like you, France would go to war to get those paintings, I promise you."

She slapped his arm playfully. "I think it is the painter, not the model. Will you paint a masterpiece of me? Shall I undress?"

Lucien felt the storeroom suddenly get very warm and his collar very itchy. "No, my sweet, we can't start today. I need to clear out these supplies, sweep. My paints and easel are at the other studio. I need to move the fainting couch down from the apartment upstairs to pose you on so you'll be comfortable."

"Will we both be comfortable on it?"

"I—we—I can start tomorrow. Will you be ready in the afternoon?"

"I'm ready now," she said. She leaned into him for a kiss. He leaned back to avoid it. There was no place he wanted to be more than lost in her embrace, but not now, in the doorway of a storage shed, with the sound of footsteps coming from the bakery.

"We need to go now," he said, taking her hand and pulling her out of the way so he could close and lock the door. As he turned the key, he said, "There's a narrow passage between the buildings to the square. Only boys use it, but it's wide enough for a determined thief, too."

When they stepped back into the bakery Mère Lessard was standing by the bread board, her arms crossed over her bosom, her jaw jutting out so she might sight accurately down her nose at her son.

"Maman!" said Lucien.

"You made your sister cry," said Mère Lessard. "She is upstairs weeping like you slapped her."

"I didn't slap her."

"A grown, married woman, weeping like a little girl. I hope you are proud of yourself."

"I did nothing, Maman. I'll speak to her." Then he composed himself, shaking off the prickly lust from a moment ago and plunging forward into the fiery recrimination coming from his mother. "This is Juliette. She's going to model for me, and I need to use the storage shed as a studio."

"*Enchanté,* Madame Lessard," said Juliette, again with a suggestion of a curtsy.

Mère Lessard said nothing for a moment but raised an eyebrow and regarded Juliette until Lucien cleared his throat.

"Is this the Juliette who broke your heart and sent you on a drunken binge? The Juliette who nearly killed you and the rest of us for having to do your work for you? That Juliette?"

Lucien really hadn't thought out the idea of getting Juliette through the bakery in the middle of the day, so excited had he been by the promise of seeing sunlight on her naked body.

"The same," said Juliette, stepping forward. "But I've changed."

Lucien nodded furiously to affirm she had changed, although he wasn't sure how.

"Lucien is my only and my ever now," said Juliette. She pulled Lucien to her by his tie and kissed his cheek.

For some reason, Lucien thought of the Crucifixion, when Christ looks down upon the Roman soldiers and prays, *"Forgive them, Lord, for they know not what they do."*

Madame Lessard's eyebrow of recrimination worked its full circuit of rising and falling, like a drawbridge to damnation, and when it settled, she said, "You know his sister Régine will get the bakery when I'm gone? So there's no fortune to be found here."

"No, Madame," said Juliette. "I wouldn't—"

"Even so, he is determined to be a painter, so he is as shiftless and lazy as are all of that breed, so even without the bakery he will likely never be able to provide for you, and you two will die penniless and starving, clutching each other's pox-ridden bodies in the street, smelling of cheap English gin and opium, and rats will eat what is left of your skinny thighs, you know this?"

Juliette fidgeted a bit herself now, the cool pool of promise that had shielded her from the heat having evaporated under Madame Lessard's scrutiny.

She ventured to say, "Madame, I assure you—"

"And I'll have you know that if you hurt my son again, if he so much as sighs sadly over his coffee, I will hire a man, a Russian, probably, to hunt you down and rip all that shiny black hair from your head, then break your skinny arms and legs, and set you on fire, and then put you out with a hammer. And should there be children from your beastly rutting, I shall have the Russian man cut them into tiny pieces and feed them to Madame Jacob's dog. Because, although he may be only a worthless, simpleminded, libertine artist, Lucien is my favorite, and I will not have him hurt. Do you understand?"

Juliette just nodded.

"Good day, then," said Madame Lessard. "Go with God." And she glided across the bakery and up the stairs to the apartment.

"I'm her favorite," said Lucien with a big smile.

Five

GENTLEMEN WITH PAINT
UNDER THEIR NAILS

Paris, May 1863

ALTHOUGH HE WOULD NOT REMEMBER IT, WHEN LUCIEN WAS BORN, the first thing he saw as he peeked over the edge of the world was Madame Lessard's bunghole. *Well that can't be right,* he thought. And he thought he might cry for the shock. Then the midwife flipped him over and the second thing he saw was the blue sky through the skylight. He thought, *Oh, that's better.* So he cried for the beauty and was at a total loss for words for almost a year. He wouldn't remember the moment, but the feeling would come back to him from time to time, when he encountered blue.

"Perhaps I'll call it *Luncheon on the Grass,* then," said Manet. "Since I've clearly forgotten to paint the model wet enough." *Édouard Manet*—Henri Fantin-Latour, 1867

ON THE DAY LUCIEN WAS BORN, PÈRE LESSARD WAS NOT TO BE FOUND IN THE bakery or the apartment above. While Madame Lessard was alternately pushing Lucien out and cursing the baker's very being, Monsieur Lessard made his way across Paris to the Palais de l'Élysée to look at paintings, or, perhaps more important, to look at people looking at paintings. Although he would not remember it later, that day, the day his only son was born, was the first time Père Lessard would encounter the Colorman.

He wouldn't have noticed them at all among the crush of people lined up to get into the *palais,* except that the woman was wearing a full veil of Spanish lace over her hat, which made her look like a specter against the white macadam paths and marble palace façade, looming, as she was, over the crooked little man in a brown suit and bowler hat. He held a stretched canvas wrapped in butcher paper under his arm. He might have been a hunchback, but his hump was in the middle of his spine and strained the buttons on his waistcoat as if the suit had been tailored for a taller, straighter man. Père Lessard sidled down the queue of people, making a great show of trying to look over the crowd while he found a position where he could hear the unlikely couple's conversation.

"But two at one time!" said the woman. "I want to see."

The little man patted the painting under his arm. "No, I have what I came for," he said, his voice like the crunch of gravel under a scoundrel's shoes. "These are not my pictures."

"They are *my* pictures," said the woman.

"No. You may not go in there. Who will you say you are? Do you even know?"

"I don't need to know. I have the veil." She bent down now and ran a lace-gloved finger down the little man's cheek. "Please, *cher.* There will be so many painters in there."

Père Lessard found himself holding his breath, hoping she would raise her veil. There were a thousand pretty women on the walkway, but there was no intrigue in getting a glimpse of their faces. He needed to see her.

"Too many people," said the little man. "Tall people. I don't like people taller than me."

"Everyone is taller than you, *cher.*"

"Yes, tall people can be annoying, monsieur," said Lessard. He didn't know why. It wasn't like him to impose himself into other people's conversations, even in his own bakery, but this woman . . . "Pardon me, but I overheard your conversation."

The little man looked up and squinted against the bright spring sky; his eyes were set so far back under his brow that Lessard could only see the faintest highlight reflecting off them, like lanterns disappearing into a dark cavern. The woman turned to look at Lessard. Through the Spanish lace veil, the baker caught sight of a blue ribbon tied at her throat and just the impression of white skin.

"You are tall, too," said the little man.

"Are you a painter?" asked the woman, a smile in her voice. Père Lessard was caught off guard; he was neither tall, nor a painter, so he was going to excuse his rudeness and move on, but even as he shook his head and prepared to speak, the woman said, "Then we have no use for you. Do piss off, if you would be so kind."

"I would," said Lessard, turning on one heel as if he'd been ordered by an army captain to about-face. "I would be so kind," he said.

"Lessard!" called a familiar voice out of the crowd. The baker looked up to see Camille Pissarro coming toward him. "Lessard, what are you doing here?"

Lessard shook Pissarro's hand. "I'm here to see your paintings."

"You can see my paintings anytime, my friend. We heard that Madame Lessard went into labor. Julie has gone up the butte to help." Pissarro and his wife, Julie, lived with her mother in an apartment at the base of Montmartre. "You should go home."

"No, I will just be in the way," said Lessard.

Later, he would exclaim to Pissarro, "How was I to know she was going to give me a son? She was making the same daughter-birthing noises she made before—casting insults on my manly parts and so forth. I love my daughters, but two is double the number a man needs to break his heart. And then a third! Well, I thought it only courteous to give her time to discuss my downfall with her mother and sisters before I looked into her little-girl eyes for the first time and lost my heart again."

"But Madame gave you a boy," said the painter. "So you are saved the heartbreak."

"That is yet to be seen," said Lessard. "You can never underestimate her trickiness."

Now, outside the palace, Lessard turned to excuse himself from the little man and the woman in Spanish lace, but they were gone, and in an instant, he had forgotten about them. "Let us go view these machines of genius," he said to Pissarro.

A cackling laugh echoed out of the great hall, and a wave of laughter washed through the crowd, even though they couldn't see what had inspired the reaction.

"Machines of the rejected," said Pissarro, for once a note of despair dampening the Caribbean lilt in his accent.

They moved into the column of people that was squeezing itself into the palace: the upper-class men in top hats, black tailcoats, and tight gray trousers, women in black crinoline or black and maroon silk, their long skirts dusted at the fringe with white from the macadam; the new working class, men in white and blue striped jackets and straw boaters, the women in bright dresses of every color, sporting frilly pastel parasols, the mandala of the Sunday afternoon of leisure, a recent gift of the Industrial Revolution.

"But you said that the Salon was made up of charlatans."

"Yes," said Pissarro. "Stodgy academicians."

" 'Slaves to tradition,' you said."

They were shuffling through the galleries now, which were packed with people and oppressively hot. The walls were hung from floor to ceiling with framed canvases of every size, with no regard for subject matter, the paintings having been hung in alphabetical order by the last name of the artist.

Pissarro paused in front of a landscape with a scandalously unremarkable red cow in it. "The enemies of ideas," said the painter.

"If the bastards had not rejected you," said Lessard, into the momentum of artistic anarchy now, "you would have been forced to remove your paintings yourself."

"Well, yes," said Pissarro, stroking his beard in the direction of the red cow. "But I might have sold a few before I removed them. If a man is to paint, he needs to eat."

And there was the rub. While being a painter in Paris was a perfectly legitimate career choice, and there were eighteen thousand painters in the city at the time, the only track for making a living as an artist was the government-sponsored Salon. Only through the Salon could an artist display his art to the public and therefore receive sales and public commissions. To be excluded was to go hungry. But this year the jury of the Salon, which was, indeed, made up of traditional academic painters, had rejected over three thousand paintings, and there had been a public outcry. Emperor Louis-Napoléon decided to placate the public by holding the *Salon des Refusés,* for the paintings that had been rejected. Pissarro was showing two paintings, both landscapes, neither with a red cow.

"You're thinking that your own paintings might have been improved by a red cow," said a woman's voice at the painter's ear. He nearly jumped, then turned to see a woman right beside him, wearing a hat with a veil of Spanish lace that covered her face.

Lessard must have moved on into another gallery, for he wasn't there.

"Then you have seen my landscapes, mademoiselle?"

"No," said the woman. "But I have a sense for these things."

"How did you know I was a painter, then?"

"Paint under your nails, *cher.* And you're looking at the paint, not the picture."

Pissarro was uncomfortable being called *cher* by this strange, enshrouded, unescorted woman. "Well there was no cow in the scene, so I didn't paint a cow. I paint what I see."

"A realist then? Like Corot and Courbet?"

"Something like that," said Pissarro. "I'm more interested in light and color than painting a narrative."

"Oh, I'm interested in light and color as well," said the woman, squeezing the painter's arm and playfully hugging it to her breast. "Particularly the color blue. A blue cow, perhaps?"

Pissarro felt sweat beading on his scalp. "Pardon me, mademoiselle, I must find my friend."

Pissarro pushed through the crowd, passing hundreds of paintings without even looking—feeling as if he was rushing through a jungle, away from some dark voodoo ritual he had stumbled upon. (Which had happened to him as a boy on Saint Thomas, and even now he could not pass any of Paris's cathedrals without suspecting that inside, some dark ritual involving bloody chicken feathers and entranced, sweat-slick African women was going on. To a secular Caribbean Jew, Catholicism was like a malevolent, mystical stepchild lying in wait.)

He caught up to Lessard in the "M" gallery. The baker was standing just outside a semicircle of people gathered around a large canvas. They were pointing and laughing.

The baker looked up at his friend. "Are you all right? You look as if you've seen a ghost."

"I've just been mercilessly flirted with by a strange woman," said Pissarro.

"All the little frogs are not at the river this Sunday then?" Little frogs, *les grenouilles,* was the term for the flirty young girls, mostly shopgirls, seamstresses, or part-time models, who spent their weekends at leisure on the banks of the Seine in (or out of) colorful dresses, in search of a drink, a song, a laugh, a husband, or often just a drunken tumble in the bushes, and generally pursuing another invention new to the working class: fun.

Pissarro smiled at Lessard's joke, then let his smile fall as he looked at the painting that was drawing so much attention. It was a nude, a young woman sitting on the bank of a river, with two fully clothed young men, their picnic lunch in disarray on the ground beside them. Some distance in the background, another young woman in white petticoats waded in the river. The nude woman stared out of the canvas, directly at the viewer, a wry smile on her lips, as if to say, "What do you *think* is going on here?"

"The painter's name is Édouard Manet," said Lessard. "Do you know him?"

Pissarro couldn't look away from the canvas. "I know of him. He was a student of Thomas Couture when I was studying with Corot."

A woman worked her way to the front of the semicircle, made a great show of looking the painting up and down, then covered her eyes and hurried away, fanning herself as if she might faint at any second.

"I don't understand," said Lessard. "There are hundreds of nudes in the exhibition. They act as if they've never seen one before."

Pissarro shook his head as he stroked his long beard, graying already, even though he was only thirty-three. He couldn't look away from the painting. "Those others are goddesses, heroines, myths. This is different. This changes everything."

"Because she's too skinny?" asked the baker, trying to understand why people would laugh at a scene that seemed so unfunny.

"No, because she's real," said Pissarro. "I envy this Manet the work, but not the discomfort he must be feeling."

"Looks to me like she's deciding which of these two she's going to bonk in the bushes."
Le Déjeuner sur l'herbe—Édouard Manet, 1863

"Him?" said a familiar woman's voice at his ear, bosoms again pressed against his arm. "He didn't have to pose bare-assed on the grass for hours on end."

ÉDOUARD MANET FELT AS IF ALL OF PARIS WERE LINING UP TO SPIT IN HIS face. "This picture will set the city on its ear," he'd told his friend Charles Baudelaire a week before. Now he wanted to fire a letter off to the poet (who was away in Strasbourg) to vent the horror he was experiencing at having people laugh at his work.

Manet was thirty-one, the son of a magistrate, with a good education and family money. He was broad-shouldered, lean-hipped, and had his blond beard trimmed according to the latest fashion. He liked to be seen in the cafés, talking philosophy and art with his friends, the center of attention—a wit, a raconteur, and a bit of a dandy. But today he wanted to fade into the very marble of the walls.

He took his butter-yellow leather gloves from his top hat and pretended to be concentrating on pulling them on as he made his way out of the gallery, hoping he might avoid attention, but just as he was sliding around a marble column into the next gallery, he heard his name called and made the mistake of looking over his shoulder.

"Monsieur Manet! Please." A very tall, well-dressed young gentleman approached, flanked on one side by a slight fellow with a light goatee in a worn linen suit and on the other by a stout young man with a full, dark beard, wearing a fine black suit, with lace shirt cuffs extending from his sleeves.

"Excuse me, Monsieur Manet," said the tall man. "I am Frédéric Bazille, and these are my friends—"

"The painter Monet," said the youth with the lace cuffs. He clicked his heels and bowed slightly. "Honored, sir."

"Renoir," said the thin fellow with a shrug.

"Are you not a painter as well?" asked Manet, noting paint on the cuffs of Renoir's jacket.

"Well, yes, but I find it better not to announce it at the outset, in case I need to borrow money."

Manet laughed. "The public can judge harshly with or without prior knowledge, Monsieur Renoir. I can attest to that today."

Behind them, a woman looking at Manet's painting giggled, while a young pregnant girl pretended to be faint and needed to be helped away from the tableau by her heroic, falsely offended husband. Manet winced.

"It is a masterpiece!" said Bazille, trying to distract the older painter from the criticism. "We all agree. We are all students at Monsieur Gleyre's studio."

The other two nodded. "Bazille just failed his medical exams," said Renoir.

Bazille glared at his friend. "Why would you tell him that?"

"So he'll feel better about people laughing at his picture," said Renoir. "Which is magnificent, even if the girl is a little skinny."

"She's real," said Monet. "That's the genius of it."

"I like a girl with a substantial bottom," said Renoir, drawing in the air the size bottom he preferred.

"Did you paint it *en plein air*?" asked Monet. They had all been painting in the open air recently, working indoors only for the figure drawings at Gleyre's studio or to copy paintings at the Louvre.

"I did the sketches in the field, but I painted it in my studio," said Manet.

"What do you call it?" asked Bazille.

"I call it *The Bath*," said Manet, feeling a little better now about the public's reaction. These were intelligent young men who knew painting, who understood what he was trying to do, and they liked the picture.

"Well that's a stupid title," said a woman's voice, suddenly in the midst of them. "She's not even wet."

The young painters stepped back. A woman draped in black Spanish lace had imposed herself into the group.

"Perhaps we've happened onto the scene before the bathing," said Manet. "The motif is classical, madame. After Raphael's *Judgment of Paris*."

"I knew the pose looked familiar," said Bazille. "I've seen an etching of that painting in the Louvre."

"Well that explains it," said the woman. "The Louvre's a little pious, isn't it? Can't throw a round of darts in there without scoring three Madonnas and a baby Jesus. And Raphael was a lazy little fop."

"He was a great master," said Manet with the tone of a disappointed schoolmaster. "Although it seems the Salon has missed the classical reference," he added with a sigh.

"The Salon is out of touch," said Bazille.

"They are pretenders and politicians," said Monet. "They wouldn't know good painting if Rembrandt himself showed it to them."

"They accepted one of my paintings this year," said Renoir.

And everyone turned to him, even the woman in lace.

"What is wrong with you?" said Bazille.

Renoir shrugged. "It hasn't sold."

"Apologies," said Monet. "Renoir is a painter who is only a painter. Polite society is a mystery to him."

Manet smiled. "Congratulations, Monsieur Renoir. May I shake your hand?"

Renoir beamed with the attention of the older artist. "Maybe she's not too skinny," he said as he took Manet's hand.

"Well she's not wet," said the woman. "This is not a picture of bathers. Looks to me like she's deciding which of these two she's going to bonk in the bushes."

Now everyone turned to the woman, the young men rendered speechless by a mix of embarrassment and titillation. Manet was simply horrified.

"Unless she's already done the deed," continued the woman. "Look, their lunch is tossed all over the place. That expression on her face—she seems to be saying, 'Absolutely, I fucked them both. In the weeds. On our lunch.' "

Manet had stopped breathing for a second. In the heat he felt light-headed and leaned on his walking stick to steady himself.

Renoir was the first to recover the power of speech. "I think her look is enigmatic. Like the *Mona Lisa's*."

"And what do you think the *Mona Lisa* was saying?" said the woman. She elbowed Monet in the ribs to punctuate her question, then leaned into him. "Hmmm? *Mon petit ours?*"

"I—uh—" He had never been called a "little bear" before and he wasn't sure how to take it. He looked at Manet, hoping the older painter might rescue him.

"Perhaps I'll call it *Luncheon on the Grass,* then," said Manet. "Since I've clearly forgotten to paint the model wet enough." He bounced his walking stick off its tip and snatched it out of the air like a magician signaling that the show should begin. "Madame, if you will pardon me, I must be off. Gentlemen, it was a pleasure. If you are free this evening, perhaps you can join me for a drink at Café de Bade on boulevard des Italiens at eight." He shook each of their hands, bowed to the woman, then turned on his heel and strode out of the gallery, feeling as if he'd just escaped an assassination attempt.

"MONSIEUR MANET WAS THE ONE ON TOP OF HER IN THE WEEDS," SAID THE woman in lace, looking over Monet's shoulder at the painting. "Don't you think?"

"It is not for me to say," said Monet. "An artist and his model—"

"You're a painter, aren't you? You're all painters, aren't you?"

"We are, mademoiselle," said Bazille. "But we prefer to paint *en plein air.*"

"Outside? In the daylight? Oh, how lovely," she said. "Just so you know, when you take your model into the weeds, put a blanket down. It's just good manners."

The bark of an angry man's voice echoed across the gallery. The woman looked up, startled.

Renoir spotted a little man in a brown suit and bowler hat pushing his way through the crowd, shouting in a language he didn't recognize.

"I think that fellow is waving to you," said Renoir.

"Oh my, it's my uncle. Such a bore. I must be going." She lifted her skirts and made a quick turn. "I'll be seeing you, gentlemen."

"But how will we know you?" asked Monet. "We don't even know your name."

"You'll know me." And with that, she hurried off, moving through the crowd like a black cloud, the little man limping after her, straining to see her around the skirts, coattails, and parasols that blocked his way.

Monet said, "Did you see her face?"

"No," said Renoir. "Just that black lace, like she's in mourning."

"Perhaps she has scars," said Bazille.

"She was wearing blue lip rouge," said Monet. "I caught a glimpse of it through the lace. I've never seen such a thing."

"Do you think she's a prostitute?" asked Renoir.

"Could be," said Bazille. "No proper lady would talk that way."

"No, I mean Manet's model." Renoir was looking at the painting again. "She's so skinny she probably has to model to supplement her whoring income."

"Could be," said Monet, now turning his full attention to the painting. "Can you imagine painting something like that in the open air? Actually capturing the moment on a huge canvas, the people life-size?"

"Well you're going to have to get a prostitute to model if you want her to sit nude on the riverbank like that," said Renoir.

"And have money to pay her," said Bazille.

"Well that's out of the question," said Renoir. "I suppose you could get a girl to fall in love with you and she would sit on the grass for free, but unless she's a proper whore I don't think she'll do the naked part."

"You're right, Renoir," said Monet, keeping his gaze on the painting. "We have to go."

"We do?" said Renoir. "We haven't even looked at your painting."

"No, we have to find that woman in the Spanish lace. She'll do it. I mean, she seemed open to the idea." A great, joyous grin bisected his beard. "A modern moment in time, caught on an enormous canvas. I shall stop time for a luncheon on the grass!" He turned and strode into the crowd with such purpose that people moved out of his way without his asking.

"But you have no money for a canvas that size," said Bazille, following his friends into the next gallery. "No money for paint or brushes."

"You do," said Monet.

Renoir looked over his shoulder and nodded. "Be sure to ask your father for enough for the whore, too."

"I'm not asking my father for money to hire a whore for you to paint," said Bazille.

"Yes you are," said Monet.

"Her name is Jo Hiffernan," said Whistler. "An Irish hellcat—skin like milk. Quick-witted for a woman, and a soul as deep as a well." *Symphony in White #1*—James McNeill Whistler, 1863

As he entered the "W" salon, Manet was immediately struck by a very tall canvas of a redheaded woman dressed all in white. There was a quality to her gaze, as if she were not only looking at you but into you and knew too much about you, owned you. His bather had the same quality, and seeing it in another painting took the edge from the criticisms he'd been enduring all day. Then he spotted the painter, holding forth in lecture to a small gathering of admirers in front of the painting.

"Whistler," Manet called. "How's your mother?"

The American bowed to the group and turned to greet his friend. He was a gaunt, dark-haired fellow about the same age as Manet, with an outrageous gondola of a mustache riding his lip and a monocle screwed into his eye like the brass porthole of a warship. He looked weaker, more pale than when they had last traded quips at Café Molière a year ago, and he was actually leaning on his walking stick as if lame, rather than wielding it as an *accoutrement* of fashion.

Whistler often joked about his puritanical mother, who reminded him with weekly letters that he was frittering away his life and the good family name by trying to live as a painter in London.

"Ah, Mother," said Whistler in English. "She's an arrangement in gray and black; her disapproval falls like a shadow across the ocean. And yours?"

Manet laughed. "Hiding in shame and praying for one of her sons to take up the law like our father."

"Our mothers should share tea and disappointment together," said Whistler.

Manet released his friend's hand and turned his attention to the painting. "The Salon rejected this? She is so bold. So real." The girl, in a long white gown, stood barefoot on the white fur of a polar bear rug, but beneath that was an Oriental carpet with a woven pattern of bright blue.

"My *White Girl*. She was turned down by the Salon *and* the London Academy. Her name is Jo Hiffernan," said Whistler. "An Irish hellcat—skin like milk. Quick-witted for a woman, and a soul as deep as a well."

"Oh, poor Jemmie," said Manet, "must you fall in love with every woman you paint?"

"Nothing like that. The wench poisoned me and right there is the evidence." Whistler waved up and down the painting. "I must have scraped the canvas a hundred times—started over. All that lead white soaks right through your skin. I still see rings around every point of light. My doctor says it will take months for my vision to return to normal. I've been in Biarritz by the sea, recovering."

That explained it. Lead poisoning. Manet breathed a little easier. "The limp, then? Also lead poisoning?"

"No, last week I was painting on the beach and I was swept out to sea by a rogue wave—pounded in the surf. I would have drowned if some fishermen hadn't rescued me."

She glided between them like a petite storm, black lace trailing behind her. "Should have stayed in London and continued to shag the redhead on the bear rug, then?" she said in English, an Irish accent.

The little color Whistler had drained out of his face. "Beg pardon, mademoiselle—"

"A bear rug's a sight more comfortable than the riverbank, eh, Édouard?" she said to Manet in French, squeezing his biceps. "At least she didn't give him syphilis, *non*?"

Manet felt his mouth moving, but no words were coming out. The two painters, both notorious raconteurs, looked at each other, speechless.

"You two look like you've seen a ghost. Oh, there's my uncle again. Have to go. Ta!"

She hurried off through the crowd. Whistler's monocle dropped out of his eye and swung from the end of its silk cord. "Who was that woman?"

"How would I know?" said Manet. "Don't you know her?"

"No. Never seen her before."

"Me either," Manet lied.

"She knew your name."

Manet shrugged. "I'm known in Paris."

He really didn't know who she was. He didn't even know *what* she was. He was suddenly feeling ill, and not because of the criticism of his painting. "Jemmie, this *White Girl* of yours wasn't the painting you were working on in Biarritz when you had your accident, was it?"

"No, of course not. That was in the studio. The Biarritz painting was called *The Blue Wave.*"

"I see," said Manet. "Of course."

"So, Whistler, how's your mother?" *Hommage à Delacroix*—Henri Fantin-Latour, 1864. (Whistler center, standing; Manet, standing center right; Baudelaire seated to Manet's left. Fantin-Latour, the painter, seated in the white shirt.)

THE BLUE WAVE HAPPENED TO BE THE TITLE OF THE PAINTING THE COLOR-man carried, wrapped in butcher's paper, under his arm as he hurried after the girl in Spanish lace.

"Where have you been?" He followed her out of the palace into the bright noon sun.

"Having fun," she said, not missing a step. "Did you see them all? These young painters! They paint in the open air—in the sunshine. Don't you know what that means?"

"Blue?"

"*Oui, mon cher. Beaucoup bleu.*"

Interlude in Blue #2:
Making the Blue

For as long as there have been painters, there have been color men. For years it was thought that the true painter, a master painter, would gather his own pigments, the earths, ochres, insects, snails, plants, and potions that went into making color, and combine them in his studio. But the truth is, the ingredients for colors were often hard to find, difficult to prepare, and rare. To be a master, a painter needs to paint, not waste the light by searching for and preparing pigment. It was the color man who delivered the rainbow into the hands of the artist.

Ultramarine, true blue, the Sacré Bleu, is made from crushed lapis lazuli, a gemstone, and for centuries, it was rarer and more valuable than gold. Lapis lazuli is found in one place in the world, the remote mountains of Afghanistan, a long, dangerous journey from Europe, where the churches and palaces were being decorated with the Blessed Virgin wearing a Sacré Bleu gown.

It was the color men who sought out the lapis and pulled the color from the stone.

First they pounded the lapis with a bronze mortar and pestle, then that powder would be sifted until so fine the grains were not visible to the naked eye. The dull bluish-gray powder was then melted into a mixture of pine rosin, gum mastic, and beeswax. Over a period of three weeks, the putty would be massaged, washed with lye, strained, then dried, until all that was left was pure, powdered ultramarine, which a color man could sell as dry pigment, to be mixed by the artist with plaster for fresco, egg yolk for tempera, or linseed or poppy oil to use as oil paint.

There are other blues, blues from plants, indigo and woad, which fade with time, and inferior blues from minerals like copper and azurite, which can go black with time, but a true blue, a forever blue, ultramarine, was made in this exact way. Every color man knew the recipe, and every color man who traveled Europe from painter to painter with his wares could swear to his clients that this was the process he had used.

Except one.

Six

PORTRAIT OF A RAT CATCHER

Paris, 1870

WHEN LUCIEN WAS SEVEN YEARS OLD, WAR CAME TO MONTMARTRE. Because of the war Lucien became the Rat Catcher and had his first encounter with the Colorman.

Of course war had come to the butte before. In the first century BC the Romans had built a temple to Mars, the god of war, on the mount, and from that point forward, you couldn't catapult a cow at Paris without someone setting up for siege on Montmartre. With her seven freshwater wells, her windmills, her vegetable gardens, and her commanding view of the entire city, everyone agreed that there was no better butte on which to be besieged.

And so it came to pass that Louis-Napoléon, feeling pressured by Chancellor Bismarck's proposing a Prussian *derrière* be put on the throne of Spain (thus putting hostile forces on borders to both the north and south of France) and buoyed by his successful campaigns against Russia and Austria, plus the reputation of his illustrious uncle as the greatest military strategist since Alexander, declared war on the Prussians in July of 1870. By September, the Prussian army had kicked nine shades of umber out of the French and Paris was under siege.

The boulevards were barricaded and the Prussian army surrounded the city. The great Krupp guns fired sporadically, which did little more than keep the city's national guard running from neighborhood to neighborhood to put out fires. Hot-air balloons were lined down the middle of the Champs-Élysées, prepared to try to smuggle out letters as soon as night fell, and most would actually make it.

An early frost had dusted the cobbles of Place du Tertre that morning, as Lucien and Père Lessard stood at the edge of the butte, behind the iron fence that crowned the square, waiting for the loaves to be done, and watched French soldiers making their way up rue des Abbesses, pulling a hundred cannons with horses.

"They will store them in the Church of Saint-Pierre," said Père Lessard. "And use them as a last resort if the Prussians try to take the city."

"Maman says that the Prussians will rape and kill us," said Lucien.

"Really, she told you that?"

"*Oui*. If the steps are not swept perfectly clean, they will rape and kill us all. Twice."

"Ah, I see. Well, yes, the Prussians are a thorough people, but I don't think you need to worry about it."

"Papa, what is raping?"

Père Lessard pretended that his pipe had gone out and fumbled with a match against one of the iron fence bars as he tried to formulate a way to answer without actually having to answer. Had it been one of his daughters, he might have sent her back to her mother, but Madame had a way of implying to the boy that all the evils and plagues of man could be blamed, more or less, on the hapless baker of Montmartre, and he was in no mood to try to explain to his only son how he had invented rape.

And damn the match, it had burned all the way to his fingertips.

"Lucien, you have heard the term 'making love'?"

"Yes, Papa, like when you and Maman are kissing and tickling and laughing. Régine said that is what you were doing."

Père Lessard swallowed hard. It was a small apartment, but he always thought the children were asleep when— That spiteful woman and her giggling. "Yes, that's right. Well, rape is the opposite. It is *making hate*."

"I see," said Lucien, mercifully satisfied with the answer. "Do you think we will get to shoot the cannons before the Prussians rape and kill us?"

"There will be no cannons for us. Our part of the fight will be feeding the hungry people of the butte."

"We always do that. Perhaps Monsieur Renoir will come and fire the cannons, now that he is a soldier."

"Perhaps," said the baker. Renoir had been drafted into the cavalry, despite having been raised in the city and having never ridden a horse. A training officer who saw Renoir trying to handle horses took pity on the painter and hired him to teach his daughter how to paint, thus keeping him out of action. Monet and Pissarro had escaped to England. Bazille was training with the army in Algiers. Cézanne, the roughest of the lot, had gone into hiding in his beloved Provence.

"With all your pets gone, perhaps a suffering wife will at last be taken dancing?" said Madame Lessard. "In a new dress of white and black stripes, as was ordained by the Holy Father."

"The Pope did not decree that you should have a striped dress to go dancing in, woman."

"Well, perhaps now that your pets are gone, you'll go to mass instead of drinking coffee all morning and talking about art, and you'll know what the Holy Father said." Madame Lessard turned then to her daughters, Marie and Régine, who stood by, pretending to mend stockings. "Have no fear, my ducklings, Maman won't let you marry a heretic."

"So I am a heretic now?"

"Who would say such a thing?" said Madame. "I will have their ears boxed by that sturdy doorman, Monsieur Robelard. I believe his price is two *francs.*" Madame held out her hand for the coins. *"S'il vous plaît."*

Père Lessard dug into his pocket. Somehow, it seemed perfectly acceptable that he should pay Monsieur Robelard, the doorman at the Moulin de la Galette, to defend his honor against the accusation of being a heretic that no one had leveled. If nothing else, Père Lessard had the business sense of an artist.

Despite a siege on the city, Madame Lessard was saving for a black and white striped dress in which to be taken dancing. But there would be no dancing at the Moulin de la Galette, or any of the other dance halls in the city. The men who stayed in the city, even those who had been able to afford to send their families away before the Prussians arrived, spent their evenings and Sunday afternoons defending the barricades, and the women, when not hiding in the cellars, went about the business of feeding and caring for their children. The grocers, butchers, and bakers went about trying to provide for the Parisians when there was nothing left to provide.

The chickens and ducks pinned in the backyards of Montmartre disappeared first. The ducks and most tender yard hens in the beginning, but once the feed grain was gone, even the laying hens were short for the pot, until not even a single time-toughened rooster remained unstewed to announce the dawn. With no trains to bring livestock from the country, the butchers for Paris's great Les Halles marketplace spent their days in cafés with their ham-sized fists wrapped around delicate cordial glasses of Pernod, until that, too, was gone. Montmartre's two milk cows, belonging to Madame Jacob of the *crémerie,* were spared for a while because they could graze on the back slope of the butte and in the fencerows of the Maquis, the shantytown by the cemetery, but when the grass was nibbled to nubs and the National Guard's horses were being slaughtered for meat, then even the sad-eyed Sylvie and Astrid found their way into the *pot-au-feu,* which Madame Jacob salted with her tears.

As the siege had fallen in the autumn, every vegetable garden in

Montmartre and the Maquis was brimming with maize and snail-scarred squash, but two weeks after the Prussians arrived, with nothing coming into the city from the countryside, only the root vegetables remained, and those so rare that a gentleman in possession of a turnip might find himself in the company of a brace of Pigalle harlots, eager to exchange a full evening of lubricious charms for the promise of a demi-tuber.

When the Prussian guns first thundered in the distance, Père Lessard knew what was coming, so he bought all the flour he could find, then gathered a dozen empty flour sacks from the storeroom and led Lucien down the butte to a cooper's shop tucked among the factories of Saint-Denis. There, for the price of asking, they were able to fill their flour sacks with the fine oak sawdust.

"You will use it to fire your ovens, no?" said the barrel maker. "Very smart. Burns very hot. But be careful. It can be explosive if the air is filled with it."

"Yes, like flour," said Père Lessard. "I will be careful." He hadn't thought of using the sawdust to fire the ovens. He shook the cooper's hand, then hired a ragpicker with a donkey cart to haul the bags of sawdust up the butte.

"If strong French oak is good enough for our wine, it will be good for our bread, too," he said to Lucien as they wound their way up Montmartre behind the cart. "The trick is to use no more than a quarter sawdust or the dough will not rise. But for piecrust, you can go as much as half."

"How did you know to use sawdust, Papa?"

"Ours is a very old profession, and no one wants to hear excuses why the baker does not have wares, so we learn tricks. Why, once there was a pair of bakers on the Île de la Cité that were killing and baking foreign students from the Sorbonne into pies. And no one who bought the pies ever complained. Only a German father who missed his son and came to investigate his disappearance finally found them out. Cannibalism, right there on the doorstep of Notre-Dame."

Lucien's eyes had grown as big as his fists at the horrific prospect of what Father was proposing. "But, Papa, I don't think I'm big enough to make students into pies. Perhaps you should have Marie and Régine do it. They are taller."

"Oh, we won't start you out on students, Lucien. They are quick and hard to knock on the head. We'll start you out with something easier, a grandmother, I think."

Lucien was having a hard time catching his breath. Why was the ragpicker smiling? Maybe he was going to be in on it. Maybe he would haul the grandmother to the bakery. Which was good. Lucien knew that unless he picked a grandmother who lived on Montmartre, he'd never get her up the hill without help.

"Maybe I can just ask a grandmother to come to the bakery. I could make up a story of how Maman needs help, and—"

"Oh, that won't be necessary, Lucien. You'll just conk her on the head. That is the proper way."

The ragpicker nodded, as if it was well-known that conking a grandmother on the head was the accepted method.

Tears began to well in Lucien's eyes. "I don't want to. I don't want to conk a grandmother. I don't want to. I don't want to. I don't want to."

"Eh, war is hell," said the ragpicker.

Père Lessard tousled Lucien's hair, then pulled the boy's head against his hip in a hug. "Shhhh, son, stop crying. I'm just fucking with you."

Now the ragpicker threw his head back and laughed in the way only a Frenchman with seven teeth and a conscience soaked in wine can laugh, the sound his donkey might make if he were a heavier smoker and had just licked the devil's ass to chase all taste of goodness from his tongue. The ragpicker wasn't a scoundrel, but scoundrels envied his laugh.

Humiliated, horrified, and not a little out of breath, Lucien flailed at Father with his fists; the first bounced harmlessly off the baker's bottom, the second plowed solidly and with great force into Père Lessard's testicles, and in that instant, time stopped for the baker, and even before the breath left his body and he crumpled to the ground in pain, he thought, *The boy has his mother's sense of humor.*

As Lucien ran up the hill toward home, Père Lessard said to the rag-picker, "He's a sensitive boy. I think he should be an artist."

Madame Lessard met him at the top of the stairs, her hands on her hips, her chin jutting like the prow of a warship. "So, you will have my son bake my mother into a pie, will you?"

"Just *a* grandmother, not *his* grandmother. I was teasing him." Although it then crossed Lessard's mind that if one were choosing a grandmother from which to make pies, Madame's mother, who, upon a sunny day, when the twin locomotives of her bosom towed her cumulus skirts through the market at Louveciennes, was followed by children and dogs seeking shade, would indeed make for a rich and prodigious filling. He would atone for the thought, he knew, whether he chose to or not.

"I adore your mother, my love. I was simply preparing Lucien to help find new sources of filling for our pastries."

"Like his grandmother?"

"Like rats," said Père Lessard.

"No . . ." said Mère Lessard, for once not feigning shock.

"You know, the rabbit is a rodent also, and delicious."

"Now you will feed me rat. Mother warned me about you."

"No, *ma chère,* the rats will be for the customers only." *But your mother should thank the saints she lives in Louveciennes or there would be fat bitch pie for everyone on the butte,* he thought.

LUCIEN DID NOT TAKE IMMEDIATELY TO THE DUTIES OF RAT CATCHER; IN FACT, for the first two days, he spent his morning chasing his quarry into the dark corners of Montmartre, only to find himself chased right back out of those same corners by a rat that had tripled in size and, if he was not mistaken, was carrying a knife.

Madame Jacob, who owned the *crémerie,* found him sulking one morning behind the Moulin de la Galette. She had gone to the north slope out of habit, to fetch her cows, but they had already passed on by then, and she was simply herding ghosts.

"No rats today, Lucien?"

"No one is supposed to know I am catching rats," Lucien said.

"Well, you aren't, are you?"

"They're huge! They tried to rape and kill me."

"Ah, but Père Lessard needs to feed Montmartre, as do I. I'll tell you what, Lucien, let me give you something easier to catch, and you bring them to me, and I will give you three traps that I have, and some garlic, which your father can use for his rat *pâté.*"

"Easier to catch?" Lucien asked. He hoped Madame Jacob wasn't going to suggest grandmothers again, because after his experience with the rats, he didn't want to imagine what kind of raping and killing an angry grandmother might visit upon him.

"*Escargots,*" said Madame Jacob. "You'll find them early morning in the cemetery, when the mist is still running over the gravestones."

"*Merde!*" said Lucien, for the first time in his life.

THE NEXT MORNING, WHILE FATHER WAS STILL PROOFING THE OAKY LOAVES for baking, Lucien made his way up rue Lepic, past the still blades of the Moulin de la Galette, and down through the Maquis, with its row upon row of tiny, ramshackle houses, splintering privies, decimated vegetable gardens fenced with pickets of rough sticks, and the occasional broken wagon or junk pile. Usually the Maquis woke up shouting, but today it was oddly still, not even a late whore or early scavenger about; no rooster crowed, no dog barked, anyone able-bodied enough to have been at work was away, camped at the barricades with the militias. Of the scores of tin chimneys, but one bled a tarry stream of smoke over the roofs, someone burning oily rags to chase the morning chill, the only sign at all that the Maquis was still alive.

Lucien shivered and hurried down the hill to the cemetery. There, among the sycamores and chestnut trees, the moss-covered monuments and blackened bronze crypt doors, he found his prey. Upon the third tomb he passed, a fairly fresh slab of basalt belonging to the late Léon Foucault, was an angry *escargot,* his horns extended, lording over his stony realm like a dragon over his hoard of gold.

"Aha!" said Lucien.

"Aha!" replied the snail.

At which point Lucien dropped his wooden bucket and ran away, flailing his arms and screaming as if he'd just seen a ghost, which he was fairly sure he had.

"Wait, wait, wait, boy!" said a voice from behind.

Lucien looked over his shoulder, although he continued to scream, so as to not lose his place. But it was neither a ghost nor a charging, angry, and talkative *escargot,* but a rather old man, skeletally thin, wearing an ochre-colored plaid suit that had seen its prime perhaps thirty years before. The old man was holding the snail, shell pinched between two fingers, offering it to Lucien.

"It's yours, boy. Come now, take it." He wore thick spectacles in tortoiseshell frames and had a long, angular nose.

Lucien crept back toward the old man, retrieved his bucket, and held it out. He'd seen this old man before, tending a small garden in the Maquis. Always in his very clean, if threadbare, plaid suit, a medal on a tricolor ribbon pinned to his chest. The old man dropped the snail in the bucket. *"Merci,* monsieur," Lucien said, bowing a little, although he wasn't sure why.

The old man was very tall, or at least he seemed so, because he was so thin, and he crouched and looked into the bucket. "There should be great thoughts in that one. I've been watching him on Foucault's tomb for an hour now."

Lucien didn't understand. "It's not for me," he said. "It's for Madame Jacob."

"Just as well," said the old man, standing up now. "They taste like dirt. And with no butter or garlic to put them in, you might as well be eating dirt. But here's the secret: only eat snails from the graves of great thinkers. Foucault here was a brilliant man. He calculated a way to measure the speed of light. And he is dead only two years. Surely his soul still trickles from the grave, to be consumed by this snail. If we eat the snail, we absorb some of that brilliance, do we not?"

Lucien had no idea, but clearly the old man expected an answer. "Yes?" Lucien ventured.

"You are correct, young man. What is your name?"

"I am Lucien Lessard, monsieur."

"Also correct. And I am Professeur Gaston Bastard. You may call me Le Professeur. I was a teacher, retired now. The Ministry of Education gave me a pension and a medal." He tapped the medal on his chest. "For excellence."

The Professeur paused again and tilted an ear, as if waiting for another answer, so Lucien said, "Excellent?"

"*Très bien!*" said the Professeur. "Come." The Professeur turned on the heel of a very broken-down boot and strode off down the path, his back as straight as a twenty-year-old's, chin high, as if he were leading a march. "You know this entire cemetery stands over a limestone quarry dug by the Romans two thousand years ago?"

The Professeur paused, turned, waited.

"The Romans," Lucien said. He was beginning to get the rhythm now. When his mother, his father, or nearly any grown-up talked to him, they were really just interested in hearing their own voice and he could let his mind wander, to his lovely Minette, or dinner, or how he might need to pee, but the Professeur required attention.

"Much of early Paris was built from the limestone in this quarry. There! There is one."

The Professeur stopped and waited while Lucien picked a fat snail off a very old tomb, completely green with moss. Then they continued.

"Later they began to mine the gypsum from Montmartre, from which they make . . . ?"

Lucien had no idea what gypsum was. He stopped breathing for a moment, trying to think. He knew that if something came out of a mine it was in the ground. He tried to think of anything he knew that was made from something in the ground.

"Onion soup?" he said.

The Professeur looked at Lucien over his glasses. "Plaster," he said. "They make plaster from gypsum. The finest plaster in the world. Perhaps you have heard of plaster of Paris?"

Lucien hadn't. "Yes," he said.

"Well it was actually plaster of Montmartre. The whole butte was once so riddled with mine shafts that it became unsafe to build on. They had to pour concrete into the old mines to make it stable. But some of the mine shafts are still down there. They open up after a strong rain or if someone digs a cellar too deep. One of them even opens into the Maquis." The Professeur raised an eyebrow, as if waiting for an answer, even though he hadn't asked a question.

"The Maquis?" Lucien said.

"Yes, not far from my house. It's hidden. It's where the best rats come from."

"Rats?" said Lucien.

They spent another hour picking the snails from gravestones and the Professeur showed Lucien how to follow pearlescent slime trails under the bushes and leaves to track down the snails who were already finding their hiding places for the day.

"They would taste better if you could put them in a tub filled with cornmeal, let them live on that for a week to purge the earth from their bodies. Alas, there is no corn. But *you* should only eat Foucault's snail, anyway."

The Professeur had insisted that Lucien keep the snail they'd plucked from Foucault's tomb in his pocket and made him promise he alone would eat it so he could absorb some of the snail-eaten soul of the great scientist.

"Now," said the Professeur, "if we could get some snails from Père-Lachaise Cemetery, there are some great thinkers buried there. Most of these you've collected graze on the souls of scalawags."

Lucien was happy that he had nearly filled his bucket with snails, but as he followed the old man back to his little house in the Maquis, he was beginning to suspect that his benefactor might be a madman.

The Professeur showed Lucien into the two-room cabin. Most of the hard-packed dirt floor of the front room was taken up by what looked like a small racetrack. Against one wall were two cages, each about knee-high. One was full of mice, the other rats. There were perhaps a dozen of each species.

"Horses and charioteers," said the Professeur.

"Rats," Lucien said with a shudder. There, in the cage, they seemed much smaller, less dangerous, less likely to rape and kill him than the ones he'd encountered in the wild.

"I'm training them to perform," said the Professeur. He reached into the larger cage and retrieved one of the rats, who seemed completely unbothered by being handled and simply sniffed at the old man's hand as if looking for food.

"I am going to teach them to perform the chariot-race scene from the novel *Ben-Hur*," said the Professeur. "The rats shall be my horses and the mice my charioteers."

Lucien didn't know what to say, but then he noticed that there were, indeed, six little chariots lined up along one side of the oval track.

"I will train them and then take my spectacle to Place Pigalle and charge people to watch the races. There may even be wagering."

"Wagering," Lucien repeated, trying to mimic the enthusiasm in the Professeur's voice.

"You have to reward them when they do what you want. I tried punishing them when they misbehaved, but the hammer seemed to crush their spirit."

Lucien watched as the Professeur hitched the rat to a chariot, then set him down and retrieved a mouse from the other cage and placed him in the chariot. The mouse immediately wandered off and started looking for an opening in the wall around the track. Soon there were rats and mice running all around the little arena, and two rats had even crawled over the wall and were dragging their chariots around the outer walls of the house, looking for an opening to the outside. The Professeur engaged Lucien's help, and they chased and replaced rat horses and mouse drivers until the two of them were kneeling over the tiny hippodrome, gasping for breath.

"Oh, they mocked me," said the Professeur. "Called me a loon. But when I achieve the spectacle, I shall be hailed as a genius. I have eaten Foucault's snails as well, you know?"

"Pardon, monsieur, but they may call you a loon anyway."

"Do you think me a loon, Lucien?" the Professeur asked with the same schoolmaster's tone with which he had asked every other question.

Fortunately, he was asking the baker boy of Montmartre, a place where loons tended to congregate, and whose father had taught him that great men were often eccentric, unpredictable, and enigmatic, and just because we did not understand the path they chose, we should not doubt their vision.

"I think you are a genius, monsieur, even if you are a loon."

The Professeur scratched his bald head with a rat as he considered the answer, then shrugged. "Well, I have my medal anyway. You should get your snails to Madame Jacob. Tomorrow you can return and help me teach the mice to hold the reins. Come, I'll show you where to catch meat for your father's *pâtés*."

MADAME JACOB HAD NOT BEEN IMPRESSED THAT LUCIEN'S SNAILS HAD FED ON the souls of geniuses, but she did give him the three rat traps she promised, as well as a braid of garlic for his father. The traps were actually little cages, cast in bronze, with a round port in the side where a rat might enter and a spring mechanism that snapped the port shut when the rat stepped on a plate inside. A brass chain with an anchor ring was attached to each trap.

The Professeur had shown Lucien the entrance to the old gypsum mine, concealed beneath a thicket of laurel bushes just above the Maquis. Lucien often played in the Maquis with his friends, and he knew the bushes, and that there were blackberry brambles with vicious thorns woven through the laurel. The thorns were probably the only reason the bushes hadn't long ago been hacked up for fuel and the mine filled in like the others.

"You'll need to go far enough into the mine for it to be dark," said the Professeur. "Rats are nocturnal and prefer to move in the dark. But don't go too far in. It may not be safe from cave-in. Just past where the light reaches. That is where I caught my charges."

The next morning, Lucien carried his heavy traps into the mouth of the mine and when the light stopped, so did he. While trying not to look at the spiderwebs overhead or stare into the pitch-black of the mine, he baited each of the traps with a tiny strip of rind from a wheel of camembert cheese, then closed the lids and wound the clockwork mechanism that set the trap, just as Madame Jacob had taught him. He pushed each trap into the dark against the mine wall, at which point the panic overcame him and he ran out of the mine as if pursued by demons.

He resolved that the next day, when it came time to retrieve his traps, he would bring a candle, and perhaps Father's butcher knife, and maybe he could borrow one of the cannons from the church if they weren't using it, but instead he brought his friend Jacques, lured him with a slight exaggeration of the value of what they would be retrieving from the mine.

"Pirate treasure," said Lucien.

"Will there be swords?" asked Jacques. "I would like a sword."

"Just hold the candle. I have to find my traps."

"But why are you looking for rat traps?"

Lucien was trying to calculate how they had come so far into the dark and still not found his traps, and Jacques's questions were distracting him. "Jacques, be quiet or we will have to rape and kill your grandmother and put her in a pie."

Lucien was fairly sure his parents would have been proud of the way he had handled the problem, but when Jacques started to sniffle, Lucien added, "Because that is what pirates do." *What a baby.* Why did children get so upset about a little pie?

"No!" said Jacques. "No you won't! I'm—"

But before Jacques could announce his intent, a scratchy voice sounded out of the dark.

"Who's there?"

And with that Jacques was off, wailing toward the entrance, and Lucien took off behind him. After a few steps, Jacques's candle went out, and after a few steps more, Lucien tripped and fell headfirst against the wall of the mine shaft. When his head hit, a splash of bright white lights fired across his vision and he heard a high-pitched note in his ear, as if someone had struck a tuning fork inside his head. When he was finally able to push himself up on his hands and knees and the points of light cleared from his vision, he was in total darkness, with no sense of which way was out of the mine. He could no longer hear Jacques's steps retreating or where they might have faded to.

He crawled a few feet, afraid that if he stood he might trip again.

The powdered gypsum on the floor of the mine was soft on his hands and knees, and after his abrupt encounter with the wall, he thought he'd take his chances closer to the ground. A few feet more and he thought he might be able to see some light, and he stood up. Yes, there was definitely light.

He stood and started toward it, probing cautiously ahead with a toe before planting each foot. He saw a shape, an orange rectangle, and thought it might be the mouth of the mine, but as he moved, the shape revealed itself as something that was illuminated from the side, not the source of the light, and he realized he'd been moving around a bend in the mine. It was a canvas, he thought, but it was the back of the canvas. He could see the nail heads on the stretchers, illuminated by the light of a single candle.

From behind the canvas, the sound of labored breathing.

Lucien moved a little farther around the corner and stopped. Stopped breathing. There was a little man there beyond the canvas, naked, brown, his feet and legs dusted with white gypsum powder, bent over something, a dark, long shape on the floor. He was scraping the dark thing with some kind of blade. The blade looked like it might be made of glass, but it looked very sharp.

Lucien started to shake from holding his breath, so he allowed himself a breath, slow, shallow, quiet. He could feel his heart beating in his temples, behind his eyes, yet he dared not move.

The little man would scrape the blade down the length of the dark shape, then he would scrape the blade into some sort of earthen jar and sigh, as if with satisfaction. It was the motion that Father used when scraping flour from his bread board after the loaves were formed.

Then the shape on the floor moved, moaned, the sound of an animal, and Lucien nearly leapt straight up in the air but managed to catch himself. It was a person, a woman, and she'd moved a leg into the narrow band of light thrown from the candle. The leg was blue. Even in the dim orange light of the candle, Lucien could see it. Now he could make out how she lay, on her side on the floor of the mine, one arm stretched out above her head until it disappeared into the black.

The little man tapped the blade into the jar, then turned and placed the blade right where the woman's face would be and pressed down. The woman moaned, and Lucien's breath caught again, this time with a bit of a yip.

The little man wheeled toward Lucien with his blade up, his eyes like black glass, in the darkness. "Who's there?"

"*Merde!*" Lucien said for the second time ever, although it came out in a very long, siren wail behind him as he bolted into the darkness, his hands held before him, and he kept trailing that audible "*merde*" until he saw the light of day and escape—the sweet green light on the thorn-bushes outside—and he was nearly there, almost there, when a long arm reached down by the mouth of the mine and snatched him up.

Part II

The Blue Nude

In each picture is a whole lifetime imprisoned,
a whole lifetime of fears, doubts, hopes and joys.
—Wassily Kandinsky, *Concerning the
Spiritual in Art*

So, for instance, if you know that it is dangerous for you to
have colors near you, why don't you clear them away for a
time, and make drawings? I think that at such moments you
would do better not to work with colors.
—Theo van Gogh, letter to Vincent
January 3, 1890

Seven

FORM, LINE, LIGHT, SHADOW

Merde!" SAID LUCIEN.

In the creation of any work of art, there is some point, no matter how much training and experience is brought to bear on the work at hand, when the artist is taken with a feeling of both exhilaration and terror, the *Oh shit. What the hell have I gotten myself into!* moment of flailing panic, akin to the feeling of falling from a great height. Lucien's *"merde"* moment came when Juliette dropped the sheet she was using as a cover and said, "How do you want me?"

And although every experience in his life had somehow added up to this moment, this very moment, and he was uniquely suited and chosen to be in this moment, he could think of nothing whatever to say.

Well, he could think of *something* to say: *On the divan, against the wall, on the floor, bent over, wrapped around, upside-down, downside-up, fast, slow, gentle, rough, deep, hard, loud, quiet, kicking over the lamps, wild, while Paris burns, again and again until there is no more breath in our bodies, that's how I want you.*

But he didn't say that. He didn't need to. She knew.

"To pose," she said.

"I'm thinking," he said.

Form. Line. Light. Shadow. He worked the words in his mind like clay. *Form. Line. Light. Shadow.*

When he first walked into Cormon's studio at age nineteen and took his seat at an easel among the other young men, the master had told them, "See form, see line, see light, see shadow. See relationships of lines. The model is a collection of these elements, not a body."

At the master's signal, a young woman in a robe who had been sitting quietly next to the stove in the back of the room climbed up on the platform and dropped her robe. There was collective intake of breath; the newcomers, like Lucien, stopped breathing altogether for a second. She wasn't a beauty. In fact, in her shopgirl clothes, he might not have given her a second look, but she was there, nude, in a fully lit room, and he was nineteen and lived in a city where a woman was not allowed to ride on the top level of the omnibus streetcars lest someone catch a glimpse of her ankle as she climbed the steps and thus compromise her modesty. True, he had taken an apartment only a block away from a licensed brothel, and the girls danced bare breasted in the back rooms of the cabarets, and every gentleman had a mistress from the *demimonde*, who was kept in some apartment across the city, hidden behind a wink and the selective vision of his wife. But hidden.

That first class he saw *form, line, light, and shadow,* just long enough to get a bit of the drawing down, but then he'd be yanked out of his work by nipples! No, not by *the nipples,* but by general nipples—of concept— the model's nipples, and his concentration would collapse in a cascade of images and urges that had nothing whatever to do with art. For the first week, as the poor girl posed, Lucien battled the urge to stand up and yell, "For the love of God, she's naked over there, aren't any of you thinking about bonking her?" Of course they were, they were men, and except for the gay ones, they were only getting any art done at all if they managed to put that feeling to bed.

The second week, the model was an old man, who tottered up to the stage, *sans* robe, his sagging sack nearly dragging the ground, his withered haunches quivering under the weight of his years. Strangely enough, the figure was easily interpreted as *form, line, light, and shadow* from then on for Lucien. And when they were, once again, working with a female model, he only needed to conjure up the image of the old man to put him back on the straight and narrow path to *form, line, light, and shadow.*

Sure, you allowed yourself a brief moment when the model first disrobed—*Oh, yes, she'd do.* And it turned out that nearly every one of them would do, even if the imaginary circumstances in which she would do had to be constructed. *Well, yes, desert island, drunk, one hour until you're hanged, sure, she'd do.* But he had never encountered anything like Juliette, not as a painter, anyway, because he *had* encountered her as a man, had had numerous tumbles with her, in fact, as new lovers they'd been ecstatic with discovery, in his little apartment, in the dark, not going out for days at a time in the weeks before she broke his heart.

This was different. She was standing there in a beam of sunlight from the skylight, veritably glowing, as perfect and feminine as any statue in the Louvre, as ideal as any beauty obtained, any goddess imagined, by man. *Oh, she'd do. If I was being gnawed by wolves, before I'd bother to stop to shoo them off, she'd do.*

"What are you doing, Lucien?" she said. "Open your eyes."

"I'm trying to picture your desiccated scrotum," said the painter.

"I don't think anyone has ever said that to me before."

"Dangling, dangling, almost there."

"Where is your paint box? I don't even see your paints."

Lucien opened his eyes, and although he hadn't gotten into a mindset of light and shadow quite yet, his erection had at least subsided. Perhaps he could work now. Better than those early days in Cormon's when he was scolded. "Lessard, why have you drawn a nut sack on this model? You are drawing Venus, not a circus freak."

"You said she was shape and line."

"Are you serious? I am here only to teach serious painters."

And then Toulouse-Lautrec would step up behind the master, adjust his *pince-nez* as if fine-tuning the focus, and say, "That *is* a serious nut sack on that Venus."

"Indeed," their friend Émile Bernard would say, stroking his mossy beard, "that is a nut sack of a most serious aspect."

And around they'd pass the opinion, nodding and scrutinizing, until Cormon would either eject them all from class or storm out of the studio himself, leaving the poor model to break pose and inspect her nether parts, just in case.

Then Toulouse-Lautrec would say, "Monsieur Lessard, you are only to *think* about the scrotum to distract yourself, not actually draw it. I feel that the maestro will be even less open to discussing modern compositional theory now. To atone, you must now buy us all drinks."

"I'm not going to be painting today," Lucien said to Juliette. "It may take several days just to do the drawing." He waved a sanguine crayon at the wide canvas he'd set up on two chairs from the bakery café, it being too large for any easel he owned.

"It is a very large canvas," Juliette said. She lay down on the fainting lounge and propped herself up on her elbow. "I hope you are planning on taking a long time to paint this if you want me to grow into it. I'll need pastries."

Lucien glanced up at her, saw the mischievous smile. He liked that she was implying that she would stay around, that there was a future for them together, after she'd bolted before. He was tempted to make some ridiculous promise about taking care of her, knowing full well that the only way he could honestly make that promise was to put down his paintbrush forever and bake bread.

"Monsieur Monet told me once that great paintings are only achieved when the painter has great ambition. That's why, he said, Manet's *Luncheon in the Grass* and *Olympia* were great paintings."

"Great *big* paintings," she giggled.

They *were* large canvases. And Monet *had* attempted his own luncheon on the grass, a great, twenty-foot-long canvas that he dragged, rolled up, all over France with a pretty model named Camille Doncieux whom he'd met in the Batignolles and his friend Frédéric Bazille to pose for all the male figures. "But don't let your ambition become too large too early, Lucien," Monet had told him. "In case you have to sneak out on your hotel bill in the middle of the night with the canvas. Camille nearly broke her neck helping me carry that canvas through the streets of Honfleur in the dark."

"How about like this?" Juliette said. She leaned back into the cushions, her hands behind her head, a knowing smile. "You can use Goya's *Maja* pose. That's what Manet started with."

"For the love of God, she's naked over there, aren't any of you thinking about bonking her?" *The Nude Maja*—Francisco Goya, 1797

"Oh no, *ma chère*," Lucien said. "Manet didn't go to Madrid to see Goya's *Maja* until after he painted *Olympia*. He didn't know what she looked like." Lucien had grown up on lectures on the famous paintings from Père Lessard; their stories were the fairy tales of his childhood.

"Not him, silly. The model knew."

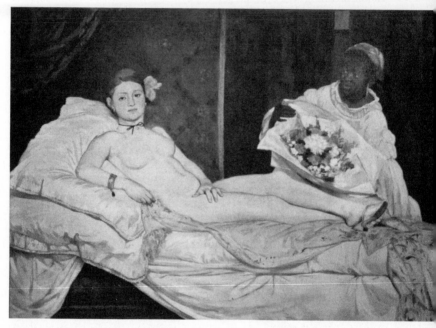

"You can use Goya's *Maja* pose. That's what Manet started with."
Olympia—Édouard Manet, 1863

What a completely disturbing thought. Olympia did look remarkably like Goya's *Nude Maja*, regarding the viewer, daring him, and Manet clearly admired Goya, using Goya's *Maja on the Balcony* as inspiration for his own painting of the Morisot family, *The Balcony*, and Goya's war paintings from Napoleon's invasion of Spain for his *Execution of Maximilian*, but those works were later, after Manet had gone to

Spain and *seen* the Goyas. It couldn't have been the model, Victorine. She was, well, she was like many models of the time, an uneducated, undowered girl who lived in the *demimonde,* the half world between prostitution and destitution. The model was like the brush, the paint, the linseed oil, the canvas. She was an instrument of the artist, not a contributor to the art.

"You know a lot about painting for a girl who works in a hat shop," Lucien said.

"So, now you'll paint me with only one brush?"

"No, I didn't mean—"

"You know a lot about painting for a baker," she said, the sparkle of a dare in her eyes.

Bitch. "Hold that pose. No, bring your right arm down to your side."

"Do it for me," she pouted. "I don't know how."

"Just move, Juliette. Now, don't move."

And he began to sketch her image nearly life-size on the canvas. First roughing out her figure, then going back, filling in contours. He lost himself in the drawing, seeing only *form, line, light,* and *shadow,* and time slipped into those dimensions until she moved.

"What? No!" Lucien dropped his crayon on the seat of one of the chairs he was using for an easel.

She stood up, stretched, yawned, fluffed her breasts up a bit, which transported Lucien out of the land of line and shape, back to a small, sunlit room with a beautiful, naked girl whom he desperately wanted to make love to, and perhaps marry, but definitely and immediately bonk.

"I'm hungry and you're not even painting."

She started to gather her clothes from a chair by the door.

"I have to have the whole motif sketched out, Juliette. I'm not going to paint you in the storeroom of a bakery. The setting needs to be more grand."

She stepped into her pantaloons and his heart sank.

"Does the *Maja* have a grand setting? Does *Olympia* have a grand setting, Lucien? Hmmm?"

And the chemise went over her head and her shoulders and the world became a dark and sad place for Lucien Lessard.

"Are you angry? Why are you angry?"

"I'm not angry. I'm tired. I'm hungry. I'm lonely."

"Lonely? I'm right here."

"Are you?"

"I am."

He stepped up to her, took her in his arms, and kissed her. And off came the chemise, off came the pantaloons, then his shirt, then the rest, and they were on each other, on the fainting lounge, completely lost in one another. There may have been pounding on the door at one point, but they didn't hear it and didn't care. Where they were, no one else mattered. When, at last, she looked down from the lounge, at him, lying on his back on the floor, the light from the skylight had gone orange, and the sweat sheen on their bodies looked like slick fire.

"I have to go," she said.

"Maybe I'll be able to start painting tomorrow."

"First thing in the morning then?"

"No, ten, maybe eleven. I have to make the bread."

"I'm going." She slid from the lounge and again gathered her clothes while he watched.

"Where are you living now?"

"A little place in the Batignolles. I share with some other shopgirls."

"Don't you have to work tomorrow?"

"The owner of my shop is understanding. He enjoys art."

"Stay. Have dinner with me. Stay at my apartment. It's closer than yours."

"Tomorrow. I need to go. The day is gone."

She was dressed now. He would have given a fortune, if he'd had it, to watch her pull her stockings up again. He sat up.

"Tomorrow," she said again. She put her hand on his shoulder and kept him from rising, then kissed him on the forehead. "I'll go out through the alley."

"I love you," he said.

"I know," she said as she closed the door.

"WELL?" SAID THE COLORMAN.

She put her parasol in a stand by the door and untied the wide ribbon that held on her hat, then set it gently on the hall tree. The apartment's parlor was small but not shabby. A Louis XVI coffee table in gold leaf and marble sat before a mauve velvet divan. The Colorman sat in a carved walnut chair from the same period and looked like a malignant, twisted burl infecting the elegant wooden form.

"He didn't paint," she said.

"I need a painting. Since we lost the Dutchman's picture, we need the color."

"That was a waste. He'll paint. He just hasn't started yet."

"I mixed colors for him. Greens and violets made with the blue, as well as the pure color. I put them in a nice wooden box."

"I'll give them to him tomorrow."

"And make him paint."

"I can't make him paint. I can only make him *want* to paint."

"We can't have another perfectionist like that fucking Whistler. We need a painting, soon."

"He needs to be handled gently. This one is special."

"You always say that."

"I do? Well, perhaps it's true."

"You smell of sex."

"I know," she said as she sat on the divan and began to unlace her shoes. "I need a bath. Where's the maid?"

"Gone. She quit."

"Frightened?" She kicked off a shoe and sat back on the divan with a sigh.

He nodded, looking at the ground, looking very simian and ashamed, as if he were the bad monkey confessing to eating the sacred banana. Again.

"You didn't try to fuck her, did you?"

"No. No. No. Making color. She came in."

"And she saw you?"

"An accident." He shrugged. "Couldn't be helped."

She grinned at him as she unbuttoned her blouse. "'Couldn't be helped'—you like it, don't you?"

"She had cooked supper already." Again the shrug. "It's on the stove. There's hot water."

The girl called Juliette shrugged off her blouse and pulled her chemise over her head. The Colorman scrutinized her breasts as she stood, unbuttoned her skirt, and let it fall.

"I like this body," he said, looking her up and down. "The skin so white, almost blue, yes? Hair black and shiny. I like. Where did you find her?"

"This one? This one is mine." She walked away in only her pantaloons and black stockings, leaving her clothes behind in a heap. "I guess I'll be drawing my own bath."

"Can I watch?" asked the Colorman. He slid out of his chair.

She stopped and looked at him over her shoulder. "Why?"

"Pretty skin. Nothing to read."

"You *like* scaring them, don't you?"

"Supper smells good, huh? Veal stew. Maybe she'll come back. She didn't seem that scared."

She turned abruptly to face him and he skipped to a stop, his face almost bumping into her belly, a near collision of the sacred and profane.

"You like scaring them more than you like fucking them, don't you?"

The shrug. "I'm old." He looked around the room, as if trying to remember something that was anywhere but where she was. "And scaring them is free."

She turned on a heel and with three long dancer's strides was in the bedroom, where there was a high-backed, enameled tub. "Oh for fuck's sake. Come on."

"*Merci*, Bleu," he said. Bleu was what he called her, how he thought of her, because it fit, no matter who she was, no matter *what* she was. He limped in behind her.

"Get us a new maid tomorrow, though," she said. "And don't scare this one."

Interlude in Blue #3:
A Frog in Time

A substance's color is generated by the absorption of light hitting it and the material's resonant frequencies. That is, when a material's molecules resonate with a certain frequency of light, the light rays are absorbed. When they do not resonate, the rays are either reflected or pass right through it. Only the reflected rays reach our eye and determine color. Natural pigments, like lapis lazuli, from which the Sacré Bleu is made, show their color by the absorption of light. Absorption of light literally transforms the orbit of the electrons in the atoms of the pigment. In short, the color doesn't actually exist, physically, as we experience it, until it is exposed to light waves. Light makes it appear, changes the surface physically.

Theoretically, if all of the light passed through a substance, an object could be invisible to the eye.

Strangely enough, truly blue pigment exists in no vertebrate creature on Earth. The fish scales, butterfly wings, peacock feathers that appear to our eye to be blue are what is called *structural color*, where surfaces are composed of microstructures that scatter very short wavelengths of blue light—refraction—the reason the sky appears blue without blue pigment.

There are, however, unconfirmed reports of a blue tree frog in the Amazon river basin. The frog has been spotted on three occasions by Western biologists, but when any attempt was made to capture or photograph the creature, it appeared to the scientists to vanish.

Native legends tell of a shaman who found one of the blue frogs dead and made an arrow poison with its skin. When he shot a monkey with the poisoned arrow, it disappeared, or so he said. But a boy from the shaman's village remembered finding a dead monkey at the edge of the village the month before, slain with an arrow exactly like the one the shaman had used, even though the shaman had not been hunting that earlier time. Somehow, the blue arrow poison had transported the animal across time.

Many Indians report that they have seen the blue frog of the Amazon vanish before their eyes, and even with a thorough search of the area have never gotten a second glimpse of the same frog. What they neglected to consider was not where to search, but when.

Eight

APHRODITE WAVING LIKE A LUNATIC

Paris, 1890

L UCIEN WORKED IN THE BAKERY BY HIMSELF UNTIL ALMOST EIGHT O'CLOCK before his sister Régine came down and found him at the front counter. There had been no sign of Mère Lessard, who was usually bustling about the shop, sweeping and fretting and arranging the cases and racks in the front well before dawn.

"Where have you been?" asked Lucien. "Where is Maman? I've barely been able to keep up with the customers and not burn the pastries."

"Maman is tired. She won't be working today."

Lucien handed a customer a *boule,* the large round loaf that was their specialty, then took the customer's coins and thanked her before turning to his sister. He could never remember his mother skipping work except to visit her own mother, or out of retribution for some offense, real or imagined, by his father.

"Is she sick? Should I send for a doctor?"

Régine smacked him in the back of the head with a baguette, which he interpreted as, "No, you do not need to send for a doctor."

Two old men who had been killing time at one of the small café tables laughed.

"Ah, Lucien, you don't need a wife, eh? Not with a sister like that."

"Family business conference," Régine said. She breezed by him in a way that seemed even more menacing than the normal breezing by of their mother (even though Régine was half her size). She caught Lucien's apron strings and pulled him backward into the kitchen.

Before Lucien could get fully turned around she was brandishing the baguette like an axe handle, ready to dash his brains out with its delicious, crunchy-chewy crust.

"How can you use that storeroom, Lucien? How can you paint in there, after what happened to Papa?"

"Papa always wanted me to be a painter," Lucien said. He didn't understand why she was so angry. "And we've always used that storeroom."

"As a storeroom, you idiot. Not as a studio. We could hear you two in there yesterday. Gilles pounded on the door when he came home from work and you ignored him."

Régine had married a carpenter name Gilles, the son of a dance-hall doorman, also from Montmartre. They lived in the apartment upstairs with Madame Lessard. "Where is Gilles? Did he not go to work either?"

"I sent him down the back stairs."

"Régine, this is going to be a great picture. My masterpiece."

The baguette came around fast and wrapped around his head. The Lessards had always prided themselves on their light, delicate crust, so Lucien was somewhat surprised at how much it hurt, even now, after all the practice.

"Ouch. Régine, I am a grown man, this is none of your affair."

"There was a woman, Lucien. With Papa."

Lucien suddenly forgot about being angry, about having to run the bakery alone or being ashamed about his sister listening to him having sex. "A woman?"

"Maman was in Louveciennes, visiting Grand-mère. Marie and I saw her, well, just the back of her as she went into the storeroom. Some red-haired slut. Marie went to see what she could. That's what she was doing up on the roof when she fell."

Régine was breathless now, and not from distress she had constructed in order to get her way. Lucien had seen that often enough to know this wasn't it.

"Does Maman know?"

"No." Régine shook her head. "No one. No one."

"Why didn't you tell me?"

"Because I didn't know anything. We just saw a woman, just the back of her, but she had long red hair, *the slut*. We saw her go in the storeroom with Papa and he locked the door. I didn't know what happened. Then when Marie fell—I didn't know what to do. It was too much."

Lucien took his sister in his arms. "I'm sorry. I didn't know. He was probably just painting her."

"Like you were painting yesterday?"

Lucien held her and patted her back. "I have to go. I really am painting Juliette today. *Painting.*"

Régine nodded and pushed him away. "I know."

"We were together, before, Régine. I thought I'd lost her. Yesterday was—was a reunion."

"I know, but you're the baby. It's sordid. Maman says she has no son now that you've ruined that poor girl."

"Two days ago she threatened to have a Russian man set Juliette on fire and feed our children to Madame Jacob's dog."

"That was before she heard you two. She won't come out of her room until lunch or you have gone to confession, whichever comes first."

"But I'm twenty-seven years old, did you think that I was never with a woman?"

"Well, you never bring them home. We thought perhaps someone had taken you to bed out of pity, maybe. And girls now *do* drink a lot."

Lucien brushed the crumbs out of his hair. "I'm not married because I'm a painter, not because I can't find a woman. I've told you, I don't have time for a wife. It wouldn't be fair to her."

"So you say. I suppose we should be grateful that you're not chasing boys like that horrible Englishman that came into the bakery."

"Oscar? Oscar is brilliant. Speaks French dreadfully, but a brilliant man."

"Go," Régine said. "I will watch the store. Go paint. And don't tell Maman what I told you. Don't tell anyone."

"I won't."

"And don't be sordid."

"I won't."

"And don't become reclusive like Papa."

"I won't."

"And leave the studio door open, so we can see what you're doing."

"I won't."

"Go," she said, gesturing with her broken baguette. "Go, go, go, little brother. Go to your slut."

"I love her."

"No one cares. Go!"

ALL MORNING, WHILE HE WENT ABOUT HIS WORK IN THE BAKERY, LUCIEN HAD been telling himself, *Today I am an artist. I will make art. I am not going to throw her on the lounge and boff her senseless, no matter how much she begs.* He really hoped she wouldn't beg, because he wasn't that sure of his resolve. *And even if I throw her on the lounge and boff her senseless, I'm not going to ask her to marry me.*

He found her waiting by the shed door when he came out of the bakery. She wore a festive white dress with blue and pink bows and a tall hat that looked more like a flower arrangement than headwear. The sort of ensemble a girl might wear to dance in the courtyard of the Moulin de la Galette on a beautiful summer Sunday afternoon, not an outfit you would put on to walk a dozen blocks so you could take it off for a painter.

"Don't you look pretty."

"Thank you. I brought you a present."

"And you've wrapped it beautifully," he said, putting a hand on her waist.

"Not that, you goat, something else. I'll show you inside."

As he unlocked the door, she took a hinged wooden box from her bag and opened it. "Look, color! The man assured me it's the finest quality. 'Pure pigments,' he said, whatever that means."

There were a dozen tubes of paint, large, 250-milliliter tubes—enough color to easily cover the canvas, unless he used the thick impasto method that van Gogh liked, and he didn't think that technique suited his subject. Each tube had a small label of paper pasted on it with a dab of the color, but there was no writing, no note on the mixture.

"But I was going to go buy paint from Père Tanguy this afternoon."

"Now you can start painting instead," she said. She kissed his cheek, set the box onto the table he'd set up for supplies, then she noticed a changing screen had been set up at the far end of the studio. *"Oh là là.* Is that to preserve my modesty?"

"It's proper," he said.

Actually, he had fetched the screen from Henri's studio on rue Caulaincourt in the wee hours, while the bread was baking, so he wouldn't be able to watch her dress or undress. He thought perhaps he would be able to keep his concentration on the painting that way.

She emerged from behind the screen wearing a white Japanese silk kimono that Henri kept around the studio for his models, or for himself, as on occasion he liked to dress like a geisha girl and have their friend Maurice Guibert take photos of him. But as far as making Juliette look like the diminutive aristocratic painter, the robe failed miserably.

"How do you want me?" Juliette asked, letting the kimono fall open.

Well now she was just *trying* to be annoying.

Lucien looked only at the canvas, made a point, in fact, of looking *only* at the canvas, and waved her toward the lounge as if he didn't have time to bother with showing her how to pose. "Like yesterday will be fine," he said.

"Oh really, shall I lock the door?"

"The pose," Lucien said. "Like yesterday, do you remember?"

She dropped the robe and reclined into the same pose she had been in the day before. Exactly the same pose, he figured, looking at the sketch. It was uncanny for a model to find the pose that quickly without direction.

He'd decided to set her in an Oriental harem, after the Algerian paintings of Delacroix. Great flowing silks and golden statues in the background. Maybe a slave fanning her. A eunuch, perhaps? He heard his masters, Pissarro, Renoir, and Monet, lecturing him: *"Paint what you see. Capture the moment. Paint what is real."* But the whitewashed storeroom would not do as a setting for this beauty, and he didn't want to paint the background black and bring up the image from darkness as the Italian masters had, as had Goya with his *Maja.*

"I'm thinking about painting it in the Florentine style, laying down all the values in *grisaille,* a gray-green underpainting, then glazing the colors on over it. It will take longer than other methods, but I think it's the only way I can capture your light. I mean, *the* light."

"Could you do the underpainting in another color, say that pretty blue the man sold me?"

Lucien looked again at her, the sun filtering in from the skylight on her naked skin, then at the canvas. "Yes, yes, I can do that."

And he began to paint.

After he'd been at it an hour, Juliette said, "My arm is going to sleep. Can I move it?" Without waiting for his permission, she started to swing her arm around in a windmill motion.

"Sure, I'll call the painting *Aphrodite Waving Like a Lunatic*."

"No one has done that before, I'll bet. You would be the first to paint a waving nude. It could start a revolution."

Now she was nodding as well as swinging her arm around; the unsynchronized motion put him in mind of one of Professeur Bastard's bizarre machines.

"Maybe we should take a break," Lucien said.

"Buy me lunch."

"I can get you something from the bakery."

"I want you to take me out."

"But you're naked."

"Not permanently."

"Let me finish your thighs, then we'll go."

"Oh, *cher*, that sounds delicious."

"Stop moving your legs, please."

"Sorry."

It was two hours before he stepped away from the canvas and stretched his back. "That seems like a good place to take a break."

"What? What? Is there a voice there? I'm faint from hunger." She threw her arm over her eyes dramatically and pretended to faint, which on the fainting couch looked terribly appropriate and made Lucien wonder if he might not have chosen the wrong pose for her.

"Why don't you get dressed while I clean these brushes?"

She sat up quickly, pushed her lower lip out in a pout. "You're bored with me, aren't you?"

Lucien shook his head; there really was no winning here, as his father had taught him was often the case when dealing with women.

"Where do you want to go for lunch?" Lucien asked.

"I have an idea," she said.

Before he could fully fathom what she had in mind, they were boarding a train at Gare Saint-Lazare and headed for Chatou, only a few miles northwest of the city.

"It's lunch, Juliette. I need to get back to work."

"I know. Trust me," she said.

From the train station she led him to the banks of the Seine; out on the river he could see people gathered on a small island, connected to the shore by a long wooden dock. Rowers and day sailors had tied their boats to the dock. There was music playing and people on the platform were laughing, dancing, and drinking, the men in bright, striped jackets and straw boaters, the women in brightly colored pastel dresses. All along the shore bathers waded, splashed, and swam, and farther up the river, Lucien could see couples lying together under the willows.

"I can't believe there are so many people out here on a weekday," Lucien said.

"Isn't it marvelous?" Juliette said, taking his hand. She pulled him down the riverbank.

Lucien saw two painters working side by side on the near bank, concentrating intensely on their work and laying down color at a mad speed. He stopped to watch and Juliette yanked him away. "Those two are—"

"Come on, it will be lovely."

Finally, he gave himself up to the experience. They ate, and drank, and danced. She flirted with various boaters and the gentlemen slumming among the rowers, who were having a look at all the young girls, and just as she'd get their interest, she would cling to Lucien's arm and profess to her suitor that the painter was her only and her ever. The resentment from the men was palpable.

"Juliette, don't do that. It's—well, I don't know what it is, but it makes everyone involved uncomfortable."

"I know," she said, and she planted a wet kiss on his neck, which made him squirm and laugh.

A fellow in a T-shirt and boater who was rowing by at the time shouted, "Ah, nothing like a Sunday afternoon at La Grenouillère, *oui?*"

"*Oui,*" said Lucien with a smile, tipping his own straw boater, which he didn't remember putting on, or for that matter owning. He was sure it was Tuesday. Yes, Tuesday.

"Let's explore," said Juliette.

They walked up the riverbank, talking and laughing, Lucien noting how the light played on the water, Juliette noting how silly everyone looked in their bathing costumes, some of the men still wearing their hats as they swam. They found a spot under a willow tree whose branches hung all the way to the ground, and there, on a blanket, they finished a bottle of wine, teased, kissed, and made love, all of it feeling very exciting and dangerous and naughty.

After they dozed in each other's arms for what seemed like the whole afternoon, they made their way back to the train station, where the last train of the day was just boarding. They took the train to Gare Saint-Lazare, leaning on one another as they looked out the window, not saying a word, but both grinning like blissful idiots.

Although he could ill afford it, Lucien paid for a cab to take them from the station back to the bakery, where she assumed her pose on the fainting lounge, and he took his seat, palette in hand, and he resumed his work, without a word, until the light from the skylight went orange.

"That's it," Juliette said.

"But, *ma chère*—"

She stood and began dressing, as if she had suddenly remembered an appointment. "That's enough for today."

"They used to call this the painter's hour, Juliette," Lucien said. "There's a softness to the early evening light, and besides—"

She put her finger to his lips. "Have you not had a good day?"

"Well, uh, yes, of course, but—"

"The day is done," she said. And in a minute she had dressed and was out the door. "Tomorrow," she said.

Lucien sat back on the little stool he'd been sitting on to work on the lower parts of the canvas. It had been a good day. A very good day. In fact, he couldn't remember ever having had such a day before.

He put down his brushes and palette and moved to the fainting couch, where he could still feel the warmth of Juliette's body. La Grenouillère: he had always heard about it, about the wonderful times. He'd seen the paintings Monet and Renoir had made there side by side. It was even more magical than he had imagined. He lay back on the couch and covered his eyes with his arm, letting the day play in his head. He wondered why, in all of his life in Paris, he hadn't spent a glorious Sunday afternoon among the boaters and the "little frogs" at La Grenouillère. Perhaps, he thought, it was because La Grenouillère had burned to the waterline in 1873, when he was ten, and had never been rebuilt. Yes, that was probably why. And for some reason, that didn't bother him at all.

Nine

NOCTURNE IN BLACK AND GOLD

London, 1865

A LIGHT FOG WASHED THE BANK AT BATTERSEA BRIDGE. BARGES MOVED like great black ghosts on the Thames, silent but for the *clop clop* of a team of draft horses on the shore echoing off the houses of Chelsea.

Out on Battersea Bridge, the Colorman looked like a pile of wool haunting the night, wrapped in an overcoat that reached all the way to the ground, the collar up higher than his ears and brushing the wide brim of a black leather hat. Only his eyes showed above a thick wool scarf.

"What kind of loony paints at night, outside, in the cold?" he said. "This bloody island is always cold and damp. I hate it here." When he spoke steam, diffused by the scarf, came rolling out from under the brim of his hat.

"He's as mad as we've made him," said the redhead. She pulled her own coat tight around her. "And it was on this island they made you a king, so don't be such an ungrateful little wanker."

"Well, fix him. If he paints at night, we'll lose him."

She shrugged. "Sometimes you lose."

She walked down off the bridge into Chelsea and up the river toward the painter, who stood at an easel with a small lantern hung from it so he could see his palette and canvas.

WHAT KIND OF LUNATIC PAINTS AT NIGHT, OUTSIDE, IN THE COLD? WHISTLER wondered. He stamped his feet to get the blood flowing in them, then washed some of the ultramarine blue across the center of the canvas with a wide sable brush.

He'd thinned the paint so much that he had to brace the canvas so that it stuck out from the easel horizontally, to keep the color from running, as if he were painting with watercolor. Just as well he was doing his nocturnes outside; the fumes from that much turpentine would have sent his head spinning if he'd tried to paint them in the studio, in winter, with the windows closed. As if being in the studio at all, with her, didn't send him spinning anyway.

Jo—Joanna, his wild redhead, his blessing, his curse. She was like some siren from an Edgar Allan Poe story, "Ligia," perhaps. Preternaturally intelligent, frighteningly beautiful in that detached, untouchable way that he so loved touching. But he was so unsettled around her, losing time, lately, going to the studio in the evening to find that he'd finished a painting that day without any recollection of having done it. At least he remembered the work he was doing on these night paintings.

But how could she be the cause of his, well, instability? And why did it subside when he worked at night?

A woman's voice behind him. "I think throwing your brother-in-law through the window might have marked the moment when it all went tits-up, wouldn't you say, love?"

Whistler turned so quickly he nearly knocked over his easel. "Jo, how did you know I was here?"

"I didn't. I was out for a walk. I thought you were probably home with your mum."

Whistler's dire, puritanical mother was visiting from the States. She'd come over to check on him when his sister wrote her to say that she was worried about his "well-being of mind," prompted, no doubt, by Whistler throwing her husband through a café window.

"Well that was stupid," Jo had told him that night.

"He said that you looked like my attending tart." He couldn't believe he had to defend defending her.

At that point she'd pulled her nightgown over her head and slid naked into his lap. "If the shoe fits, love," she said. "If the shoe fits."

He lost most every argument to her that way.

Upon finding out his mother had arrived in London, Whistler and Jo quickly removed from the house all evidence of what Mother would have called his "decadent life"—from his collection of Japanese prints, to his bar, to Jo herself, whom he moved into his studio a few blocks away.

As soon as he'd been out of Jo's company for a few days, he started to feel different, as if a part of him that had been lost had returned, but he also started to have vivid, detailed dreams of working on paintings that didn't exist, of going places with her he had never been. But now, in the cold, damp London night, rather than feeling obsessed by her, inspired by her, or overwhelmed by her, he was . . . well . . . he was afraid of her.

With his palette still in hand, Whistler went to her and kissed her on the cheek. "Sorry, I've been experimenting with the points of light on the river, using washes of oil to produce atmosphere."

"I see," she said. "Does Mum think you're mad, then?"

"No, just deeply corrupted."

"I'll take that as a compliment," she said, snaking her arm around his waist. "You've had supper?"

"I did. One dines early when the Lord is expected at every meal. He's on a tight schedule, evidently."

"Come back to the studio, Jimmy. I'll make you a treat."

"Thank you, but I'm not hungry."

"Who said anything about food?"

He stepped out of her embrace and up to the canvas. "No, Jo, I need to work."

"It's not like you have to capture the bloody light; it's dark as a black dog's ass out here. Come in and warm up."

"No, you go. I'll try to stop by the studio to see you tomorrow." But he wouldn't be stopping by. If things went as he'd planned, he'd be on a steamer to South America tomorrow. He unfolded and sat on a three-legged stool before the easel, pretended to be engrossed in his painting.

She said, "That creepy little brown chap came by the studio today. He said you owe him a painting."

"I'm beyond that, Jo. My work is selling. I can't trade a painting for a few tubes of paint."

She nodded and removed her gloves with more care than was really required, as if considering what would come next. "I think you know it's more than a few tubes of paint."

"Fine then, I'll pay him in cash. If he comes by again, tell him I'll be in the studio on Monday."

By Monday he'd be in the middle of the Atlantic, steaming his way to Chile to paint the war there. His mother haranguing him about his dropping out of West Point to become a painter, as well as his brother's noble service as a surgeon in the Confederate army, had given him the idea. He wondered what it said about a man that he would actually go into a war zone to avoid his mistress.

She went to him, ran her hand through his hair, traced the fringe on his forehead with her fingernail. "You're not still angry about my posing for Courbet?"

They'd gone to Normandy with Whistler's friend and mentor the French Realist painter Gustave Courbet, and one afternoon James returned from painting fishing boats on the beach to find Jo spread out naked across one of the beds, the sun through the window lighting up her red hair like copper fire, and Courbet at his easel, painting her. Whistler didn't say a word at the time. They were artists, after all, and Courbet's mistress was in the next room doing needlework, but he'd exploded at Jo as soon as they were alone.

"No, I'm not angry," he said, not looking up from the nocturne he was painting. "His picture wasn't as good as mine of you."

"Ah, so that was the issue. That explains it." She ruffled his hair, then took the crown of his head in one hand and his chin in the other and held his head against her breast. He didn't push away, but he didn't lean into her embrace.

"Ah, Jimmy, you're such a love." She bent then and held his head tightly as she whispered in his ear. "Good night, my love."

She kissed his cheek, stood, and walked away toward Battersea Bridge.

He watched her go and realized that he had been holding his breath from the time she'd first touched his chin. He thought for a moment about painting her as a shadowy figure in the fog, but then it spilled back on him, the lead poisoning, the wave that nearly killed him, the temper tantrums, the loss of memory, the deep unsettledness that always seemed to follow his painting her, and he shivered and put his brush into the tin he'd hung from the easel.

She turned back toward him then. He couldn't even see her face, just the corona of red around her head, the gaslights of Chelsea reflecting off her hair. "Jimmy," she said in a whisper, which he heard as if it were coming from inside his head instead of from fifty yards away. "That day in Normandy? I'd just fucked Gustave, right before you came in. He had

"Ah, Jimmy, you're such a love." *Weary*—James McNeill Whistler, 1863

both of us, me and Elise, one after another, and we had each other while he watched. I thought you should know. That was a lovely painting you did of the fishing boats, though. One of my favorites. I gave it to the Colorman. Don't be angry. You don't know it, but Gustave saved your life. Tonight. *Bon voyage*, love."

"Well?" said the Colorman.

"No painting," said Bleu.

"But soon, yes? No more painting in the dark? A painting soon, yes?"

"No. He's leaving. I went by his house. There are trunks in the foyer.

He ordered enough color for a whole season from Windsor and Newton. The bill came to the studio, but the delivery went to the house."

"Those fucks at Windsor and Newton. They're using Prussian colors." He spit off the bridge to show his disdain for those fucks at Windsor and Newton, Prussian colors, and the river Thames in general. "Where are we going?"

"You and I are going to France. I don't know where he is going."

"You're going to just let him get away?"

"I have someone else in mind," she said.

"But who? Who will you be to him?"

"That's the beauty of it. He's already taken with Jo." She did a half curtsy as if presenting herself. "I don't even have to change shoes."

"Sounds dodgy," said the Colorman. "Let's use this one up."

"No, Courbet is very talented. A great painter."

"You always say that."

"Perhaps it's always true," she said.

They went to France, they found Gustave Courbet working in Provence, where it was warm, which made the Colorman happy. Jo would be Courbet's mistress and model on and off for ten years, after which the man who had once been called France's greatest painter was exiled to Switzerland, and there, broke and alone, drank himself to death.

"See," the Colorman would say. "That could have been that fucking Whistler. We could have fed him to a Saint Bernard."

The Colorman had never really cared for Whistler.

Ten

RESCUE

COUNT HENRI-MARIE-RAYMOND DE TOULOUSE-LAUTREC-MONFA BURST into the room, drew his weapon, and shouted, "Madame, I demand you unhand this man, in the name of France, Le Boulangerie du Montmartre, and Jeanne d'Arc!"

Juliette quickly covered herself with her robe; Lucien looked up from his canvas and held his brush at port arms.

"Really, Henri, 'Jeanne d'Arc'?"

"Well, we don't have a king anymore."

Juliette said, "Why is he waving that cordial glass at me?"

"Oh balls," said Toulouse-Lautrec. Instead of his sword cane he had grabbed his flask cane, which concealed a flask of cognac and a cordial glass (a gentleman does not drink directly from his walking stick) for visits to his mother, and he was, indeed, brandishing a crystal cordial glass at the naked girl.

"Because a snifter would not fit into my cane," he said finally, as if that explained everything.

"I thought you were at your mother's in Malromé."

"I was. But I have returned to rescue you!"

"Well that's very thoughtful of you."

"You've grown a beard."

Lucien rubbed his cheek. "Well, I've stopped shaving."

"And you've stopped eating as well?" Lucien had been thin before, but now he looked as if he hadn't eaten the entire month that Henri had been gone. Lucien's sister had said so much in a letter she'd sent to Malromé:

> *Monsieur Toulouse-Lautrec, he has stopped making the bread.*
> *He won't listen to my mother or me. And he physically threatened*
> *my husband, Gilles, when he tried to intervene. He locks himself in*
> *the studio every morning with that woman, and he drags himself*
> *out in the evening and leaves through the alley, without so much as*
> *a* bonjour *for his family. He rants about his duty as an artist and*
> *won't be reasoned with. Maybe he will listen to another artist. M.*
> *Renoir is in Aix, visiting Cézanne. M. Pissarro is in Auvers, and*
> *M. Monet never seems to leave Giverny. Please, help, I do not know*
> *the other artists of the butte, and Mother says they are all useless*
> *scalawags anyway and wouldn't be able to help. I disagree, as I*
> *have found you to be a very kind and useful scalawag, and overall*
> *a very charming little man. I implore you to come help me save my*
> *brother from this horrible woman.*
>
> *Regards,*
> *Régine Robelard*

"You remember Juliette, from before?" said Lucien.

"You mean *before* when she ruined your life and reduced you to a miserable wretch? Before that?"

"Before that," said Lucien.

"Yes." Henri tipped his hat with the cordial glass, now feeling quite silly for holding it. "*Enchanté*, mademoiselle."

"Monsieur Toulouse-Lautrec," said Juliette, still in pose, dropping the silk robe to offer her hand.

"Oh my," said Henri. He looked over his shoulder at Lucien, then back at Juliette, who smiled, calmly, almost beatifically, not as if she wasn't aware that she was naked, but as if she were bestowing a gift upon the world. He forgot for a moment that he had come here to rescue his friend from her villainy. Her lovely, lovely villainy.

Henri bowed quickly over her hand, then wheeled on a heel. "I must see your painting."

"No, it's not ready." Lucien caught him by the shoulders to keep him from moving behind the canvas.

"Nonsense, I'm an artist as well, and your studio mate; I have special privileges."

"Not on this one, Henri, please."

"I have to see what you've done with this—this—" He was waving toward Juliette while trying to get a look at the canvas. "The form, the luminosity of the skin—"

"Lucien, he's talking about me like I'm a thing," said Juliette.

Lucien crouched and sighted over his friend's shoulder. "Look at the subtlety of the shadows, soft blue, barely three levels of value between the highlights and the shadows. You'd never see that except with indirect sunlight. With the surrounding buildings diffusing it, the light is like this most of the day. It's only for an hour either side of noon that the highlights become too harsh."

"Lucien, now you're talking about me like I'm a thing."

"Nonsense, ma chère, I'm talking about the light."

"But you're pointing at me."

"We should put a skylight in the studio on rue Caulaincourt," Henri said.

"There's an apartment upstairs, Henri. I fear the effect wouldn't be the same."

"Good point. Is this the pose? You should do her from the back when you finish this one. She's a finer ass than Velázquez's *Venus* in London. Have you seen it? Exquisite! Have her looking over her shoulder at you in a mirror."

"Still here," Juliette said.

"Put a naked cherub on the couch with her to hold the mirror," said Henri. "I can model if you need."

The idea of Henri as a hirsute cherub seemed to jolt Lucien out of his enchantment with the light on Juliette's skin, and he steered the count to the door. "Henri, it's good to see you, but you have to go. Let's meet at the Chat Noir this evening for a drink. I need to work now."

"But I feel as if my rescue has been, well, somehow less than satisfactory."

"No, I've never felt so thoroughly rescued, Henri. Thank you."

"Well, this evening, then. Good day, mademoiselle," he called to Juliette as Lucien pushed him out the door.

"*À bientôt,*" the girl said.

Lucien closed the door behind him and Henri stood there in the little weed-choked courtyard, holding a crystal cordial glass with a heavy brass knob on its base, wondering exactly what had just happened. He was sure that Lucien was in grave danger; otherwise, why had he hurried back from Malromé? Why had he come to the bakery? Why, in fact, was he even awake at this ungodly, midmorning hour?

He shrugged, and since he was holding the cordial glass anyway, he worked the long cylinder of the silver flask from his cane and poured himself a cognac to steel his nerves for the next stage of the rescue.

Inside the studio, Juliette resumed her pose and said, "Have you ever seen the Velázquez Venus, Lucien?"

"No, I've never been to London."

"Perhaps we should go see it," she said.

TOULOUSE-LAUTREC WAITED ACROSS THE SQUARE IN MADAME JACOB'S *CRÉMERIE*, watching the alley next to Lessard's *boulangerie*. The girl appeared at dusk, just as Lucien's sister said she would. He quickly chomped on a bit of bread spread with Camembert that he had left, drained his wine, placed some coins on the table, and climbed down from the stool.

"*Merci,* madame," he called to the old woman. "Good evening."

"Good evening, Monsieur Henri."

Henri watched as the girl made her way across the square and down rue du Calvaire toward the bottom of the butte. Henri had never had cause to follow anyone before, but his father was an avid hunter, and despite Henri being a sickly child, he had grown up stalking animals. He knew that it was folly to follow too closely, so he let his prey get two blocks ahead before he limped along behind. Fortunately, her trail was all downhill, and he was able to keep up with her easily, although she didn't dawdle or stop at any stalls or markets as did most of the other shopgirls crowding the sidewalks on their way home from work.

She actually passed his studio on rue Caulaincourt, and Henri was tempted to stop in and refresh himself with a cognac before continuing, or more likely, not continuing, and finish his evening out at the Moulin Rouge, but he fought the urge and followed her around Montmartre Cemetery and into the Seventeenth Arrondissement, to the neighborhood known as the Batignolles. This was one of Haussmann's new neighborhoods, with wide boulevards and standardized buildings, six stories tall, with mansard roofs and balconies on the second and top floors. Clean, modern, and devoid of much of the squalor that had marked old Paris, and for that matter, Montmartre.

When they had gone perhaps twenty blocks southwest, most of it with Henri huffing and puffing to keep up, the girl turned abruptly off rue Legendre to a side street that Henri did not know. He hurried to the corner, as fast as his aching legs would carry him, so as not to lose her, and nearly ran into a young girl in a maid's uniform who was running the other way. Henri excused himself, then removed his hat and peeked around the corner. Juliette was not ten feet away. Beyond her stood the little Colorman.

"Was that our maid?" asked Juliette.

"Accident," said the Colorman. "Couldn't be helped."

"Did you scare this one, too?"

"Penis," he explained.

"Well there's really no excuse for that, is there?"

"Accident."

"You can't just accidentally penis someone. She better have made supper and drawn me a bath before you frightened her off. I'm exhausted and I'm taking Lucien to London tomorrow, where I'm going to bonk him in every corner of Kensington."

"How do you bonk someone in the Kensington?"

She growled something in a language that Henri didn't understand, unlocked the gate, and led the Colorman up the stairs. Henri stepped around the corner and watched the gate swing shut.

So that was it. She *was* connected to Vincent's little Colorman. But how? Father, perhaps? Tomorrow. Tomorrow he would find out. Now he had to be back on the butte at the Chat Noir to meet Lucien. He limped to avenue de Clichy and a cabstand, then rode back up the hill in the back of a carriage.

He waited for Lucien at Le Chat Noir until nearly ten, then, when the baker did not show, made his way to the Moulin Rouge, where he drank and sketched the dancers until someone, he thought it may have been the clown La Goulue, poured him into a taxi and sent him home.

THE NEXT MORNING, AT WHAT HE CONSIDERED A SAVAGE HOUR, HENRI crouched in an alley off avenue de Clichy, with a portable easel, paint box, and folding stool, waiting for the girl to pass. Every few minutes, a boy he had hired would bring him an espresso from the café around the corner, he would splash a bit of cognac into the cup, then he would shoo the boy away and resume his watch. He was three espressos and a cigar into the mission when he spotted Juliette as she rounded the corner, wearing a simple black dress and parasol and a hat decorated with iridescent black feathers with a smoke chiffon scarf as its band, which trailed behind her as she walked. Even from a block away her blue eyes were striking, framed by all the black silk and white skin, and he was put in mind of Renoir's vibrant, blue-eyed beauties, all of the color, but none of the softness, at least not here, on the street. In Lucien's studio yesterday, well, there her edges had softened.

He ducked into the alley and extinguished his cigar on the bricks, then flattened himself against the wall. As a boy, he had sat in hunting blinds with his father, on their estate outside of Albi, and although he'd spent most of his time in the blind sketching the trees, the animals, and the other hunters, the count had taught him that stillness and patience could be as vital to a hunt as the stealth and agility of the stalk. "If you are still enough," his father would say, "you become part of your surroundings, invisible to your prey."

"*Bonjour*, Monsieur Henri," Juliette called as she walked by.

Well fuck the count—great, eccentric, inbred lunatic that he is, anyway, thought Henri.

"*Bonjour*, Mademoiselle Juliette," he called back. "Tell Lucien I waited for him last evening."

"I will. Forgive him, he had an exhausting day. I'm sure he's sorry he missed you."

He watched as she was carried away by the stream of people on the avenue, then signaled to the coffee boy, on whom he loaded up the easel, the stool, and the paint box.

"Come, Captain, we are on to Austerlitz!"

The boy rattled along behind him, dragging the legs of the easel and barely able to keep himself from tripping over the stool and the paint box. "But, monsieur, I am not a captain and I am not allowed to go to Austerlitz. I have school."

"It's just an expression, young man. All you need to know is you shall receive twenty-five *centimes* for your efforts, providing you don't dash my poor paint box to splinters on the cobbles."

After a few blocks Henri led the boy down the street where he'd followed Juliette the night before, then paid the boy to set up his easel on the sidewalk opposite her building. It occurred to him, then, that if he were going to pretend to paint, for perhaps hours, that he was going to have to actually paint. Should the Colorman appear after watching him out the window for hours, he'd actually have to have some color on the canvas.

He had only one small canvas in the holder in his paint box. A bit of a dilemma. He hadn't painted *en plein air* very often, but the master of the method, Monet, said that no decent painter should ever work outdoors on a single painting for more than an hour at a time, lest he be trying to paint light that is no longer there. Even now, the master was probably in Giverny or Rouen with a dozen canvases set up on a dozen easels, moving from one to the next as the light changed, painting exactly the same subject, from the same angle. If someone thought he was painting haystacks or a cathedral, Monet would have thought them quite the dimwit. "I'm painting moments. Unrepeatable, singular moments of light," he would say.

Fortunately for Henri, this little street looked as if it held one single, intolerably dull moment. Although just two blocks off the bustling avenue de Clichy, it might have been a street in a ghost town. There wasn't even the obligatory bent-backed oldster sweeping his or her front step, which he was certain was an ordinance in Paris. A whore, a shitting dog, or an oldster sweeping the steps—one or all was required by law. He'd run out of cognac before he ran out of canvas, unless something exciting happened, like a cat decided to jump onto a windowsill.

He sighed to himself, set up his stool, poured a bit of linseed oil into one of the little palette cups, some turpentine into the other, then squeezed out a small dollop of burnt umber onto the wooden palette, thinned it with the turpentine, and began to sketch the Colorman's front door in oil with a thin bristle brush.

Having decided that the theme of this picture would be a deserted street, he was almost disappointed to hear footsteps from the courtyard of the Colorman's building. The building's concierge, a wizened widow, appeared at the first-floor window, then ducked behind a curtain as the gate latch clanked. Every apartment building in Paris had a concierge who, by some sort of natural selection, was both extraordinarily nosy yet loath to be accused of it.

The Colorman backed his way through the wrought-iron gate, pulling behind him the wooden case nearly as large as himself.

Henri could feel the hair stand up on the back of his neck and he wished he hadn't become so engrossed in his painting that he'd completely forgotten to drink, because he could have used another cognac to still his nerves. Now he leaned into his canvas and pretended to be meticulously working on an edge when, in fact, he very seldom worked up close to the canvas and preferred long-handled brushes.

"Monsieur!" said the Colorman, crossing the street, his great case bumping his heels as he moved. "Remember me from avenue de Clichy? Monsieur, can I interest you in some color? I can tell from your excellent hat that you are a man of taste. I have only the finest earths and mineral pigments, none of that false Prussian shit."

Henri looked up from his painting as if he'd been awakened from a dream. "Ah, monsieur, I did not see you. I tell you honestly, I do not know the state of my paint box today. Perhaps I will have need of your wares." Henri pulled his paint box out from under the easel, unsnapped the latches, and opened it. As he'd planned, it was a sad cemetery of crushed and depleted paint tubes, twisted sacrifices to beauty.

"Ha!" said the Colorman. "You need everything."

"Yes, yes, one of everything," said Henri. "And a large tube each of lead white, ivory black, and ultramarine."

The Colorman had opened his own case on the street, but he stopped. "I don't have a large tube of ultramarine, monsieur. Only a very small tube." His eyes were set so far back under his brow that Henri had to bend down to see what emotion was there because the Colorman's voice sounded full of regret. Not what Henri expected.

"No matter, monsieur," Henri said. "I will take what you have, a small tube is fine. If I need more blue I can always—"

"None of that Prussian shit!" barked the Colorman.

"I was going to say that I can always use stand oil and glaze what little I have over white."

The Colorman cocked his head. "No one does that anymore. That's the old way. You new fucks putting paint on with a trowel, that's the way now."

Henri smiled. He thought of Vincent's calculatedly violent palette-knife paintings, paint so thick it would take half a year to dry, even in the arid South. Then his thought of Vincent went dark as he remembered the letter. The Colorman had been in Arles.

"Well," Henri said, "better the old ways than use that Prussian shit."

"Ha! Yes," said the Colorman. "Or that synthetic *French ultramarine*. I don't care what they say, it's not the same as the blue from lapis lazuli. It is not the sacred blue. You will see. You will never find a finer color, monsieur."

At that moment, seeing the color in the case, the pentimento that had been rising in Henri's mind became a clear, vivid image. He had seen them together, one time outside of his studio, Carmen and the Colorman. How had he forgotten? "Actually, I have used your color before. Perhaps you remember?"

The Colorman looked up from his case. "I would remember selling to a dwarf, I think."

Henri wanted right then to bash the twisted little creature's brains in with his walking stick, but he calmed himself enough to just snap, "Monsieur, I am not a dwarf. I am fully seven centimeters taller than the requisite for a dwarf, and I resent your implication."

"So sorry, monsieur. My mistake. Still, I would remember selling to you."

"Your color was obtained through a girl who modeled for me, a Mademoiselle Carmen Gaudin. Perhaps you remember her."

"Is she a housemaid? My maid quit yesterday."

"Your standards were perhaps too demanding for her?"

"Penis," explained the Colorman with a shrug.

"Ah, I understand," said Henri. "Mine refuses to do windows. No, Mademoiselle Gaudin was a laundress by trade. A redhead, perhaps you remember?"

The Colorman lifted his derby and scratched his head as if trying to conjure a memory. "Sure, maybe. The redheaded laundress. Yes, I wondered where she got the money for color."

Actually, at the time, Henri had wondered that as well, since she'd brought him the paint as gifts. "For *our* pictures," she said.

"Do you know where she is now?" asked Henri. "She used to work at the laundry near Place Pigalle, but they haven't seen her."

"That one was called Carmen, right?"

"Yes, Carmen Gaudin."

"She got very sick. I think maybe she died."

Henri felt a blow to the heart. He hadn't intended to ask about her at all. He thought he was through with her. But there was a loss, in that instant, at hearing the Colorman's words.

The Colorman put his hat back on. "She had a sister who lived in the Third, not far from Les Halles, I think. Maybe she went there to die, huh?"

"Perhaps. How much for the color?" said Henri. He took the paint tubes and laid them across the bottom of his paint box, then paid the little man what he asked.

The Colorman pocketed the bills. "I should be making more blue soon, if you run out. I'll come around to your studio."

"Thank you, but I prefer not to be disturbed at my studio. I will come to you, now that I know where you live," Henri said.

"I move a lot," said the Colorman.

"Really, have you ever been to Auvers-sur-Oise?" *Aha!* Henri thought. *I have you now.*

"Auvers?" The hat came off, more head scratching, looking at the upper floors of the buildings for an answer. "No, monsieur, why do you ask?"

"A friend of mine wrote me a letter from there, saying he had purchased some fine oil paints from someone who looked like you. He was a Dutchman, dead now, sadly."

"I don't know any Dutchman. I don't do business with fucking Dutchmen. Fuck Dutchmen and their Dutch light. No. I have to go." The Colorman snapped his case shut, then hefted it onto his back and started to make his way down the street.

"*Adieu,*" Henri called after him.

"Fucking Dutchmen," grumbled the Colorman as he wrestled his case around the corner.

Carmen had moved in with her sister in the Third Arrondissement? If he took a taxi, Henri could be there in thirty minutes. No one had to know.

But first, he needed to find out about the color.

Eleven

CAMERA OBSCURA—

London, 1890

While Henri had spent the day stalking the mystery of the Colorman, Lucien had spent a week in London looking at art and bonking Juliette in every corner of Kensington.

"If you bolt on the hotel bill after only one night they don't even bother with the police," Juliette had said.

"But shouldn't we change neighborhoods?" Lucien had stayed in very few hotels in his life, and he had never run out on the bill.

"I like Hyde Park," Juliette said. "Now come to bed."

There had been a lot of firsts on his first trip to London, not the least of which was the realization that France and England had been at war since, well, since they had been separate countries, really. Outside of the National Gallery, at Trafalgar Square, he looked at the great pillar built to Admiral Nelson, in honor of his victory over Napoleon's navy (and the Spanish) at Trafalgar. The painter Courbet had been exiled for rallying to destroy Napoleon's version of the column outside the Louvre (supposedly at the urging of his Irish mistress, Jo).

"Courbet was a tosser," Juliette said. "Let's go look at pictures."

Lucien didn't ask how she'd known he was thinking about Courbet, or when she started using the English term "tosser"; he'd given up on that sort of thing and had just given himself over to her will. In a few minutes they were through the rotunda and Juliette led the way, breezing by masterpieces like they were leprous beggars, until they stood in front of Velázquez's *Venus*.

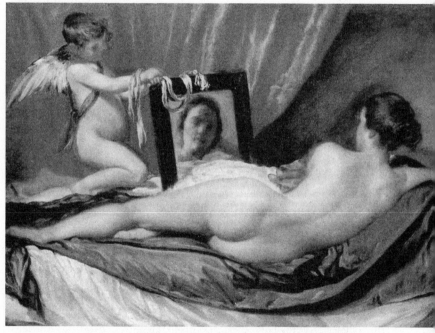

"Put a naked cherub on the couch with her to hold the mirror," said Henri. "I can model if you need." *Venus at Her Mirror*—Diego Velázquez, 1647

She lay on a chaise lounge with her back to them, her skin a smooth, peach-kissed white, and although Henri had been right, her bottom was not quite so fine as Juliette's, she was a beauty to be sure, and because she was looking at you looking at her, in a mirror held by a cherub, there was just the slightest feeling of naughtiness, the voyeur exposed. But she didn't regard you, size you up and dismiss you the way Manet's Olympia did. She didn't tease you the way Goya's *Maja* did. She was just watching you watch her do what she did, which was display the most sublime backside in art. But for all the real dimension, tone, and even light in her skin, on her back and legs, her face in the mirror was dark, out of focus, as if she watched you from a different place, through a window, not really a mirror.

"He must have used a camera obscura," Lucien said. The camera obscura: an actual camera that existed before film. The lens flipped the image and projected it onto a sheet of ground glass, often with a grid etched into it, so the artist essentially painted what had already been reduced to two dimensions in a real, living version of a photograph.

"Why would you say that?" Juliette asked.

"Because her face is out of focus, but her bottom is sharp. I mean, soft, but sharp. That's not the way he paints the cherub, whose face is in vivid focus but in the same plane as the mirror—because he was painted from imagination, or from a different sitting. Your eye changes focus when you look at the different elements of a scene, regardless of distance, but the camera can only focus on a certain range of depth. If he had painted it by just his eye, her face would be in focus."

"Maybe he just couldn't see what she looked like."

Lucien turned to her. "Don't be silly."

"Me? You're the one making up machines."

He laughed, then looked from her, to the painting, then all around the gallery, at all the paintings, then to her again. "Juliette?"

"Yes?"

"Thank you for showing me this—these paintings."

"Lot of good it does you if you won't see them." She grinned and began to walk away. He followed her, as he was supposed to, but then stopped in front of a very large canvas, a Renaissance Madonna.

"Holy mother of . . ."

"What? What?" She stopped.

"It's a Michelangelo," Lucien said. The picture, while almost ten feet tall, looked to be part of a larger piece, perhaps an altarpiece, with the Madonna in the center and the Christ child, a toddler, reaching for a book that she was holding. Her breast was exposed, for no apparent reason, as she was otherwise fully covered by her robe. The shadow of her robe had been shaded in black, but otherwise it had never been painted.

"I wonder why he didn't paint her robe," Lucien said.

"Maybe he got tired," said Juliette.

"Strange." He wandered away from her then, on to the next painting, this one also a Michelangelo. "Look at this."

It was a pietà called *The Entombment,* and in this one, the Holy Mother's robe had been left unpainted as well, while the rest of the painting was finished.

"He didn't finish this one either," said Lucien. "In fact, there's no blue in the painting at all." Excited at seeing a masterpiece stopped in prog-

"He didn't finish this one either," said Lucien. "In fact, there's no blue in the painting at all." *The Manchester Madonna* and *The Entombment*—Michelangelo Buonarroti, 1497

ress, he put his arm around her waist and pulled her close. "You know the Virgin's cloak had to be painted blue. It was called Sacré Bleu, because it was reserved for her."

"You don't say," said Juliette. "Maybe we should go look at the Turners, since we're in England and all."

"Why would he finish the whole painting but not use any blue?"

"Maybe because he was an annoying little poofter," said Juliette.

"A master wouldn't stop in the middle of painting to be annoying."

"And yet here I am, almost four hundred years later, annoyed."

"At Michelangelo?" Lucien had never been annoyed by a painting. He wondered if that might be yet another element of a masterpiece that he might never be able to produce. "Do you think someday I could be that annoying?"

"Oh, *cher*," she said. "Don't sell yourself short."

"What do you mean?"

"Nothing," she said, and off she glided to look at the Turners and the Constables, or *ships and sheeps,* as she liked to think of them.

She was being kind, really. Lucien hadn't a chance of ever being remotely as annoying as Michelangelo Buonarroti. For one thing, Lucien was, at heart, a sweet man, a kind and generous man, and with the exception of a bit of self-doubt about his painting, which served to make him a better painter, he was delightfully unburdened by guilt or self-loathing. Michelangelo, not so much.

Rome, Italy, 1497

THE FLORENTINE HAD BEEN ABOUT THE SAME AGE AS LUCIEN WAS NOW WHEN she'd first come to him. And like Lucien, he had not dealt with the Colorman directly. She found him in Rome, working on *The Entombment of*

Christ, which was to be an altarpiece for the Church of Saint Agostino. He was alone in his workshop, as was often the case.

She was a young girl, wide-eyed and fresh faced, wearing the gown of a peasant, loosely laced and low cut. She carried the color, freshly mixed and packaged in sheep's bladders, twisted off to size and tied with catgut, in a basket padded with unbleached linen.

The painter didn't even look from his work. "Go away. I don't like anyone around when I work."

"Excuse me, Maestro," she said with a curtsy. "But I was asked to bring you these paints by the cardinal." He was painting for the Church; there had a be a cardinal involved somewhere.

"What cardinal? I have my own color man. Go away."

She crept forward. "I don't know which cardinal, Maestro. I don't dare look up when I am addressed by a prince of the Church."

He finally looked at her. "Don't call me maestro. Not when I'm doing this. I'm not even a painter, I'm a sculptor. I find the spirit in the stone, guided by the hand of God. I work in paint only in the service of God."

Not another one, she thought. The reason she'd left Florence was she had lost Botticelli to his religious conscience, spurred by that maniac Dominican monk Savonarola and his Bonfire of the Vanities. Botticelli himself converted and threw some of his best paintings, *her paintings,* on the fire. But Michelangelo had been here in Rome for a year. How had he heard of the teachings of Savonarola?

"I'm sorry, but I must deliver these colors or I will be punished."

"Fine, fine, then. Leave them."

She moved to where he sat on a three-legged stool and slowly knelt with the basket, making sure one knee pushed out of her skirt, baring a thigh, and the front of her gown fell open. She held the position for what she thought was long enough, then shyly looked up into his face.

And he wasn't even looking. "Oh for fuck's sake," she said in English, because she thought it the best language for swearing. "You're not even bloody looking, are you, you pooft?"

"What? What?" said the painter. "That is no way for a young girl to behave, showing her body. You should read the sermons of Savonarola, young lady."

"You *read* them?" She snatched up her basket. "Of course, you read them." She stormed out of the workshop.

The Colorman was right; no good was going to come of that printing press invention of Gutenberg's. Fucking Germans and their inventions.

The next day, when Michelangelo looked up from his painting, it was a young man, little more than a boy, who carried the basket of color. This time he wasn't quite so dismissive. In fact, as the young man, Bleu was able to inspire him for weeks while he worked on the two altarpieces, as well as some smaller pictures that the Colorman was happy to take, and they followed the maestro back to his workshop in Florence. A month in, it started to go wrong.

"I can't get him to paint," Bleu said to the Colorman.

"What about those two big paintings he's been working on?"

"He won't finish them. He refuses to even touch blue color. He says it takes him away from God. He says there's something unholy in it."

"But he is fine having you in his bed?"

"That, too, has come to an end. It's that charlatan monk Savonarola. He's ruining every painter in the city."

"Show him old Athens or Sparta. They were religious and they *loved* to bugger each other. He'll like it."

"I can't show him anything if he won't paint. And he's not going to. They've just moved the biggest block of marble I've ever seen into his workshop. His apprentices won't even let me in the shop."

"I will go see him," said the Colorman. "I'll make him paint."

"Of course," said Bleu. "What could go wrong with that plan?"

It was months before the Colorman could get access to Michelangelo, and he finally did by convincing the apprentices who guarded the maestro's shop that he dealt in stonecutting tools, not color.

Michelangelo was on a ladder, working on a huge statue of a young man. Even in the rough, unpolished form, the Colorman recognized the model was Bleu.

"Why the huge head?" asked the Colorman.

"Who are you?" said the Maestro. "How did you get in here?"

"A merchant. His melon is gigantic. Like those simpletons who eat dirt at the convent."

Michelangelo put his chisel in his belt and leaned against the statue. "It's for perspective. When viewed from below, the head will appear the perfect size. Why are you here?"

"Is that why you made the penis so tiny? Perspective?"

"It's not."

"If you like the tiny penis, you should try girls. Most have no penis at all."

"Get out of my shop."

"I've seen your paintings. You're a much better painter. You should paint. The figures in your paintings are not such freaks as this."

"He isn't a freak. He is perfection. He is David."

"Isn't he supposed to be *carrying* the huge head?"

"Out! Angelo! Marco! Throw this devil out of here."

"Devil?" said the Colorman. "Screw the devil. I tell the devil what to do. The devil licks the dust from my scrotum. Donatello's David carries the big head. You can't do better than Donatello. You should paint."

Michelangelo started down the ladder, his hammer in hand.

"Fine, I'm going." The Colorman hurried out of the workshop, chased by two apprentices.

"Did you convince him?" Bleu asked.

"He's annoying," said the Colorman.

"I told you."

"I think it's because you have a big head."

"I don't have a big head."

"We need to find a painter who likes women. You're better at women."

Back in London, in the National Gallery, Lucien was standing before a J. M. W. Turner painting of a steamship caught in a storm, a great maelstrom of color and brushstrokes, the tiny ship seeming to be swallowed in the middle by the pure fury.

"This is where real painting starts, I think," said Lucien. "This is where object gives way to emotion."

Juliette smiled. "They say that he went mad and tied himself to the mast of a steamship that was headed out into a snowstorm, just so he could see the real motion of a storm from inside it."

"Really?" said Lucien, wondering how a shopgirl knew so much about painting.

"Really," Juliette said. Not really. Turner hadn't tied himself to the mast of the ship at all. *"It will be fun,"* she'd told him. *"Hold still, I have to get this knot."*

They were a week in London and returned to the studio in Montmartre without anyone having ever seen them leave. Lucien walked in and collapsed facedown on the fainting couch. Juliette rubbed his neck until she was sure he was asleep, then kissed him on the cheek and took the studio key from his pocket so she could lock the door on the way out.

When she stepped out into the warm autumn evening she saw a glint of movement from her right. There was a blinding flash, then nothing.

The sound, like the striking of a muted, broken bell, rang through the neighborhood, causing even the few bachelors who were sharing in a dinner of *pot-au-feu* (beef stew) across the square at Madame Jacob's *crémerie* to look at each other with a *What the hell was that?* expression.

Back in the alley, Juliette lay in the doorway of the studio quite unconscious, her entire forehead turning into a purple and black bruise.

"Maman," said Régine, "I think you killed her."

"Nonsense, she'll be fine. Go check on your brother." Madame Lessard stood over the model, holding a heavy steel *crêpe* pan from the bakery.

"But shouldn't we bring her inside or something?"

"When Gilles comes home he can carry her in."

"But, Maman, Gilles is working on a job in Rouen, he won't be home until tomorrow."

"Ah, the air will do her good." She stepped over Juliette and into the studio. "Lucien, wake up. Your sister is worried about you," said Madame Lessard.

Twelve

LE PROFESSEUR DEUX

É MILE BASTARD LIVED IN A SMALL HOUSE HIS FATHER HAD LEFT HIM IN the Maquis, just below the Moulin de la Galette, above the cemetery, on the northwestern slope of Montmartre. Since his father's death, he had installed a wooden floor and plumbing, and removed the tracks and cages for the rodent reenactment of *Ben-Hur,* but the abode was no less eccentric than it had been under Le Professeur I. The miniature hippodrome had given way to tables and shelves filled with all manner of scientific *bricolage,* from tiny steam engines, to measuring instruments, to laboratory glass, bottles of chemicals, mineral samples, batteries and Tesla motors, human skulls, unborn animals in jars, dinosaur bones, and clockwork machines that could perform all sorts of diverse and often useless tasks, including a windup insect that could scurry around the floor and count dropped nutshells, then report the number as a series of chimes on a tiny bell.

Like his father before him, Émile Bastard was a scientist and an academician, who taught at the Académie des Sciences and did field research in several disciplines. He was considered a bit of a Renaissance man by the Académie, and an eccentric and harmless loon by the people of Montmartre. Like his father before him, they called him Le Professeur.

Le Professeur was at his writing desk, organizing some notes he'd taken on a recent cave-exploring expedition, when he was startled by a knock at his door, which almost never happened. He opened the door to find a very short but well-dressed man, in a derby hat, with a leather satchel slung from a strap on his shoulder. It was a warm day and the little man had his coat draped over his arm, his sleeves turned back to the elbow.

"*Bonjour,* Monsieur Bastard, I am Henri de Toulouse-Lautrec, artist." He held out his card. "I am here in the interest of our mutual friend, Monsieur Lucien Lessard."

Le Professeur took Henri's card and stepped aside for Toulouse-Lautrec to enter. "Come in, please. Please, sit." He gestured to a divan on which was perched the partially reconstructed skeleton of a sloth. "You can just push the sloth to the side. A project I'm working on."

Le Professeur pulled the chair from his desk and sat across from the divan. He was as tall as Henri was short, and very thin—when wearing a tailcoat, he put people in mind of a praying mantis with muttonchop whiskers.

Henri cringed as a hazelnut shell crunched under his shoe.

"Sorry," said Bastard. "I have a machine that counts the shells."

"But why do you have the shells all over the floor?"

"I just told you, I have a machine that counts them. Would you like to see a demonstration?"

"Perhaps another time, thank you," said Henri. He removed his hat and laid it over the skull of the sloth, who had a disturbingly melancholy look on his face, probably because he was only partially assembled. "The matter of Lucien Lessard."

"Yes, how is the boy?"

"You've known him a long time?"

"Over twenty years. I met him when he was very little, during the Prussian War. My father had sent him alone to catch rats in the old gypsum mine by the cemetery. When I found out I went to retrieve him. I caught poor Lucien as he was running out of the mine, terrified. A brilliant academic, my father, but he did not always use the best judgment in dealing with children. He treated them like small adults. No offense."

Henri waved off the comment. "I'm concerned about Lucien. It's difficult to explain, but I feel he may be under the influence of some sort of drug." At that, he opened the satchel and retrieved a handful of paint tubes. "I believe that these tubes of color may contain some sort of hallucinogen that is affecting Lucien's health and sanity."

"I see," said the Professeur, who took the tubes from Henri, uncapped them one at a time, and sniffed each in turn. "Smells like linseed oil is the medium."

"Professeur, can you test them at the Académie, perhaps, find out if there is anything harmful in them?"

"I will, but first, tell me what kind of behavior has caused your concern. Normal oil color contains substances that can be toxic, cause the symptoms of madness."

"He's locked himself in the studio behind the bakery with a beautiful girl and he almost never comes out. His sister is most concerned. She says he's stopped baking the bread and he doesn't even seem to eat anymore. She says all he does is screw and paint."

The Professeur smiled. Lucien had spoken to him of his friend the count and his proclivity for dance halls and brothels. "Respectfully, Monsieur Toulouse-Lautrec, is that so different from your own life?"

"Please, Monsieur le Professeur, I have done some experiments with absinthe, and I can attest that it has dangerous hallucinogenic powers, in particular the ability to make homely women appear attractive."

"Well, it's eighty percent alcohol and the wormwood in it is poisonous; I suspect what you are seeing are glimpses of your own death."

"Yes, but with exquisite bosoms. How do you explain those?"

"That is a question," said the Professeur, who, in contrast to all rationality, loved looking for answers to even the most absurd questions.

"Anyway," continued Henri, "I suspect there is something in this color that does the same thing, and our friend Lucien is under the influence of it. I believe I, too, have been under the influence of this very same drug in the past."

"But not currently?"

"No, now I'm simply a libertine and a whoremonger. In my past there was obsession and love, which are the spells under which I believe our Lucien has fallen."

"And who do you think is drugging him?"

"I believe it is a conspiracy of the girl and her partner in crime, a dealer of color."

"And their motive?"

"To seduce Lucien."

"And you said that she is beautiful?"

"Exquisite. Radiant. Irritatingly so."

"Monsieur Toulouse-Lautrec, I understand why someone might conspire to seduce you. You have a title and are heir, I presume, to a significant fortune, but Lucien is the poor son of a baker, and while he is a talented painter, as you know, there is no guarantee that he will ever find success or financial reward. So, again, what would be the motive?"

Henri stood and began to pace in front of the divan, crunching hazelnut shells with every other step. "I don't know. But I can tell you this: When something like this happened to me, Lucien and some other friends removed me from the situation and the obsession passed. But I lost time. Significant amounts of time. Memories. I have months at a time that I cannot remember. I have paintings that I don't remember having painted, and I remember painting others that I do not have. I have no other explanation. Perhaps if you can find something in the paint that explains the loss of time, we will find a way to stop it."

"Stop your friend from painting and making love to a beautiful woman?"

"When you say it that way it doesn't sound like such a good thing."

"No, it is. Monsieur Toulouse-Lautrec, you are a good friend to Lucien. Better than you know. Did Lucien's sister tell you how their father died?"

"No, and Lucien only speaks of his father's love for painting."

"His sister thinks it was a similar love for painting that killed him. I will test the paint. It will take a few days, but I will find out the elements from which it is formulated, but even if I find something, if Lucien doesn't want to be rescued, you will be in a difficult position removing him from the danger."

"I have a plan," said Henri. "I know two doormen from the Moulin Rouge, stout fellows who know their way around a billy club. If you find something, we'll burst into the studio, knock Lucien out, drag him off of her, and tie him up in my studio until he comes to his senses."

"You're a better friend than I even thought," said the Professeur. "Shall I call on you at your studio when I have my results?"

"The address is on the card, but I'm often out, so if you'll just send word," said Henri. "Lucien has spoken of you in terms he reserves for his artist heroes, and even his mother has kind words for you, which is a bit of a miracle in itself, so I know I can trust you to keep this confidence between us. I have reason to suspect that the Colorman is dangerous."

Just then there was a whirr of motors and something scuttled out from under the divan. Henri screamed and jumped up onto the couch. A brass insect about the size of a squirrel was running around on the floor, from nutshell to nutshell, clicking at each one, then moving on with a whirr.

"Ah, it must be noon," said the Professeur.

"Time for a cognac," said Henri breathlessly. "Join me, Professeur?"

EVEN THE *THOUGHT* OF CARMEN CLOUDED HIS JUDGMENT; HE SHOULD HAVE recognized that. Otherwise, why would he think he could find a single redheaded laundress whom no one had heard from in three years, and in an *arrondissement* where nearly a hundred thousand people lived! He had a lithograph he should be doing for the Moulin Rouge, a poster of Jane Avril, and if a true and gallant friend, he would be trying to make another attempt to rescue Lucien, but the vision of Carmen pulled him to the Third. Was it the vision? She was pretty but not beautiful, but she had a quality of rawness, of reality, that touched him, and he had never painted better. Was that it? Was it the girl or the painting?

"Are you in pain, little one?" she would say, the only woman other than his mother he allowed to call him such a thing. "Shall I rub your legs for you?"

He didn't even know if she was still alive. What if, as the Colorman said, she had perished—perhaps from grief, when he'd gone away? Abandoned her.

Jumping from laundry to laundry, with the taxi waiting for him at each, he found himself deep in the Marais, the Jewish neighborhood on the Right Bank of the Seine. By no means a ghetto, this area had been renovated by Baron Haussmann like most of Paris's neighborhoods and the architecture was the same, uniform, six-story buildings with mansard roofs, so the only indication of any economic or ethnic disparity was the preponderance of goldsmiths, the signs in Hebrew in the bakery windows, and the ubiquitous Hasids out and about in their long coats, even in the August heat. There was a furtiveness to the movement of the people in the Marais these days, as anti-Semitism was rising as a political force in the city, and a Jew wandering in the wrong circles might find himself berated by some drunken gentleman for some imagined offense, or the center of some paranoid conspiracy theory. Much to his chagrin, Henri's friend the artist Adolphe Willette, otherwise a man of great humor, had run for mayor of Montmartre on the anti-Semite platform and, fortunately, had been soundly defeated.

"Willette, you dolt," Henri had told him, "I would love to support you, but being of noble birth myself, if I were to discriminate based on the accident of birth I'd have to eschew the company of all you horseshit commoners, and then who would I drink with?"

It was sometimes difficult to reconcile a man's talents with his personality. Even the great Degas, who, as an artist, was a hero to Henri, and probably the best draftsman of all the Impressionists, had turned out, in person, to be a complete prick. Henri had even lived for a while in the same apartment building as Degas, but instead of being able to glean some bit of wisdom from the master, all he got was disdain. At first, a simple dismissive harrumph in the courtyard as they passed, but later, when Henri encountered Degas at an exhibition where they were both showing, Degas, acting as if he didn't see Henri standing nearby, said, "These redheads of Toulouse-Lautrec's, they all look like syphilitic whores."

"You say that like it's a bad thing," Henri said over his shoulder, but he was hurt. Insulted by his hero, he limped away to a corner of the gallery where people were not so surly. Degas inspired him, and he'd been open in his admiration, showing Degas' influence in his own art, and that made the rejection all the more painful. Henri was preparing to shrug off his friends and go get outrageously, scandalously drunk in some working-class dance hall when he felt a hand on his shoulder and looked up to see a thin, white-goateed man in his fifties looking at him from under the brim of a rough linen hat: Pierre-Auguste Renoir.

"Monsieur, take heart. Degas hates everyone. He may be the best sculptor alive, now that his eyesight is too far gone to paint, but I will tell you a secret. His dancers are *things* to him. Objects. He has no love for them. Your dancers, monsieur, they live. They live on canvas because you love them, no?"

Henri didn't know what to say. He was stunned, having gone somehow from a grinding self-loathing at the hands of Degas to an electric numbness at Renoir's extraordinary kindness. He felt faint and had to steady himself on his walking stick.

"No. I mean, yes. I mean, *merci beaucoup*, Monsieur Renoir, I think you know . . ."

Renoir patted his arm to quiet him. "Watch. In a moment I will go tease him about his hatred of the Jews until he storms out like a spoiled child. It will be fun. Degas is always separate from his subjects. He separates himself by choice. Always has. He doesn't know what it is to laugh with a fat girl, but we do, don't we?"

A bit of a satyr's grin under the hat brim, a sparkle of joy in his eye. "Don't let Degas' ugliness bring you down. Camille Pissarro, my friend, he is a Jew. You know him?"

"We have met," said Henri. "We both show at Theo van Gogh's. I share a studio with Lucien Lessard, who is close with him."

"Yes, Lucien. A student of mine. Always drawing pictures of dogs humping. I think there was something wrong with that boy. Maybe all that time in the bakery—perhaps he had a yeast infection. Anyway, Pissarro, he looks like a rabbi with his big beard and his hook nose, but a pirate rabbi, always in those high boots of his. Ha, a pirate rabbi!" Renoir laughed at his own joke. "When he comes to Paris now, he has to hide out in a hotel room because he looks so Jewish, people will spit on him on the streets. What pettiness! Pissarro! Master of us all. But what they don't know, that I know, is that from his hotel room window, he is doing the best painting of his life. You do that, Monsieur Toulouse-Lautrec. Take Degas' petty treatment and make great paintings from it."

Henri felt that he might begin to weep if he stood there any longer. He thanked Renoir again, bowed deeply, and excused himself to leave for an engagement he had only just then made up, but Renoir grabbed his arm.

"Love them all," said Renoir. "That is the secret, young man. Love them all." The painter let go of his arm and shrugged. "Then, even if your paintings are shit, you will have loved them all."

"Love them all," Henri repeated with a smile. "Yes, monsieur. I will do that."

And he had tried, still tried to show that in his work, but often his separation from his subjects wasn't driven, like Degas, by disdain for humanity, but by his own self-doubt. He loved them for their humanness, their perfect imperfection, because that was what they all shared, what he shared. But only one had he really loved, perhaps the only one as imperfect as he. He found her in the third laundry he visited in the Marais.

The proprietor of the laundry was a scruffy, haggard man who looked as if he might have been hanged and revived at some point. He was badgering a delivery boy when Henri came through the door.

"Pardon, monsieur, but I am the painter Toulouse-Lautrec. I am looking for a woman who modeled for me several years ago, and I have lost track of her. Does a Mademoiselle Carmen Gaudin work here?"

"Who is asking?"

"Forgive me, I didn't realize you were both deaf and a buffoon. I am, as I was ten seconds ago, the Count Henri-Marie-Raymond de Toulouse-Lautrec-Monfa, and I am looking for Carmen Gaudin." Henri was finding the detective work did not agree with his constitution as it involved talking to people who were odd or stupid, without the benefit of the calming effect of alcohol.

"I don't care if you have a fancy name and a title, there's no Carmen here," said the scruffy man. "Now fuck off, dwarf."

"Very well," said Henri. Usually his title would ease this sort of resistance. "Then I will have to take my business elsewhere, where I will be forced to hire an assassin of launderers." Times like these, Henri wished he had the bearing of his father, who, although a loon, carried himself with great pomp and gave no second thought to pounding a counter with his walking stick and calling down nine hundred years of aristocratic authority upon the head of any service person unwise enough to displease him. Henri, on the other hand, dropped his empty threat and limped away.

As he reached the door, a woman's voice called from behind him. He turned to see her coming through the curtain from the back room.

"I am Carmen Gaudin," she said.

"Carmen!" Just the sight of her wholly unnaturally red hair, pinned up in a haphazard *chignon,* with two great scimitar bangs swooping down and framing her face, made his heart race, and he walked, light with excitement, back to the counter.

"Carmen, *ma chère,* how are you?"

She looked confused. "Excuse me, monsieur, but do I know you?"

Henri could see that her confusion was real, and, apparently, contagious, because now he was confused. "Of course you know me. All the paintings. Our evenings? It's Henri, *chérie.* Three years ago?"

"I'm sorry," she said.

"Now go away," said the scruffy man. "She has work to do."

Carmen's gaze went from demure and confused to furious, and she directed it at her boss. "You wait!" To Henri, she said, "Monsieur, perhaps if we stepped outside for a moment."

He wanted to kiss her. Hold her. Take her home and cook dinner for her. That quality of being both strong and fragile at the same time was still there, and it appealed to a part of him that he normally kept hidden. Take her home, eat with her, and sip wine, laugh softly at sad things, make love to her and fall asleep in her arms: that's what he wanted to do. Then wake up and put all that melancholy sweetness on canvas.

"Please, mademoiselle," he said, holding the door for her. "After you."

On the sidewalk she quickstepped to the doorway of an apartment building next door, out of sight of the laundry, then turned to him.

"Monsieur, three years ago I was very sick. I was living on Montmartre, working in Place Pigalle, but I don't remember any of it. I forgot things. The doctor said the fever hurt my brain. My sister brought me to her house and nursed me back to health, but I remember almost nothing I did in the time before that. Maybe we met then, but I am sorry, I do not know you. You say I modeled for you? You are a painter?"

Henri felt his face go numb, as if he'd been slapped, but the stinging lingered. She *really* didn't know him. "We were very close, mademoiselle."

"Friends?" she asked. "Were we friends, monsieur?"

"More than friends, Carmen. We spent many evenings, many nights together."

Her hand went to her mouth, as if she were horrified. "Lovers? We weren't lovers."

Henri searched her face for some hint of deception, some glimmer of recognition, of shame, of joy, but he found nothing.

"No, mademoiselle," he said, the words as painful to him as having a tooth pulled. "We worked together. We were more than friends. An artist's model is more than a friend."

She seemed relieved. "And I was your model?"

"The best I've worked with. I could show you the paintings." But even as he said it, he knew he couldn't. He could show her *a few* of the paintings. But he had only three. Yet he remembered, or thought he remembered, painting a dozen. He could see the nude he painted of her, and remember how reluctant she had been to pose for it, but he couldn't remember selling the painting, and he certainly didn't have it now. "Perhaps you could come to my studio. Perhaps I could do some sketches of you, and perhaps your memory will return when you see the paintings."

She shook her head, looking at her feet as she did. "No, monsieur. I could never model. I can't believe I ever modeled. I am so plain."

"You are beautiful," he said. He meant it. He saw it. He had put it on canvas.

The proprietor of the laundry stepped out on the street then. "Carmen! You want a job or you want to run off with a dwarf, it is no matter to me, but if you want a job, go back to work, now."

She turned from him. "I have to go, monsieur. I thank you for your offer, but that time is forgotten. Perhaps it is best."

"But . . ." He watched her hurry by the boss into the laundry. The boss snarled at Henri as he closed the door.

Toulouse-Lautrec climbed into the taxi, which had been waiting.

"Another laundry, monsieur?" asked the driver.

"No, take me to the brothel at rue d'Amboise in the Second. And easy around the corners. I don't want to spill my drink."

Thirteen

THE WOMAN IN THE STOREROOM

MÈRE LESSARD HAD NEVER REALLY USED VIOLENCE AGAINST ANOTHER person before. Of course, living on Montmartre, where bohemians, working people, and the bourgeoisie mixed in the dance halls and cafés, she'd seen many fights and had nursed cuts and bruises on her own men. And during the Prussian War, she had not only endured the shelling of the city and helped with the wounded, but she had also seen the riots after the war, when the Communards took the cannons from the Church of Saint-Pierre, overthrew the government, then were massacred against a wall at Père-Lachaise. Certainly she had always implied, even threatened, that she was capable of violence, and had more or less convinced her family and most of the artists on the butte that she might go berserk at any moment and slaughter them all like an angry she-bear, a reputation of which she was proud and had worked hard to achieve. But smacking Juliette in the forehead with a *crêpe* pan was her first *real* act of violence, and she found it wildly unsatisfying.

"Perhaps a different pan," Régine said, trying to console her mother.

"No," said Mère Lessard. "I could have used the copper one from our own kitchen, the one with the tin lining, which is lighter, and better, I think, for *crêpes*, but the one from the bakery is perfect for braining a model. Heavy, yet not so heavy that I cannot swing it. And I didn't want to use a rolling pin. The point was to knock her unconscious, not crush her skull. No, the pan was perfect."

They had carried Lucien upstairs to the apartment and sat next to the bed where he lay as still as death.

"Perhaps if there were more blood?" said Régine. "The way we allow just a touch of the fruit to show by venting the piecrusts."

"No," said Madame. "I think the blow was perfect. She went out like a candle, and not a drop of blood. She *is* very pretty, and blood would have stained her dress. No, I think that conking someone on the head is like the sex: a thankless task we must perform to keep the peace." She sighed, wistfully, as she looked at the photo of Père Lessard on the bed-side table. "The joy is in the threatening. Threats are like the love poems of head conking, and you know what a romantic I am."

"*Mais oui*, Maman," said Régine. She stood and cocked an ear toward the doorway. "There is someone on the stairs."

"Take the *crêpe* pan," said Mère Lessard.

Régine got to the top of the stairs at the same time as did a bull-shouldered man in work clothes, who caught her around the waist with one arm, spun her around, then pressed her to the wall and kissed her unmercifully while she squirmed, his three-day stubble scratching her face.

"My sweet," said Gilles, her husband. "My flower. I thought to sur-prise you, but you are ready to make *crêpes* for me. My little treasure."

"The pan is for hitting you. Put me down," said Régine. She wriggled in his embrace and he pressed her harder against the wall. "My little love pig, I missed you."

"It's Gilles," Régine called to her mother.

"Hit him," said Mère Lessard. "He deserves it for coming home early."

"Oh," said Gilles, dropping Régine like a poisoned apple. "Your mother is here."

"Good evening, Gilles," said Mère Lessard, a dismissive chill in her voice, for although she liked the burly carpenter very much, there was no advantage in letting him know that.

Gilles stepped into the bedroom. "What is wrong with Lucien?"

"That woman," said Régine.

"What woman?" Gilles had been blissfully oblivious of the goings-on around the bakery for the last month, as he had been away most of the time, working on a public building in Rouen.

"There is a girl lying unconscious in the doorway of the storeroom," said Mère Lessard. "You were supposed to bring her in."

"Of course," said Gilles, as if he'd been a complete cad for not realizing how utterly useless he was. "I will go now." To Régine, he said, "Keep my *crêpes* warm, my sweet." And he was off down the steps.

"The pan was for hitting you," Régine reminded him.

"I'm sorry," said Mère Lessard. "I have failed you, my child. I let you marry a complete dimwit."

"Yes, but he's strong, and he doesn't care at all about art," said Régine.

"There *is* that," said Madame.

Downstairs, in the storage-shed-turned-studio, Gilles stood before the painting of Juliette. While it was true he didn't give a toss about art, he was a great enthusiast when it came to the naked female form.

"*Sacré bleu!*" he exclaimed, with no irony whatsoever.

"Do you need help?" Régine's voice came from the bakery kitchen.

Gilles backed away from the painting. "No. She's not here. There's no one here."

"She was right here," said Régine, now standing in the studio doorway.

Gilles turned so quickly he nearly lost his balance. "*Chérie*, you startled me. Did you know this shed had a skylight? I've never seen a shed with a skylight. Why would you have a skylight here?" He shrugged at the mystery of it all.

Régine held her hand to her mouth as if suppressing a sob, then said, "Come inside, Gilles. I need to tell you something."

THE COLORMAN HEARD THE KEY RATTLING IN THE LOCK AND OPENED THE door for her.

Bleu entered the apartment and gingerly pried up the brim of her hat. "Ouch, ouch, ouch, ouch."

"You need to finish with him," said the Colorman. "Someone is getting suspicious."

"Ouch!" said Bleu with a great blast of air as she pulled off her hat and tossed it to the hall tree. She bent over until she was eye to eye with the Colorman, whose deep-set eyes bulged out a bit as he got a good look at her puffy, purple forehead. "You think?" she said.

"What happened?"

"What do you think happened? Someone hit me."

"The baker?"

"No, not the baker. His mother, I think. I didn't see it coming."

"Did you kill them?"

"Yes, I don't know who hit me, but I killed them all the same."

"You're cranky when you're bruised. You want wine?"

"Yes, wine, food." She collapsed on the divan. "Do we have a maid?"

The Colorman turned to her, sheepishly, and shrugged.

"Oh for fuck's sake. Fine, bring me some wine, then. Who do you think is suspicious?"

"The dwarf. The little painter. He was here. He bought color from me. He was asking about the Dutchman, about Auvers."

"Surely he hasn't connected us with the Dutchman. How would he do that?"

The Colorman shrugged again, then handed her a heavy crystal goblet of wine.

"I don't know. A letter maybe? The Dutchman was mad. And not in the usual way. Maybe we should kill the dwarf, just to be safe."

"How is that safe? He wouldn't even be suspicious if you hadn't murdered the Dutchman."

"Accident. Couldn't be helped," said the Colorman.

"Well, we're not going to kill him. We'll hide."

"What about the baker? He suspects?"

"No, he doesn't suspect anything. He's exhausted. I had him in London for a week today. It's his family."

"Did you get the painting?"

"Does it look like I got the painting? I brought this." She threw a partially used tube of paint on the coffee table. "This is all the blue that is left."

"Why didn't you get the painting?"

"Because someone just brained me and the painting is fucking huge, isn't it? It's still wet, I couldn't cut it from the stretchers and roll it up. And I might have been noticed, making my way across Montmartre with a bigger-than-life-size nude of myself, don't you think?"

"I was just asking. London makes you cranky."

"London does not make me cranky. Losing months of work, getting knocked on the bloody head, and having to talk to you makes me cranky."

"Oh," said the Colorman. "I don't like London."

"Noted." She drained her glass. "There's food?"

"Roast chicken. I saved you half. So, we get the painting, then kill the baker and his family to cover our tracks."

"No, we don't kill them. What is with you and the killing? Did you get a taste of it with the Dutchman and now you want to keep trying it? This isn't like scaring away the maids with your penis. If you keep murdering artists someone will notice, you know?"

"You think I can scare painters away with my penis?" He rolled his eyes to the ceiling at the wonder of the possibility. Bleu didn't know that he had tried it once with the painter Artemisia and she had threatened to saw his head off; insane Italian tart.

"No, but you can't kill them, either. Not all of them. Not that way."

"We'll use the color. And if you go with me they won't remember."

"Of course they won't bloody remember, they'll be dead." Then she called him a name in a dead language that translated, roughly, to "poop on a stick," but sounded more succinct, like this: "Of course they won't bloody remember, they'll be dead, Poopstick."

"We can move, hide. The dwarf asked about the redheaded laundress. Maybe you should find her again for him. He paints fast."

She shook her head. "No, we'll hide, but I have to finish with Lucien."

"You want a bath?"

"Food."

"Then a bath? I lit the heater. The water will be hot."

"You can't watch."

"Just a little? Your forehead is turning Tyrian purple. I like it against the white skin."

"Tyrian purple? That specific? Really?"

He shrugged eloquently, his *Oops, I accidentally frightened the maid with my penis and shot the one-eared Dutch painter, couldn't be helped* shrug.

"Colorman," he explained.

"Bring me food, Poopstick," she said.

"IS HE GOING TO DIE?" RÉGINE ASKED HER MOTHER.

They sat at Lucien's bedside. Gilles stood in the doorway of the tiny bedroom.

Mère Lessard did not answer Régine but turned directly to Gilles. "If he dies, you must find that woman and strangle her."

Gilles knew he and Régine should have found their own house. If they had moved to that little apartment near Gare Saint-Lazare that his boss had offered, he wouldn't be in this position. Régine could have walked to the bakery in less than twenty minutes, there were good markets, and most of the trains to the west, where he had been working, left from Gare Saint-Lazare. He could have belched without being scolded, asked for what he wanted for supper, and most important, no one would be asking him to strangle a pretty girl. He had never stood up to his mother-in-law, but in this case, he might have to. Was he not a man? Was he not the master of his own house? Régine was his wife, this was his house, and he was finished taking orders, damn it.

"Did you throw some water on him?" Gilles asked.

"No," said Mère Lessard. "We dragged him up the stairs, undressed him, and got him into bed. He didn't wake up through that, a little water isn't going to wake him."

"I'll get some water," said Gilles. Perhaps if he showed he was useful for other things, she would forget about having him strangle the girl.

Régine followed him to the kitchen and took the pitcher from his hand. "Forget the water. You sit."

She sat across the table from him and took his big, rough hands in hers. There were tears in her eyes. "Gilles, when I tell this thing that I must tell you, you have to promise not to leave me."

"I promise." He was not a man of great imagination, but what could she say that would be so horrible? He had shared a house with her mother, after all, what could be worse than that?

"I have killed my sister, my father, and now my sweet brother, Lucien," she said.

Although that hadn't at all been what he expected, Gilles nodded knowingly. "Your pot roast?" he said.

In an instant she was on her feet, snatching up a tea towel, a trivet, a sugar bowl, and flinging them at his head. "No, not my fucking pot roast, you idiot. What a stupid thing to say, 'pot roast'!"

"Don't kill me," said Gilles. "I love your pot roast."

When Mère Lessard came out of the bedroom to check on the commotion, Régine attenuated her tantrum, took Gilles by the hand, and dragged him back down the steps to the bakery to confess what she felt were her crimes.

MARIE HAD NOT JUST BEEN HER SISTER, SHE HAD BEEN HER BEST FRIEND, AND every time she was reminded of her, Régine had to fight back tears, which was difficult in a city where every fourth or fifth woman you met was named Marie.

"Papa loved painters and painting," said Régine. Gilles had fetched the tall stool from behind the counter in the front, and Régine perched on it by the heavy, marble-topped table where much of the pastry was made. "Maman was always scoffing and teasing Papa about his artist pets, and Lucien, even when he was little, told him that he should paint, but Papa always resisted. The two of them had their own little religion built around the artists on Montmartre—like the painters were a canon of saints. Saint Monet of Le Havre, Saint Cézanne of Aix, Saint Pissarro of Auvers, Saint Renoir of Paris—sometimes it felt like we were feeding every artist on the butte.

"Finally, when I was about nineteen, something happened. I came downstairs one morning and Papa was sitting right here at the pastry table, with a paint box open on his lap, just looking at the colors like they were holy relics. Lucien was at his side, and the two of them seemed like they were in a trance. They hadn't even fired the ovens yet, and we were about to open. I don't know where the box of paints had come from. It was too early for them to have gone down to Père Tanguy's shop in Pigalle, and it hadn't been there the night before. Lucien looked at me and said, 'Papa is going to be a painter.'

"That was the last they spoke of it for weeks, but Papa and Lucien cleared out the storage shed, and every day, after the bread came out of the ovens, Papa would disappear into the shed and stay there until supper time. Soon, Lucien took over all of the baking so Papa could paint. One day, Papa came storming through the bakery, ranting about having to have light and how color doesn't exist without light."

"Is that why there's a skylight in the shed?" asked Gilles, who was hoping he could steer the confession toward issues of carpentry, where he had some expertise.

"Yes! Yes!" said Régine. "I thought Maman would throw him out, she was so angry. But the more she complained, the more Papa locked himself in the new studio, and poor Lucien was caught in the middle. He was running the bakery, going to school, taking his painting lessons at Monsieur Renoir's studio around the corner—too much for just a boy. Marie and I should have helped more, but Maman had divided the family into two camps, not the *men* and the *women*, as you would think, but between artists and real people. We were only allowed to help Lucien enough to keep the bakery running, and no more. He, like our father, was a foreign creature, and until he came to his senses, we were to treat him as such."

"I thought that's how she felt about every man," said Gilles, feeling sorry for Lucien and Père Lessard, who had, for the carpenter, taken on a mythical quality. Mère Lessard spoke of him in alternate tones of adoration and disdain. One moment he was so pure and heroic that no man could ever live up to his memory, the next a feckless, irresponsible dreamer who should serve as an example of how far a man-turned-fire-bringer could fall from grace.

Régine patted her husband's arm. "Whatever you do, you must never tell Maman what I am about to tell you."

"Never," said Gilles.

"Maman was away at Grand-mère's—she'd been gone for days. There was a woman. A young woman, a redhead, I think. I didn't get a good look at her, just a glimpse, but I saw Papa lead her through the bakery and out to his studio one day. They went in and locked the door. Papa didn't come out for supper that evening, and he didn't answer the door when we called for him to come up. The next morning, he didn't even check on Lucien while my brother made the bread.

"By the next evening Marie was ready to burn the shed down, she was so angry, but I said we couldn't be sure. He might just be painting her. After all, he didn't even flirt with girls who came into the bakery like all the other business owners on the butte. Marie said that she was going to check.

"It was midwinter, and it had been snowing for two days. We could see smoke from Papa's stove out our bedroom window, but little more. Marie put on her winter boots and climbed out onto the roof and made her way to where she could look down through the skylight. I tried to stop her, pull her back into the window, but she would not hear of it. She walked on the peak of the roof, a foot on each side. It was so slippery, she nearly lost her footing with every step. She got to where she could see in the skylight and her eyes went wide, and not as if she were frightened, but in a big smile, like Christmas morning. She turned to say something to me, lost her footing on the peak of the roof and began to slide toward the street. I saw her go over the side and could feel the ground shake when she hit."

"That's two stories," said Gilles.

"She must have landed flat on the back of her head. The doctor could find no broken bones, and there was no blood, but she was unconscious."

"And did your father come out then?"

"No. I screamed and ran out to Marie. Some of his artist friends, Cézanne and Pissarro, who were down from Auvers, were warming themselves across the street at Madame Jacob's *crémerie;* they came running and helped move her into the bakery. Lucien was at his lesson and Maman wasn't due back until the next morning. Madame Jacob's daughter ran for the doctor. Cézanne and Pissarro pounded on the studio door but got no answer. When I assured them that Papa was inside, they broke down the door. We found him there, lying on the floor with a handful of brushes and loaded palette, alone. Dead."

"*Mon Dieu!*" said Gilles.

"The doctor said it was his heart, but he was dried up, like he'd been in the desert without water for days. Marie lingered for three days and never woke up."

"And the girl? The one you saw go into the studio?"

"I never saw her come out."

"But the painting? Couldn't you find her from that? Find out what happened?"

"There was no painting," said Régine, dabbing her eyes. "Not one. Empty canvases. Papa had been painting for months by that time, hours and hours every day, and we never saw a painting. Not even Lucien saw one."

Gilles took her in his great arms and held her while she sobbed against his chest. "It is not your fault, *chérie*. Bad things sometimes happen. You couldn't have known."

"But I did know. I could have stopped them. I could have stopped Lucien when he first took that girl into the studio. It was just like Papa. I just watched. They love the painting so much, I couldn't. I couldn't."

"And your mother never knew why any of this happened."

"No. It would have only hurt her more. She can never know, even if Lucien doesn't wake up, she can never know." She broke down again then, and Gilles held her tighter.

"Never?" said Mère Lessard from the staircase.

Gilles wondered how a woman of such substantial size could move so quietly, even on a creaky staircase.

Fourteen

WE ARE PAINTERS, AND
THEREFORE SOMEWHAT USELESS

LUCIEN LAY UNCONSCIOUS FOR EIGHT DAYS. AS WORD OF HIS CONDITION spread around the butte, neighbors and friends stopped by the bakery to offer food, help, and relief for Mère Lessard, who did not want to leave her son's bedside.

"If he wakes," instructed the matriarch, "first make him drink some water, then remind him that his mother told him that girl would lead to no good."

Régine was able to keep the bakery running, with the help of Gilles, who rose early and kneaded the bread dough in the heavy oak tray.

Two Parisian doctors were called, examined Lucien, found no reason for his coma, and each went away murmuring prescriptions of "wait and see." Mère Lessard would not allow Lucien to be taken to the Hôtel-Dieu, the ancient hospital next to Notre-Dame Cathedral.

"That is a place where you go to die, and my son is not going to die."

But by the end of the week, the visitors were taking on the aspect of mourners, offering to light candles and say prayers, and there was little talk of recovery, hope, or Lucien's future. Mère Lessard and Régine took turns squeezing water from a cloth over Lucien's cracked lips, and from time to time he would swallow, so drop by drop he was kept from dying of thirst.

On the seventh day, Régine took the morning train to Auvers-sur-Oise to fetch Dr. Gachet. She returned that afternoon with not only the good doctor, but Camille Pissarro, who had been visiting. Dr. Gachet, whose practice bent toward homeopathy, began adding tinctures of herbs to the steady drip administered by the women, and on the eighth day Lucien opened his eyes to what looked like the white-bearded face of God.

"Welcome back, Rat Catcher," said Pissarro.

Mère Lessard pressed a handkerchief to her mouth and hurried from the room to hide her tears.

"Oncle Camille," said Lucien. "How?"

"I came with Gachet. I was in Auvers, painting with Gauguin."

"Is Minette with you?" Lucien's voice was dry as dust.

Régine held a cup to Lucien's lips and he took a sip of water, which gave Pissarro time to recover from the reminder of his daughter, dead now eighteen years. He looked to the doctor and raised an eyebrow, as if to ask if he should speak the truth to the boy, who was obviously still disoriented.

Dr. Gachet stroked his pointed red beard for a second, as if the friction might yield a prognosis, then nodded.

"Minette is gone, Lucien," Pissarro said. "Many years ago. Don't you remember?"

"Blue!" said Lucien, sitting up quickly, grabbing Pissarro by the lapels of his jacket. "Did it take her?"

Pissarro looked past Lucien to the corner of the room. There was nothing there to look at, just paint on the walls, but he couldn't look at Lucien, whose gaze was begging for answers. The old painter's vision glazed over with tears.

"She was sick, fever," he said. He shook his head and looked down at the floor, ashamed. "A long time ago, Rat Catcher."

Lucien looked to Dr. Gachet. "Did it take her?"

The doctor pulled a stool up next to the bed and sat. "Lucien, you've been unconscious for over a week. Do you know what happened to you?"

"I'm fine," Lucien said. "I was painting. Wait. Juliette? Oh, Oncle, the painting! You must see the painting!"

Pissarro shook off his distress and looked at Gachet with a smile. "He'll be fine," he said, as if *he* were the physician now.

"I'll be the judge of that," said Gachet. "Lucien, did you eat anything different? Any shellfish, maybe? Mushrooms you didn't know?"

"I had fish and chips. In London. With Juliette," said Lucien. "Where is Juliette?"

"Mother brained her with a *crêpe* pan," said Régine, who had been standing in the doorway. "She hasn't been back."

"But I love her," said Lucien. "And the painting isn't finished."

Gachet stood. "Why don't you rest a bit, Lucien. Camille and I will go look at your painting."

IN LUCIEN'S STUDIO, DR. GACHET AND CAMILLE PISSARRO STOOD IN FRONT of the blue nude of Juliette.

"Extraordinary," said Gachet.

"It reminds me of Renoir's olive trees. In those days he had gone to the South and was working through a theory that all shadows were made of blue light—he would paint them no other color. His whole palette was built up from blue."

"Really, Camille? She reminds you of olive trees? Let me check your pulse, my friend, you may be dead."

"I meant the colors."

The studio door opened and they turned to see Henri de Toulouse-Lautrec, looking quite rumpled, as if he had been recently unpacked after having been stuffed in a small box for a long time.

"*Bonjour,* messieurs." Henri had met Pissarro at Theo van Gogh's gallery, where both were showing paintings. The moment Toulouse-Lautrec entered, the air in the studio had changed from the rich, nutty smell of linseed oil, with the slight astringent note of turpentine, to a choking miasma of patchouli, musk, absinthe, tobacco, and secretions of well-ripened lady-parts, possibly of the deceased. Dr. Gachet surreptitiously wiped his hand on his trousers after shaking Lautrec's hands.

"I have seen your work, monsieur," said the doctor. "Your lithographs in particular are very striking. I am a printmaker myself."

"I have heard," said Henri. "I look forward to seeing your work. But now Lucien, I was told that he is awake?"

"An hour ago, perhaps," said Gachet.

"Then he will recover?"

"It appears so. He's very weak. Dehydrated."

Henri removed his hat and wiped his brow with a handkerchief. "Thank God. I tried to rescue him but was unable to convince him of the danger."

Pissarro, who had been looking at the painting since Henri had entered, trying to keep his mind off the atrocious odor, said, "Rescue him? From what?"

"From her," said Henri, nodding to the painting.

"Danger is not the first impression she inspires," said Gachet.

"Not just her," said Toulouse-Lautrec. "The Colorman, too."

Now both Gachet and Pissarro looked to the diminutive painter.

"They are together," said Lautrec.

"Vincent said something about a color man right before he died," said Gachet. "I thought it was just delirium."

"Vincent knew him," said Henri. "A very specific color man. Small, brown, broken looking."

"And this girl, Lucien's model, is associated with him?" asked Pissarro.

"They live together in the Batignolles," said Henri.

Pissarro looked to Gachet. "Do you think Lucien is strong enough to talk?"

Lucien studied Gachet's eyes, which were large and always a bit doleful, as if he could see some sadness in the heart of everything.
Portrait of Doctor Gachet—Vincent van Gogh, 1890

RÉGINE FED LUCIEN BROTH AND A LITTLE BREAD—THE COLOR GRADUALLY returned to his cheeks. Madame Lessard brought in a basin and shaved him with a straight razor while Pissarro and Dr. Gachet looked on. When she left the room, Dr. Gachet closed the door behind her and took a seat on the stool by Lucien's bed. Pissarro and Toulouse-Lautrec stood by.

Lucien looked to each of them, then grimaced. "Good God, Henri, is that smell coming from you?"

"I was going to come right over as soon as I heard you were awake, but the girls insisted upon giving me a bath first. I sat vigil for you for a week, my friend."

"One sits vigil *over* the dying, not ten blocks away, on a pile of whores, out of his mind on opium and absinthe."

"Each grieves his own way, Lucien. And since you are going to survive, it appears that my method may have therapeutic benefits. But I will defer to the good doctor's judgment." Henri looked over his *pince-nez* at Gachet.

"No, I don't think that's the case," said the doctor.

"My apologies, then, Lucien, you aren't going to survive."

Gachet was nonplussed. "That's not what I was saying—"

"If not, may I have the new painting? It is your masterpiece."

"It's not finished," said Lucien.

"Should we go?" Pissarro asked the doctor, gesturing to himself and Toulouse-Lautrec.

"No. I may need you two to help me diagnose Lucien's trouble."

"But we are painters—"

"And therefore somewhat useless," said Lautrec.

The doctor held up his finger to stop him in his place. "You will see." To his patient, he said, "Lucien, when you first woke up, you asked about Minette. You said 'the blue' and asked if it had taken her. What did you mean?"

Lucien tried to think, but there were things muddled up in his head. He remembered London, and seeing the Turners and Velázquez's *Venus,* but he had never been to London. Everyone was sure of it but him. They said he'd been in the studio for days before they found him, and no one had seen him leave.

"I don't know," Lucien said. "Maybe it was a dream. I don't remember. I just felt Minette, gone. Like it had just happened and something had taken her from me."

"You asked if *'blue'* had taken her," said the doctor.

Lucien studied Gachet's eyes, which were large and always a bit doleful, as if he could see some sadness at the heart of everything.

"That doesn't make sense, does it?" said Lucien.

"The boy is tired," said Pissarro. "Let's let him rest."

"Not to worry," Gachet said. "But you don't remember, do you? You don't remember Minette being sick?"

"No," said Lucien. He could feel the heartbreak of her loss, but he didn't remember his first love falling ill. Only the arrow to the heart when they told him of her death. He could still feel it.

"And you don't either?" Gachet said to Pissarro.

The painter shook his head and looked at his hands. "Perhaps it is a blessing."

"Yet you both were there," said the doctor. "I treated Minette for her fever. I remember, you were both there."

"Yes," said Pissarro. "I had done several paintings of Lucien, so I . . ." Pissarro lost his thought.

"Where are they?" asked the doctor.

"What?"

"Camille, I've seen nearly every painting you've done. I've never seen a portrait of Lucien."

"I painted them. Three, maybe four. I was teaching him while I painted. Teaching my own son Lucien, as well. Ask him."

Gachet looked to Lucien. "Do you remember those sessions?"

Lucien tried to remember. It had to have taken hours and hours of sitting still, back in a time when sitting still was a very difficult thing to do, yet all he could bring up was a sense of anxiety, rising to almost a panic from his core. "No. No, I don't remember."

"And you've never seen the paintings?"

"No."

Pissarro grabbed his friend's arm. "Gachet, what is this about? Minette died eighteen years ago."

"I have lost memories, too," said Toulouse-Lautrec. "And I know others, well, one other, a model. It's the color. Isn't it?"

"*What* is the color?" said Pissarro, his grief turning to exasperation. "We don't remember because of what color?"

"I don't know, let us examine this." Gachet patted Pissarro's hand to reassure him. "This color man, have you had dealings with him, Camille? Specifically, back in the time when you were painting Lucien?"

Pissarro closed his eyes and nodded. "I remember such a man. Many years ago. He came to Lessard's bakery the day Père Lessard was raffling off one of my paintings. I paid him no mind. He gave me a tube of paint to try. Ultramarine, I think. Yes, I remember seeing him."

"Did you use the paint?"

"I don't remember. I suppose I would have. Those were lean times. I couldn't afford to let color go to waste."

"And, Lucien," said the doctor. "Do you remember this color man?"

Lucien shook his head. "I remember a pretty girl won the picture. I remember her dress, white with big blue bows." Lucien looked away from Pissarro. "I remember wishing that Minette had a dress like that."

"Margot," said Pissarro. "I don't remember her surname. She modeled for Renoir. His swing picture, and the big Moulin de la Galette picture."

"I knew her," said Gachet. "Renoir called me to Paris to treat her. Marguerite Legrand was her full name. Do you know if Renoir bought color from this color man?"

"Why?" asked Toulouse-Lautrec.

"Because he has had these lapses in memory," said the doctor. "Whole months that he lost, as has Monet. I don't know about Degas, or Sisley, or Berthe Morisot—the others among the Impressionists—but I know these Montmartre painters have all had these memory lapses."

"And Vincent van Gogh as well?" said Henri.

"I'm beginning to think so," said Gachet. "You know that oil color can contain chemicals that can harm you? The mercury in vermilion alone could drive a man to what is called the 'hatter's madness.' We all know someone who has been poisoned by lead white. Chrome from chrome yellow, cadmium, arsenic, all elements of the colors you use. That's why I've always discouraged my painter friends from painting with their fingers. Many of those chemicals can enter the body just through the skin."

"And Vincent used to eat paint," said Henri. "Lucien and I saw him do it at Cormon's studio. The master scolded him for it."

"Vincent could be . . . well . . . passionate," said Lucien.

"A loon," said Henri.

"But brilliant," said Lucien.

"Absolutely brilliant," agreed Lautrec.

Gachet looked to Pissarro. "You know how Gauguin was saying that he and van Gogh had fought in Arles? Vincent became so violent that he cut off a piece of his own ear. Gauguin was forced to return to Paris."

"Van Gogh committed himself to a sanitarium after that, didn't he?" said Pissarro.

Lucien sat up now. "Vincent was not well. Everyone knows that."

"His brother said he has had spells for years," said Toulouse-Lautrec.

"Vincent didn't remember the fight," said the doctor. "Not at all. He told me that he had no idea why Gauguin left Arles. He thought Gauguin had abandoned him over artistic differences."

"Gauguin said he had fits of temper that he didn't even remember the next day," said Pissarro. "The lapses were more disturbing than the temper."

"Drinking?" said Lucien. "Henri loses weeks at a time."

"I prefer to think of them as *invested*, not lost," said Toulouse-Lautrec.

"Gauguin said he hadn't been drinking that day," said the doctor. "He said that Vincent thought his distress had something to do with a blue painting he had made. He would only paint with blue color at night."

Lucien and Pissarro looked at each other, their eyes widening.

"What?" asked Gachet, looking from the young painter to the older and back. "What, what, what?"

"I don't know," said Pissarro. "When I think of that time, I feel something terrible. Frightening. I can't tell you what it is, but it seems to live just outside of my memory. Like a phantom face at a window."

"Like the memory of a dog that's been mistreated," said Henri. "I mean, that is how I feel about the time I lost. I don't understand what happened, but it frightens me."

"Yes!" said Lucien. "As if the more I think about it, the more the memory runs away."

"But it's blue," said Pissarro.

"Yes. Blue." Lucien nodded.

Gachet stroked his beard and looked back and forth again, searching the painters' faces for some hint of irony, amusement, or guile. There was none.

"Yes, there's that, the blue," said Henri. Then to the doctor, "What about hallucinations? Remembering things that never happened, maybe?"

"It could all be caused by something that this color man put in the paint. Even trace amounts from breathing fumes could have caused it. There are poisons so powerful that the amount you could put on the head of a pin could kill ten men."

"And you feel that this is why Vincent killed himself? That he had bought color from this little color man?" asked Lucien.

"I'm not sure anymore," said Dr. Gachet.

"Well," said Henri, "you will be more assured soon. I've commissioned a scientist from the Académie to analyze color I bought from the Colorman. We should know any day."

"That's not what I meant," said Gachet. "I mean, yes, he may have been under the influence of some chemical compound, but I'm not sure that Vincent killed himself."

"But your wife said he confessed it when he came to your house," said Pissarro. "He said, 'This is my doing.'"

"That was enough for the constable, and at first, I didn't question it. But think: who shoots himself in the chest, then walks a mile to the doctor? This is not the action of a man who wants to end his life."

Fifteen

THE LITTLE GENTLEMAN

THREE DAYS AFTER LUCIEN AWOKE FROM HIS COMA, TOULOUSE-LAUTREC arrived at Lessard's bakery to find the young painter not only on his feet, but forming great, disc-shaped loaves and laying them on trays to be proofed. The kitchen was rich with the smell of yeast and the sweet aroma of fruit *confits* that were simmering on the stove.

Before venturing a greeting, Henri fished a gold watch from the pocket of his waistcoat and checked the time.

"Oh thank God, when I saw the bread I thought it might be before dawn."

Lucien smiled. "These are not today's loaves, Henri. Those came out of the oven hours ago. I'm going to proof these loaves twice, the second time overnight. It's an Italian recipe. They call it *focaccia*. The bread becomes dense but not heavy, good for carrying sauces, cheese, meats."

"French bread is superb for cheese and meat, Lucien. What is your sudden fascination with the Italian way of doing things? I noticed you used thin glazes on your painting like the Italians."

"They were the masters, Henri. They say that the Italians taught the French to cook. That when Catherine de Medici married King Henry the Second, she brought a whole brigade of Italian chefs to France, toured them around the country holding banquets and teaching the people how to cook."

"Blasphemy!" said Toulouse-Lautrec. "It is accepted science that God himself gave the French the gift of their cuisine, and while he was downstairs, cursed the English with theirs."

"But the painting—"

"Fine, there were a few Italians who could paint." Henri had made his way over to the stove and scooped a handful of steam off a cherry *confit* and inhaled it. "This is delightful."

"Régine will put it in croissants tomorrow. Taste it if you'd like."

"No, the aroma is enough for now."

Lucien turned the last of the loaves on the floured table and plopped it onto the proofing tray. "Speaking of which, you are slightly less aromatic than when we last met."

"Yes, apologies. One loses perspective after a week in a brothel. I have since returned home, bathed in my own apartment, without the help of my maid, who left me, I might add."

"Well, when you don't go home for weeks at a time, without notice . . . servants need to be paid, Henri."

"That wasn't it. I had paid her in advance, thinking I would be away at Mother's for the whole month."

"Then what was it?"

"Penis," explained Toulouse-Lautrec.

"Pardon?"

"I was conducting an experiment. A theory based on information I had recently obtained, for which I sought confirmation. I strolled out of my bedchamber, *au naturel,* and the maid tendered her resignation on the spot—with far more histrionics than was called for, I thought. The woman is sixty-five years old—a grandmother—it's not as if she's never seen one."

"I assume you were wearing your hat?"

"Of course, what am I, some philistine?"

"And were you, if it's not too personal to ask, in a state of readiness?"

"For the accuracy of the experiment, yes. I would say I was approaching two o'clock—half past at the least. A condition I attained, I might add, completely without her assistance, as she was dusting the parlor at the time."

"And still, she bolted on you? It sounds as if you're lucky to be rid of her."

"Well, yes, the bitch refused to do the windows. Fear of heights."

"And penises."

"Evidently. But to be fair, I had brought Guibert along to record the experiment with his camera. It was his first time working inside with the flash and he overloaded the pan a bit with magnesium powder. The resulting explosion and fire may have contributed to her exit."

"Fire?"

"*Un petit peu.*" Henri held his thumb and forefinger a centimeter apart to show just how little fire was required to frighten away the maid.

"I remember when you limited your experiments to ink and paper."

"Say you, as you prepare that Italian bread abomination."

"*Touché,* Count Monfa."

Henri whirled on his heel and peered over his *pince-nez* at Lucien. "So, you are recovered?"

"I need to find her," said Lucien.

"So, *no,* then."

"I'm fine. I need to find Juliette."

"I understand. But if I may ignore you for a moment, we need to speak to Theo van Gogh."

"So you're not going to help me find her?"

"I thought I made it clear that I was ignoring you on that count. We can't just burst into the gallery and start interrogating him about his brother's death. I do have pictures hanging there, as do you, I believe, but I can't think of how to move the conversation from our pictures to Vincent without seeming uncouth."

"Heaven forbid," said Lucien.

"We need to take him your painting."

"No, it's not finished."

"Nonsense, it's magnificent. It's the best thing you've ever done."

"I still have to paint in a blue scarf tied around her neck, to direct the eye. And I have to get some more ultramarine from Père Tanguy."

"I'll fetch you a tube from the studio."

"It's not just that, Henri . . ."

"I know." Toulouse-Lautrec took off his hat and wiped his forehead with a handkerchief. "Why is it so hot in here?"

"It's a bakery. Henri, I'm afraid of the painting."

"I know," said Toulouse-Lautrec, his head bowed, nodding somberly in sympathy. "It's the penis, isn't it?"

"There's no penis!"

"I know, I was just trying to lighten your mood." Henri clapped his friend on the back and flour dust rose from Lucien's shirt. "That shall be our conceit to Monsieur van Gogh. We will take your painting to him and ask his opinion about adding the scarf. He will see that it is a masterpiece, be flattered that we asked, then, while his guard is down, I'll ask him what he knows about the circumstances leading up to his brother's death."

"That's a horrible plan."

"Yes, but I have chosen to ignore that."

BECAUSE HE SELDOM APPEARED ON THE BUTTE DURING THE DAY, MANY OF THE boys of Montmartre had actually never seen the "little gentleman." He was rumor, a myth, a legend. They had, of course, heard of him; they knew he was of royal birth, an artist and a *bon vivant,* and they had concocted tales that they shared among themselves, that he was actually a troll, the cruel master of a circus, and possibly a pirate, but the things they all knew to be true about him—by way of warnings from their mothers—were that he was always to be referred to as "the little gentleman," was never to be teased, whispered about, or laughed at, because he was, in fact, a gentleman, always polite and well dressed, usually generous and charming, and Madame Lessard had promised that any child caught being unkind to the little gentleman would be disappeared, never to be seen again except as an unappetizing pie with eyelashes in the crust. (Madame Lessard was only slightly less mysterious than the little gentleman himself, but more menacing, as she could deceive you by giving you a treat today, only to set you up for a proper poisoning later, or so the story went.)

But now, the legend had materialized, better than a bear on a bicycle eating a nun: the baker and the "little gentleman" were carrying across Place du Tertre a large picture of a naked woman who had recently been murdered by Madame Lessard, and the boys of the butte were drawn to the spectacle like sharks to blood.

"I don't see why we couldn't ask van Gogh to come to the studio," said Lucien, trying to cantilever his end of the painting into the wind. (There were reasons why windmills had been built on Montmartre.) They were progressing across the square in a sideways, crablike manner, to keep the painting from being ripped from their grasp. Thus, because of the length of the canvas, nearly eight feet, and the crowd of boys who had gathered to look at the nude as it progressed, they were displacing the space normally required to allow passage for three carriages, with horses, and were going blocks off course to accommodate the wind and their entourage.

"Why don't we hire some of these urchins to help?" said Henri. "You would help, wouldn't you, urchins?"

The urchins, who were also moving in a crablike manner, their eyes pinned on the blue nude as if attached by mystic cords, several, unashamed, tenting their trousers with innocently stiffened peckers (they knew not the cause, only that the sight of the blue nude was simultaneously pleasant and unsettling, the exact effect she had on adults, *sans* trouser tents), nodded. "We'll help," said one boy, his finger far enough up his nose to tickle a memory nesting in his frontal lobe.

"Not a chance," said Lucien. "The paint's not even dry. They'll get their dirty little hands all over her. Back, urchins! Back!"

"Was she blue in real life?" one boy asked Henri.

"No," said Toulouse-Lautrec. "That is merely the artist's impression of the light."

"Did you touch her boobies?" another urchin asked.

"Sadly, I did not," answered Henri, grinning at Lucien and bouncing his eyebrows, the very caricature of a light-opera lecher.

"Why didn't you make them bigger?" asked Nose-finger.

"Because he didn't paint her!" barked Lucien. "I painted her, you annoying little maggot. Now fuck off, all of you. Off you go. Pests! Vermin!" Lucien couldn't wave them away without letting go of his end of the painting, but he was doing some powerful head tossing and eye rolling.

"Well, if you're going to shout at us, we're not going to help you anymore," said Nose-finger.

"Lucien," Henri said, "it is still a crime to beat a child to death, but if you feel you must, I will prevail, on your behalf, upon a team of lawyers my family retains for just such emergencies. My father is notoriously careless with firearms."

"Is that why Madame Lessard killed her?" asked one urchin, who, for some reason, Lucien had begun to think of as Little Woody. "Because you were painting her instead of baking bread like you're supposed to?"

"That's it," said Toulouse-Lautrec. "I'll do the beating. Shall we lean the painting against this wall?"

Lucien nodded and they carefully set the painting on its edge. Henri had been holding his walking stick braced against the back of the canvas stretcher, but now he waved it with a great flourish and closed his eyes as he drew the brass pommel. A collective gasp rose from the urchins. Henri ventured a peek.

"Would you look at that?" he said. There, instead of the cordial glass he was nearly sure he would be holding, he was brandishing a wicked spike of a short sword. "I'm glad I didn't offer to console you with a cognac, Lucien. *En garde,* urchins!"

He thrust the sword in the direction of the boys, who let loose with a cacophony of shrieks as they scattered to every corner of the square. Henri looked over his shoulder and grinned at Lucien, who couldn't help but grin back.

"She's too skinny," came a voice from where had once stood a thistle of street urchins. A slight man, today wearing a broad straw hat and buff linen jacket and trousers, his gray goatee trimmed and combed, and an amused smile in his blue eyes: Pierre-Auguste Renoir.

"Monsieur Renoir," said Toulouse-Lautrec. *"Bonjour."* He sheathed the sword in his cane and offered his hand to the older painter.

Renoir shook it and nodded a *bonjour* to Lucien. "You are better, then?"

"Much better," said Lucien.

"Good. I heard you were going to die over some girl." Renoir looked again at the painting. "This skinny blue girl?"

"I was just exhausted," said Lucien.

"Well, Rat Catcher, I guess you *did* learn something."

Lucien looked at his shoes, feeling himself blush at the master's comment.

"I like big butts," Renoir explained to Toulouse-Lautrec. "This one is too skinny, but that's not Lucien's fault." Renoir took a step back from the canvas, then another, and another, until he was across the street, then retraced the steps and bent down until his nose was nearly touching the paint.

He looked up at Lucien, who was still steadying the canvas against the breeze. "This is very good."

"*Merci,* monsieur," said Lucien.

"Very, very good," said Renoir.

"It's nothing," said Lucien.

"Ha!" Renoir slapped his leg. "It's no humping dogs, but it's very good." Renoir pushed his hat back and he broke into a wide grin, a gleam in his eye betraying something joyful surfacing in his memory. "Do you remember moving that big picture of the Moulin de la Galette across the butte with me, Lucien?"

"Of course," said Lucien, now sharing the smile.

"It was a big canvas," Renoir said to Henri. "Not as big as this one, but too big for one person to carry. Caillebotte has it now."

"I know the painting," said Henri. Of course he knew it. He'd been so impressed with it that he'd painted his own version of it a few years ago.

"Anyway, I wanted to paint a party, all the life that happened on a Sunday at the Moulin de la Galette—dancing, drinking, gaiety. It was going to take a big canvas. And I could only work on Sundays because my models, Margot and the others, all worked during the week. So every Sunday, Lucien and I would walk the big canvas from my studio on rue Cortot to the dance hall, and I would paint while my friends posed. After the rough sketch, I could only keep them still one or two at a time. It was like herding cats. They wanted to drink, dance, celebrate, the very things I was trying to capture, and I was making them pose. I'd paint all day, doing a little of each model until they got impatient. Except little Margot. She would pose like a statue for as long as I needed her to. Then in the late afternoon, we would move the canvas back across the butte to my studio. *Oh là là,* the wind. We had to pick leaves and pine needles out of the paint every week, and I would fix each little scar, just to have a new set to fix the next week. You remember, Lucien?"

"*Oui*, monsieur. I remember."

"You remember that white dress with the blue bows Margot wore?" Renoir asked, the gleam in his eye now going misty."

"*Oui*, monsieur."

"I loved that dress, but I had already painted her in it for my swing picture, and another picture of her dancing in it. I painted her in the blue stripes for *Le Moulin de la Galette*. Margot in blue." A tear streamed down the painter's face and he looked away, ashamed. "I'm sorry, messieurs, I don't know what has come over me. Seeing your picture, Lucien—see what you've done."

"I'm sorry, Monsieur Renoir," Lucien said. He was sorry for his mentor, but he didn't know how to comfort him. This was not the realm of their relationship. They were student and master. Best now, as men do, to pretend that nothing had happened.

Henri stepped over to Renoir, took a clean handkerchief from his breast coat pocket, and offered it to the master even as he turned to look the other way.

"These winds make my eyes water," said Toulouse-Lautrec to no one in particular. "The dust, I think, and the soot from the factories in Saint-Denis. It's a wonder a man can even breathe in this city."

"Yes," said Renoir, wiping his eyes. "The soot. Used to be we only had to put up with the coal soot in the winter. Now it's all the time."

"Monsieur Renoir," said Henri. "About those days, when you painted Margot. Dr. Gachet said he treated her?"

Lucien picked up his end of the painting and began blinking furiously, shaking his head in tiny jerks to signal Henri to come on and let Renoir go about his day, but because Toulouse-Lautrec was ignoring him, Lucien looked instead as if he had suddenly developed a very elaborate facial tic.

"I was very fond of Margot," said Renoir. "She fell ill with a fever and I had no money for a doctor. I wired Gachet and he came immediately. He tried, but he couldn't help her."

"I'm very sorry," said Henri. "I can tell from your paintings she was extraordinary."

"I would have married her if she had lived," said Renoir. "She was such a sweet little thing. But I know as the years passed, her bottom would have gotten huge. She was lovely."

"Did you ever lose time with her?" Henri asked.

Lucien nearly let the painting drop. "We should go, Henri. Let Monsieur Renoir get back to his day."

Renoir dismissed Lucien's distress with a wave of his delicate hand (his fingers were starting to knot with arthritis). "It was a long time ago. That whole time is a blur for me. I painted all the time. After Margot died I just traveled and painted. Just changing scenes to clear my head, I think. I don't remember much of it."

"I'm sorry to bring up a painful time, monsieur," said Toulouse-Lautrec. "I only hope there is something that we younger painters might learn from your experience. Lucien has suffered a heartbreak recently."

"I have not," said Lucien.

"Your mother didn't really kill this girl, did she?" asked Renoir. "That's just Montmartre milling rumors, right?"

"No, monsieur, just rumor. She is fine. We should go now. Please give my best to Madame Renoir and the children."

"Wait," said Henri, sounding desperate now. "In those days, did you ever buy color from a strange little man? Smaller even than me. Dark, almost apish? Broken?"

Suddenly, whatever sweet melancholy had animated Renoir a moment ago drained from his face.

"Oh yes," he said. "I knew the Colorman."

"I like big butts." *Self-Portrait*—Pierre-Auguste Renoir, 1910

Tʜᴇᴏ ᴠᴀɴ Gᴏɢʜ's ɢᴀʟʟᴇʀʏ sᴛᴏᴏᴅ ɪɴ ᴛʜᴇ sʜᴀᴅᴏᴡ ᴏғ ᴛʜᴇ ʙᴀsɪʟɪᴄᴀ ᴏғ Sᴀᴄʀᴇ́-Coeur, the white, Moorish–meets–Taj Mahal fairy-tale church built on Montmartre by the state to atone for the army massacring the Communards (the leaders of whom came from Montmartre) after the Franco-Prussian War. Like Paris's other architectural anomaly, the Eiffel Tower, Sacré-Coeur would often cause neck-wrenching double takes to those new to the city. But because it was visible from the entire city, it provided a convenient landmark to help travelers find Montmartre and patrons to find the Boussod et Valadon gallery, run by Theo van Gogh. "It's right behind that big, white, mosque-looking thing on the butte," they would say.

"Have you ever been tempted to paint Sacré-Coeur?" Henri asked Lucien as they swung the blue nude around to fit it through Theo's door. The gallery had a glass storefront framed in red and a wide red canvas awning with the words ART DEALER sewn on its outside edge.

"You mean paint the whole thing or make a painting of it?"

"Make a painting of it."

"No."

"Me either."

"My mother says that God wouldn't be caught dead in that garish harlot of a church."

"A moment, Lucien, I may have just had a religious epiphany," said Toulouse-Lautrec.

They rested the canvas on its edge as Lucien opened the door.

Theo van Gogh, thirty-three years old, thin, sandy haired, with a meticulously trimmed beard, wearing a houndstooth suit with black cravat, was sitting behind a desk at the rear of his gallery. When he heard the door open he rose and hurried to the front to help.

"Oh my. Henri, is this yours?" Theo said, holding the door out of their way as they carried the painting in. His French was slightly clipped by a Dutch accent.

"Lucien's," said Henri.

"*Bonjour,* Monsieur van Gogh," Lucien said with a nod as he steered the painting to the middle of the gallery. Lucien knew Theo, had sold some paintings in the gallery, but remained a bit formal with him out of respect for his position. The younger van Gogh looked thinner than when Lucien had last seen him, alert to the point of being almost jumpy but not healthy. Pale. Tired.

"Shall I fetch an easel?" asked Theo. "I don't know if I have one large enough."

"The floor will be fine. Just a wall to lean it against. The paint is still wet, I'm afraid," said Lucien.

"And you carried it here uncrated? Oh my," said Theo. He ran to the back of the gallery, grabbed the chair he had been sitting on, and brought it to Lucien. "Lean the stretcher against this."

The entire gallery, which took nearly the whole lower floor of the four-floor brick building, was hung floor to ceiling with paintings, prints, and drawings. Lucien recognized the paintings of Toulouse-Lautrec and Pissarro, as well as Gauguin, Bernard, and Vuillard; drawings by Steinlen and Willette, the butte's leading cartoonists; the odd Japanese print by Hokusai or Hiroshige; as well as many, many canvases by Theo's brother Vincent.

Once they had the painting in place, Theo stepped back to take a look.

"It's not finished, I—" Lucien started to explain about wanting to add the blue scarf, but Henri signaled for him to be quiet.

Theo took a pair of spectacles from his waistcoat and put them on, then crouched down and looked more closely at the canvas. He removed the spectacles and stepped back again. Here, for the first time, really, Lucien could see in the younger brother the intensity he'd seen in Vincent. Theo tended to be a bit fussy, often had the air of a clerk, assessing, accounting, measuring, but now he was evincing the sort of burning concentration that Vincent seemed to wear constantly, like a mad prophet. Henri had teased him that he knew he could always find a seat at a party next to Vincent because the Dutchman's gaze had frightened everyone away.

Lucien was beginning to fidget under the pressure of Theo van Gogh's silence when the gallery owner finally shook his head and smiled.

"Lucien, I don't know where I could hang it. As you see, the walls are full. Even if I took down all of the prints—it's so large."

"You want to hang it?" Lucien said. He hadn't really heard Renoir's praise over the piece, so now, for the first time, he looked at it as something besides a reminder of Juliette.

"Of course I want to hang it," said Theo. He offered his hand to Lucien, who took it and endured a shoulder-wrenching handshake. "You know, Vincent used to say that someone needed to do for figure painting what Monet had done for landscapes, and that no one had. I think you have."

"Oh, come now, Theo," said Henri. "It's a nude, not a revolution."

Theo smiled at Toulouse-Lautrec. "You're just jealous."

"Nonsense, this painting is shit," said Henri.

"It's not shit," said Lucien, really having trouble trying to figure out what, exactly, was their plan. It might not be a masterpiece, but it wasn't shit.

"It's not shit," van Gogh confirmed.

"Thank you, Theo," Lucien said. "Your opinion means a lot to me, which is why we've brought the painting to you unfinished. I'm thinking of painting a scarf—"

"Do you have all of Vincent's paintings here now?" interrupted Henri.

Theo looked startled at the mention of his brother. "Yes, I have them all here in Paris, although not hanging, obviously."

"In the lot of his last paintings, were there any figure paintings? Any paintings of women?"

"Yes, one of Madame Gachet; three, I think, of the young girl whose family owns the inn at Auvers, where Vincent was living; and one of the innkeeper's wife. Why?"

"Often, when an artist is tormented, a woman is involved."

Surprisingly, Theo van Gogh smiled at this. "Not just artists, Henri. No, when Vincent first went to Arles he mentioned a woman briefly in one of his letters, but it was the way you talk about a pretty girl you see walking in the park, wistful, I think you would call it. Not as if he knew her. Mostly he wrote about painting. You know him—knew him. Painting is all he talked about."

"Was there something about his painting that would have—that was causing him distress?"

"Enough distress to kill himself, you mean?" Now Theo lost his semblance of gentlemanly detachment and gasped as if unable to catch his breath.

"I'm sorry," Lucien said, steadying Theo with a hand on his back.

In a second van Gogh snapped back into his clerk aspect, as if they were talking about the provenance of a painting, not the death of his brother.

"He kept saying, 'Don't let anyone see *her*, don't let anyone near *her*.' He was talking about a painting he sent from Arles, but I received no figure painting from Arles."

"And you don't know who '*she*' was?"

"No. I don't. Perhaps Gauguin knows; he was there when Vincent had his breakdown in Arles. But if there was a woman, he never mentioned her."

"So it wasn't a woman . . ." Henri seemed perplexed.

"I don't know why my brother killed himself. No one even knows where he got the pistol."

"He didn't own a gun?" asked Henri.

"No, and neither did Dr. Gachet. The innkeeper only had a shotgun for hunting."

"You were a good brother to him," said Lucien, his hand still on Theo's back. "The best anyone could expect."

"Thank you, Lucien." Van Gogh snapped a handkerchief from his breast pocket and ran it quickly under his eyes. "I'm sorry. I'm still not recovered, obviously. I will find a place for your picture, Lucien. Give me some time to put some of the prints in storage and sell a few paintings."

"No, that's not necessary," said Lucien. "I need to work on her. I meant to ask you, as an expert, do you think I should paint a scarf tied around her neck? I was thinking in ultramarine, to draw the eye."

"Her eyes draw the eye, Lucien. You don't need a scarf. I wouldn't presume to tell you how to paint, but this picture looks finished to me."

"Thank you," said Lucien. "That helps. I would still like to work on the texture of the throw she is lying on."

"You will bring it back, then? Please. It really is a magnificent picture."

"I will. Thank you, Theo."

Lucien nodded to Henri, signaling him to pick up his end of the painting.

"Wait," said Henri. "Theo, have you ever heard of the Colorman?"

"You mean Père Tanguy? Of course. I have always bought Vincent's paints from him or Monsieur Mullard."

"No, not Tanguy or Mullard, another man. Vincent may have mentioned him."

"No, Henri, I'm sorry. I know only of Monsieur Mullard and Père Tanguy in Pigalle. Oh, and Sennelier by the École des Beaux-Arts, of course, but I've had no dealings with him. There must be half a dozen in the Latin Quarter to serve the students, as well."

"Ah, yes, thank you. Be well, my friend." Henri shook his hand.

Theo held the door for them, glad that they were going. He liked Toulouse-Lautrec, and Vincent had liked him, and Lucien Lessard was a good fellow, always kind, and, it seemed, was turning into quite a fine painter. He didn't like lying to them, but his first loyalty must always be to Vincent.

"THE PAINTING IS NOT SHIT," SAID LUCIEN.

"I know," said Henri. "That was just part of the subterfuge. I am of royal lineage; subterfuge is one of the many talents we carry in our blood, along with guile and hemophilia."

"So you don't think the painting is shit?"

"No. It is superb."

"I need to find her, Henri."

"Oh for fuck's sake, Lucien, she nearly killed you."

"Would that have stopped you, when we first sent you away from Carmen?"

"Lucien, I need to talk to you about that. Let's go to Le Mirliton. Sit. Have a drink."

"What about the painting?"

"We'll take the painting. Bruant will love it."

FROM INSIDE A RECESSED DOORWAY AT THE REAR OF SACRÉ-COEUR, SHE watched them walk her picture out the door of the gallery. They moved like a pair of synchronized drunkards, up the middle of the street, sideways, trying to keep the edge of the painting pointed into the breeze. Once they rounded the first corner she quickstepped down the stairs, across the small square, and into Theo van Gogh's gallery.

"*Mon Dieu!*" she exclaimed. "Who is this painter?"

Theo van Gogh looked up from his desk at the beautiful, fair-skinned brunette in the periwinkle dress who appeared to be climaxing on his gallery floor. Although he was sure he hadn't seen her before, she looked strangely familiar.

"Those were painted by my brother," Theo said.

"He's brilliant! Do you have any more of his work I could see?"

Sixteen

IT'S PRONOUNCED BAS'*TAHRD*

"He was two parts talent, three parts affectation, and five parts noise."
Aristide Bruant (poster)—Henri Toulouse-Lautrec, 1892

O H LOOK, IT IS THE GREAT PAINTER TOULOUSE-LAUTREC ACCOMPANIED by some dog-shit unknown bastard!" cried Aristide Bruant as they entered the half-lit cabaret. He was a stout, stern-faced man, in a grand, broad-brimmed hat, high-heeled sewer-cleaner boots, a black cape, and a brilliant red scarf. He was two parts talent, three parts affectation, and five parts noise. Le Mirliton was his cabaret, and Henri Toulouse-Lautrec was his favorite painter, which is why Henri and Lucien were dragging the blue nude into the bar in the middle of the day.

"When you break a tooth on the gravel in your blackberry tart," Lucien called back, "it will be a present from that same dog-shit unknown bastard!"

"Oh ho!" shouted Bruant, as if speaking to a full house of revelers instead of the four drunken butchers falling asleep over their beers in the dinge of the corner and a bored barmaid. "It appears that I have failed to recognize Lucien Lessard, the dog-shit baker and sometime dog-shit painter."

Bruant wasn't being particularly unkind to Lucien. Everything at Le Mirliton was served with a side order of abuse. It was Bruant's claim to fame. Businessmen and barristers came from all the best neighborhoods of Paris to sit on the rough benches, rub elbows on greasy tables with the working poor, and be outwardly blamed for society's ills by the anarchist champion and balladeer of the downtrodden, Aristide Bruant. It was all the rage.

Bruant strode across the open floor of the cabaret, snatching up his guitar, which had been resting on a table, as he went.

Lucien set down his end of the painting, faced Bruant, and said, "Strum one chord on that thing, you bellowing cow, and I will beat you to death with it and dismember your corpse with the strings." Lucien Lessard may have been tutored by some of the greatest painters in France, but he hadn't ignored the lessons from the butte's finest crafter of threats, either.

Bruant grinned, held the guitar up by his face, and mimed strumming. "I'm taking requests . . ."

Lucien grinned back. "Two beers with silence."

"Very good," said Bruant. Without missing a step, he turned as if choreographed, docked the guitar on an empty table, and headed back to the bar.

Two minutes later Bruant was sitting with them at a booth, and the three of them were looking at the blue nude, which was propped up against a nearby table.

"Let me hang it," said Bruant. "A lot of important people will see it in here, Lucien. I'll put her up high, over the bar, so no one will get any ideas about touching her. They might not buy it, because their wives won't let it in the house, but they'll see it and they'll know your name."

"You have to show the painting, Lucien," Henri said to Lucien. "We can put together a show later—maybe Theo van Gogh will sponsor it, but that will take time. I can't organize it. I need to go to Brussels, and to show with the Twenty Group, and I have promised to print new posters for the Chat Noir and the Moulin Rouge."

"And he owes me a cartoon for *Le Mirliton*," said Bruant. He irregularly published an arts magazine with the same name as his cabaret, and all of Montmartre's young artists and writers contributed to it.

"All right, then," said Lucien. "But I don't know what to ask for it."

"It shouldn't be for sale," said Henri.

"I would agree," said Bruant. "That's the power of the coquette, isn't it? Make them want it, but don't let them have it. Just tease."

"But I need a sale." And therein lay the artist's dilemma: to paint for filthy lucre was a compromise of principles, but to be an artist who didn't sell was to be anonymous as an artist.

"If she'll sell now, she'll sell later," said Henri. "The bakery makes enough money for you to live."

"Fine, fine," Lucien said, throwing his hands up. "Hang her. But if someone makes an offer, I want to know about it."

"Excellent," said Bruant, hopping up from his seat. "I'll go borrow a ladder. You can supervise the hanging."

When the singer had gone, Henri lit a cheroot with a wooden match and leaned into the cloud of smoke he'd just expelled over the table.

"Before he returns, Lucien, I need to tell you something—warn you."

"Don't be so ominous, Henri. It doesn't suit you."

"It's just that, Juliette—while I will help you find her, if you wish—I need to warn you—you may not want to find her."

"Of course I want to find her, Henri. I'm a wreck without her."

"I think you're romanticizing your time with her. You were a wreck when you were with her, too."

"I was painting."

"That's not the point."

"That's always the point."

"She was definitely living with the Colorman."

"Are you saying she was secretly his mistress? That can't be. Who lets his mistress spend so much time with another man?"

"I'm saying they have an arrangement."

"He's her pimp, then? Is that what you're saying? Are you saying that the woman I love is a whore?"

"You make it sound so sordid. Some of my best friends are whores."

"That's not the point. She is not a whore, he is not her pimp. You think everyone is a pimp. That's why you always lose the game."

Henri liked to play a game he called Guess the Pimp in the ballroom of the Moulin de la Galette. He and a group of friends (sometimes Lucien included) would sit at the edge of the crowded dance hall and try to guess which men in the booths were pimps tending to their girls and which were simply workingmen or rascals trying to make time with a pretty thing. They would place their bets, then one of the Moulin's doormen would come by and confirm or disprove their suspicions. Henri almost always lost.

"Not her pimp," said Henri. "I don't know what he is to her, but what I need you to ask yourself is, what if you found Juliette and she didn't know you?"

"What?"

"Lucien, you know after I followed her to the Colorman's apartment, I spoke to him."

"I know this, Henri. You thought he was lying about knowing Vincent."

"I'm sure he was lying about Vincent, but what I didn't tell you is I asked about Carmen."

"Carmen? Why?"

"When I saw him outside of the Dead Rat, the day you ran into Juliette, I remembered seeing Carmen with him."

"No!"

"You know I couldn't remember much of my time with Carmen."

"Absinthe," said Lucien. "That's why we sent you to your mother's. It was for your own good."

"Damn it, Lucien, it wasn't the absinthe. You heard Dr. Gachet. Renoir, Monet, all of them have had these moments of memory lapse, of hallucinations, going back years. Renoir remembers the Colorman but nothing about him. You've had them, and you haven't been drinking absinthe, have you? It's the color. Something in the color. And it doesn't just affect the painter. I *found* Carmen, Lucien. I found her and she had no idea who I was. She blamed it on a fever. She almost died after I left."

Lucien felt his face go numb at the revelation, both over what he had done to Henri and what it might mean to him and Juliette. He, Maurice Guibert, and Émile Bernard had physically dragged Henri out of his studio, bathed him, dressed him, then Guibert and Bernard had taken Henri to his mother's castle and stayed there with him until he sobered up.

"You were killing yourself, Henri."

"I was painting."

"We were trying to be good friends to—"

"She doesn't know me, Lucien," Lautrec blurted out. "She doesn't remember ever having met me." He ground his cheroot out on the floor (as Bruant not only allowed but required), then removed his *pince-nez* and pretended to wipe the fog from the lenses on his cravat. "That's what I've been trying to say. Juliette may not even know you."

"She will. We'll go to the Batignolles now. We'll save her—break whatever kind of hold the Colorman has over her. She'll understand about my mother braining her with a *crêpe* pan. You'll see."

Henri shook his head. "You think I haven't gone back? You were unconscious for a week, Lucien, and we were certain she was the cause. Of course I went back to where she lived. They are gone."

"I thought you were drunk in a brothel the whole time I was out."

"Well, yes, I was drunk, but I wasn't always in a brothel. I took a taxi to their apartment—but I did take two whores with me in case of an emergency. The concierge said that when she checked on them one morning, the Colorman and the girl were just gone. Not a word."

"We'll find her," said Lucien, realizing even as he said it that they'd both been this way before.

"Like we found her when she left two and a half years ago? Like I found Carmen after I came back from Mother's?"

"But we did find them."

"We found them because of the Colorman."

"Then we'll find the Colorman again."

"We are painters," said Henri. "We don't know how to find things."

"Speak for yourself. I'll find her."

Henri sighed and drained his beer, then looked to the bar. Bruant hadn't returned from wherever he'd gone to fetch the ladder. The butchers still dozed in the corner. The barmaid had her head propped on her hands and was on her way to dozing off as well. "Fine, then. Let's move your painting behind the bar. Then we'll go see your friend Professeur Bastard."

"Le Professeur? But he's a lunatic."

"I don't think he is," said Henri. "I think he is just eccentric."

"Well his father was a lunatic," said Lucien, draining the last of his beer as well.

"So is my father and so was your father."

"Well, yes, he was eccentric."

"Then shall we go see if Le Professeur has found the secret of our Colorman's paints?"

"SHOULDN'T WE BE GOING TO THE ACADÉMIE?" ASKED LUCIEN AS THEY MADE their way down the back of the butte and through the Maquis. It was well past midday now and there was all manner of industry, from goat milking to rag picking to rat racing, going on in the shantytown. (Yes, real rat racing. The old Professeur had never been able to train his rats to perform *Ben-Hur,* but when he died, the junior Bastard gave the track and the race-trained rodents to some local boys, who started a betting operation. They were grown men now and had staged twenty races a day for nearly fifteen years. In doing so they had also managed to prove that even in the most squalid slum, full of bandits, beggars, whores, con men, lechers, drunkards, layabouts, and egregious weasels, it was possible to attract an even more unsavory element. Le Professeur Deux, pioneering the budding demi-science of sociology, had done a study.)

"He told me he would be home today," said Henri, who snatched up his walking stick and tapped on Le Professeur's weathered plank door with the brass pommel. There was the sound of steam being vented, as if several espresso machines were all winding down at once, and the Professeur Émile Bastard opened the door and stepped awkwardly out of the doorway, nearly bumping his head on one of the open ceiling rafters.

"Gentlemen. Welcome. Come in, please. I've been expecting you. Lucien, so good to see you."

"And you," said Lucien.

Toulouse-Lautrec limped in but looked over his shoulder at Lucien and whispered, "I stand corrected. He *is* a lunatic."

Lucien nodded in agreement as he shook hands with Professeur Bastard. The Professeur was a very tall man—his thin, aquiline aspect put one in mind of a tweedy wading bird of some sort, an academically inclined egret, perhaps—but today he stood at least a foot taller than his normal height. He had to duck under each ceiling joist as he led them into the parlor in halting, careful steps. Bastard was wearing some kind of stilts under his trousers, fitted with shoes to appear to be his own feet. They crunched hazelnut shells strewn across the floor as he walked.

"Gentlemen, please sit down." Bastard gestured to two chairs, then reached into his trouser pocket and activated some sort of switch. Again there was the sound of gases venting, and Bastard lowered into a sitting position in a series of pneumatic jerks.

Lucien and Henri did not sit, they just stared. While Le Professeur *was* sitting, he wasn't sitting *on* anything. He was simply maintaining a sitting position in midair, like one of those annoying street performers one encountered around Paris who were always walking in the wind, or climbing imaginary stairs, or getting trapped in invisible boxes from which they could only be extracted by the donation of a ten-*centime* piece or a *gendarme* with a billy club.

"Sit, sit, sit," said Le Professeur.

"But, monsieur?" said Lautrec, waving at the Professeur in the manner of a magician presenting a freshly bisected assistant. "You are—"

"I am quite comfortable," said Bastard. He reached into his pocket, clicked some sort of switch, and with a hiss and a click, he stood to attention, his head barely missing a ceiling beam. He lifted his trouser cuffs to reveal, extending from his shoes, a leg-shaped frame of brass rods, with pistons suspended in the center. "What do you think?"

"You are certainly tall," said Henri.

"I built them for you," said the Professeur. "They are entirely too tall for me. They'll still have to be fitted to you, but I think you'll find they function quite efficiently."

"For what?" asked Henri.

"For effortless ambulation, of course. I call them Loco-ambulators, or steam stilts."

There was another hiss of steam being released and Lucien thought he smelled something burning.

"Help me out of them, I'll show you."

With the Professeur's instruction, they first lowered him to the floor, so he was sitting splay legged, then helped him unfasten leather straps and buckles until he was able to wriggle out of his trousers, leaving the steam stilts on the floor and the Professeur to pace in his underwear and socks as he lectured.

"I had noticed, when you visited before, that walking came to you with great difficulty and pain. Given your royal lineage, I deduced that this problem was one caused perhaps by your parents having been too closely related by blood."

"And I fell off a horse and broke my legs when I was a boy," said Henri, somewhat amused by the Professeur's pompousness, despite that he was wearing a tailcoat and no pants. (The tailcoat had concealed a small condensation chamber that was part of the steam stilts and rested across the small of the back.)

"Just so," said the Professeur, charging on, lifting the steam stilts to their feet as he spoke, so they stood there, a gleaming bronze skeleton (sans torso) with its trousers around its ankles. "I thought to relieve you of some of the effort, since you live on Montmartre, and climbing stairs and hills obviously caused you pain. At first I thought, *wheels,* but soon I realized that not only would wheels be conspicuous in company, they were useless on stairs. I designed the first set of walkers with Tesla motors, but the battery that would be required to run the machine would have been so heavy as to preclude your actually accompanying your legs."

"So my legs might have gone out drinking without me?"

"Possibly," snapped the Professeur. "Then it was clear that combustion was the only way to release enough energy to power you and still have the machine compact enough to be concealed. Steam was the answer. I designed the steam stilts so that by merely making the movement you normally make by walking, your legs would activate a series of switches and valves that extend and contract these pistons. You put out no more effort than if you were moving your legs underwater."

"I see," said Henri. "Now I must ask you, before you go any farther, and this is important: Do you have any brandy or cognac in the house?"

"Is something burning?" asked Lucien.

"Ah, the boilers are in the shoes," said the Professeur. "They burn powdered coal at a low smolder, but unfortunately there is some wasted heat. If you stand in one place for long, there is a danger of charring the rug."

Henri had begun to chuckle and was trying to conceal his amusement.

"At first, I wasn't sure how to shield your feet from the heat, then I thought, Of course, Monsieur Toulouse-Lautrec wouldn't mind being a bit taller. We'll simply extend the rods of the calves so that you are suspended above the heat of the boilers, and *voilà!* You are six feet tall."

"But everyone knows I have short legs. Would you have me leave Paris so I could use your walker?"

"Men trust their perceptions, not their memories. Your trousers will conceal the mechanism. You would only have to slip away a few times an evening to add fuel to the shoes. Perhaps more if there is dancing."

Henri was giggling now, barely able to contain himself. "So I'm to shovel coal into my shoes hoping no one notices, while the smoke and steam—what of the vapor?"

"There's little more smoke than a cigar, and the steam would be barely visible by gas lamp. It vents out the back of your trousers, under the tail of your coat."

"Marvelous!" said Henri. "I use a similar port for my own vapors. I want to try them, immediately. Well, as soon as we've heard the results of your analysis of the colors."

"Ah, yes," said the Professeur, "the colors. Let me get my papers."

He went into the back room, which Lucien thought might have once been the bedroom, yet there was no sign visible through the doorway that there was a bed in there, only worktables and scientific instruments.

Lucien leaned over to Henri and whispered, "Are you really going to try those legs of his?"

"Absolutely," Henri whispered back. "But no special trousers to conceal them. I'm wearing them on the outside. Did you hear that, Lucien? Dancing. On my mechanical, steam-farting legs. I shall be the toast of Pigalle."

"Oh balls," Lucien said.

"What?"

"I think your miraculous new feet are on fire."

And indeed, flames were shooting out of the tops of the Loco-ambulators' shoes and licking the brass legs.

"I'll get water," said Lucien, jumping up and running to the kitchen.

"Bring back liquor," said Henri.

Five minutes later the flames were out and the three sat, sadly looking at the charred remains of the steam stilts, which now stood just outside the door, in the dust, like the charred skeleton of a cannonball catcher, his torso carried off to parts unknown by the last shot.

"Perhaps a clockwork design," said the Professeur wistfully.

"As long as the pendulum is enormous," said Henri with a grin. "I have a reputation to maintain."

"So, Professeur," said Lucien. "About the colors."

"Yes," said Henri, "is there some kind of drug in them?"

The Professeur shuffled his papers until they seemed suitably disorganized.

"As you know, there have been theories since Newton that every material has its own unique qualities of light refraction, but beyond the visual analysis, there is no way to quantify that uniqueness."

"Which means?" asked Henri.

"To our eye, different red things will appear red," said Lucien.

"Exactly," said the Professeur.

"Is it obvious for me to point out that it does not require a scientist to point out that that is obvious?" asked Henri.

"Exactly," said the Professeur. "Which is why I used a new process discovered by a Russian scientist called liquid chromatography, where substances are suspended in a liquid and then either placed on paper or in thin tubes, and the level to which each substance migrates is unique. So in a color made of different colored minerals, say an orange composed of red ochre and yellow ochre, the two minerals will migrate to different levels, and if the red were made from another mineral, or an insect compound, like cochineal beetles, it too would find a different level in the liquid."

"And what about compounds that weren't part of the color, like a drug, perhaps?"

"Yes, that too," said the Professeur. "But liquid chromatography is a new process, and no one has done any indexing of the behavior of the elements, so I did a simple comparison. I went to Gustave Sennelier's shop near the École des Beaux-Arts. He makes all of his paint from pure, dry pigments, mixed to the order of each artist's preferences. Since we knew what went into each of his paints, I was able to compare the ingredients of each of his colors with those of your Colorman."

"And?" asked Lucien.

"Each of Sennelier's colors is composed of the same elements as those of your Colorman, mostly purely mined minerals, except the blue."

"I knew it," said Henri. "What is in the blue? Wormwood? Arsenic?"

"I don't know."

"That doesn't help," said Lucien.

"We compared every blue pigment that Sennelier had, as well as mineral samples I got from the geology department at the Académie. I also tested any element that appears blue under different light, or can be changed to blue by oxidation, like copper. I can tell you it's not azurite, and it's not lapis lazuli, the most common elements used to make blue. It's not indigo and it's not woad, nor any other plant or animal pigment that I could find. It's an unknown."

"That must be it, then," said Lucien. "There is some kind of drug in the blue compound. Can you test that?"

"Well, there wasn't much in that small tube Monsieur Toulouse-Lautrec gave me, but I suppose we could give it to some rats and see if they behave differently."

"Dr. Gachet said that even a very tiny amount might affect the mind—what might be absorbed through the skin or inhaled as you are painting. Henri and I certainly didn't eat any paint."

"I see. And you would have both been exposed to the compound over a longer period of time?"

Lucien looked at Henri, trying to measure the reality of it. If, indeed, both Juliette and Carmen had somehow been complicit in exposing them to the Colorman's blue, then it would have been over a period of years. But he didn't paint Juliette before, in the time before she went away. Or maybe he just didn't remember painting her.

"Henri, do you remember, when I was with Juliette before, did I paint her?"

"I never saw a painting, and you didn't speak of it, but now I wonder. You don't know?"

"Gentlemen," interrupted the Professeur, "you believe something in this pigment affected your memory? Correct?"

"Yes," said Lucien. "And perhaps it caused us to have false memories."

"I see." The Professeur shuffled through his notes for a moment, then stopped, stood, and quickstepped to a bookshelf in the corner of the room, where he snatched up a leather-bound volume and quickly flipped through the pages until he seemed to find what he was looking for. "Aha!"

"Aha, what?" asked Henri.

"This Austrian doctor writes of a process he uses on his patients to access what he calls 'suppressed memories.' Have you ever heard of hypnosis?"

"Mesmerism?" said Henri. "That's a carnival trick they use to make people behave like chickens. A service that, I can attest from experience, can be attained at the rue des Moulins brothel by slipping an extra three *francs* to the madame."

"Really?" said the Professeur.

"Four *francs* if you require an egg to be laid."

The Professeur seemed perplexed by Henri's revelation and rolled his eyes toward the ceiling as if the great gears of his mind were being strained by the mathematics of the scenario. "Seems rather dear for an egg," he said finally.

"Forget the egg," said Lucien. "Are you saying that you can help us remember?"

"Well, I can certainly try," said the Professeur. "I have hypnotized subjects."

"Professeur Bastard," said Henri, "I'm not sure I understand. You are a chemist, a geologist, you dabble in engineering, build machines, and now psychology; what exactly is your field of study?"

"Truth, Monsieur Toulouse-Lautrec, does not confine itself to a cage."

There came a whirring sound from under the Professeur's chair and the rat-sized brass nut-counting machine scurried out into the room and skittered from shell to shell and gaily chimed its findings.

"Ah, it's two o'clock," said the Professeur.

Seventeen

IN THE LATIN QUARTER

DID YOU FIND US A PAINTER?" ASKED THE COLORMAN WHEN SHE CAME in. He was sitting on the divan, feeding a carrot to Étienne, the donkey, who was wearing a straw boater with holes cut out for his ears.

The Colorman had rented them an apartment in the Latin Quarter, on rue des Trois-Portes, just off boulevard Saint-Germain.

"What is he doing here?" she said, unpinning a rather complex hat from her hair, and in the process releasing several silky black tendrils from her *chignon*.

"He was on holiday," said the Colorman.

"Not what is he doing in Paris, what is he doing on the divan?"

"Eating a carrot. I am eating a carrot as well. We are sharing."

She had already folded her parasol and put it in the stand by the door, so she thought perhaps she could use the Colorman's walking stick to drive into his eye socket and out through the back of his head. Only the thought of trying to get brain stains out of the rug stopped her, as they, of course, had not yet found a maid.

She was annoyed. The Colorman was annoying, made more annoy-ing, perhaps, because it was a warm autumn day and she'd been out stroll-ing through the Jardin du Luxembourg, looking for a new painter, and she was sweating under the ridiculous layers of skirts, corsets, petticoats, and other *accoutrements* required of the fashionable, modern woman. A bustle! Who had thought of that? Two of the city's finest painters had declared this bottom exquisite, had they not? Had this bottom not been favorably compared to the finest bottoms in art and been judged supe-rior? Had she not willed it to be thus? So why, why, why did she have to strap a pumpkin-sized tumor of silk and taffeta to her backside to appear acceptable to Paris society? Sweat was running down the crack of her ass and it was annoying. The Colorman was annoying, this new apartment was annoying, and Étienne, sitting on the divan, his front hoofs on the floor, crunching away at his carrot, was annoying.

"Take him outside," she snapped.

"His stall isn't ready. The concierge is going to have her man clean it out."

The new building had a stable and carriage house for the residents' horses, a feature that was becoming a rarity in the city.

"Well take him out with your color case and *you* find us a new painter."

"I can't go out. We have an appointment."

"An appointment? You and Étienne have an appointment? Here?"

The Colorman pulled another carrot out of a flour sack and chewed off the tip, then held the rest out for Étienne. "We are interviewing a maid."

"And Étienne has to be here because . . . ?"

"Penis," explained the Colorman.

That was it. She'd just have to clean the brains out of the carpet her-self. She snatched the Colorman's walking stick out of the brass stand and assumed an *"en garde"* posture, the cane's silver tip aimed at the little man's eye.

"Mine doesn't frighten them like it used to," said the Colorman mournfully. "I think I am losing my touch."

Étienne nodded sadly, or it seemed sadly, but to be fair, he was actually just signaling that he was ready for another carrot. Juliette let the tip of the cane drop, then sighed, whirled, and plopped down on the couch between the two pathetic penis plotters.

"Besides," said the Colorman, "we're out of the blue. I gave the last I had to the dwarf. He would be easy for you. And he paints fast. Find another redheaded laundress to tempt him."

Yes, he would be easy, but she did not want to return to Toulouse-Lautrec, despite his talent. She didn't want any of the painters in the park, or the dozen with their easels lined up like dominos on either side of the Pont-Neuf. She wanted Lucien. She missed Lucien. She had been sleeping with a shirt she had stolen from him, snuggling it to her face and breathing in his unique yeast-and-linseed-oil-mixed-with-man aroma. It was a problem.

"This apartment is rubbish," she said.

"It's nice," said the Colorman. "It has two bedrooms and a bath. You should take a bath. Étienne hasn't seen this one naked. He'll like her."

"There are too many bloody cathedrals. Every way I turn here, it's like gargoyles are biting my ass." The rue des Trois-Portes was, in fact, situated in the midst of three large churches. A hundred or so meters to the southeast stood the Church of Saint-Nicolas-du-Chardonnet (patron saint of wine in a box); to the west was the Church of Saint-Séverin; and a hundred meters to the north, perched on the Île-de-la-Cité, riding up the middle of the Seine like the bridge of a great warship, stood Notre-Dame Cathedral. And that wasn't even counting Sainte-Chapelle, another two blocks from Notre-Dame, the jewel box of stained glass that she had helped inspire. And although they had avoided it in the case of Sainte-Chapelle, probably because the Colorman had established himself as an imbecile bell ringer up the street at Notre-Dame at the time, it was the burnings that she'd hated about cathedrals. And the windows. And being the Mother of God. But mostly the burnings.

Chartres, France, 1174

DAWN. THE SPIRES OF THE CATHEDRAL ROSE BLACK AGAINST THE SUNRISE AND cast long, knife-shaped shadows across the town.

The Colorman led the girl to a wide, calm spot in the Eure River where a simple crane made of long wooden poles was levered out over the river with its nose dipped into the water like a drinking bird. The girl was thin, and only a little taller than he, with dirty ginger hair that hung in tangles around her face. She might have been thirteen or twenty, it was hard to say, as her face was the blank, unprimed canvas of a simpleton, portraying no interest in what was going on around her. Her green eyes and a thin sheen of drool on her lower lip were the only things about her that reflected light; the rest of her was muted by a patina of filth and stupidity.

He'd found her the morning before, squatting beneath a cow, squirting a stream of milk into her mouth from the udder. There'd been a wooden pail there, ready for the morning milking, but she'd never gotten to it, as the Colorman had lured her away from her task with a bright red apple and a shiny piece of silver dangling from a string.

"Come along, now. Come on."

He backed his way across the village, leading her to a stable he'd rented, where he'd given her the apple, and beer, and wine spiced with a narcotic mushroom that made her sleep until he'd awakened her today. The promise of another apple lured her to the riverbank.

"Take that off. Off," said the Colorman, showing her the gesture of lifting her frock over her head.

She made the same gesture but failed to grasp the idea she was supposed to actually remove her dress, a grimy, woven wool arrangement that was tattered at every seam.

The Colorman held the apple up in one hand, then tugged at the cord tied at her waist as a belt.

"Off. Take it off. Apple," said the Colorman.

The girl giggled at his touch, but what concentration she had was trained on the apple.

The Colorman uncinched her belt with his free hand, then held the apple just out of her reach as he alternately tickled her and worked her dress up to her shoulders and her arms out of the sleeves as she flinched and giggled. Finally he put the apple in her mouth and yanked her dress over her head with both hands as her full being seemed to fold over and around the apple. She stood in the mud, completely naked, except for the small silver coin suspended from a string around her neck.

She was laughing as she gnawed into the apple, and from the noises she was making the Colorman feared that she might choke before he finished his work.

"You like apples, huh?" he said. "I have another one for you after that one."

He unslung a leather satchel from his back and removed the materials he would need. The blue was in an earthenware jar no bigger than his fist, still in the dry, powdered form, as it had to be for the glassmakers. For this, since it didn't need to dry, or last very long, he would bind the color in olive oil, which he poured from a bottle into a shallow wooden cup to mix with the Sacré Bleu.

He stirred the mixture with a stick, until it was a smooth, shiny paste, then, with the distraction of another apple and another piece of silver, he applied the blue to the girl's body as she squirmed and giggled and crunched away on her apple.

"She is going to be angry when she sees you," said the Colorman, stepping back from the girl and checking over his work. "Very angry, I think."

There was a large, flat stone tied at the end of the wooden crane, just at the level of the Colorman's chest, and he pressed down on it the best he could, but the end of the crane in the water remained there. He grunted and hopped and swung back and forth, and still the crane only lifted a few inches.

"Girl, come here," he said to the simple girl, who was watching him with the fascination of a cat regarding the workings of a clock.

He trudged over to her, took her by the hand, then led her to the large stone.

"Now, help me push." He mimed pushing down on the stone. The girl watched him, having returned both her hands to guiding the apple into her mouth. Nothing.

He tried to get her to jump up on the stone, but there was no strategic placement of the apple that could get her to do that, and finally, when he couldn't get her to grasp the concept of boosting him up onto the stone, he lashed her to it with her belt slung under her arms, then scrambled up her body and knelt on the stone as he used the girl for leverage while she made a distressed mooing sound approximating the call of a calf caught in a thicket of thorns.

But the wooden crane moved, and its far end lifted out of the water a charred, twisted mass that looked like a statue of a suffering saint fashioned in pitch. It streamed soot and muddy water back into the river. Here in Chartres, it was the tradition to both burn and drown the witches, so at least he wasn't sifting bones out of an ash pile, as had been the case in the past.

The Colorman cringed, then chanted something that sounded more like a grunt than a prayer, repeating it until the black mass at the end of the crane cracked, showing pink, burned flesh beneath the surface.

The simple girl stopped mooing, took a great gasping breath, and stepped away from the stone counterbalance, slipping out of her rope belt as she moved. The Colorman was catapulted upward, his twisted form describing a gentle arch in the air before he plopped, ass first, onto the muddy riverbank.

"Oh for fuck's sake," said the simple girl, backing away from the whole apparatus.

"I knew you'd be angry," said the Colorman.

"Of course I'm angry," said the girl. "I've been burnt up." There was light in the girl's eyes now, the dullness gone. She wiped the drool from her lips with her arm and spit out the blue pigment.

"I brought you an apple," said the Colorman, pulling the last apple from his satchel.

The girl looked at him, smeared with the oily blue, then at her own body, covered head to toe in blue, then at him. "Why are you all covered in the blue? You better not have bonked me before you brought me back."

"Accident," said the Colorman. "Couldn't be helped."

"Oh, what is that?" She crinkled her nose and held her arms out from her sides as if they were foreign, foul things and she could actually escape them if she showed enough disgust. "I smell of shit? Why do I smell of shit?"

"I found you under a cow."

"Under a cow? What was she doing under a cow?"

"She's a little slow."

"You mean I'm an imbecile?"

"Not anymore," said the Colorman cheerily, holding out the apple, wishing that it would work on Bleu the way it had worked on the slow girl. But no.

"You painted the village idiot blue and bonked her before you pulled me up?"

"Being burned up makes you cranky."

The filthy, naked blue girl stomped into the muddy river with a growl. When she got to waist level she began to scrub herself and a blue stain floated on the water around her. "Why don't they ever burn you? You're involved. You're part of it. You're the one making the fucking color." She punctuated every sentence by splashing a great swan of muddy-blue water at the Colorman.

They had been working around the cathedral glassmakers for two hundred years now, moving from camp to camp with them, from Venice to London, as they built their furnaces and made the glass for the windows at each cathedral site. The Colorman provided the pigment to make a unique hue of blue, the Sacré Bleu, and she seduced the glassmakers. Unfortunately, the furnaces were usually built out in the open, or near a forest where wood could be easily harvested, and the glass, too, was stored either in the open or in makeshift tents, forcing them to make the blue in the open as well, where people could stumble upon them in the process. It was a disturbing process to watch. Medieval people reacted badly to the sight.

"You're the blue one," said the Colorman.

"You could have rescued me."

"I just did."

"Before the burning."

"I was busy. Couldn't be helped. I rescued you that time in Paris. At Notre-Dame."

"Once! Out of how many times? Peasants have no imagination. No other solutions." She splashed her point home. "Crops fail? Burn the blue girl. Fever in the village? Burn the blue girl. Badgers ate the miller? Burn the blue girl."

"When did badgers eat the miller?"

"They didn't. I'm just using that as an example. But if they did, you know the villagers would burn the bloody blue girl as a remedy. 'Witch' this and 'witch' that? It's not like it's easy seducing a glassmaker into thinking you're the Virgin bloody Mary and then screwing him into inspiration. I'm telling you, Poopstick, this guilt strategy the Church is working is not good for art."

"Maybe we should find a new camp of glassmakers," said the Colorman.

She ducked under the water, scrubbed her hair as long as she could hold her breath, then surfaced with a shudder. "Oh, you think? I don't guess we can stay here, can we, since everyone knows me as the village idiot? Not much I can do except eat dirt in the square and bonk the sodding priest, is there?"

"You can change."

"No, I refuse to be burned more than once in the same village; find me a clean frock and we'll go."

And so they did.

For eight hundred years, it was thought that the formula for making the blue glass in the windows of the cathedral Notre-Dame de Chartres was lost, when it had simply moved on. For Bleu, the burnings had more or less taken the charm out of Gothic cathedrals.

THE SAYING GOES, "THE MIND OF PARIS IS ON THE LEFT BANK, THE MONEY IS ON THE RIGHT," and the mind of the Left Bank was the Latin Quarter, so called because the common language spoken by the university students was Latin and had been for eight hundred years.

"I don't like the Latin Quarter," Juliette said. She took a carrot from the Colorman's bag and crunched off the tip. Étienne made a move to bite the carrot greens and she nudged his nose away with her elbow. "All the students are annoying, with their brooding and their spotty faces. And the good painters are all over on Montmartre or in the Batignolles."

"Then go find a new painter and live with *him*," said the Colorman.

It was her fault he'd had to take an apartment in the Latin Quarter, where he had cached secrets and power she didn't know about. He wanted to tell her that it was her fault for not getting the Dutchman's painting, and it was her fault for leaving the baker's painting behind, and if she hadn't done that, they might have gotten a nice place in the First Arrondissement, with better shops, Les Halles market, and the Louvre nearby, but she was in that mood she got in sometimes, the mood where heat and memories of playing the Mother of God annoyed her so that she would stab you in the eye with a walking stick, and he didn't want to press her.

"If we have no blue, what good is a new painter?" Juliette said.

"And the Dutchman's brother. You don't think he has our paintings? You know if the Dutchman told the dwarf about us, he told his brother."

"If he has it, he wouldn't show it to me. I looked at a hundred of Vincent's canvases. None painted with Sacré Bleu."

"You need to fix the brother's memory."

"I can't go back to Montmartre looking like this anymore. When the family starts conking you on the head, it's time to change strategies. If you want me to go back, I need the blue."

"If we can get the color, you need to clean this up." The Colorman took off his hat and scratched his head, a patchy carpet of coarse black hair. He could, perhaps, get the color, but he didn't want her to know the source, which was going to be awkward, since he'd need her to help him make it. Maybe he should just buy a new gun and start shooting painters. It was much simpler that way. "If you can't make them forget, the baker and the dwarf, the Dutchman's brother, then you need to finish them."

"I know." She pulled her carrot greens away from Étienne, who snapped at her in protest. Then she noticed that his great erect donkey dick was jutting damply out from under him and off the edge of the sofa. She smacked its tip with her carrot and the donkey brayed like a broken bellows in protest.

"He missed you," explained the Colorman.

Eighteen

TRAINS IN TIME

"I's two thirty. It's two thirty. It's two thirty."

"You're supposed to use the watch as a point on which to focus," said the Professeur, who was swinging his pocket watch by the chain in front of Lucien's face. "Not to continually check the time."

"You didn't say that." Lucien squinted at the watch. They'd been at this for a half an hour, trying to access Lucien's earliest memories of the Colorman, but all they'd discovered was the time. "You just said concentrate on the watch. I thought you'd want to know what time it was."

"When does he start to behave like a chicken?" asked Henri. "I need to get to the printers."

"A subject for hypnosis must be suggestible," said the Professeur. "Perhaps we should try it on you, Monsieur Lautrec."

"And waste the thousands of *francs* I've spent on alcohol trying to destroy the very memories you are trying to raise? I think not. I have an idea, though, that may work on Lucien. Could we try an experiment?"

"Of course," said the Professeur.

"I'll need what is left of the blue oil color I gave you for analysis."

The Professeur retrieved the color from the bedroom/laboratory and gave it to Lautrec, who uncapped the tube.

"I'm not eating paint," said Lucien.

"You don't have to eat it," said Henri. "You merely have to look at it." And with that, he squeezed a dollop of paint out onto the Professeur's watch and smeared it around on the face.

"This was my father's watch," said the Professeur, frowning at his newly painted timepiece.

"In the name of science!" pronounced Toulouse-Lautrec. "Now try it." He limped off to the kitchen. "Don't you at least keep some sherry for cooking?"

The Professeur dangled the watch in front of Lucien's face. "Now, if you just concentrate on the watch, on the blue."

Lucien sat bolt upright on the couch. "I don't see the point of this. What am I going to remember?"

Henri was returning to the parlor with a very dusty bottle of brandy in hand. "We don't know what you're going to remember until you remember it."

"You think it will help me find Juliette?" And therein lay the resistance. Lucien was afraid that the Professeur might, indeed, be able to conjure up lost memories, but what if Lucien remembered that his Juliette was some sort of villain? He couldn't bear it.

"Wait. Henri, you said that Carmen didn't remember you, but she wasn't unkind to you, right? She didn't seem to be trying to hide from you? Perhaps she was an unwilling participant in the Colorman's scheme. Perhaps she loved you deeply and he made her forget. Perhaps Juliette, too, is being manipulated against her will."

"Perhaps," said Lautrec absentmindedly, "but she is too beautiful, I think, to not be inherently evil."

Henri was ambling around the room looking in various nooks and crannies, moving different machines and instruments, and finally settled on a small graduated cylinder. He began to pour brandy into it.

"Monsieur," said the Professeur, shaking his head. "That was last used for a substance that is quite poisonous."

"Oh balls," said Lautrec. He snatched the skull of a small animal, a monkey, it appeared, from the Professeur's desk and poured a dollop of brandy into it, then slurped off the top.

"Henri!" scolded Lucien.

"May I suggest a *demitasse* from the kitchen," said the Professeur. "I prepare my own coffee in the morning."

"Oh, right," said Henri, draining the monkey skull and replacing it on the desk, then limping back to the kitchen.

"Why don't you just drink out of the bottle?" Lucien called after him.

Henri's head popped back around the corner. "Please, monsieur, what am I, a barbarian?"

When they were all settled again in the parlor, Henri with his brandy, the Professeur with his watch, Lucien with his foreboding, the process began again. This time the Professeur spun the watch slowly on its chain while he recited the litany of relaxation, concentration, and sleep to Lucien.

"Your eyelids will feel heavy, Lucien, and you may close them when you wish. When you do, you will fall into a deep sleep. You will still be able to hear me, and answer me, but you will be asleep."

Lucien closed his eyes and his head slumped forward onto his chest.

"You are completely safe here," said the Professeur. "Nothing can harm you."

"If you feel you need to scratch around looking for worms, we will understand," said Henri.

The Professeur shushed the painter with a finger to his lips, then whispered, "Please, monsieur, I am not going to make him think he is a chicken." To Lucien he said, "How are you, Lucien?"

"I am completely safe and nothing can harm me."

"That's right. Now I'd like you to go back, travel back, back in time. Imagine you are going down a flight of steps, and with each step you take, you go back another year. You will see your past go by, and remember all the pleasant moments, but keep moving until you first encounter this Colorman."

"I see him," said Lucien. "I'm with Juliette. We are drinking wine at the Lapin Agile. I can see him out the window. He is standing across the street with his donkey."

"And how far back have you traveled?"

"Perhaps three years. Yes, three years. Juliette is radiant."

"Of course she is," said the Professeur. "But now you need to continue your journey, down the stairs, until you see the Colorman again. Down, down, back through time."

"I see him!"

"And how far have you gone?"

"I'm young. Maybe fourteen."

"Are you secretly aroused by the nuns at school?" asked Henri.

"No, there are no nuns," said Lucien.

"Perhaps it was just me," Henri said.

"No, it wasn't just you," said the Professeur, with no further explanation. "Go on, Lucien, what do you see?"

"It is early morning, and it is raining. I have been out in the rain, but now I'm under a roof. A very high glass roof."

"And where is this roof?"

"It is a train station. It's Gare Saint-Lazare. I have been carrying three easels and a paint box for Monsieur Monet. He is still standing out in the rain, talking to the Colorman. The Colorman can't get his donkey to come under the awning of the station. Monsieur Monet says he has no money for color. He says he is going to capture the fury of smoke and steam. The Colorman hands him a tube of ultramarine. He says this is the only way, and Monet can pay him later. I can't hear what the Colorman says next, but Monsieur Monet laughs at him and takes the paint."

"Is the Colorman working with a girl?" asked Henri. "Do you see a girl?"

"Yes. Not *with* the Colorman, but nearby. She is inside the station, but it's very early, and there is almost no one else around."

"What does she look like?"

"I can't see. She is holding an umbrella so I can't see her face. She's small, thin. From her dress and posture I would say she is fairly young."

"Can you move closer?" said the Professeur. "See if you can get a look at her."

"I set down the easels and walk toward her. She peeks around her umbrella, then hurries away, out toward the rue de Rome exit. As she steps into the rain she has to lift the umbrella. Yes, she's young. Pretty."

"Do you know her?"

"Can you touch her bosoms?" asked Henri.

"Monsieur Toulouse-Lautrec, please," said the Professeur.

"What? It's an illusion, there are no rules of propriety."

"It's Margot," said Lucien. "The girl who Monsieur Renoir has been painting at the Moulin de la Galette. She is leaning over, talking to the Colorman behind her umbrella. They leave together, down the boulevard. I will try to follow them."

Paris, 1877, Gare Saint-Lazare

"I AM THE PAINTER MONET," MONET ANNOUNCED TO THE STATION MANAGER. The usher, who had presented Monet's calling card, stood by the manager's desk, frozen in a half bow to the grandiose gentleman. Lucien stood in the doorway, drooling, as he had been instructed, and haphazardly juggling the three easels, Monet's paint box, and a broad wooden case for carrying wet canvases.

"I am the painter Monet. I have decided to paint your station."
Claude Monet—Pierre-Auguste Renoir, 1875

Monet wore a velvet jacket and a silk waistcoat bound with a gold watch chain; lace cuffs draped his wrists; a black silk cravat was tied at his throat, pinned with a pearl stickpin—every inch the gentleman, dandy, and master of his universe. His lapel bulged a bit, betraying half a baguette that he had concealed in his coat, the remains of the breakfast Mère Lessard had sent along to him, since he had no money for food.

"I have decided to paint your station," said Monet. "I must admit, I was torn between Gare du Nord and your station, but I believe your station has more character, so it is Gare Saint-Lazare that shall be honored."

The station manager, a thin, nervous, balding man—a man built for bureaucracy—was flustered. He stood at his desk in his suit of yellow ochre plaid and began to fuss with papers, as if something on his desk might confirm his station's worthiness.

"This is my assistant, Lucien," Monet announced, turning on a heel and leading the way out of the office into the great chamber of the station. "He is a simpleton, but I allow him to be my porter so he does not starve. Don't be alarmed if you see him eating paint. I allow him half a tube a day."

"*Bonjour*," drooled Lucien.

The station manager and the porter nodded uncomfortably to the boy, then skated by him in the doorway as if he might be poisonous to the touch and followed Monet onto the platform under the grand clock.

"I wish to paint the steam and smoke, the fury of the engines preparing to depart. I will paint fog, you see, capture on canvas that which has never been captured."

The station manager and the porter nodded in unison, but didn't move otherwise and seemed to have no intention of doing so, as if they were overwhelmed by the painter's bearing.

"Lucien, set up my easels," said Monet, pointing. "There! There! There!"

The painter's barking of orders seemed to wake the station manager from his daze. Of course, if there was going to be steam, the locomotives would need to be fired. "Bring engine number twelve under the roof. Tell the engineers down the line to get their engines up to steam."

"I will need them to vent it at once, if they can," said Monet.

"Tell them to vent the steam on my signal," the station manager instructed the porter, who hurried off down the train tracks. To Monet, the manager said, "Monsieur, may I suggest that you only have one train at a time release its steam. On a wet day like today, the entire station might be so filled with fog you couldn't see to paint."

"Fine, I want a storm of steam. Turner's ghost should stir at the storm I capture today," said Monet. "Let me know when all is ready." He took his palette from his paint box and began to load it with color, while Lucien set blank, primed canvases on the easels, then looked to the master with an eyebrow raised, waiting for approval.

Monet stood behind each canvas in turn and looked at his view of the station, then adjusted them so he had nearly the same perspective at each spot. Then he took a broad, flat brush, wet it with turpentine in the palette cup, then loaded it with lead white and dipped just the corner in the Colorman's ultramarine. In a second he was washing the top of each canvas with a pale blue, going from one easel to the next and back.

"But, Monsieur Monet," said Lucien, confused. "The trains are not ready yet. How can you capture the moment if the moment is not happening yet?" How was he to learn anything from his masters if they changed their method without notice? Monet never tinted his canvases before beginning a painting, or at least Lucien had never seen him do it.

"Just watch, Lucien. And don't forget to drool when the station manager returns."

Monsieur Monet was mad, Lucien thought. Well, not really, but others would have thought it a mad undertaking. Lucien had been present when Monet and Renoir were having coffee at the bakery, shortly after the first Impressionists show, when one of the reviewers had written, *"Monsieur Monet seems to view the world through a cloud of fog."*

"I'll show them," Monet said to his friend. "I'll paint fog."

"You're mad," Renoir had said.

"You'll see."

"You really think you can do it?" asked Renoir.

"How would I know?" said Monet. "No one has ever done it."

In the station, smoke from the steam engines was beginning to billow against the glass roof and moved in great waves out into the morning sky. Lucien looked from canvas to locomotive, and back to canvas. He had seen Monet lay down color with mad, frenetic precision, faster than any of the other painters, but he couldn't see how he could capture a subject as ethereal as steam from a locomotive.

When the painter saw that he had the stationmaster's eye across the platform, he waved his brush, now loaded with tinted ultramarine, as a signal to begin. The stationmaster signaled, in turn, to porters, who signaled to each engineer down the line, and three locomotives, one under the roof and two out in the yard, released great clouds of smoke and steam, their whistles sounding all across the city.

Monet painted. Lucien stood behind him, trying to watch, trying to learn, seeing him build up each canvas, moving from one to the next, laying down blues and greens and browns, the dark lines describing the engines and the structure of the great roof rising up out of pools of pastel color. The whistles sounded again and Lucien looked at the big station clock above the ticket windows. A half-hour had passed.

Monet stood back from three finished paintings and checked the scene again for any detail he might have missed. "Let's clip these canvases and put them into the case, Lucien," the painter said. "We should give the stationmaster back his station." He slid his palette into the grooves of his paint box and lay the brushes into a tin-lined tray for Lucien to clean, then wiped his hands and strutted toward the stationmaster's office to thank him.

Lucien opened the case to stow the new paintings. Its inside was fitted with rails that kept the paintings from touching while being transported. It would be a week, maybe two, before they could be touched, months before they would be dry enough to varnish.

The case already held three completed paintings. That couldn't be right. Lucien slid the top canvas part of the way out on its rails. Yes, it was a newly painted canvas of the station. The turpentine smell was rising from it. He touched the paint near the edge of the canvas, an area that would be obscured by a frame. Fresh, wet paint. Somehow, Monet had painted six paintings in thirty minutes. By the time Lucien had all of the paintings stowed, the easels broken down, and had given the painter's brushes a perfunctory cleaning with turpentine and linseed oil, Monet was standing over him, grinning.

"You did it," said Lucien. "You really did it."

"Yes," said Monet.

"*How* did you do it?" asked Lucien.

The painter ignored Lucien's question and instead picked up the case with the finished paintings. "Shall we go? Renoir will just be finishing his breakfast. I think we should go show him what a madman can do."

He led Lucien out of the station onto the boulevard, just pausing a moment to pull his hat down in the rain.

"Turner's ghost should stir at the storm I capture today," said Monet.
Gare Saint-Lazare in Paris—Claude Monet, 1877

THE PROFESSEUR COUNTED LUCIEN OUT OF HIS TRANCE. "THREE, TWO, ONE, and now you are awake."

"You can't be remembering it correctly," said Henri.

Lucien looked around the Professeur's dingy parlor and blinked as if he'd just come in out of a bright sunlit day. "I think I am," he said.

"I have seen one of Monet's Saint-Lazare paintings," said Lautrec. "I don't think even the great Monet could paint one of them in half an hour, let alone six. You made some mistake in recalling it."

"The question is," said Lucien, "why am I remembering it at all? The Colorman was there, and Margo was there, but the Professeur asked about a memory of the Colorman, not Monet painting the station."

"Perhaps your mind filled in the details," said the Professeur. "Our memories sometimes conform to a logical narrative, and details are constructed to make sense, like the passage of time being compressed."

"But I didn't construct this. I didn't remember any of this until now. Something strange did happen with the time, and it has to do with the color. The same blue you put on the watch, Monet used to wash the canvases. It wasn't my memory that was affected, it was reality."

"How do you know that?" asked Henri.

Lucien downed the *demitasse* of brandy that Henri had poured for him and set the cup on the coffee table. "I know because it's not raining out."

"I don't understand," said the Professeur.

"Look at your shoulders. Touch the top of your head. You two have been in the rain. So have I."

They weren't soaked by any means, but there were moist spots on their heads and shoulders, as if they had run through the rain to catch a taxi. Henri checked the tops of his shoes, which were still spotted with beading water droplets.

"It hasn't rained in Paris in a week," said Henri.

"It's been even longer since it rained in my parlor," said the Professeur.

"Six paintings in a half an hour," said Lucien.

"Yes, but what does that tell us? What does that mean?" asked the Professeur.

"It means that Lucien can't be reasonable and behave like a proper chicken when he is hypnotized like everyone else," said Henri.

"It means I am going to see Monet," said Lucien. "I'm taking the first train to Giverny in the morning."

"I can't go with you," said Henri. "I have to go to Brussels. Octave Maus is showing my work at his exhibition of the Twenty. I have to be there."

"There is a painter named Octave Maus?" asked the Professeur.

"He's a lawyer," said Henri.

"Oh, that makes more sense," said the Professeur.

"No it doesn't," said Lucien. "Octave Maus is still an absurd name, even for a lawyer. Wipe that blue off your watch, Professeur, it's affecting your judgment."

"It was a very small monkey in a very large park." *Sunday Afternoon on the Island of La Grande Jatte*—Georges Seurat, 1884

JUST BEFORE DAWN THE COLORMAN AND ÉTIENNE STOOD BY THE TRACKS AT Gare de Lyon waiting for a train that had departed a day ago from Torino, and before that, Genoa, Italy. There was raw color on the train, gouged fresh from the hills of Italy: tan and umber earths from Siena; red, yellow, and orange ochres from Verona, Naples, and Milan. Most makers of oil color would wait, have the wholesaler deliver the crushed minerals to their shops, but the Colorman wanted to pick the very rough ores of the earth from which his color was born. Sacré Bleu was his power, but he was a man of all colors. He even performed some of the ritual when making the other colors, not because it was necessary, but because it frightened the maids.

As the train's brakes hissed and squealed and the great beast stopped, the Colorman noticed another man by the tracks, a slight fellow with a goatee, wearing a light gray plaid suit and hat that was entirely too fine for a stevedore or porter, and except for the Colorman, no one else was to be found this far down the tracks, away from the passenger platforms. The man in gray held a *pince-nez* and seemed to be trying to read the sides of the train cars.

"What are you looking for?" asked the Colorman.

"This is the train from Italy, I'm told," said the man, eyeing Étienne's boater hat suspiciously. "I'm expecting a shipment of colored ores, but I don't know where to find it."

"It's probably that one," said the Colorman, pointing to a train car he was sure it wasn't. "You are a painter?"

"Yes. Georges Seurat is the name. My card."

The Colorman looked at the card, then handed it to Étienne, who thought it tasted fine.

"You painted that big picture of the monkey in the park."

"There was a very small monkey in a very large park. *Sunday Afternoon on the Island of La Grande Jatte.* That painting was about placement of color."

"I liked the monkey. You should buy your paints from a color man."

"I work in pure hues," said Seurat. "After Chevreul's theory of mixing color in the eye, rather than on the canvas. Dots of complementary color placed next to each other cause an instinctual and emotional response in the mind of the viewer—a vibration, if you will. Something that can't be achieved by color muddied on the palette. I need the colors as raw as can be."

"That sounds like bullshit," said the Colorman.

"Chevreul was a great scientist. The world's premier color theorist, *and* he invented margarine."

"Margarine? Ha! Butter with the flavor and color taken out. He's a charlatan!"

"He's dead."

"So you see, then," said the Colorman, thinking he had made his point by not being dead. "You should buy your pure color from a color man. Then you can have more time to paint."

Seurat smiled then, and tapped his walking stick on the bricks. "You are a color man, I presume?"

"I am *the* Colorman," said the Colorman. "Only the finest earths and minerals, no filler, mixed to order, in whatever medium you like. I like poppy oil. No yellowing. Like margarine. But if you want linseed or walnut oil, I have them." The Colorman rapped his knuckles against the big wooden case strapped on Étienne's back.

"Let me see," said Seurat.

The Colorman wrestled the case off of Étienne's back and opened it on the bricks. "I'm out of blue, but if you want, I'll have some delivered to your studio." The Colorman handed the painter a tube of Naples yellow.

"Very fine," said Seurat, squeezing a worm's-head length out of the tube and turning it to catch the light of the rising sun. "I think this will do. I wasn't looking forward to grinding ores all day, anyway. What is your name?"

"I am the Colorman."

"I understand, but your name? What do I call you?"

"The Colorman," said the Colorman.

"But your surname?"

"Colorman."

"I see. Like Carpenter or Cooper. An old family trade then? And your first name?"

"*The,*" said the Colorman.

"You are a very strange fellow, Monsieur Colorman."

"You like to paint the women as well as the monkeys, right?" asked the Colorman, making a gesture that didn't look at all like he was painting.

"You are a color man, I presume?"
Georges Seurat—Ernest Laurent, 1883

Nineteen

THE DARK CARP OF GIVERNY

MÈRE LESSARD PREPARED A BASKET OF BREAD AND PASTRIES FOR Lucien to take with him to Giverny. "Give my warmest regards to Madame Monet and the children," the matriarch said, tucking croissants into a nest of white tea towels. "And remind Monsieur Monet that he is a wastrel and a ne'er-do-well and to please stop by the bakery when he is in Paris."

Régine stopped him at the bakery door and kissed his cheek. "I don't think you should be going so soon, but I'm glad you're not out looking for that horrible woman."

"You are the only horrible woman allowed in my life, *chérie*," he said, hugging his sister.

It was two hours on the train from Gare du Nord to Vernon, and during the ride Lucien sat near a young mother and her two little daughters, dressed as finely as fancy dolls, who were traveling to Rouen. He sketched them and chatted and laughed with them, and people who passed down the aisle of the train smiled at him and wished him good day, and generally, he thought that during his time locked away in the studio with Juliette he had developed some new form of magical charm, when in fact it was just that he and his basket smelled of freshly baked bread and people like that.

From the station at Vernon, he walked the two miles into the country-side to Giverny—less a village, really, than a collection of small farms that happened to perch together just off the river Seine. Monet's place lay on a sunny rise above a grove of tall willows that had once been a marsh that the painter had converted into a water garden, with two wide lily ponds with an arched Japanese bridge at their intersection.

The house was a sturdy two-story of pink stucco with bright green shutters.

Madame Monet, who was, in fact, not yet Madame Monet, met Lucien at the door. Alice Hoschedé, a tall, elegant, dark-haired woman, her *chignon* now beginning to streak with gray, had been the wife of one of Monet's patrons, a banker. She had now been with the painter for fifteen years, but they were not married. Monet had been living and painting commissions on the Hoschedés' estate in the South when the banker suddenly fell into ruin and abandoned his family. Monet and his wife, Camille, invited Alice and her four children to live with them and their own two sons. Even long after Camille died, and she and Monet had become a couple, Alice, a devout Catholic, insisted they keep up the ruse that their relationship was platonic, and they still kept separate bedrooms.

"These are lovely, Lucien," she said, accepting the basket of baked goods. A teenage daughter, Germaine, whisked them off to the kitchen. "Perhaps we can all share them for lunch," said Alice. "Claude's in the garden, painting."

She led him through the house, the foyer and dining room of which were painted bright yellow. Nearly every wall was covered with framed Japanese prints by Hokusai and Hiroshige, with the odd Cézanne, Renoir, or Pissarro hung here and there among them as accents, or vice versa. Lucien peeked into a large parlor as they passed, the walls of which were lined floor to ceiling with Monet's own work, but Lucien didn't dare stop to lose himself in the master's paintings as Alice was already on the back porch, presenting the garden with a wave, as if ushering an ascended soul into paradise.

"I think he's back by the bridge today, Lucien."

Lucien walked through the back garden, rows upon rows of blooming flowers, built from the ground up on trellises and tripods, so that from eye level to the lawn, there was nothing but color, roses and daisies and dahlias the size of dinner plates, all mixed wildly by color, if not species, so that there was no gradation, no pink next to a red, no lavender next to a violet, but contrast in size and color, blues over yellows, oranges nesting among purples, reds framed in greens. Lucien realized that from any window at the back of the house, one could look out upon nature's palette exploding across the landscape. This was a garden designed by and for a painter, someone who loved color.

He came out of the mounds of color and into a cool grove of willow trees, and there, by the two mirror-calm lily ponds, he found Monet at his easel. Lucien made no attempt to approach in stealth; instead he shuffled his feet on the path and cleared his throat when he was still a good twenty meters away from the painter. Monet glanced quickly out from under the wide brim of his straw gardener's hat, then went right back to applying paint to canvas. A finished painting leaned against the trunk of a nearby willow.

"So, Lucien, what brings you out to the country?" There was welcome and warmth in Monet's voice, but he did not pause a second in his work. Lucien took no offense. Once, while painting his enormous *Luncheon on the Grass,* near the forest of Fontainebleau, with Frédéric Bazille and his beloved Camille as models, Monet had become so engrossed in his work that he'd neglected to notice a team of athletes had come to the field to practice, and so had been quite surprised when an errant discus shattered his ankle. Bazille had painted the scene of Monet convalescing, his leg in traction.

"I'm looking for a girl," said Lucien.

"Paris has finally run out, then? Well, you could do worse than a girl from Normandy."

Lucien watched the master laying down the color, the white and pink of the water lilies, the gray-green of the willows reflected on the surface of the water, the muted umber and slate blue of the sky in the water. Monet worked as if there was no thought process involved at all—his mind was simply the conduit to move color from his eye to the canvas, like the court stenographer who might transcribe a whole trial, every word going from his ear to the paper, yet remain unaware of what had transpired in the courtroom. Monet had trained himself to be a machine for the harvest of color. With brush in hand, he was no longer a man, a father, or a husband, but a device of singular purpose; he was, as he had always introduced himself, *the painter Monet.*

"A particular girl," said Lucien, "and to find her, I need to ask you about blue."

"I hope you're going to stay the week, then," said Monet. "I'll have Alice make up the guest room for you."

"Not blue in general, Oncle. The blue you got from the Colorman."

Monet stopped painting. There was no doubt in Lucien's mind that he knew *which* Colorman.

"You have used his color, then?"

"I have."

Monet turned on his stool now and pushed back the brim of his broad hat so he could look at Lucien. His long black beard was shot with gray, but his blue eyes burned with a fierce intensity that made Lucien feel as if he'd been stripped naked for some sort of examination. He had to look away.

Monet said, "I told you never to buy color from him."

"No you didn't. I didn't remember ever seeing you with him until yesterday."

Monet nodded. "That happens with the Colorman. Tell me."

And so Lucien told Monet about Juliette and painting the blue nude, about Henri and Carmen, about their loss of memory, about the Professeur's hypnotic trance and the phantom rain on their shoulders, about the death of Vincent van Gogh and the letter to Henri, how Vincent had been afraid of the Colorman and had tried to escape him by going to Arles.

"So he's gone now, you think?" asked Monet.

"Along with Juliette, and I have to find her. You know, don't you, Oncle? When you painted Gare Saint-Lazare, six paintings in a half an hour, you knew?"

"Not a half an hour, Lucien, four hours. For me it was four hours, maybe more. You know what time is like when you are painting."

"I looked at the station clock."

"The Colorman's blue can stop time," said the painter, as if he were declaring something as obvious and accepted as the sky being blue.

Lucien sat down in the grass abruptly, feeling as if his knees would not support him; the nerves in his legs had been suddenly severed. "That's not possible."

"I know. Nevertheless, it's true. You've used it, so you know. It's in the feel of the paint, the behavior of the surface. Critics never see that, never account for that. They always think we are trying to say something with the paint; they don't know the paint itself speaks to us, by touch, by reflection. You have felt it, no?"

"Oncle Claude, I don't understand. We thought there was some kind of drug in the color, that we were hallucinating."

"I understand. And at the time, I thought I had gone mad, but I pushed through. An artist can't let madness stop him from making art, he simply has to channel it. That's what I thought I was doing."

"For how long? How long did you think you were mad?"

"Until about two minutes ago," said the older painter.

"You never said anything."

"What was I to say? *'Oh, Lucien, by the way, I realize the clock has only moved a half an hour, but I managed to paint six paintings of Gare Saint-Lazare, and the smoke was kind enough to hold still while I painted.'"*

"I suppose I would have thought you mad," said Lucien.

"That was the only time I bought paint directly from the Colorman. That day at Gare Saint-Lazare. And he knew what I was trying to do. I remember him saying that if I washed my canvas with his blue, it would make what I was doing easier."

"You said that was the only time you got color *'directly'* from him. You had used his color before?"

"Before and after then. My wife, Camille. It was Camille who brought it to me, and it was she who paid for it. I fear in more than just money."

Lucien shuddered. He hadn't bought paint from the Colorman either. It had always come through Juliette. He might never have connected the two of them if Henri hadn't pointed it out. He said, "So your Camille knew the Colorman?"

Monet slouched on his stool and looked at the ground in front of him. "From when I met her, the early days, running out on hotel bills, dragging that twenty-foot canvas all over France with me, Camille was like some wild wood nymph, but always interested in the painting, pushing me to go farther, do more, even after she became pregnant and it would have been so much easier for us if I had taken other work. But I remember how she brought me a box full of color early on, right after I first met her, and from then on, she would coyly present me with tubes of paint, like little love gifts. 'Make me a beautiful picture, Claude,' she would say. Sometimes we would go on adventures and I would paint for what seemed like months, in the forest at Fontainebleau, or the beaches at Honfleur and Trouville, and I would wonder why the innkeeper at the Cheval Blanc was putting up with us for so long, only to find out that we had been on his books for only a day or two. It went on for years like that. Camille would go for months playing the role of the dutiful wife, the good mother—she would fret about money and the future—then suddenly she would be the carefree girl again, and we would be like new lovers, at each other every moment I wasn't painting and she wasn't taking care of the children. I would lose weeks in the color and in her flesh, happy, ecstatic to do so. I would get to where I was about to drop with exhaustion, and suddenly she would be the responsible wife again, taking care of the family while I either recovered, as if from a fever, or simply slept for days."

"And you think it was the Colorman's blue that made her this way?"

"I didn't at first; who would have thought such a thing? But after the Gare Saint-Lazare paintings, I came to believe it. But even then, if someone had told me I was somehow cheating time, I don't know that I would have changed anything. I was painting. Always painting. Painting well. Why would I change that? How could I? But eventually, I think the painting killed Camille."

Monet's voice broke at the end, almost as if he was suppressing a sob. Lucien didn't know what to do. Should he embrace his mentor? Offer sympathy? Pat his arm and tell him all would be well? As it had been with his own father, Lucien felt wrong consoling his painter "uncles." They were pillars of strength, resolve, and genius—how could he presume to offer them anything but admiration? But then he thought of his friends who were painters, Vincent, Henri, Bernard, even Seurat, walled into his intellectual fortress of color theory and optics—all were plagued by fits of hubris followed by soul-crushing self-doubt. Were Monet, Pissarro, and Renoir any different? Really?

Lucien said, "Everyone knows it's not easy to be the wife of an artist, but you—"

Monet held up his paintbrush to interrupt Lucien. "Your girl, this Juliette? Is she ill?"

"What?" Lucien was casting his gaze around the lily pond, looking for some order to manifest itself. What had he expected to hear? "Juliette? No, she wasn't sick."

"Good," said Monet. "Perhaps she left you before it happened. With Camille it was years and years. But I tried to save her. I did hope."

At that, Monet set his palette on the ground, dropped his brush into a can of turpentine that hung from a chain on his easel, and stood.

"Come with me." Monet led Lucien back through the garden to a large, plain block building adjacent to the house. The painter unlocked the door with a key on his watch chain and let them into a studio with high ceilings and skylights draped with white linen to diffuse the light, not unlike the lighting in Lucien's own storeroom studio.

There were wooden racks against one wall to keep canvases separated while they dried, but dozens upon dozens of paintings, most of Monet's garden and the countryside around Giverny, were hung edge to edge all the way to the ceiling on the end wall. Finished canvases were leaned at the foot of the wall in rows, ten-deep, with the painted side facing in so dust couldn't settle on the surface before it had cured enough for varnishing.

"I suppose I should ship most of these off to Durand-Ruel," said Monet. "It's not good to keep so many in one place. Pissarro lost sixteen hundred paintings when the Prussians took his house during the war. They used his paintings as aprons in the slaughterhouse they set up. Lined the floors with them against the blood."

Lucien shuddered at the thought. "I heard Monsieur Renoir's brother-in-law used some of his paintings to waterproof the roofs of his rabbit hutches. Madame Renoir boxed her brother's ears and you could hear the commotion all over the butte."

"Ah, Aline," said Monet. "Renoir was lucky to find that one when he did."

Monet flipped through the stacked canvases and finally stopped and pulled out a portrait of a woman. He stood it against the others, then stepped back. She was sleeping, her face surrounded by a storm of color, slashes of blue and white, laid down even more furiously than Monet's usual style. "See," the painter said. "I tried to save her. I tried to bring her back."

Lucien didn't understand. The face in the portrait wasn't clearly rendered, just the hint of features among the color. "Madame Monet?" he asked.

"Camille on her deathbed," said Monet. "The last time I used that blue. Alice's daughter Blanche was in the room. She had been caring for Camille. I thought she would think I was some kind of ghoul. My wife slips away and I am painting her corpse. I told her I had to capture the shade of blue Camille was turning, before it went away. She never questioned it. She just left me to paint. But I was trying to bring her back, trying to stop time the way that I had stopped it at Gare Saint-Lazare that day, the way it had stopped all those times when Camille and I were traveling, when she was modeling for me. Anything, just to have another moment with her, to keep her with me."

The painting changed for Lucien now. He could see in the brushstrokes what Monet had always stated as his purpose: *to capture the moment.* He was trying to keep her alive.

"Make me a beautiful picture, Claude. Make me a beautiful picture."
Madame Monet on Her Deathbed—Claude Monet, 1879

He could think of nothing to say about the painting. To comment on it as art would have seemed cold; to comment on the subject, well, nothing was really enough in the face of such grief. "I'm sorry," Lucien said finally, and let that hang in the air for a moment before pressing on.

He remembered Madame Monet from when the Monets had lived on Montmartre, and although he hadn't known her well, she had always been kind to him. "How did you know? She had been sick for a long time, hadn't she? How did you think to try to use the blue again?"

"She told me," said Monet. "She was fighting for breath, gasping, and she had been for a time. Not even life enough to cough. But then she took my hand, and the light came back into her eyes; just for a moment, she was that wild girl who had been coming to me all those years, and she said, 'Make me a beautiful picture, Claude. Make me a beautiful picture.' That is how I knew. All those years, she hadn't been saying make a beautiful picture *for* her, she was asking me to make her *into* a picture. It sounds mad, even now, saying it out loud."

"No," was all Lucien said, and he let the silence settle on the room.

Monet tucked the picture of Camille back into the stack, then shuffled about, arranging brushes in jars, gathering rags, and rolling up paint tubes, while Lucien pretended to be looking at the paintings on the wall so he didn't see the tears in his mentor's eyes.

Lucien had a thousand questions, but he didn't want his fear for Juliette to drive him to be unkind. When he heard Monet strike a match to light his pipe, he let fly.

"What of the others? Renoir? Cézanne? Did they do business with the Colorman?"

Monet puffed on his pipe as if considering an academic question, not something so close to his heart as his Camille. "You remember Renoir's Margot, don't you?"

"Of course. She lived on Montmartre."

"She died a few months after Camille. Her death nearly destroyed Auguste, he was so heartbroken. I came to her funeral, and that night we drank, Renoir and I, and some of the others, and he talked about painting her, about not being able to find paintings that he knew he had made of her. It was so close after the time Camille died that I thought then his false memories might be caused by that same blue—that Renoir had somehow discovered by accident what I had. But I didn't have the courage to ask him, and soon he went away, traveling all of the Mediterranean, I think to escape it. We have never spoken of it since."

"And the others?"

Monet rolled his eyes and drew a spiral in the air with the stem of his pipe, as if he were directing the orchestra of his memory. Finally he said, "Could be everyone, could be none of them, Lucien. You know painters. If the Louvre should offer to buy this *Blue Nude* of yours, declare it a national treasure, would you look for some way to give credit to this magical paint?"

"No, I suppose not, but Pissarro—"

"Lucien, look." With his pipe, Monet directed Lucien's gaze to the wall of paintings, touching each in the air as if it were a musical note on a staff. "In my lily ponds, there is a big gray carp. I think he must have come in from the Seine when we first built them. He is the same color as the mud at the bottom of the pond, the same color as the shadow of the willows. Sometimes all you can see of him is a light gray line that is the edge of his dorsal fin. Every time I paint the garden, I paint the light on the surface of the pond, the reflections, the lilies floating above, the sky and sun reflected on the water, and even as I paint, he is there. I have to look to see him, and sometimes I don't know he's there until he moves, but he is there. There's no image of him in any of these paintings, but he is in every one of them, under the surface. I know he was there. I can feel him there in these paintings, even if you cannot see him. Do you understand?"

"I think so," said Lucien. He didn't understand at all.

"The Colorman is like that carp, Lucien. In all of our paintings, Pissarro's, Renoir's, Sisley's, Morisot's—even poor Bazille, before he was shot in the war—even back then, from the first days when we all met in Paris, he is there, in all our art, just below the surface."

BELOW THE SURFACE OF BOULEVARD SAINT-GERMAIN, THE COLORMAN LIMPED across the limestone floors of a chamber that had been cut into the Left Bank nearly two thousand years before. He held a storm lamp above his head, looking for the carved stone that marked the position and level of the room, but the space was so vast that the light evaporated into relentless murk.

"We need to follow the wall," he said to Étienne, who didn't particularly like going down steps or through narrow passageways, who thought that the dark was a signal to sleep, not something you should travel around in, and generally that this whole underground expedition was complete bullshit. Étienne was along because the Colorman didn't like being alone in the dark, and he couldn't allow Bleu to know about this place.

The entire Latin Quarter was undermined like this, in the most literal sense of the term. These remnants of quarries for limestone, clay, and sand went down ten levels. The upper levels were the oldest, dating back to the time of the Gauls, even before the Romans, but as each generation dug into the banks of the Seine for stone to expand the city, the miners would have to dig deeper, using the floor of the earlier quarry as the ceiling for the newer one, until 1774, when a huge sinkhole opened in rue d'Enfer, swallowing up a whole block of buildings, and a man named Charles-Axel Guillaumot was commissioned by Louis XVI's royal architects to survey, excavate, and repair the quarries before the entire Latin Quarter sank into the earth. Over twenty years, even through the revolution, when few bureaucrats survived the guillotine, Guillaumot rebuilt the underground, shoring up each level, marking each chamber and passageway to correspond with the street above, until he had reconstructed a stable, safe underground city that plunged twice the depth that any structure at the time stretched to the sky. When the city's cemeteries began literally to burst at the walls from the weight of centuries of the dead, the bones of millions were moved to the chambers under Montparnasse to make way for the *nouveau* dead, and the ossuary was christened the "Catacombs" after the ancient crypts of Rome.

The Colorman had entered through the Catacombs' entrance at boulevard Saint-Jacques. In a quarter-hour he and Étienne had stumbled past the stacked femurs and fibulas of history and were making their way into the deepest part of the underground city where no one ever went.

They came to the carved stone that marked their location and the Colorman set his lamp on the floor, pulled a parchment map from his pocket, and spread it out on the floor.

"Not far now," he said to Étienne, who was looking at a strand of cobwebs that was streaming from the brim of his new hat, which he felt was just another indicator of what complete bullshit this mission was.

They were so deep now that even the scurry of rats had ceased as there was nothing to draw them down here. The Colorman skirted a wall for the equivalent of a city block, leading Étienne by a rope, until he came to a bronze ring set in the stone about the level of his knees.

"Shhhhh," shushed the Colorman. He cocked his head and listened. Étienne turned his ears away from the wall and scanned the great room: the sound of their breathing, and a very distant sound of dripping water.

"Did you hear footsteps?" asked the Colorman.

Étienne didn't answer, as was his policy. However he thought he might have heard the scrape of a shoe; maybe not.

The Colorman grasped the bronze ring, and as his body described the shape of the letter C, he pulled on the ring. There was a scraping sound and a panel in the wall swung away. It was, in fact, a thick oak door, only faced with limestone tiles to match the wall.

"*Voilà!*" he said, holding the lantern high. The chamber inside was no bigger than the parlor in their apartment, and the lantern illuminated it entirely. Except for a bronze charcoal brazier that shone brightly, and scores of canvases leaning against the far wall, the room was empty. The Colorman shuffled to the canvases and picked one that was nearly as tall as he was, a Manet, a nude of a fair-skinned, dark-haired woman, painted under window light. She was sitting at her vanity in front of an ornate gold mirror, looking back over her shoulder at the painter as if she had expected someone to walk in on her and was pleased about it. More importantly to the Colorman's purposes, the delicate chair on which she sat was draped with luxurious ultramarine velvet. It was a rare composition and would have been a national treasure as well as a scandal if anyone had known it existed, even now, eight years after the painter's death. The Colorman, Manet, and the model had been the only ones to ever see the painting.

It was a treasure for the Colorman, too, and he did not like having to use it, but they needed the blue. He carried the painting out into the greater room and leaned it against the wall while he pushed the stone-clad door closed.

"I should hang the lamp from your neck," the Colorman said to Étienne. "I need both hands to carry this."

He wrestled with the lamp, tried to tie it around Étienne's neck, only to find that the smell of burning donkey hair was not something his equine companion was willing to endure.

"We're going to have to use Goya's trick," said the Colorman. He had packed a half dozen thick candles into his satchel, which he attached to the brim of Étienne's hat, then lit, so that the donkey was the one who led their way out of the underworld, looking like a long-eared birthday cake, while the Colorman stumbled along behind, trying to steer the canvas through the passageways.

"Did you hear something?" asked the Colorman when they were almost back to the entrance of the Catacombs.

Étienne did not answer, because he hadn't been listening, and he wouldn't have said anything if he had, because now his new hat was ruined by melted wax, which proved, he thought, that this trip was complete bullshit.

The Colorman threaded the canvas through a narrow door and into a chamber that was lined floor to ceiling with human skulls. "We'll take the painting to the flat, Étienne, then we'll go to market and buy you some carrots. I need to buy a new pistol, too. Bleu is not properly cleaning up after herself."

Twenty

BREAKFAST AT THE BLACK CAT

UPON HIS RETURN FROM THE SHOW IN BRUSSELS, HENRI DRAGGED LUCIEN out of the bakery and across the butte to Le Chat Noir cabaret for breakfast.

"But I own a bakery," Lucien said, still squirming out of his apron as they crossed the square. "The Chat Noir isn't even open for breakfast."

"Today, they are," said Henri. "Rodolphe Salis has commissioned me to decorate the walls of his cabaret. I must inspect the canvas."

"You've been in Le Chat Noir a thousand times."

"Yes, but today I shall be sober! And I need your opinion."

"You're a lunatic."

"On what I should paint."

"Right. Sorry. Lead on, then."

Rodolphe Salis, a dark-bearded, formally dressed man of forty, unlocked the cabaret for them and led them to a booth where they could see the walls Henri was to paint. Salis had moved the Chat Noir from its location up the street so he might appeal to a higher class of clientele, and the *décor* in the cabaret, carved Louis XIV tables and chairs—red velvet, gold leaf, and crystal adorning anything that wasn't moving—reflected his intent. Behind the marble-topped bar was an enormous mural by Adolphe Willette, a cartoon, really, depicting a modern-day bacchanalia, with bankers in tailcoats gunning each other down over half-naked, fairy-winged showgirls at the margins, while the bulk of the revelers danced, drank, and groped in a maelstrom of oblivious debauchery in the center. It was a satirical indictment of Le Chat Noir's clientele, Paris patricians slumming on Montmartre with their working-poor mistresses, the artist, Willette, simultaneously celebrating the *joie de vivre* and biting the hands that fed him.

"I know," said Salis, waving to the painting. "It's quite a painting to have your work in company with. Thank the stars no one actually looks at the art."

"I'm flattered for the opportunity," said Henri. "Perhaps a glass of wine for Lucien and me while we discuss the motif." He patted a leather briefcase he carried with him.

"I'll send it over," said Salis, heading off to his office.

"You said breakfast," Lucien whispered furiously.

"Yes?" said Henri, looking perplexed. He lit a cheroot and pulled a stack of mail from his briefcase. "All this in just two weeks. Oh look, a letter from Grandmama in Albi."

"I'm worried to death about Juliette," said Lucien. "I can barely sleep."

Their wine arrived with a thin, redheaded girl who looked too young to be working in a cabaret, perhaps thirteen. She curtsied as she backed away from the table.

"Don't look at her," said Henri. "She's Salis's daughter. I don't know why she's not away at a boarding school. Salis certainly has the money. But she's a redhead, so she's probably evil, even at her tender age."

"I thought you liked redheads."

"I do. What's your point?"

"Nothing."

Henri slurped his wine and returned to his mail. "How sweet, Grand-mère wishes me luck with the show in Brussels. Listen. *'I would like to hope that my grandson's brush, when he shows his work in public, will always be in good taste.'*"

"She doesn't know how you live in Paris, does she?"

Henri dismissed the question with a wave of his cigar and regarded the empty plaster panels over their booth. "I want to paint a picture of a clown fucking a cat."

"I'm not sure that will work, even on the walls of Le Chat Noir," said Lucien.

"All right, a ballerina. One of the *petits rats* from the opera that Degas paints so often."

"With a clown?"

"No, fucking a cat. It's a theme, Lucien. The name of the place is Le Chat Noir."

"Yes, but when you did the poster for the Moulin Rouge you didn't do a clown fucking a windmill."

"Sadly, no, they rejected my first drawings. And I'm good friends with one of the clowns there, Cha-U-Kao. She would have modeled for me. She's both a clown *and* a lesbian. At the same time! Art weeps for the missed opportunity."

"You could still paint her," said Lucien.

"No. She hates cats. But what magnificent symbolism that would be. I tell you, Lucien, these symbolists, Redon and Gauguin, they're on to something."

"You said Gauguin was a self-important tosser," said Lucien.

"I did?"

"Many times."

"Well I meant *theorist*. He's angry at me because I won't join any of his movements. *Cloisonnism?* What is that? Fencing your colors up in line. That's just Japanese printmaking with a new name."

Lucien poured Henri another glass of wine from the carafe, because if he couldn't somehow force his friend to slow down and listen, he was afraid he was going to have to choke him.

"I suppose we'll have to drug the cat, or have the ballerina hide a trout in her tutu."

"I went to Giverny," Lucien said. "Monet says the blue color can stop time. Literally stop time for the painter."

"Oh," said Henri. "So what you remembered, when the Professeur hypnotized you, with the trains, that happened?"

"Yes," Lucien said. "Monet really painted six paintings in a half an hour. To him it was hours. The Colorman told him what would happen that day. But before then, and after, the color always came by way of his wife, Camille."

"But she died, didn't she?" said Henri.

"Monet says they all die, Henri. There's always a woman and she always dies."

Henri twirled his cigar in the crystal ashtray, paring off the snowy powder of ash and punishing the ember, daring it to go out. He looked over his *pince-nez* at Lucien, studying the baker as if he were a painting, analyzing the brushstrokes that formed his eyelashes. Lucien feigned a cough and looked at the table, unable to hold his friend's gaze.

"Not always," Henri said, his voice soft, the voice of a friend, not the outrageous painter Toulouse-Lautrec. "They don't always die. Carmen went away. She's fine. Juliette went away, before, and she came back. Maybe she'll come back again."

"But you said yourself that Carmen nearly died. What if Juliette is sick somewhere? What if the Colorman has locked her up? Who knows what he does to them?"

"Carmen knows," said Henri. "We could ask her what the Colorman does, where he goes."

"But she doesn't remember anything."

"And neither did you, until the Professeur did his parlor trick with the blue watch."

"We don't have any more blue."

"Yes we do, Lucien. We have your *Blue Nude*. Remember how Renoir reacted when he saw it? It was as if he were transported back to his Margot. We'll ask Carmen to remember while she's looking at your painting."

"I will try anything, Henri, but won't seeing Carmen be painful for you?"

"If she remembers me as I remember her, no. If not, well, I'll be heartbroken, but she's a redhead, it's to be expected. Tomorrow morning you can get your painting from Bruant and bring it to my studio. That gives me time to do some sketches for Salis and run by the brothel at rue d'Amboise for some light evening debauchery. In the morning, I'll go to the Marais and bring Carmen back to question her before the *Blue Nude*. Perhaps Le Professeur will help."

"He's gone away, exploring some newly discovered cave in Spain."

"Do you know if he fixed my mechanical stilts?"

"I know he had been working on them. He said he would leave them at your studio. They weren't there?"

"I don't know. I haven't been there. I wanted to have breakfast before I started work."

"She's both a clown and a lesbian. At the same time! Art weeps for the missed opportunity." *La Clownesse Cha-U-Kao au Moulin Rouge*—Henri Toulouse-Lautrec, 1895

THE COLORMAN UNLOCKED THE DOOR AND WALKED THE MANET SIDEWAYS into the flat. It was dark, not a single gaslight was lit, yet he could see Juliette by the moonlight streaming through the windows. She stood at the stove, stirring something in a pot. It smelled like stew, lamb maybe.

"*Chérie,* why are you standing in the dark like a ninny? Come look at what I have. I'll bet you don't remember this one." He leaned the painting against the wall, then took a box of matches from the mantel, climbed on a chair under one of the gas sconces, turned the valve, and lit a match. Even on the chair, he could not reach the lamp. Somewhere there was a brass extension rod that a match could be clipped on for lighting the overhead lamp, but he wasn't going to find it in the dark.

"Come help me."

She dropped her spoon and moved across the room in awkward, mechanical steps. She took the match from him and held it to the mantel, which sizzled into a white-hot glow.

She stepped back and stood there, still holding the lit match. The Colorman blew it out before it burned her fingers. She wore the periwinkle dress. A note was pinned on ruffles at her bosom. It read DO NOT BONK THE JULIETTE in bold yet elegant script.

The Colorman sighed and climbed off his chair. So Bleu had moved on to another body.

The Colorman said, "The concierge wouldn't let Étienne come upstairs, the bitch. But I left some carrots with him in the stable. And I got a new pistol." He pulled the small revolver from his waistband and waved it in the air like a tiny broken buckaroo.

Juliette said nothing, but turned to watch him as he tucked the pistol away and went to the stove to taste the stew.

"You remember this Manet?" He moved the painting into the light. "Berthe is nearly as pretty as you, eh? Darker eyes, though."

Juliette blinked, that was all. He knew she wasn't going to answer. This kind never talked, which, truth be told, he liked better than when Bleu was in residence. Although this was a rare occurrence, happening only when she created a model from scratch. Most of the time she just moved from one body to another, even back and forth, often leaving the person whose body she had used confused and unable to remember where she had been while Bleu was in control. Sometimes, however, as she had with Juliette, Bleu simply found the meat, a corpse (this one had been a drowned woman in the morgue on Île de la Cité) and she would shape it into a whole new living, breathing creature. Juliette had never existed before Bleu made her, so when Bleu moved on, the Juliette shell became little more than a doll. She could move and would take instructions, do simple tasks, and she would eat, drink, and go to the lavatory without being prompted, but she had no will of her own.

"I didn't need the note," said the Colorman. He went back to the stove and ladled out two shallow bowls of the stew. He placed the bowls on the table and went back to the kitchen for spoons and a baguette. "Come, sit. Eat," he said.

Juliette went to the table, sat down, and began to eat.

"Slowly," the Colorman said. "It's hot. Blow on it." He showed her how to blow on a spoonful of stew before eating it and she followed him in the gesture, blowing on it exactly four times, as he had, before putting each spoonful in her mouth. A drop of brown gravy ran down her chin and dripped onto the tablecloth.

The Colorman climbed down from his chair, snapped up her napkin from the table, and tucked it into the high collar of her dress, taking the care to smooth the bib over her breasts several times to make sure it was secure.

"There, you won't ruin your dress. See, I didn't need the note."

She stared blankly at a spot in the middle of the table but smiled faintly after she swallowed each bite. She really was lovely. And so pleasant to be around without Bleu inside being sarcastic and barking rules.

He knew he needed to respect Bleu's wishes, however. There had been a few times when he had not, and she'd found out, and he'd woken up on fire, which was unpleasant. But they did need a maid, didn't they?

"Maybe after supper, you can do a little cleaning," he said. He tore off a piece of bread and tossed it in her bowl. She picked it up and nibbled it like a squirrel worrying an acorn.

The note only said not to *bonk* the Juliette. It didn't say she couldn't clean the flat. And it didn't say that she had to be wearing any clothes while she cleaned, did it? No, it did not.

"You can clean and I'll see if I can frighten you," said the Colorman. "If Bleu isn't back by morning, you can come with me to Montmartre to shoot the baker and the dwarf. It will be fun."

He'd forgotten how much he liked it when Bleu left one of her empty shells wandering around the house. Except for the being set on fire, of course.

As it turned out, finding another painter hadn't been that difficult. She'd found the perfect one, one she'd known before, known his desires, but for him to be of any value, she needed the blue, and to get that, she needed to get to Montmartre, and as it turned out, getting a taxi at midnight in the Latin Quarter was very difficult indeed, especially if you were a fourteen-year-old Polynesian girl, which is how Bleu currently appeared.

The taxi driver was snoring in his seat, the horse was dozing in his harness.

"Excuse me, monsieur," she said, tugging gently at the cuff of the cabbie's trousers. "Excuse me."

The taxi driver's head lolled in a full circle before he identified where the voice was coming from, despite the tug on his cuff. Sleeping *and* drunk.

"Can you take me to Montmartre, please, monsieur?" she said. "Boulevard de Clichy. I'll need you to wait while I pick up something, then return here."

"No, that's too far. It's late. Go home, girl."

"I can pay."

"Fine, twenty *francs*."

"That's robbery!" She stepped back to get a better look at the cab-driving pirate.

"Or we could work something out, my little chestnut," said the cabbie with a lecherous sneer that, if not practiced, showed great natural ability.

"I'm worth twenty *francs*, then? How about we have a tumble in the back of your cab, you give me the twenty *francs*, then I'll hire a sane taxi driver to take me to Montmartre for two *francs* and I'll send the rest to my mother in Tahiti, who has leprosy?" Bleu lifted her very plain gray skirt and gave the cabdriver a look at her ankles, resplendent in brown wool stockings. "How about it?"

"Twenty *francs*? I could have ten girls in Pigalle for twenty *francs*!"

"I thought it seemed generous of you, but I am just an ignorant island girl who probably doesn't have leprosy, what do I know?"

"Fuck off, girl. It's late."

"Exotic island beauty," she said, teasing, showing a little more ankle, and in the process releasing the full seductive power of a brown woolen sock. "Woo-woo," she said, thinking that might be something an exotic island beauty might say. "*Oh là là*," she said.

"I'm tired. I'm going home for the night," said the cabbie.

"Look, you were the one who said we could work something out. That was your idea," said Bleu.

"I was still sleepy and hadn't gotten a good look at you. And that was before I knew about your mother's leprosy. Twenty *francs*."

"Fine," she said, climbing into the cab. "But I'm not paying you until you bring me back here. Take me to the cabaret Le Mirliton on avenue de Clichy."

To be a woman at all, in these times, was to be treated like an object, of either scorn or desire, or both, but it was certainly easier making your way around Paris as a beautiful brunette dressed as a proper lady than it was as an island waif barely scratching womanhood. In retrospect, she might have been hasty in changing so soon, but she needed to divert the Colorman's attention from Lucien, and the best way to do that was to convince him that she had found a new painter, one for whom this little Tahitian girl was the model of perfection.

The streets were nearly deserted so it took only a half an hour to get across the city to the base of Montmartre. A half an hour of the horses' hooves on the cobbles, the smell of coal smoke, horse shit, yeast from loaves proofing in the bakeries, garlic, soured wine, and meat grease from last evening's cooking, plus the pervasive odor of dead fish and something deeply green rising in the fog off the Seine. In the back of the hack she bounced like an echo in a rolling pumpkin as the cabbie seemed determined to hit every rut and pothole in the city, and she was giggling at the absurdity of it by the end, which saved the driver's life.

"Here you go," the cabbie called as he pulled up in front of the darkened cabaret. "Twenty *francs*."

"Wait in that alley." She tossed her head toward the next corner; a wave traveled down her long, blue-black hair with the gesture. "I'll pay you when I'm finished."

"You'll pay me now, if you want me to wait."

Bleu reconsidered trying to lure him into the cab for a tumble, then snapping his gritty neck. Certainly the island girl didn't have the seductive charms of Juliette, but men were pigs and could be depended upon to give in to their most base instincts, which is why she felt the need to slaughter one now and then. Perhaps she shouldn't have played the leprosy note quite so hard. She really didn't want to leave a corpse in a waiting cab and then have to drive herself across the city, which would undoubtedly attract attention.

Yes, life was hard for a woman in Paris, harder still if you were several women. She sighed, a heavy, existential sigh that would become all the rage in Paris in fifty years.

"Half now," she said, handing up a ten-*franc* note. "Half when you take me back to boulevard Saint-Germain. Now wait for me around the corner."

The driver scoffed at her and left the cab sitting where it was.

"Fine," she said. The dolt didn't know enough to be afraid. She'd show him.

She strode up to Le Mirliton's double oak doors and kicked them at the center of the jamb. The plan, the picture she saw in her mind, what should have happened, was that the doors should have splintered around the locks and sprung open, for despite the diminutive size of her current body, she was very, very strong. What actually happened was the doors, held closed by a padlock and chain threaded through the door handles inside, flexed a bit, gave just enough to absorb the impact of her kick, and she landed on her ass on the sidewalk, while the doors remained quite intact.

The taxi driver laughed. She leapt to her feet and growled at him.

"Maybe you should just knock," the driver said. "I'll wait for you around the next corner." He snapped the reins and the horse clopped a half a block and turned down a narrow street.

A stained glass and oak transom over the two doors had been left open a crack. She eyed it, then shimmied up the front of the right door, using the hinges for footholds; popped the transom open; and slid into the cabaret headfirst, turning a somersault in the air and making a cat-like landing on her feet, but with her skirt upturned over her head.

"*Oh là là!*" A man's voice, somewhere in the dark.

She fought the tangle of her skirt down, even as she realized that her island girl was wearing no knickers and had just treated the room to a full display of her exotic bare bottom and bits. The child really had been an innocent.

"Oh for fuck's sake," she said to the bartender, who had apparently been sleeping on the floor behind the bar and had popped up like a surprised puppet when he'd heard her kick the door, just in time to see her stick her landing *sans culottes*.

He was young, and even in the dark she could see he was lean and handsome, with a shock of blond hair that fell over one eye and a red waistcoat that made him appear a bit like a sleepy yet dashing outlaw.

"*Bonsoir*," she said, so as not to be impolite. She was across the bar in an instant. She stretched up and kissed the surprised bartender chastely on the lips, just a peck, then snatched a bottle out of the well and hit him over the head with it three times fast. Miraculously, the bottle did not break. The bartender, however, was quite unconscious and bleeding from his scalp in two places. Enchantment and seduction were fine means of persuasion, but when time is short, an awkward but quick concussion could better serve a girl's purpose.

"Sorry," she said. "Accident. Couldn't be helped." No wonder the Colorman always said that; she felt much better about having bludgeoned the bartender, who had really done nothing more than *oh là là* her naughty bits. She bent and kissed him on the cheek, then leapt up onto the bar to inspect the *Blue Nude*.

She could just reach it, and she gently touched the paint at the edge. Still tacky, even after weeks. Damn Lucien, using stand oil cut with clove oil for a medium—it might take months to dry completely. She wouldn't be able to razor it off the stretchers and roll it up; she'd have to take the whole bloody life-sized thing.

Standing on a chair on the bar, she was able to unhook the painting and get it down without marring the paint. She found the key to the padlock and chain in the barman's pocket and was standing on the sidewalk with the painting less than five minutes after she'd exited the cab.

The *Blue Nude* was nearly as wide as she was tall, and the only way she could carry it was to hook the very tips of her fingers onto the inside of the top stretcher frame and hold her hands over her head while she stepped sideways down the sidewalk. She performed that awkward waltz for a half a block, until she got to the corner where the cab had turned, only to find a street that was empty of all traffic in general, and a waiting taxi in particular. The greasy cabdriver had abandoned her to the deserted, wee hours of the morning, with no way to get the painting home.

"Oh balls," she said. Now she'd have to find some other way of getting the Colorman's mind off of Lucien.

Twenty-one

A SUDDEN ILLNESS

LUCIEN WAS BREATHLESS.

The whore said, "Oh, Monsieur Lessard, I have seen your painting at Le Mirliton. It is so beautiful."

Lucien bent over and braced his hands on his knees while he tried to catch his breath. The three whores in the brothel parlor were all waiting for him to say something. He'd just run all the way from Bruant's cabaret, where he'd found the front door open, the bartender unconscious on the floor, and the *Blue Nude* gone.

"Toulouse-Lautrec?" he gasped.

"Fourth room at the top of the stairs," said a tall, blond whore in a pink negligee. "Your bread is very good too, but I think you should have a go at painting."

Lucien nodded his thanks for the advice and tipped his hat to the ladies before bounding up the swooping staircase.

The fourth door was locked, so he pounded. "Henri! It's Lucien. The *Blue Nude*. It's gone!"

A rhythmic yipping noise with bedspring-squeak counterpoint emanated from behind the door.

"One moment, Lucien," called Henri. "I'm boinking Babette and if she comes I get a discount."

The yipping and squeaking paused. "He does not."

"Ah, she is such a tease. My allowance has not arrived this month, so I am—"

"He's a little short!" the whore giggled.

"Oh, I will have my revenge now."

"Would you two hold still!"

"Feel my wrath, tart!"

More squeaking, more giggling. It sounded like there was more than one woman in there.

Lucien felt as if he might faint, more from anxiety than the lack of breath; his pulse pounded in his temples. He fell forward, allowing his forehead to rest against the door. "Henri, please! Someone has stolen my painting. We need—"

The door was yanked open and Lucien fell headlong into the room.

"*Bonjour,* Monsieur Lessard," said Mireille, the short, plump whore from Lucien's last visit. She stood over him, naked but for an oversized black beret. Several colors of oil paint streaked her body here and there and she was brandishing a wide bristle brush loaded with Naples yellow, much of which had found its way to her nipples.

"Get off me, you horny puppet," said a different woman's voice from the bed.

Before Lucien could look up there was a thump and Count Henri-Marie-Raymond de Toulouse-Lautrec-Monfa was lying on the floor before him, quite naked, except, of course, for his hat and *pince-nez*. (He was a count, for fuck's sake, not some crazed cannibal pygmy!)

"Lucien, you look distressed."

"I *am* distressed. Someone has taken the *Blue Nude* from Le Mirliton."

"And you're sure it wasn't Bruant? Perhaps he took it to a private showing. There's been quite a buzz, you know. I heard Degas himself was interested in coming to look at it."

Lucien moaned.

"I know how you feel," said Mireille. "My painting is ruined."

Lucien turned his head just enough to see that she was standing next to an easel, on which was propped a number thirty canvas painted with crude figures that looked to Lucien like dogs fighting. He moaned again.

"Oh my." A woman's face—a cute brunette with improbably large brown eyes—popped over the edge of the bed and looked down at Lucien. "He sounds forlorn, Henri. Shall I get him a drink or suck him off or something?"

"Lucien, have you met Babette?" Henri said.

"*Enchanté,* mademoiselle," Lucien said, returning his forehead and his gaze to the carpet. "Thank you, but I think I will stop breathing soon. Very kind of you to offer, though."

"Please, Lucien," said Henri. "My treat. While I am currently cash-poor"—he glared up at the grinning Babette, daring her to reprise her "short" joke—"my account here is in very good standing."

"Not anymore," said Babette. "Not after you had us up all night trying to charge up your fancy mechanical shoes."

Lucien surfaced from his sea of woes for a moment to raise an eyebrow at the prostrate prostitute above him. "What?"

She tossed her head toward the corner of the room, where Professeur Bastard's steam stilts stood gleaming like the lower half of a lonely mechanical man. "He says that they are powered by suction, yet all night we sucked and sucked while he stood on them and they never worked."

"We took turns," said Mireille. "To charge them up."

Lucien looked to Henri. "They're steam powered, not vacuum."

"Le Professeur's note said these were the improved version."

Lucien shook his head, buffing his forehead on the rug in the process. "He mentioned something about building a clockwork set, not vacuum powered."

"Well, we tried that, but having one's manhood wound like a clock key is less pleasant than it initially sounds."

"Monsieur Henri," said Babette. "You deceived us!"

"That is not true, my little *bonbon*," said Henri. "I am an artist, not an engineer, such things are a mystery to me, and in my defense, absinthe and cocaine were involved."

"And laudanum," giggled Mireille, poking Lucien in the ribs with her toe, as if making him party to some inside joke.

Babette vaulted off the bed, landed with a bit of a bounce, snatched a silk robe from the bedpost, and wrapped it around herself. "Monsieur Henri, I am a professional. I cannot abide such unethical behavior."

"*Chérie*, it was a favor for a friend."

"You will be receiving my bill," she said, stomping out of the room, nose in the air, letting loose a hint of a giggle when she said, "Good day, monsieur!"

Mireille watched her colleague's melodramatic exit and seemed to be searching for what to do next. After a second of the two painters looking at her, waiting, she said, "I can't work with you people. You are shit as models!" She turned on a heel and marched out of the room, head high, her paintbrush leaving a yellow arc on her thigh as she went.

Henri sighed and said, "I'm teaching her to paint."

"Trousers?" Lucien replied. "Please."

Henri retrieved his trousers from a chair and slipped them on. "We should get coffee. If we're to find your painting, I fear I will be forced to sober up and a hangover is likely to descend very soon."

"You think we can find the painting?"

Henri pulled on his undershirt, and when he had replaced his hat, said, "Of course, you know the Colorman had to have taken it. We'll get it back from him."

"The bartender said it was a young girl. A Tahitian girl, he thought. I don't even know where to start looking. Without the painting, we have no way to find the Colorman, or Juliette. I've lost my best painting *and* the love of my life."

Henri turned slowly from the dresser, where he had been collecting his watch and cuff links, and sat on the red velvet vanity stool. "And we won't be able to use your *Blue Nude* to help restore Carmen's memory to ask her."

"That too," said Lucien.

"I'm sorry, Lucien," said Toulouse-Lautrec, genuine sadness in his voice. "Perhaps we should have a cognac to console ourselves. Shall I call the ladies back?"

Lucien sat up on the floor, leaned back against the bed. "I haven't painted anything since she left. I'm not even a baker anymore. Régine is finishing the bread today. That painting was not only the best I've ever done, it's the best I'll ever do. Nothing. I have nothing. I *am* nothing."

"That's not so bad," Henri said. "Sometimes, during the day, when there are no men here, and it's just the girls, they forget I'm here. They brush each other's hair, or whisper about times when they were young, or they wash out their stockings in a basin. They nap in each other's arms, or just collapse on a bed and snore like puppies, and I sit in the corner, with my sketchbook, saying nothing. Sometimes the only sound is the scratching of my charcoal on the paper, or the gentle splashing of water in the basin. This becomes a world without men, soft and unthreatening, and the girls become as tender as virgins. They are not whores, as they would be if they took a step outside, or as they will be when they are called downstairs again by the madame, but they are nothing else, either. They are between. Not what they used to be, and not what they have become. In those times, they are nothing. And I am invisible, and I am nothing too. That is the true *demimonde,* Lucien, and the secret is, it is not always desperate and dark. Sometimes it is just nothing. No burden of potential or regret. There are worse things than being nothing, my friend."

Lucien nodded, trying to find some sort of value to the emptiness, to the sheer cold vacuum he felt inside since Juliette had left. His "nothing" didn't feel as painless as Henri's and his harlot friends'. He said, "And Carmen?"

Henri took off his *pince-nez* and seemed distracted by cleaning the

". . . and snore like puppies." In the Bed—Henri Toulouse-Lautrec, 1893

lenses on his undershirt. "Carmen? No, she was something. We were something. When I remember those times, when we would go off into the country together, we *ran* through fields, we climbed hills, we made love standing up—me with my back against a tree, holding her up. I can remember the bark digging into my back, and I only cared for her comfort, that I could hold her legs away from the tree, letting the backs of my hands be scraped to blood while she kissed me. She and I, together."

"I didn't know," said Lucien.

"In those times, I was strong. In those times, Lucien, I was *tall*. Now she doesn't remember who I am."

"Your paintings of her are exquisite," Lucien said. "Your best, I think."

Henri smiled. "I am the *painter* Toulouse-Lautrec."

"Better than nothing," said Lucien.

Henri slid off the vanity stool and offered his hand to Lucien to help him up. "Let's get some breakfast and go see Theo van Gogh. He always knows what is going on in the art market and will know if the *Blue Nude* is being offered somewhere. We'll find the bitch who took your painting, then we'll find your Juliette. I promise."

"I am the *painter,* Toulouse-Lautrec."
Self-Portrait—Henri Toulouse-Lautrec, 1883

WHEN HE HAD BEEN A SAILOR, PAUL GAUGUIN HAD DREAMED OF FIELDS OF yellow corn, red cows grazing in meadows, and rusty peasants sleeping on haystacks. When he was a stockbroker he dreamed of ships becalmed in flat, aquamarine seas, their sails as flaccid and pale as shrouds. Now a painter, he slept alone in his tiny Paris apartment and dreamed of tropical islands where buttery brown girls moved in cool shadows like spirits, and despite the chill autumn night, his sheets were soaked with sweat and entangled him like kelp round the drowned.

He sat up on the edge of the bed and wiped his face with his hands, as if he might be able to rub away the vision. The nightmare wasn't the girl. He'd dreamed of island girls since he'd returned from Martinique three years ago, but this one was different, a Polynesian, in a crisp white and blue mission dress, white flowers in her long hair. The girl didn't frighten him at all. She was young and pretty and innocent in the wild unspoiled way of the Pacific, but there was a shadow there, behind her, something small and dark and menacing.

He had dreamed of this particular girl before. She wasn't some general spectre of lust, although she did come naked into his dreams at times and he would wake with an ache in his loins as well as the trembling of the night terror—the dark figure always lurked there; she was a specific personage, with features that he was sure had been conjured out of his imagination as a symbol. He was sure he had never actually seen the girl, but her face was as distinct and real in his mind as that of his wife, Mette, whom he'd abandoned in her native Copenhagen along with their four children, years ago. He could have drawn her from memory.

He stood and crossed the room by the moonlight through the window. It was late, he could tell. The gaslights out on the street had been extinguished and he couldn't hear the orchestra or revelers at the Folies Bergère a block away. A drink of water, and perhaps he'd be granted a few hours of dreamless sleep before he made his way up Montmartre to see if Theo van Gogh had sold any of his paintings—if there would be money for tobacco and oil color this week.

He poured himself a glass of water from a porcelain pitcher in the little kitchenette, just a burner and a sink, really, drank it off, then noticed as he set the glass down that he'd left the door into the hallway ajar. He'd grown careless, either because the building's concierge was a vigilant busybody or because he had nothing left to steal, it didn't matter. He pulled the door closed and headed back to bed with a bit of a shudder—sweat drying in the autumn air.

One step to the bed and he saw her, at first just her dark face and arms against the white sheet—only the pinpoint sparkles in her eyes in the dark, like distant stars. She threw back the sheet, opened it to him, and her dark body was spread across the bed like a shadow in the moonlight—a familiar shadow that evoked a yearning in his loins and an electric-blue bolt of fear up his spine.

"Monsieur Paul," said Bleu. "Come to bed."

"—the dark figure always lurked there—" *Nevermore*—Paul Gauguin, 1897

THEY ATE CROISSANTS AND SAUSAGES AT THE DEAD RAT AS THE WORLD whirled back into focus for Henri with a vivid, vicious sharpness. He wore a *pince-nez* with dark lenses that he'd had made for just such hangover mornings and made him look like a small and miserable undertaker.

"Lucien, as much as I enjoy the convenience and company at Le Rat Mort, I believe our favorite restaurant has begun to provoke nausea in me."

"Perhaps it has less to do with the restaurant and more to do with circumstance. The last few times we've been here, you've just spent the night in drunken depravity at a brothel."

Lucien held his *demitasse* of espresso aloft and toasted his friend, who cringed at the sound of the cups clicking.

"But I like brothels. My friends are there."

"They aren't your friends."

"Yes they are, they like me just as I am."

"Because you pay them."

"No, because I'm charming. Besides, I pay all of my friends."

"No you don't. You don't pay me."

"I'm going to buy breakfast. On my account. Besides, I only pay them for the sex, the friendship is free."

"Don't you worry about syphilis?"

"Syphilis is a wives' tale."

"It is not. You get a chancre on your manhood, then later you go mad, your limbs drop off, and you die. Manet died of syphilis."

"Nonsense. Syphilis is a myth. It's Greek, I think—everyone has heard of the myth of syphilis."

"That's the myth of *Sisyphus*. He spends his whole life pushing a large stone up a hill."

"With his penis? No wonder he has a chancre on it!"

"No, that's not the story."

"So you say. Shall I order more coffee?"

They had taken a booth at the back of the restaurant, away from the windows, due to Henri's self-inflicted sensitivity to light, but now there was a commotion near the front. A large, ruddy-skinned man with a long hooked nose and a black mustache, wearing a long embroidered Breton jacket, had entered the restaurant and was going from table to table, imparting some news that was distressing the patrons; a few of the ladies held handkerchiefs to their mouths to cover their dismay.

"Gauguin," said Henri. "Don't let him see us. He'll try to get us to join one of his movements."

"But this would be a perfect time to ask him if Vincent was in contact with a woman in Arles."

As if he'd heard them, Gauguin looked up, spotted them, and slalomed between the tables toward them.

"Here he comes," said Henri. "Tell him we've decided that we are staunch adherents to the Incohérents movement. We will not be persuaded."

"You and Willette just made that movement up to annoy him." Henri and other artists who inhabited Le Chat Noir had formed the Incohérents as a response to the Salon des Artistes Français and all the overly earnest, humorless art movements that had risen since the Impressionists.

"That's not true," said Henri. "We made it up to annoy everyone, but yes, Gauguin in particular."

Gauguin arrived at their booth and slid into the seat next to Lucien without being asked.

"Lautrec, Lessard, did you two hear? Theo van Gogh is dead."

"Murdered?" asked Lucien.

"A sudden illness," said Gauguin.

"Now the painter, he slept alone in his tiny Paris apartment and dreamed of tropical islands where buttery brown girls moved in cool shadows like spirits." *Self-Portrait*—Paul Gauguin, 1888

Twenty-two

THE END OF THE MASTER

I DIDN'T BONK THE JULIETTE," SAID THE COLORMAN. "I DIDN'T."

"What's she doing bent over the back of the couch naked?"

"Dusting?" He shrugged.

"She doesn't need to be naked to dust."

The island girl, Bleu, began to gather Juliette's clothes from the floor and throw them at the Colorman. "Help me get her dressed." To Juliette she said, "Get dressed." The living doll straightened up and moved with clockwork awkwardness to retrieve her clothes as well.

"But I was going to make the color."

"You can make the color with this body," said Bleu. She didn't care which body he used to make the color. She would be entranced during the process either way, not completely oblivious, but not completely present, either. There was a dreamlike separateness in it, ecstatic, blissful, removed, and essentially helpless. But unlike the Juliette body, who was just sort of a stringless puppet, if Bleu vacated the island girl's body now, the girl would find herself in the midst of this strange scene with no memory whatsoever of how she'd gotten there. At best she would be reduced to a drooling lunatic, at worst she might dive through a window in terror. Sacré Bleu might be the essence of beauty, but making it was not a beautiful process.

"Wait," Bleu said. Juliette paused, stood, and held her silk chemise between her breasts, posed like the statue of a shy Venus, as if she would happily wait a thousand years for the next command.

To the Colorman, Bleu said, "How are you going to make the color? We don't have a painting."

Bleu wasn't about to tell the Colorman about the current state of Lucien's *Blue Nude*.

"Remember this?" The Colorman dragged a large canvas from behind the divan where Juliette had been bent over. She really had been dusting, dusting the surface of an oil painting with her chemise.

"Berthe?" said Bleu, a little stunned. She stepped away from the painting and sat down gently on one of the Louis XVI chairs. "I thought you used this painting twenty-five years ago. Where . . . ?"

Making Sacré Bleu required a painting, a stained glass window, an icon, a fresco—some work of art that had been made with the color, but when she was entranced, she didn't always know which work of art the Colorman had used. But the color had to be made. Without it neither she nor the Colorman could go on. There was always a price, and the paintings were part of it. She had never expected to see this painting again.

"I had it lying around," said the Colorman. "She is lovely, no?"

"Don't try to distract me, Poopstick. If you had this lying around, why did you have to shoot Vincent? Why the panic about Lucien's painting? Why all this drama and desperation?"

"I think maybe she is finer even than your Juliette," said the Colorman. "The dark eyes—the fair skin—beautiful *and* clever."

Berthe Morisot had, perhaps, next to Juliette, been the most beautiful woman Bleu had inhabited, certainly in the modern era, but Manet had painted this so long ago—how and why was it here now? She tried to calm herself, her anger at the Colorman.

"He really did adore her," she said after a moment.

"It looks like he wanted to walk into the painting and die with her."

"He did," said Bleu.

"You were the best of them, Berthe," he said. *Berthe Morisot*—Édouard Manet, 1872

Paris, April 1883

MANET WAS DYING. HE WAS SWEATING, SHIVERING WITH FEVER, AND THE stump, where they had severed his left foot a week ago, felt as if it was on fire. His wife, Suzanne, begged him to take the morphine for the pain, but he would not have it. He would not give up the clarity of his last hours on earth, even if the only vivid element left was pain.

The doctor called it locomotor ataxia because a gentleman's physician does not tell a grieving wife that her husband is dying of late-stage syphilis.

Until the disease descended, he'd been at the height of his abilities. Only two years ago the state had made him a *chevalier* of the Legion of Honor, fulfilling a lifelong aspiration, but even now, those paintings that had earned him the honor, *Luncheon on the Grass* and *Olympia,* attracted scandal whenever they were exhibited. The revolution he had started but had never joined, Impressionism, was coming into its own, with those students who had gathered around him like puppies at the 1863 Salon des Refusés—Monet, Renoir, Pissarro, Cézanne, and Degas—all becoming lions in their own right, as painters, anyway, if not yet financial successes. They all had come and gone from this room, paid tribute and said their good-byes, although none would admit that was what he was doing. But no more. No one should see the painter Manet like this.

"Suzanne, *chérie,* no more visitors. Please, give them my regrets and my thanks, but send them away."

Suzanne sent them away, and amid the tears she cried every day, between the breathless moments of loss that she was already feeling, a few were tears of relief, of triumph, of joy—and immediately she felt ashamed. *She* had not come, would not come. Victorine, who had posed for those paintings so long ago, the haughty whore-model from the *demimonde,* had not come. Victorine, whose gaze Suzanne had borne over a thousand evenings as the nude stared down from the canvas, judging. *Olympia,* hung in the parlor, with the tiny, taut Victorine always watching the stout Suzanne lumber around her own house like an ox, going about the mundane business of caring for her home and her husband. Édouard's greatest work. Victorine would be immortal, and ever thin, and poor Suzanne a lonely, fat, grieving footnote: the Dutch piano teacher who married her student. Édouard loved her, she knew that, she felt that, but there had been something else, a part of him she had never known, and she could see, every day, when she looked into the eyes of the woman in *Le déjeuner sur l'herbe* and *Olympia*, that Victorine had.

The bell rang and Suzanne heard the maid let someone in.

"Madame Morisot Manet," the maid announced, leading Berthe in from the foyer. Berthe wore a dress of lavender silk, trimmed in white lace, and a hat with a diaphanous white chiffon veil. Berthe, so often dark of demeanor and aspect that Suzanne could not think of her except in black Spanish lace, as if eternally grieving, but today, bless her, she had come calling dressed like a bright spring flower.

"Suzanne," said Berthe, rolling back her veil and embracing Édouard's wife, kissing her cheeks. She stepped away but held on to Suzanne's hands, squeezed them as she said, "How can I help?"

"He's in so much pain," said Suzanne. "If I could just get him to take the morphine."

"I heard that he wasn't seeing visitors."

Suzanne smiled. "No, but he will see *you*. Come."

Before they entered the bedroom, Suzanne turned to Berthe and whispered, "His color is bad, don't let him see that you're distressed."

Berthe dismissed the thought with a nod. Suzanne opened the door.

"Édouard, look who has come to call. It's Berthe."

Manet fought to push himself up in the bed and despite the painful effort, he smiled.

"Berthe!" He said nothing else.

There was a sparkle of joy in his eyes and seeing it brought tears to Suzanne's. She squeezed his hand and turned away. "Let me fetch us all some tea," she said, and she hurried out of the room, closed the door, and once in the hall was wracked by a great, heaving, silent sob.

"How are you, Édouard?" asked Berthe, a sweet smile there, just barely. "I mean, beyond the obvious."

Manet laughed until he coughed. "Well, beyond that, I couldn't be better."

"I've brought you something." She reached into her bag, a drawstring affair fashioned of black satin covered in Spanish lace, and retrieved a small canvas; a short-handled, fine sable brush; and a tube of paint. She laid them on his chest, and he swiped at them feebly, as if he didn't have the strength to even lift the tiny brush. Instead he caught her hand.

"You were the best of them, Berthe," he said. "You are still the best of them. If you were a man, your paintings would already be in the Louvre. You know that?"

She patted his hand, then placed the brush in his fingers. She propped up the little canvas on his chest and squeezed some of the blue color out onto it. "So you've told me. You don't remember painting the nude, do you?"

He looked at her, distressed, as if his mind was already slipping away. He held the brush like it was a foul, foreign thing.

"Sketch me, Édouard," she said. "You are the painter Manet. Now paint."

And even as he protested, his hand began to move, the brush traced lines over the canvas. "But I'm dying."

"That's no excuse, love, you're still and shall ever be the *painter* Manet. Now paint."

He fell to sketching her, from the jawline up, the soft brush and creamy blue barely making a noise in the room as her face appeared on the canvas. She made it no easier on him, her smile broadening as he worked so he had to revise the sketch.

"Poor Suzanne," said Berthe. "Victorine haunts her."

"The passion she's jealous of was for the work, not the woman," he said.

"I know," said Berthe. She *did* know. She'd been there. She had been Victorine Meurent in those times, modeled for those paintings. As Victorine she had seduced, enchanted, inspired, and ultimately killed him, for it was Victorine who had given him the syphilis. But he had never loved Victorine. It was as Berthe Morisot that she had inspired his love and his greatest painting. The painting that only she, Manet, and the Colorman had ever seen. The painting that had been stored in underground Paris for over twenty years.

"Do you remember now?" she asked, the blue starting to take effect.

"Yes. Oh yes."

She took his hand and led him to the forest at Fontainebleau, where they rented a cabin with a sunroom and she posed on a daybed during the day while he painted, where they made love with the sun on their skin. She led him to a little inn at Honfleur, where the Seine met the sea, and there they drank wine in a café on the mirror-calm harbor, painted side by side, and walked the beach at sunset. She led him to a sunny villa in Provence, near Aix, and she smiled at him from under the brim of a white straw hat, her dark eyes shining like gemstones while he painted.

Only one other time had Bleu been both the model and the painter, both the inspiration and the creator, and not a woman, then. Berthe's artistic talent had nothing to do with Bleu, and was profound, and out of time. Women didn't paint, and if they did, they weren't recognized for it. But Berthe had been accepted among the Impressionists from the start—had painted alongside them all. In the evening, when they retreated to the cabarets and cafés to discuss art, ideas, and theory, she would go home, sit with the other women, where it was proper, despite the fact that she was, as Manet had said, *the best of them*. Bleu had seen through Berthe's painter's eye, and seen Berthe through Manet's eye, in his paintings. He adored Berthe, before Bleu possessed her and after she had left. He had gone to great lengths to arrange the circumstances for Berthe's marriage to his younger brother, Eugène, just so he might be near her—all very proper and aboveboard. She the lady, he the gentleman of society. It was only when Berthe was inhabited by Bleu that Manet's passion was able to manifest in art and love. Bleu, as Berthe, had taken the painter to places he would have never gone, even as she led him now.

They stayed in the South for a month together, painting and laughing and lounging in the blue shade of olive trees, until Suzanne returned to Édouard's bedside with the tea.

"He's gone," Berthe said. "He was sketching, and then suddenly he gasped and he was gone. It was so sudden, I didn't even have time to call for you."

Suzanne stumbled and Berthe caught the tea tray and steered it away to the bureau, then was back at Suzanne's side.

Berthe gently pried the canvas from Manet's hand, smearing the oil sketch as she did, just enough so that it might have been an image of any woman.

"He called your name," Berthe said. "He said he wanted to sketch you, and he began drawing with the brush, then he gasped and called your name, 'Suzanne.'"

"SYPHILIS HAS BEEN GOOD TO US," SAID THE COLORMAN.

"Very good," Bleu said.

"Not satisfying, though," he said.

"Speak for yourself."

"It's slow; sometimes you don't want to wait and a pistol is better."

"A pistol doesn't always work for us, as you proved with Vincent," said Bleu. Then it occurred to her that it might have worked perfectly. What if the Colorman had hidden the painting Vincent had made with the Sacré Bleu, the same way he had hidden the Manet nude? What if he'd shot Vincent to keep *her* from knowing the painting's location? What if he had found some new trick to play on her while she was in a trance or in character and couldn't watch him? He was sneaky to start out, and he'd had a lot of time to get sneakier. He might have been caching paintings away for years, and she would have never known.

"You need to get ready now," said the Colorman. He closed the drapes and unfolded an oilcloth over their dining table.

"Really? You're going to do it on the table?" asked Bleu.

"Yes. It's a sturdy table. Why not?"

"Because you'll have to stand on a chair—chairs. Dangerous. We should use the divan." She started gathering cushions from the couch, and upon lifting the third one discovered a small, nickel-plated revolver stuffed in the gap by the arm. She quickly replaced the cushion before the Colorman noticed she had seen. "Or the floor," she said. "The floor is best."

She swept the oilcloth off the table and spread it out over the floor between the dining room and the parlor. As she undressed, she said, "I found Gauguin, the painter who shared Vincent's yellow house in Arles. As soon as we have the blue, he is ours. He has a weakness for Polynesian girls."

The Colorman stripped off his jacket, then unlaced his shoes and kicked them across the room. "I wondered why you picked this one. There is another painter, too, who bought color from me. Called Seurat, a theorist, though; he may be slow."

"Gauguin will be fast. He had the vision he was going to paint before he even met this girl."

"Good, we just need to clean up from the last one, then, yes?" The Colorman was nude now, except for a loincloth made of tattered linen, his bent spine and spindly twisted limbs making him appear like the product of a giant rat crossbred with a chanterelle mushroom. Coarse black hair like a boar's peppered his umber skin. He was setting four small braziers around the oilcloth, building small charcoal fires in each. To the side, he had placed two round earthenware jars the size of pomegranates, each had a leather cord at its neck and a wide cork lid.

"No cleanup to do," she said. She was nude now, too, standing aside as the Colorman prepared the site. "Vincent's brother is taken care of."

The Colorman turned slowly toward her, holding a long, black obsidian knife, the hilt wrapped with some sort of tanned animal skin. "The art dealer? You shot the Dutchman's brother?"

"Syphilis," she said. A smile then, looking shy on the naked island girl as she peeked out from behind a curtain of hip-length hair. "See, it's not always slow, but slow enough to ask them questions before they die."

The Colorman nodded. "Good, then we only have to shoot the baker and the dwarf and it's all done."

"Yes, that's all," she said. *Damn it.* This was not at all what she had expected. Not at all.

"I'm ready," he said. "Lie down." He uncapped one of the jars and hung it around his neck like a medallion.

She lay on her back in the middle of the oilcloth and stretched her arms above her head. The Colorman sprinkled powder into the braziers and a rich aromatic smoke filled the flat. Then he ran about the room hopping on chairs and turning down the gaslights, so that the girl was barely visible in the dim glow of the braziers. He began to chant as he stepped around her, waving the knife over her face. The chant didn't consist of words, as such, but rhythms, animal sounds given meaning by cadence.

"No shagging the Vuvuzela," said Bleu.

He stopped chanting. "What the fuck is a Vuvuzela?"

"That's this girl's name. No shagging her." Sometimes the trance was so deep for both of them that when Bleu emerged she was relatively sure she'd been molested. There was never any proof. He was careful and covered his tracks, so to speak, but still, she suspected.

He looked a little disappointed. His thick brow hung over his eyes a little more than normal. "Maybe when we're done you can leave her and I can frighten her, no?"

"Maybe. Make the color, Colorman."

He laughed, a wheezing cough of a laugh, and resumed his chant. The girl's eyes rolled back in her head and she convulsed several times in rhythm to the Colorman's chant, then she went rigid, bent-backed, and locked that way; only her shoulder blades and her heels still touched the oilcloth. The Manet painting began to glow then, a dim, throbbing blue light that shone over the whole room.

The Colorman chanted, danced his wounded-bird march, the painting glowed, and slowly, ever so slowly, the girl began to turn blue as the color rose on her skin. Even the soul-empty body of Juliette looked wide-eyed at the scene as the Colorman lay the blade of the black glass knife on the girl's skin and began to scrape the blue powder.

The knife was sharp, but not so sharp that it would shave, and for all his broken-spider awkwardness, the Colorman wielded the knife with smooth precision, shaving the powder off of every surface of the girl's body, even off her eyelids, and scraping it into the earthenware jar. He rolled her on her side and scraped the delicate curves of her back, rolling her again, back and forth, breaking into a sweat, so that the blue powder covered his own hands, his feet, his thighs. Meanwhile the painting, the masterpiece Manet that almost no one had ever seen, faded by degrees as the Colorman filled his jar. The painting—the passion, the suffering, the intensity, the skill, the time, the life that Manet had put into it, guided by his inspiration—all came out on the girl's skin as the powder, as the Sacré Bleu. There was always more color from the painting than had gone into it. Sometimes a small painting might yield two jars of the color, especially if it had been created with great sacrifice, great suffering, and great love, for that, too, was part of the formula.

The Colorman chanted and scraped until the Manet painting was just a blank canvas. It had taken more than an hour. He capped the jar and unslung it from his neck, setting it by the blank canvas.

The girl relaxed by jerky degrees, like the tension being released in a spring with each click of some cosmic gear, until she lay flat again, peaceful. She opened her eyes, now the only bit of her body not covered in the flat, blue ultramarine powder—even her long dark hair was dusted with the color from the Colorman stepping on it as he worked. She turned on her side and looked at the Colorman, then at the blank canvas.

"Just one jar," said the Colorman. He was rolling his glass knife up in a piece of rawhide.

She was exhausted, felt as if someone had dragged the very life force out of her, which, essentially, someone had. "But there is enough color for a painting?"

"For many," said the Colorman. "Unless they paint impasto, like that fucking Dutchman."

She nodded and climbed to her feet, stumbled, then caught herself. She looked at Juliette, who was looking back, as blank-faced as a mannequin. Bleu could hear footfalls outside on the landing. The nosy concierge, no doubt, brought up by the Colorman's chanting, just as she thought.

"You want to share a bath?" asked the Colorman, leering at the island girl, his loincloth now covered in blue and looking rather more alert than it had during the making of the color.

"One minute," she said. Bleu padded to the kitchen, leaving powdery blue footprints on the parquet floor. She wiped her hands on a tea towel, then returned to the parlor. "Did you light the fire under the water?"

The Colorman grinned. "Before we even started." He was folding up the oilcloth, coaxing the last of the blue powder into its creases so he could pour it into a jar.

"Good," she said. "Then we can clean up." She went to the writing desk in the foyer, listened—yes, the concierge was still out there—then she pulled a roll of bills out of one of the desk's pigeonholes, took it to Juliette, and stuffed it in the girl's bag.

"Your hat," said Bleu to the Juliette doll. "The one with the black chiffon band and train." The hat was on the oak hall tree by the door and Juliette retrieved it and put it on. When she turned back around, Bleu was placing the jar into Juliette's bag on top of the money.

"Perfect," said Bleu. She padded over to the couch, reached between the cushions, and pulled out the Colorman's revolver. To Juliette she said, "Scream."

Juliette screamed, a pathetic little toot of a scream.

"What are you, a baby chicken?" said Bleu. "Louder and longer!"

Juliette screamed, much louder and longer this time.

"What are you doing?" asked the Colorman.

"Cleaning up," said Bleu. She pointed the revolver at him and fired. The bullet hit him high in the chest and knocked him back. She cocked the revolver and fired again.

"Ouch," he said. Blood fountained from a hole in his sternum.

"Keep screaming," she said to Juliette. She cocked and fired again, three more times, until the Colorman lay motionless on the oilcloth, his blood pooling around him in the ultramarine powder. She cocked the revolver, pointed it at his head, and pulled the trigger. The gun just clicked.

"Hmmm. Only five shots. Okay, stop screaming and open the door."

Juliette pulled open the door to reveal the concierge, a large, severe woman, who peered into the room, her eyes wide with horror.

And Bleu jumped bodies into Juliette. The island girl dropped the gun and began to scream hideously.

"I came in from the other room and he was attacking her," said Bleu as Juliette. "The poor thing had to save herself, I don't know what horrible thing he was doing to her. I'll go get a policeman."

Juliette whisked by the concierge, down the stairs, and out into the Paris morning.

Part III

Amused

All varieties of picture, when they are really art, fulfill their
purpose and feed the spirit.
—WASSILY KANDINSKY, *CONCERNING THE SPIRITUAL IN ART*

He made painting his only muse, his only mistress, his sole
and sufficient passion. . . . He looked upon woman as an
object of art, delightful and made to excite the mind, but
an unruly and disturbing object if we allow her to cross the
threshold of our hearths, devouring greedily our time and
strength.
—CHARLES BAUDELAIRE, ON THE DEATH OF DELACROIX

Twenty-three

CLOSED DUE TO DEATH

THE SIGN ON THE DOOR OF THE BOUSSOD ET VALADON GALLERY READ CLOSED DUE TO DEATH. The three painters stood by the front window, looking in on the small array of paintings displayed in the window, among them one by Gauguin of some Breton women in stiff, white bonnets and blue dresses, threshing grain, and an older still life that Lucien had painted of a basket full of bread. One of Pissarro's landscapes of Auvers' wheat fields stood between the two.

"I would paint more farms," said Toulouse-Lautrec, "but they always put them so far from the bar."

"That bread still life will never sell," said Lucien. "That painting is shit. My best work is gone. Gone . . ."

"How will I survive now?" said Gauguin. "Theo was the only one selling my paintings."

Hearing Gauguin's selfish lament, Lucien suddenly felt ashamed. Theo van Gogh had been a young man, just thirty-three. He had been a friend and supporter to them all, his young wife with a baby boy not even a year old would be distraught, yet the painters whined like kittens pulled from their mother's teats, blind to anything but their own cold discomfort.

"Perhaps we should call on Madame van Gogh at home," said Lucien. "Pay our respects. I can fetch a basket of bread and pastries from the bakery."

"But is it too soon?" said Gauguin, realizing, like Lucien, that Theo van Gogh's death was not a tragedy crafted for his personal misfortune. "Let a day or two pass. If I could prevail upon one of you for a small loan to tide me over."

"You came here to ask Madame van Gogh for money?" asked Lucien.

"No, of course not. I had heard of Theo's death in Père Tanguy's shop only minutes before I saw you at Le Rat Mort, I was simply—" Gauguin hung his head. "Yes."

Lucien patted the older painter's shoulder. "I can spare a few *francs* to get you through until a proper amount of time has passed, then you can go see Madame van Gogh. Perhaps they will find a new dealer to run the gallery."

"No," declared Henri, who had been looking through the door into the gallery. He turned to face them, cocked his thumb over his shoulder, and looked over the top of his dark *pince-nez*. "We go see the widow now."

Lucien raised an eyebrow at his friend. "I can also lend you a few *francs* until your allowance arrives." Then Lucien followed the aim of Henri's thumb to the red frame of the door. There, at exactly Henri's eye level, was a single, distinct thumbprint in ultramarine blue—long, narrow, delicate—the thumbprint of a woman.

JOHANNA VAN GOGH ANSWERED THE APARTMENT DOOR WITH A BABY ON HER hip and a look of stunned horror on her face. "No! No! No!" she said. "No! No! No!"

"Madame van Gogh—" said Lucien, but that was all he got out before she slammed the door.

Toulouse-Lautrec nudged Gauguin. "This may not be the opportune time to ask for money."

"I wasn't going to—" began Gauguin.

"Why are you here?" Madame van Gogh said through the door.

"It is Lucien Lessard," said Lucien. "My deepest sympathy for your loss. Theo was a friend. He showed my paintings at the gallery. Messieurs Gauguin and Toulouse-Lautrec here are also painters who show at the gallery. We were all at Vincent's funeral. Perhaps you remember?"

"The little man," said Johanna. "He must go away. Theo told me I must never let the little man near Vincent's paintings. Those were his last words: 'beware of the little man.'"

"That was an entirely different little man," said Lucien.

"Madame, I am not little," said Henri. "In fact, there are parts of me—"

Lucien clamped his hand over Henri's mouth, knocking his *pince-nez* askew in the process. "This is Henri Toulouse-Lautrec, Madame van Gogh, a good friend to Vincent and Theo. Surely Theo mentioned him."

"Yes," said Johanna, the hint of a sob in her answer. "But that was before—"

"He *is* very small," said Gauguin, looking a bit tortured now at the grief in the widow's voice. "Forgive us, Madame, it is too soon. We will pay our respects another time." Gauguin turned and began to walk down the hall toward the stairs.

Henri twisted out of Lucien's grip, losing his hat in the process. "My deepest condolences," he said, glaring at Lucien and straightening his lapels as he did. "I assure you, I am not the person to whom your husband was referring. Go with God, Madame." He turned and followed Gauguin.

Lucien could hear Madame van Gogh whispering to the baby on the other side of the door.

"We will call again," said Lucien. "Very sorry, Madame." He started to walk away but paused when he heard the door unlatch.

"Monsieur Lessard. Wait."

The door opened a crack and Madame van Gogh held out a small, cardboard envelope, big enough to hold a ring or perhaps a key. "A girl came here, very early this morning. She left this for you."

Lucien took the envelope, feeling a completely unjustified euphoria rush through him as he did. Juliette? Why? How?

"A girl?" he said.

"A young Tahitian girl," said Madame van Gogh. "I have never seen her before."

"But why?"

"I don't know, Monsieur Lessard, the doctor was here, my husband was dying. I couldn't even remember who you were at the time. Now please, take it and go."

"Madame, one thing. Did the doctor say the nature of his sickness?"

"He called it dementia paralytica," said Madame van Gogh, and she quietly pushed the door shut.

"*Merci*, Madame."

Lucien tore the top off the envelope and dumped it into his open hand: a tin tube of paint, almost completely used, and a small, folded note. He felt a hand on his shoulder and looked around to see Gauguin, holding out his hand.

"I think that is mine," said Gauguin.

"In a monkey's red ass, it is," said Lucien.

It was then, with great force and no little glee, that Henri Toulouse-Lautrec swung the weighted pommel of his walking stick into Gauguin's shin.

"*En garde!*" said the count.

It was some time before Gauguin was able to join his fellow artists outside on the sidewalk.

"I THINK YOU CHIPPED A BONE," SAID GAUGUIN. THEY MADE THEIR WAY DOWN rue Caulaincourt toward Toulouse-Lautrec's studio, two of the three limping, one emphatically.

Henri said, "You know, for a man of forty-three, you are surprisingly good at hopping downstairs on one foot."

"You will pay for that, Lautrec," said Gauguin. To Lucien, he said, "That envelope is mine."

Lucien held up the envelope to show the writing on the side. "Despite my name on it and Madame van Gogh saying that the girl left it for me, it is yours?"

"Yes. I know the girl who delivered it."

"You know her? A random Tahitian girl? You know her?"

"Yes, she said that she would be bringing me color, and that was a tube of paint in the envelope, was it not?"

Henri stopped and snagged Gauguin by the sleeve of his brocade jacket, nearly spinning him around. "Wait, how do you know this girl?"

Gauguin shook his sleeve out of Lautrec's grasp. "I just know her."

"Where did you meet her?"

"I met her only recently."

"Recently where? Under what circumstances?"

Gauguin looked around, as if searching for an answer in the sky. "She may have appeared in my bed last night."

"Appeared?" Lucien loomed over Gauguin, curious to a point that was beginning to look threatening.

Gauguin backed away from his fellow painters turned inquisitors, who, it seemed, were behaving much more intensely than the situation dictated.

"I got up to get a drink of water, and when I returned to bed she was there."

"And you didn't find that at all strange?" said Lucien.

"Or convenient?" added Henri, a recriminating eyebrow bounding over the lens of his *pince-nez* like a prosecutorial squirrel.

"It was as from a dream," cried Gauguin. "What is wrong with you two?" He limped away to escape them, heading back the way they had come.

"She was perfect, then?" said Lucien. "As if conjured from an ideal?"

Gauguin stopped. "Yes. Exactly."

"Come," said Henri. "You're going to need a cognac." Henri led them another block, stopped in a doorway to unlock his studio, and led them inside. Dust motes hung in the beam of light through the door's single oval window, making the open space seem deserted, despite the canvases leaning against every wall. There were perhaps a hundred different sketches of the angular entertainer Jane Avril in different poses strewn about the floor and tacked on the walls.

"So," said Gauguin. "Jane Avril?"

"A professional interest," explained Toulouse-Lautrec.

"Professional?" inquired Gauguin.

"She smells suspiciously of lilac and can put either leg behind her head while singing 'La Marseillaise'*and spinning on the other foot. I thought further study was called for."

"Bonking," explained Lucien.

"Infatuation with *aspirations* of bonking," Henri clarified.

"I see," said Gauguin.

"Sit," said Henri, gesturing to the café table and chairs he kept for just such emergencies. Crystal snifters were set around and cognac poured from a cut-crystal decanter.

"So there was a girl in your bed," said Henri. "What of the Colorman?"

---

*The French national anthem.

"I told you," said Gauguin. "I went to see Père Tanguy this morning. I have an account at his shop—"

"Not Tanguy, *the* Colorman. Surely Vincent spoke of him to you."

"The little bent brown fellow Vincent went on about?"

"Yes," said Lucien. "That's the one."

"No." Gauguin waved in the air as if to fan away Lautrec's silliness. "I thought that was some Dutch folktale Vincent had conjured up from his childhood. He said that the little man had pursued him from Paris to Saint-Rémy, then to Arles. He was mad."

"Vincent wasn't mad," said Lucien. "Such a man exists. Was there a girl?"

"A girl? You mean with Vincent?"

"Yes, was Vincent seeing a woman?"

"No. What woman would have him? No money, out of his mind half the time, drunk and melancholy the other."

"He might not have seemed to spend much time with her. Perhaps he spoke of a model." Lucien thought of all the time he had spent with Juliette out of time, just the two of them. Henri and Carmen, Monet and Camille, Renoir and his Margot, all had experienced the slip of time while alone together. Perhaps it was possible that there had been a woman with Vincent and Gauguin had never seen her.

Gauguin threw back his brandy and closed his eyes as he waited for the burn to pass. "Vincent painted landscapes, still lifes, the odd café scene, but no portraits in Arles that I remember, other than one of me and a self-portrait. No women."

Lucien pressed. "Perhaps he spoke of someone. In passing."

Gauguin twisted the end of his mustache mindlessly, as if wringing a stubborn memory from it. "On the day before I left we had a terrible row. It started with differences in color theory. Vincent had been trying to paint without using any blue. For a while he would use ultramarine only when painting at night. He said that darkness drained the color of its evil. It was absurd. Worse than trying to talk theory to you, Lautrec."

"A woman?" Henri reminded him. He sloshed more cognac into Gauguin's snifter.

"That's the thing. Vincent became violent, screaming about blue, then he took his razor and cut off half of his ear. He waved the bloody piece around shouting, 'This will be for her! This is her price!'"

"Oh no," said Lucien.

"What?" said Gauguin. "Does that mean something? He was ill, right?"

"It means," said Henri, "that you must leave Paris. Go far away. And if you see the girl who came to your bed last night you must run like you are being pursued by a demon."

Lucien nodded to confirm Henri's warning.

"But I must paint her. It's why I was out so early to get color. I *need* to paint her."

"You need to run, Paul," said Lucien. "If you paint her, she is going to die. Or you are."

"Possibly of tedium," said Henri. "If you inflict your painting theories on her."

"That's not what I'm saying at all," said Lucien.

THEY SENT GAUGUIN ON HIS WAY WITH ALL THE MONEY THEY HAD LEFT IN their pockets and his promise that he would avoid the girl from his bed and leave Paris as soon as he could secure fare to Tahiti. He might give up on his ideal island girl, but he wasn't going to give up on the idea of painting island girls altogether.

"What does the note say?" asked Henri.

"It says '*Lucien, Sketch me.*' It's signed '*Juliette.*'"

"Rather *Alice in Wonderland* cryptic. She's a beautiful girl, Lucien, but her epistolary skills are shit."

"There's barely enough color here for a sketch."

"Perhaps we should save it. When Le Professeur returns he can use it to hypnotize you. Or we can fetch Carmen and hypnotize her as we had planned."

"No, I'm going to sketch Juliette."

Henri shrugged. "There's some cardboard in the top drawer of the print cabinet. We don't have any small canvases primed."

Lucien went to the print cabinet and pulled out the wide, flat drawer, and shuffled around the brown cardboard pieces inside until he found a piece about the size of a postcard. "This should do it."

"Do you have a photograph to work from?"

"I'll draw from memory. I think that's what she meant for me to do."

"There was evidently subtext to her letter that I did not perceive."

Lucien took a number two brush from a jar of brushes, took a small jar of linseed oil from the top of the print cabinet, and sat down at the table to draw.

"No white?"

"I'm only going to do a line drawing. If I start painting highlights I'll run out of blue before I have the figure."

"Drawing Juliette may not be the smartest thing to do, Lucien, you know that?"

"Yes, I know, but I love her."

"Very well, carry on, then," said Henri, toasting his friend. "I will catch up on my smoking and drinking while you work."

On unprimed cardboard there would be no correcting, no rubbing out, no wiping and repainting, no blending, no overpainting. He mixed some of the blue into a drop of linseed oil on the tabletop, imagined Juliette's exquisite jawline, and the brush fell to cardboard. Her neck, another line, ever so lightly at first, but then reinforced, contoured by brush hairs, and Juliette's face began to grow up from the cardboard. Lucien's hand was the conduit from the vision in his mind's eye, and he began to lay down the lines like an automated loom weaving a tapestry of silk.

His eyes rolled back in his head and he toppled over in his chair, clutching the drawing in one hand, the brush in the other, and he held them as he lay on the floor, twitching.

LUCIEN OPENED HIS EYES TO SEE HENRI EYE TO EYE WITH HIM, HIS CHEEK pressed to the floor. The two were curled up like battling twin fetuses facing off for in utero fisticuffs.

"Well, that looked unpleasant," Henri said.

"I went away."

"I gathered. Where?"

"I saw Berthe Morisot naked."

"The painter? Really? Nude?"

"In a gypsum mine."

"Not my first choice for a rendezvous, but it is *your* hallucination."

"She was covered in blue."

"Have you tried strawberry jam? Although the seeds can be annoying."

"The Colorman was there too. Also naked."

"Well, now you've lost me. Was he being greedy, if you get my meaning?"

"He was scraping the blue powder off of her body with a knife."

"Interesting. I have no desire to try that. This may be a first for me."

"It's disturbing to me."

"I imagine so. But, tell me, did you get to have a go at Berthe?"

"I was seven."

"Feet tall? Well that's just obscene."

"No, seven years old. It wasn't a hallucination, Henri, it was a memory. I'd forgotten it all. I was in that gypsum mine back during the war, hunting rats. The entrance is in Montmartre Cemetery."

"You actually saw Berthe Morisot naked and painted blue? Well that's going to be awkward if you run into her at a gallery show. I mean, she's still a handsome woman, brilliant painter, but—"

"I think we need to go to that mine."

"Perhaps some lunch first. You were unconscious for quite a while. We ran out of cognac."

"Why are you lying on the floor?"

"Solidarity. And we ran out of cognac. This is my preferred *out of cognac* posture."

"Fine. Lunch first. Then we're on to the mine."

"Splendid! Onward!"

"You can't stand up, can you?"

"The floor is cool against my cheek. I'm rather enjoying the sensation."

"After we've procured some lanterns, eaten, had coffee, and you've taken a bath. Then?"

"A bath? Really?"

"You smell like a whorehouse."

"Yes?"

"Which is inappropriate unless one is actually *in* a whorehouse."

"A bath it is, then. Splendid! Onward!"

"You'll still have to stand up."

"We really should have a maid in to wash these floors."

IT WAS NEARLY SUNDOWN BEFORE LUCIEN WAS FINALLY ABLE TO GET HENRI sobered up enough to make an assault on the mine. Each carried a storm lantern and Lucien had candles and matches in his jacket pockets. Henri had his cane with the sword in the hilt (Lucien had made him check that it wasn't the one with the cordial glass), and Lucien had a long, hook-tipped brush knife he'd borrowed from a neighbor who used it for keeping weeds at bay in the hedgerow of his backyard garden.

"Perhaps we should wait until it's not so dark," said Henri, ducking under a low archway of brambles.

"It's a mine, it's always dark." Lucien hacked away at some blackberry bushes with the brush knife, losing some skin from his knuckles on the thorns in the process.

"Well we should have brought a pistol. I have an uncle in Paris who would gladly lend us one."

"We won't need a pistol."

"That's probably what Vincent thought that last day he went out to paint."

Lucien started to argue, but instead said, "Strange, what Gauguin said about Vincent wanting to use blue only in night scenes."

"Poor Vincent," Henri said.

They had reached the mouth of the mine. Lucien knelt and pulled a match from his jacket pocket. "We should light the lanterns. Give me yours."

"I'll watch for rats," said Henri.

"They won't come out where it's light. That's why I had to go in here in the first place. To set my traps."

"Why were you hunting rats?"

"For food."

"No, really?"

"For my father's pastries."

"No, really?"

"The city was under siege. There was no other food."

"Your father made rat pies?"

"The plan had been tureens—country *pâté*—but then there wasn't enough bread to eat them with, so he made pies. The crusts were about half sawdust. Yes, rat pies, like Cornish pasties."

"But I love your meat pasties."

"Family recipe," said Lucien.

They crept into the mine, lanterns held high. There was scurrying in the deep shadows.

"Was Berthe as beautiful as I imagine her?" asked Henri.

"I was seven. I was terrified. I thought the Colorman was torturing her."

"I hope she's here. I have a small sketch pad in my pocket."

"She's not going to be here. That was twenty years ago. She lives in Montparnasse with her husband and her daughter."

"Oh, and all of a sudden we are bound by time and the possible."

"Good point."

"Thus, I brought a sketch pad."

Suddenly a match ignited only a few feet in front of them and they both yelped and leapt back. Henri tripped over a rotting timber and scrambled to look around.

"My heroes, I presume," said Juliette, holding the match to the wick of a lamp. She sat on a crate in her periwinkle dress; the *Blue Nude* was propped up against a timber behind her.

"Juliette," said Lucien. He stumbled to her; his eyes filled with tears as he took her in his arms.

Twenty-four

THE ARCHITECTURE OF AMUSEMENT

THIS WAS GOING TO REQUIRE SOME DELICACY, A CERTAIN FINESSE, A BIT more subtlety than her normal strategy, which, in most cases, was to remove her clothes. As she kissed Lucien by the orange lantern light in the mine—felt him trying to wrap his very soul around her with his arms, pour it out to her from his heart, in tears, now damp and slick on their faces, as they shared breath and warmth, the moment frozen not by some magical means, but by the exclusive singularity of their embrace, where nothing existed that was not them—she thought: *It's so much easier when you toss up your skirt, shout, "Voilà!" and you're off to the races.* This was going to be complicated.

Toulouse-Lautrec cleared his throat loudly and glanced over his shoulder as if he'd been casually browsing around at the edge of the darkness and had only just noticed his friend voraciously snogging a girl down a mine.

Juliette broke the kiss, nipped Lucien's ear, then pulled his head tight to her bosom and said, *"Bonjour,* Monsieur Henri." She winked.

"*Bonjour,* mademoiselle," said Henri, tipping his bowler hat, which was dusted with the white gypsum powder from the mine.

Lucien seemed to come awake, then, and pushed Juliette away, held her at arm's length by her shoulders. "Are you all right? I thought you might be ill."

"No, I'm fine."

"We know all about the Colorman—how he controls you, all the models over the years. How they lose their memory and become ill. We know all of it."

"You do?" She suppressed the urge to throw up her skirt and try for a bit of misdirection, but with Toulouse-Lautrec there and . . . well, it would be awkward. "You know all of it?"

"Yes," said Lucien. "Camille Monet, Renoir's Margot, even Henri's Carmen—who knows how many there have been? We know he somehow enchants them—you—with his blue color, how time seems to stop. I was worried you wouldn't even remember me."

Juliette took Lucien's hands and stepped away from him. "Well, that is very close to the truth," she said. "Perhaps we should sit for a moment and I'll explain." She looked to Henri quickly. "Do you have a drink?"

Toulouse-Lautrec produced a silver flask from his jacket pocket.

"What is it?" she asked.

"In this one? Cognac."

"Give," she said.

Henri unscrewed the cap and handed the flask to Juliette, who took a quick sip and sat back down on her crate.

"You brought more than one flask?" Lucien asked Henri.

"We didn't have a pistol," said Henri with a shrug.

"Leave him alone, he's rescuing me," said Juliette, sitting splay-legged now, elbows on her thighs in the manner of pirates conspiring over a treasure map in the dirt. She toasted the two painters with the flask and took another drink. "Sit, Lucien."

"But the painting—"

"Sit!"

He sat. Luckily there was a small barrel behind him at the time.

Toulouse-Lautrec found a perch on a fallen timber and availed himself of his second flask.

"So, you probably have some questions," she said.

"Like, why are you sitting in a mine?" said Henri.

"Including why I am sitting in a mine." She continued. "You see, I needed Lucien to remember his first encounter with the blue, his very first encounter, back when he was a boy. I knew that he would remember this place, and I knew he would feel compelled to come here."

"How did you know?" asked Lucien.

"I know you better than you think," she said. She took another sip from the flask and held it out to him. "You'll be wanting some of this."

"I don't understand," said Lucien, taking the flask. "You knew about me coming to this place when I was a child? Seeing the Colorman? You couldn't have been any older than I was."

"Yes, well, I was there."

"Did you see Berthe Morisot naked and covered in blue?" asked Henri, quite excited now.

"In a manner of speaking. I *was* Berthe Morisot naked and covered in blue."

"Sorry?" said the two painters in unison, tilting their heads like confused dogs.

She shook her head, looked at the chalky dirt between her feet, thought of just how much simpler it would be if she could just shift time and make them both forget that this had ever happened. But alas, no. She said, "You were partially right about the Colorman being connected to all of those women, those models. But I am not *like* them, I *was* them."

They both waited, each took a drink, looked at her, said nothing. Dogs watching Shakespeare.

"The Colorman makes the color—we call it Sacré Bleu—but I take over the models, enter them, as a spirit, control them, and when the

Sacré Bleu goes onto the canvas, I can stop time, take the artists to places they have never been, show them things, inspire them. I *was* Monet's Camille, I *was* Renoir's Margot, I *was* Manet's Victorine, many others, and for a very long time. I have been them all. When I leave them, they don't remember because they weren't there, I was."

"You?" said Henri, who seemed to be having trouble catching his breath. "You were Carmen?"

She nodded. "Yes, *mon amour.*"

"Who—what, what are you?" said Lucien.

"I am a muse," said Juliette.

"And you—you? What do you do?"

"I amuse," she said.

She thought it best to let that sink in for a moment, as both of the painters looked mildly nauseated, as if they had consumed too much information and were fighting the need to purge it. She thought that revealing her nature this way, after keeping it a secret for so, so long, she would feel unburdened, liberated. Strangely, no.

"This would have been easier for you if I was naked, wouldn't it? I thought about it, but lying around naked in a dark mine until you showed up, well, it seemed a little creepy. Look at Lucien's painting, which is lovely, by the way, before you answer." She grinned, to no effect at all. *Oh balls,* she thought, *this could be going better.*

"I mean," said Lucien, "what does Juliette do, when she's not possessed by you?"

"I am Juliette."

"Yes, you've said that," said Henri. "But who is the real Juliette?"

"And when are you going to wipe her memories and kill her?" asked Lucien.

Balls! Balls! Balls! Great, fiery, dangling balls of the gods!

She took a deep breath before continuing. "Juliette is different. She didn't exist before I created her. I really *am* her, she is me."

"So you conjured her out of thin air?" asked Henri.

"Not exactly out of thin air. I have to start with something. I need the meat, so to speak. I found the body of a drowned beggar in the morgue and I shaped Juliette out of that and made her live. I created her for you, Lucien, to be exactly what you would want. To be with you, perfect, just for you."

"No." Lucien rubbed his eyes as if pushing back a rising migraine. "No."

"Yes, Lucien, my *only*, my *ever*, for you."

He looked distressed. "So I've been shagging a drowned beggar from the morgue?"

"And at the same time you were with me?" Henri said. "Possessing Carmen?"

Lucien leapt to his feet. "Slut!"

"Drowned, dead, duplicitous slut!" Henri added.

"Wait, wait, wait," she said. "Not at the same time."

"But Henri was seeing Carmen at the same time I was seeing you for the first time!"

"Not at exactly the same time. I can't do that. I can only go from one to another."

"So it's like changing trains for you?" said Lucien. "Get off at one artist, get onto another."

She nodded. "That's not a bad way to put it."

"That's a horrible way to put it," said Lucien. "What happens to the train you were just on, I mean the body you leave to go to another?"

"They carry on with their lives. I went from Camille Monet to others dozens of times, back and forth."

"But you said Juliette doesn't have another life. She's you? What happened to Juliette when you took over Carmen?"

"She sleeps a lot," said Juliette.

"When you were first around, Carmen spent weeks with me," said Henri.

"I said *a lot*."

"And when you left?" said Lucien. "When you went away? Broke my heart, where did you go?"

"Vincent was a great talent," she said. "I didn't want to go. I don't always get to choose."

"You left Paris to go after Vincent? As Juliette?"

"Yes, as Juliette. Juliette always has to be nearby now, no matter what body I'm in, so I had to go. The Colorman wanted him to paint with the Sacré Bleu. I had to go. I'm sorry."

"And Carmen nearly died when you left her," said Henri forlornly.

"That's what she does," spat Lucien. "She takes them, she uses them, uses the artist, then she leaves and they die, not knowing what has happened to them. You leave the artists broken, grieving."

"There's always a price, Lucien," she said softly, looking down. She wasn't prepared for him to be angry with her. It hadn't occurred to her that he could be, and it hurt. It confused her and it hurt.

"A price? A price?"

"Yes," she said. "Do you think great art comes at no cost? There's a price to be paid."

"And how will you collect for my painting of you? Kill this person, this *thing* I call Juliette?"

Now she stood and slapped him, pulling the force of the blow at the last second so she didn't shatter his cheekbone.

"It's him! It's the Colorman who decides. I am a slave, Lucien! I am bound to him, to his power to make the blue. I do what he wants. He makes the color, I inspire the artist to paint, then the Colorman uses the painting to make more Sacré Bleu. More goes into it, must go into it, than just the paint. Love, passion, the force of life, even pain goes into the Sacré Bleu, and the color keeps the Colorman alive forever. Forever, Lucien! And without the Sacré Bleu, there is no Juliette. No muse. Without it, I don't exist. So I do what he wants, and I live, and others grow sick, and suffer, and die because of it." She was crying now, screaming at him through tears, feeling as if he was falling, spinning away from her.

"That's the price, and he always demands it, and I collect, but it is not my choice. I am a slave."

Lucien snatched her hand out of the air and held it to his heart. "I'm sorry."

She nodded, furiously, but turned her face away from him so he wouldn't see her. Suddenly Toulouse-Lautrec was beside them, snapping a crisp linen handkerchief from his breast pocket and presenting it to her.

"Mademoiselle, *s'il vous plaît*," he said.

She took the handkerchief and dabbed her eyes and nose, sniffled into it, hid behind it, taking her hand from Lucien's chest to fuss with strands of her hair that were sticking to her face. Then she peeked over the handkerchief and noticed that Henri was grinning at her. She looked to Lucien, who was grinning as well.

"What?" she said.

"Nothing," said Lucien.

"What? What?" she said. Wretched creatures, men. Were they laughing at her pain? She looked at Henri. "What?"

"Nothing," he said.

"You're grinning at me like lunatics? I am a creature of awesome power and divine aspect. I am the spark of invention, the light of man's imagination. I raise you drooling monkeys from rubbing your own pathetic shit on the rocks to bringing beauty and art to your world. I am a force, the fearsome muse of creation. I am a fucking goddess!"

"I know," said Henri.

"And you're grinning at me?"

"Yes," said Lucien.

"Why?"

"Because I nailed a goddess," said Lucien.

"Me too," said Henri, grinning enough now to unseat his *pince-nez*. "Although not at the same time."

"Oh for fuck's sake," said the muse.

ONCE IT WAS DETERMINED THAT LUCIEN AND HENRI WERE, INDEED, WRETCHED creatures with ethical compasses that pivoted around a point at their groins, which is to say, men, and that Juliette was also a creature of abstract, if not altogether absent, ethics herself, although with some fealty to beauty, which is to say, a muse, it was further determined, by unanimous consent, that in order to proceed with her revelation, more alcohol would be required, which left only to be decided the matter of where.

They wound their way up the butte with no particular destination in mind.

"We're out of cognac at the studio," said Henri, wanting very much to ask Juliette if somewhere, somehow, he might see Carmen, *his* Carmen, again.

"My apartment is too small," said Lucien. "And the bakery is out of the question." He wanted to be alone with Juliette, to lose himself in her presence, but his desire was somewhat dampened by the fear that she might murder him.

"How *is* your mother?" asked Juliette, wondering if there might not be a perfect amount of cognac that would ease the struggle of making a confession without releasing the impulse to kick portholes in the kidneys of her confessors and get on about her day.

"She sends her regards," said Lucien.

"Was that a breadboard she hit me with?"

"*Crêpe* pan."

"She's a strong woman."

"She didn't really send her regards. I was making that up."

"She's always been very kind to me," said Henri. "But I've never almost killed her son."

"Or broken his heart," said Lucien.

"It was for art, you know? I'm not a monster," said Juliette.

"You take people's lives, their health, their loved ones," said Lucien.

"I'm not *always* a monster," she said, pouting.

"A monster with an exquisite bottom," said Henri. "Speaking from a purely aesthetic point of view."

They were just passing by a tobacco shop where a gruff-looking woman stood in the doorway and scowled at them, rather than nodding the usual *bonsoir*.

"Perhaps we should discuss my bottom in a more discreet locale," said Juliette.

"Or not at all," said Lucien.

"You painted an enormous nude of me, Lucien. Did you think no one would notice?"

"It's hidden down a mine."

"It was the only place I could think to hide it that was close to Bruant's club."

"I have a fully stocked bar at my apartment," said Toulouse-Lautrec.

And so they found themselves in Toulouse-Lautrec's parlor, drinking brandy and discussing the awkward business of modeling for classical motifs.

"You know what I hated most about posing for *Leda and the Swan*?" said Juliette. "The part where you have to bonk the swan."

"If it's all about the painting, why don't you just become the painter?" asked Henri.

"I've done that a couple of times, become the painter. It doesn't seem to work to make the color. It turns out I have no artistic talent. Although I was able to inspire paintings also as a model at those times."

"Berthe Morisot?" asked Lucien.

"Yes." Juliette drained her glass and held it out for Henri to refill. "Don't misunderstand, I loved standing there with the others, our easels all lined up, painting the same motif. Cézanne, Pissarro, Monet, Renoir, sometimes Sisley and Bazille as well. Cézanne and Pissarro dressed in their high boots and canvas jackets, like they were on an expedition in the country. Cézanne wearing that ridiculous red sash to show he was from the South, not a Parisian, and Pissarro carrying that heavy walking staff, even if we were only on the banks of the Seine, painting Pont-Neuf. Me in my spring dress, looking completely out of place among all the men, but one of them, accepted by the Rejected."

She sighed and smiled. "Lovely Pissarro. Like everyone's favorite uncle. I remember one time we were all at a showing of our work at Durand-Ruel's gallery, and one patron saw me among the male painters and called me a *gourgandine,* a hussy. Pissarro punched the man in the face and stood over him with Renoir and the others while he lectured him, not about my lady's honor, but about my value as a great painter. Gentle Pissarro. So fierce in truth. So gallant." She raised her glass and drank to Pissarro.

"You really have great affection for him, don't you?" asked Lucien.

"I love him. I love them all. You have to love them all." Again she sighed, rolled her eyes like a dreamy teenager. "Artists . . ."

"Renoir says that," said Henri. "He says you must love them all."

"Who do you think taught him that?" She smiled over her snifter. Her eyes shone from the brandy, sparkled with mischief, reflected yellow highlights from the gaslights, which threw a spectral halo off her dark hair as well. The painters were having a hard time following the conversation and not getting lost in the way the light fell on her.

"You taught him?" said Lucien. "As his Margot?"

She nodded.

"Wait, wait, wait," said Henri. "If Berthe didn't make the painting for the Colorman, then—"

"Manet," said Juliette. "He worshipped Berthe and painted her—me—her, often. And I was Victorine before that, for his *Olympia* and *Déjeuner sur l'herbe.* That was about the sex, like a bunny with Victorine. Manet and his models made a lot of the Sacré Bleu for the Colorman."

"But as far as I know, both Berthe Morisot and Victorine Meurent are alive and healthy," said Henri. "You said there was always a price."

"Manet's suffering over never being able to be with Berthe and, finally, his own life." She became melancholy as she said it. "Dear, dear Édouard paid the price."

"Manet died of syphilis," said Lucien. "Henri and I were just discussing it."

"Yes," she said. "It's often syphilis."

"I don't understand," said Lucien. "Why syphilis?"

"It's a way for their dick to kill them. I'm a goddess, Lucien, there's nothing we like better than irony. It's really the only sense of order we have." She drained her snifter and held it out for a refill. "It's slow, but before all the madness and amputations set in, so many paintings!"

"Well that's depressing," said Henri. "I was sure it was a myth."

"But Vincent?" said Lucien. "Him you shot?"

"I don't shoot people. The Colorman did it. What a waste. Vincent's pain should have been the Colorman's payment."

"Then he painted you as Juliette?" asked Lucien.

"They don't have to paint me for me to inspire them. They just have to paint."

Lucien and Henri stared across the parlor at each other, each wondering how it was that they could discuss the murder of their friends and heroes over brandy, with a goddess. An increasingly drunken goddess.

"We need to drink more," said Lucien.

"A toast!" said Henri.

"To Vincent!" said Lucien, raising his glass.

"And Theo!" said Henri, raising his.

"And Theo's syphilis!" said Juliette, raising her glass and sloshing brandy all over Henri's rug.

Lucien lowered his glass slowly. "Theo too?"

"And syphilis!" said Juliette, toasting gaily.

"Theo wasn't even a painter," said Henri, ruining a perfectly good toast.

"Well I had to do something." She was both slurring and sloshing her brandy for emphasis. "The Colorman wanted to kill you all, both, everyone. Not that it matters to the little turd. He still wanted to shoot you. To clean up, he said. Which is why I took the last of the Sacré Bleu and ran away."

"So you're free."

"Not exactly. He just hasn't found me yet. That's why I had to hide in the dark. If I'm in the dark, he can't find me. The Sacré Bleu doesn't really work in the dark. That's why we couldn't paint in Henri's dismal studio." She sloshed what was left of her brandy at Toulouse-Lautrec. "That studio is dismal, Henri. No offense. You're a painter, you need light. Aw, remember that window in your other studio, such nice light—"

"But you're not in the dark now," Henri said, interrupting her musing. "Won't he find you?"

"No. Because I shot him."

"But that doesn't make any sense, and you said you didn't shoot people," said Lucien.

"What are you, a painter or the people-shooter counting person man? I fucking shot him. In the chest. Five times. Maybe six times. No, five." She leaned in close to Lucien and started to fall forward out of her chair. He caught her but then had to catch himself and ended up rolling back onto the divan as she fell onto him, her face in his lap.

"So you're free?" said Henri.

She answered, but her voice was muffled by Lucien's crotch. He kissed the back of her head, then turned her face toward Henri, who was accustomed to being around the intoxicated and so repeated himself automatically.

"So you're free?" he said.

"It's not that simple."

"Of course not," said Lucien. "And I was worried that everything was getting entirely too simple."

"Hey, fuck-bubble, am I the muse of sarcasm? No! No, I'm not. You are out of order, Monsieur Lessard. Out of fucking order." She tried to push herself up to look him in the eye but settled for fixing a steely gaze into his middle waistcoat button.

"I have never heard a goddess swear before," said Henri.

"Fuck off, Count Tiny Pants!" said the muse, who braced her forehead into Lucien's groin against her next expulsion.

"Or vomit," said Toulouse-Lautrec. "Look, it's blue."

Twenty-five

THE PAINTED PEOPLE

Britannia, Northern Frontier of the Roman Empire, A.D. 122

QUINTUS POMPEIUS FALCO, PROVINCIAL GOVERNOR OF BRITANNIA, WAS pacing the veranda of his villa at the edge of the frontier as he dictated a letter to his secretary, a report to Emperor Hadrian. It was a simple report, but one he was not happy about making. He had lost the Ninth Legion of the Roman army.

> *Most Exalted Caesar:*
>
> *It is with great consternation I report that having been sent into the south of the Caledonia district, in the northernmost territories of Britannia, to restore order to savage people we have come to call the Picts, and bring them under the Empire's control, that the Emperor's Ninth Legion, numbering four thousand legionaries and officers, has failed to send any dispatches for thirty days and is presumed lost.*

"What do you think?" Falco asked his secretary.

"'Lost,' sir?" said the scribe.

"Right," said Falco. "Somewhat vague, isn't it?"

"A bit."

Thus, the governor continued:

> And by "lost," I do not mean to imply that the Ninth is
> somehow wandering around this accursed, sunless, moldering
> shithole of a province, trying to solve a navigation problem; what I
> mean is they have been wiped out, defeated, decimated, destroyed,
> and murdered to a man. The Ninth has ceased to be. The Ninth has
> not been misplaced; the Ninth is no longer.

"That clears it up, don't you think?" asked Falco.

"Perhaps some context, sir," suggested the secretary.

The governor grumbled, then continued:

> In the past, the Picts have met our expansion into Caledonia
> with sporadic resistance from small bands of the savages with
> no apparent organization or bond beyond their common
> language. However, recently, their forces have united into a large
> army. They seem to be able to anticipate our tactics and attack
> our troops in the roughest countryside, where our war machines
> cannot travel, and our ranks are necessarily broken by terrain,
> as well as coordinated attacks and feints by multiple small
> bands of attackers. One prisoner, captured a fortnight ago, told
> us through a slave who understands their abominable language
> that the tribes have been united by a new king that they call the
> Colorbringer, who travels with a mystical warrior woman, who
> leads their army. Primitive myths or not, these "Painted People"
> represent a formidable threat to the Empire here at the end of our
> supply lines, and without troops to replace the Ninth, as well as

another two legions with provisions, I fear that we may not be able to hold the northern border against them.

    I eagerly await your instructions.

In fealty,

Quintus Pompeius Falco

Governor, Britannia

Falco walked to the edge of the veranda and stared out over the hills. In his mind's eye he saw olive trees, lemon trees, a vineyard ripening under the warm Etruscan sun. What he really saw were gray stones jutting like jagged teeth through the mossy hills and a low fog creeping through the valleys under ash-colored clouds.

"Enough context?" asked the governor. "Or shall I go on about the immediacy of securing this miserable bog and subduing these blue-stained apes for the glory of Rome?"

"Is it true, sir?" asked the secretary. "About the Picts uniting under a king?"

Falco turned on his heel to face the scribe, who flinched under the scrutiny. "They swallowed up a Roman legion, the most awesome engine of war the world has ever known; who cares if it's true? They are dangerous."

"So, we are sure the Ninth is lost to the Picts?"

"You didn't see their message then?"

"No, sir. I don't leave the villa."

"Sentries found the head of the legion's commander on a stake. Outside of the walls of the fort—not on the edge of the frontier, but right here at my home. His crested helmet was still in place, and tacked to it a message written on a sheepskin in their infernal blue paint."

"Written, sir? The savages have writing?"

"It was written in Latin. As perfect as if you had drawn the letters yourself, scribe. It read: 'Sorry. Accident. Couldn't be helped.'"

"What does it mean?" asked the scribe.

Just then a cry came out of the sky, like a hundred hawks calling at once, and Falco saw a jagged blue line forming out of the mist at the top of the hills to the north—a line of warriors. Another call, and the tops of the hills to the east were outlined in blue. Another screech, and the western hilltops were turning blue with warriors, moving like a torrent down on the fort, and the Roman garrison within its gates.

"It means we are never going to see Rome again," said Falco.

THEY HAD WALKED OUT OF THE FOREST AND INTO ONE OF THE VILLAGES OF the Picts, having traveled across Europe to get there—following a rumor, a whisper, a secret passed under the breath of those who had been conquered and then enslaved by the Romans.

"These crazy fucks paint themselves blue all over," said Bleu. "I'm telling you, Poopstick, these are our people. They're going to fucking love us!"

She wore only a loincloth threaded over a wide leather belt and two wasp-waisted Roman short swords she'd taken off dead legionaries in Iberia. Her hair was woven into five long plaits, encrusted with the Sacré Bleu, which was also smeared over her skin in rough, finger-shaped streaks. She had once been a girl of the tall, fair-skinned, Teutonic tribes that lived above the Rhine, but for months now she had been only Bleu.

"It's wet and cold here," said the Colorman.

He wore an ankle-length, unsheared sheepskin tunic that was snarled with sticks, leaves and burrs at its fringe, and a sheepskin hat that came down to his eyes. From a distance, he looked like an abused and unattractive lamb.

"You'll see," said Bleu. "They're going to love us."

They gave all the Sacré Bleu they had carried with them to the Picts, who mixed it with animal fat and painted each other's faces and bodies and found themselves, as a tribe, in communion with a goddess, sharing visions of passion and glory and beauty and blood, for theirs was the art of war.

The Greeks had called her a *daemon* (who inhabited artists and stoked them with fires of outrageous invention), the Romans called her a *genius* (for they believed not that one *was* a genius but that one *had* a genius, a patron spirit of inspiration, that must be fed with brilliance of mind, lest it move on to a more spritely host, leaving one as stagnant and dull as ditch water), but the Painted People called her Leanan Sidhe, a singular force, a goddess-lover who rode you, man or woman, into the ecstatic light and took life and love and peace as her price for a momentary glimpse of eternity. All would rise and fuck and fight and die for Leanan Sidhe! Sing praise! Howl and rake your nails across the moon in the embrace of Leanan Sidhe! Dash yourself on the rocks, lick the sweet nectar of death from the breasts of Leanan Sidhe! Fall upon your enemies with the spark of an immortal in your eye! For the Painted People! For the Colorbringer! For Leanan Sidhe!

And when they were spent, lying exhausted in slick mounds of flesh and fluids, the Colorman built his fires, sang his chant, stomped his awkward dance, and with a wicked black glass blade, scraped the sacred blue from the very skin of the writhing Leanan Sidhe.

She was right. They fucking loved them.

THE PAINTED PEOPLE CAME OUT OF THE HILLS IN A GREAT BLUE WAVE. Leanan Sidhe and the Colorbringer, their king, stood on their fighting litter atop the backs of two oxen, led by a dozen men with shields. The king was in front, strapped to a frame at his waist, quivers of javelins at his sides. Leanan Sidhe held a timber crossbeam behind the king, with a rack of the heavier *gaesum* spears at her back, their cruelly barbed brass points, as wide as shovels, looking like pickets in Death's garden fence.

No Roman lookout had survived long enough to raise the alarm until the Picts were already in sight of the fort. By the time the cavalry was mounted and the archers on the walls, the Pictish horde had closed off any escape from the compound.

At the edge of bow range, the Picts began to circle, swinging clay pots of flaming pitch around their heads on lanyards and hurling them into the kill zone between their lines and the walls, until the ground around the Roman fort was a black, smoking hell and the Picts but blue demons beyond the fire.

Pict arrows came down on the Romans from every direction. Legionaries sought cover from one threat, only to find death raining down from another. The cavalry was sent through the gates to break the Pict ranks, but no sooner was the column outside before the oxen-borne litter rumbled out of the flames and the screech of the blue-woman atop it caused their horses to rear.

Her first spear took a cavalry captain in the chest, knocking him back like he'd been tied to a stake. The Colorbringer hurled a javelin from each hand, taking an archer off the wall with the first, the second driving through the wooden rampart to impale a slave carrying water to douse the flames on the walls. A cry went up from the Picts at the sight of their king's kills, and the whirling mass of blue warriors closed in on the fort.

Roman arrows thunked into the wooden litter around them. A Pict shield bearer fell and was trampled by the heavy oxen. Leanan Sidhe took an arrow in the thigh, and her next thrown lance cleaved the archer's helmet and took off the top of his head. As she wrenched out the arrow, the Colorman was hit in the chest with one—two—three arrows, their iron tips passing through to stick out his back.

A cry of fury went up among the Picts. The Romans had the range now and a half dozen arrows pinned the Colorman to the wooden frame to which he was strapped.

"Ouch," said the Colorman. "I hate arrows."

"I know," said Leanan Sidhe. She reached forward and snatched out the arrows that protruded from his back, held the bloody shafts aloft, and screamed at the Romans. The scream echoed across the ranks. The Colorman slumped in his harness, his head lolling with the movement of the oxen. She pulled the rest of the arrows from his chest, threw them aside, then grabbed the little man by the ears and shook his head.

"Up, Poopstick, up!" she said. "They have to see you take the arrows and rise again. Fight!"

The Colorman opened one eye and his head came up. "It's cold. I hate the cold," he said, grabbing a javelin in each hand and sending them sailing over the walls into the fortress. "And I hate arrows."

When the litter reached the walls, Leanan Sidhe leapt from her perch, caught the top of the rampart, and vaulted to her feet atop the wall just as an arrow caught her in the side. She whirled, drawing her swords as she did, and looked into the wide eyes of a terrified archer, who was trying to nock another arrow. He turned to run as she fell on him and took off his arms, leaving him to bleed out, then hacked her way through Roman flesh as the Picts placed their ladders and came over the walls in swarms of blue bloodlust.

A half-hour later, every Roman had fallen, every slave taken from Caledonia had been freed, and the crooked little king of the Picts stood on the roof of the villa, a few arrows still protruding from his chest and back, holding aloft the head of Quintus Pompeius Falco, provincial governor of Britannia, whose last thought had been: *These crazy fucks really are painted blue.*

Behind the Colorbringer, the muse, Leanan Sidhe, smeared Sacré Bleu over the golden Roman eagle staff and held it over her head as the Painted People chanted her name.

Paris, Île de la Cité, 1891

WITH ONLY THE POWER OF A FEW CACHED PAINTINGS, AND NOT THAT OF TEN thousand blue-painted Pictish warriors, it took the Colorman until the next evening before he could regenerate from the gunshot wounds Bleu had inflicted upon him. Fortunately, a morgue worker who was sweeping up got too close and now lay desiccated and dead on the floor, the life drawn out of him.

The Colorman slid off the morgue slab to the cold floor. Bullets pooped from his wounds and plopped on the stone as he limped naked around the room looking for something to wear. All the dead were either naked, too ripe, or too tall for him to use their clothes, so he settled on a white mortician's coat that trailed out behind him as he went. The morgue attendant pretended not to see him as he passed, figuring that a spontaneous reanimation would require paperwork that he did not wish to fill out.

It was only three blocks back to the flat, and while it was a very public three blocks, and in the early evening, a time when all classes were out on the street, he went just the same. Gentlemen looked past him and ladies averted their gaze as he crossed the bridge from Île de la Cité into the Latin Quarter. He was near Notre-Dame Cathedral, where often were found cripples and freaks looking for charity, so the crooked little man with the overhanging brow, dragging the tails of a long white coat, attracted no more attention than any other unfortunate soul.

He rang the bell at the building on rue des Trois-Portes and the concierge yelped and leapt back when she answered the door, a woman whose size and cynicism had caused many years to pass since her last yelp *or* leap. The novelty pleased the Colorman to no end, and he had the urge to pull open his coat for a full penis presentation in celebration, but feared it might be gilding the lily, so he pressed on.

"*Bonsoir,* Madame," said the Colorman. "Could you let me in? I seem to have forgotten my key."

"But, Monsieur," said the concierge, raising a professionally buoyant eyebrow of suspicion. "I thought you were dead."

"A scratch, only. Accident. Couldn't be helped. The new maid was cleaning the gun and it fired."

"You were shot five times. I heard the shots."

"She's not a very good maid. I think we will have to let her go."

"Your niece said you were attacking the girl."

"Scolding her for her bad cleaning. Madame, let me in, please."

"The whole flat is covered in blue powder, monsieur."

"It is? That's the last straw. That maid is fired."

"She was naked. She barely spoke any French. The police took her away wrapped in a sheet."

"I will give you fifty *francs*, Madame, but my money is in the flat, so you have to let me in first."

"Welcome home," said the concierge, swinging the door wide and stepping aside.

"Did you feed Étienne?" asked the Colorman.

Paris, Montmartre, 1891

"SO YOU SEE, SHOOTING HIM IS NOT ENOUGH," SAID JULIETTE. "I HAVE TO GO back."

They were sharing a baguette and butter with coffee at the Café Nouvelle Athènes in Place Pigalle. Juliette had volunteered to buy breakfast, since she was the only one with any money left.

Outside, around the fountain in the square, models, young women and a few men, were lined up waiting to be hired. Artists in search of a model need only come to the "parade of models" to find a subject, and with a few *francs*, the contract would be sealed. Those girls who were not lucky enough to be hired by an artist might move down the boulevard to sell their wares in a different way. There was a fluid line between prostitute and model, dancer and whore, mistress and madame; all were denizens of the *demimonde*.

"You're really not hungover at all?" asked Lucien, who experienced something akin to seasickness every time he turned his head to look around the café.

"Muse," explained Henri. Then to Juliette, he said, "So, you and the Colorman are the reason Hadrian built his wall across Britain?"

She nodded modestly. "Inspiration is my business."

"He built that wall because he was *afraid* of the Picts," said Lucien, jealous that he was not emperor of Rome and could not build a wall across a country for her.

"Or annoyed by them," said Henri.

"*Mon Dieu!* For painters, you don't understand inspiration at all," said the muse.

"You're not Jane Avril, are you?" asked Henri, recoiling from the bite of a shifty suspicion.

"No," said Juliette. "I have not been the pleasure of her company."

"Oh good," said Henri. "Because I think she is very close to going to bed with me, and I would like to think she responds to my charm and not a proclivity for the color blue."

"I assure you, Henri, it is your charm," said Juliette, laughing musically, leaning over and brushing Henri's hand with her fingertips.

"Perhaps then, mademoiselle, you and Lucien can accompany me to the Moulin Rouge this evening and help convince the lady to view me on the horizontal, as that is where my charm is most compelling."

"It's like breakfasting with a goat," said Lucien.

"I'm sorry, Henri, but I can't," said Juliette.

"A goat in a hat," said Lucien.

"I really have to return to the Colorman. I have no choice."

"You can't," said Lucien. "Stay with me. Make him come after you. I'll defend you."

"You can't," she said.

"Then we'll run away. You're the one who travels through time and space, right? We'll go hide somewhere."

"I can't," she said. "He can compel me to return to him. I told you, I am a slave."

"Well, what then?" Lucien nearly fell out of his chair trying to move to her side, then caught himself on the table.

"I won't be free as long as he lives."

"But you said yourself, he can't be killed," said Henri.

"He can't be killed as long as there are paintings made with unharvested Sacré Bleu. That is my theory. When I saw the Manet nude, I thought that was my chance. I thought that painting must be what protected him, but now I know there are others, or it's something else. He's alive. I can feel him pulling me back."

"I don't understand," said Lucien. "What can we do?"

She leaned into the center of the table and the two painters leaned in for the conspiracy. "I've taken the Sacré Bleu we made with the Manet nude. It's in the mine with your *Blue Nude*. He'll need more. Gauguin is leaving for Tahiti, so I will go to the artist he's found for me. A Monsieur Seurat."

"Seurat's a *peintre optique*," said Henri. "He paints with tiny dots of pure color. Enormous canvases. He'll take years to complete a painting."

"Exactly," she said. "The Colorman will have to go wherever he has the other paintings hidden. I know they have to be close, because I was only gone a day before he came with the Manet. And the canvas wasn't rolled, it was on the original stretchers, so he couldn't have traveled far with it. There was no crate. When he goes to get another to use for the making of the Sacré Bleu, then you can follow him, destroy the paintings, and make him vulnerable."

"And why haven't you done that?" asked Henri.

"Don't you think I've tried? I can't. One of you has to do it."

"And if we do this, you will be free?" asked Lucien. "And we can be together?"

"Yes."

"And Jane Avril will go to bed with me?" asked Henri.

"That has nothing whatever to do with this," said Juliette.

"I know, but I was wondering if you might intercede on my behalf, since you have broken my heart. Just *influence* her until we're in bed, out of gratitude for helping you to gain your freedom."

"No!" said Lucien.

Juliette smiled. "Dear Henri, she will be yours and there will be no enchantment but your delightful presence."

"Fine then, I'm in," said Henri. "Let's rid the world of this Colorman."

"Oh, my heroes," she said, taking each of their hands and kissing them. "But you must be very careful. The Colorman is dangerous and crafty. He's been the end of hundreds of painters."

"Hundreds?" said Henri, a quaver in his voice.

"She smells suspiciously of lilac and can put either leg behind her head while singing 'La Marseillaise' and spinning on the other foot." *Jane Avril at the Jardin de Paris* (poster)—Henri Toulouse-Lautrec, 1893

Interlude in Blue #4: A Brief History of the Nude in Art

Hey, have a look at these!" said the muse.

Twenty-six

THE THE, THE THE, AND THE
COLOR THEORIST

JULIETTE BREEZED INTO THE FLAT AS IF MAKING A STAGE ENTRANCE. SHE paused by the hall tree for applause, which, not surprisingly, did not come, since it was only her and the Colorman in the flat.

"You're angry, aren't you?" said the Colorman.

"No, not at all," she said. "Why would you say that?"

"You shot me. Five times."

"Oh, that. No, that wasn't me. That was the island girl. I jumped into this body to help Juliette adjust her hat, and before I looked around, Vuvuzela had a gun and was shooting you. Where did she get a pistol, anyway?"

"It was mine. Five times."

"I'm sorry, I wasn't thinking. Juliette is so peaceful when she's unoccupied, I'd forgotten how disturbing it can be to suddenly wake up naked, painted blue, with a crooked little monster standing over you holding a knife."

"What are you trying to say?" Sometimes she was more subtle than he liked.

"That to a young girl, you can be a horrifying nightmare." She smiled.

"In what way?"

"Penis," she explained.

"But of course." He grinned.

The Colorman didn't remember exactly what had happened, except that it had hurt and he had been surprised, but the concierge said the island girl *had* been the one holding the gun when she came in.

"Well, where have *you* been?" he asked. "Where is the Sacré Bleu? Why didn't you come get me out of the morgue?"

"I thought you might be angry," said Juliette. She was fussing with the black chiffon scarf tied around her hat and noticed that there were still a few streaks of white gypsum dust on it where she'd brushed against something while in the mine. She went to the bedroom and made a show of pulling a hatbox from the closet. "I've been to Montmartre. The Sacré Bleu is gone. I used it to clean the memories of Lucien and Toulouse-Lautrec. They have no recollection of us ever having existed."

"But I was going to shoot them," the Colorman said, tapping a pistol, which he had gone out just that day and purchased from a scoundrel near the market at Place Bastille. The police had taken away his first one.

"Well, now there is no need."

"You used all of the Bleu for that?" He seemed to remember, although he was not sure, that they had made quite a lot of the color. It had been a big painting that had taken Manet a long time. "What did they paint? Where are the paintings?"

"No paintings. They painted me. In the old way. Right on my body. With olive oil."

"Both at the same time?"

"*Oui.*"

"*Oh là là.*" The Colorman rolled his eyes, imagining it. He liked the idea of painting the color on this Juliette body; then it occurred to him. "You washed it off?"

"I couldn't very well take a taxi across the city while painted blue, could I?" She wiped a finger behind her ear and the nail came out with a bit of blue pigment. "See, I missed some."

The Colorman scampered over to her, grabbed her hand, and put her finger in his mouth, then ran his tongue around her fingertip as he rolled his eyes. Yes, it was the Sacré Bleu. He spit her finger out.

"If you washed it off, we can't make more of the color. What about the painting the baker did of you? Did you get that?"

"Burned, so they couldn't use it to remember."

The Colorman growled and stomped around the room. "Well, you're going to have to get the island girl back, because Gauguin—"

"He's gone."

"What?"

"He's already purchased a ticket to the South Seas. He'll never finish a painting before he leaves. And the girl's family won't let her out of their sight."

"Well you need to find someone for this theorist Seurat to paint, and quickly. Maybe his wife, I don't know. And when you switch, drown this Juliette body."

"No," she said. "This body will be perfect. I have an idea."

IT WAS JUST AFTER DAWN ON MONTMARTRE. THE LOAVES HAD BEEN OUT OF the oven for only ten minutes and were still warm. Lucien felt the baguette hit him just above the right ear but wasn't quick enough to dodge the crumbs that went in his eyes as the loaf wrapped around his head.

"*Voilà!*" said Mère Lessard as she pulled the loaf away and surveyed the crunchy-chewy wiggle of the broken crust. "Perfect!"

"*Merde*, Maman!" said Lucien. "I'm twenty-seven years old. I know how to make bread. You don't have to hit me in the head with a loaf anymore to make sure it's right."

"Nonsense, *cher*," said Madame Lessard. "The old ways are the best. That's why we do them. And it is so good to have you back baking again. Your sister can do the job, but it takes a man's inborn carelessness to make a perfect baguette. Baking is art."

"I thought you hated art."

"Don't be silly." She lovingly brushed the breadcrumbs from his eyebrows, applying just a touch of mother spit to smooth them down. "Are these the hips of a woman who doesn't appreciate the art of baking?" The movement she made sent a wave traveling down her skirts, which snapped at the hem, sending up a small whirlwind of flour from the floor.

Lucien pulled out of her grasp and bolted out to the front with a basket of baguettes to avoid having to even consider his mother's question. He preferred to not think of his mother as having hips. He preferred to not think of her as a woman at all, more as a traveling mass of loving annoyance—a mother-shaped storm that inhabited the bakery and, in bringing rain for the growth of the living things over which she hovered, didn't mind scaring the piss out of them with a few thunderbolts from time to time.

He'd thought this way, had carried this mystical view of his mother, since he was a boy. In those days, the painter Cézanne would come into the bakery, usually with Monet, Renoir, or Pissarro, and he would almost hide behind his friends until Madame Lessard went to the back room, then the Provençal would wipe the sweat from his bald head with his sleeve and frantically whisper, "Lessard, you must get your wife under control. The way the tendrils are always falling from her *chignon,* and the way she smiles and sings in your shop—well, I'll say it: Lessard, your wife always appears freshly fucked. It's unnerving. It's indecent."

Père Lessard, along with the other artists, would laugh at the chagrined Cézanne. Little Lucien, as the son of a baker, thought that anything that was "fresh" must surely be a good, and would only learn later what Cézanne had been talking about, and then, after having a soul-chilling shudder, he would choose not to think of it again. Ever. Until, of course, for some reason, this morning she reminded him.

Lucien handed the basket of bread to Régine, who had been working the counter. "We need to hire a kid for Maman to hit with the baguette," he said. "You were supposed to have children by now for just that reason."

Régine looked at her brother, aghast that he would say such a thing, and without her saying a word, Lucien knew he had hurt her feelings.

"I'm sorry, *ma chère,*" he said. "I am a cad."

"Yes," she said.

She was about to elaborate on just what variety of cad he was when someone at the counter snarled, "Bread!"

Lucien looked over to see a bowler hat floating just over the counter, and beneath it, the simian visage of the Colorman.

Lucien took his sister by the shoulders, kissed her on the forehead, then steered her through the curtain into the back. "I'm sorry, I'm sorry, I'm sorry. Now, please, for the love of God, stay back here."

Lucien came back through the curtain wearing a big smile. "*Bonjour,* monsieur, how may I help you?"

"You are the painter, no?" said the Colorman.

"I am the baker," said Lucien, extending his hand over the counter, "Lucien Lessard."

The Colorman shook Lucien's hand while squinting at him and tilting his head, as if trying to lever his way past Lucien's smile to the lies behind it, or so it felt to Lucien. What was he doing here?

"I am the Colorman," said the Colorman. "I sell color."

"Yes, but what are you called? Your name?" said Lucien.

"The Colorman."

"But what is your surname?"

"Colorman."

"I see," said Lucien. "How may I help you, Monsieur Colorman?"

"I know where the girl is."

"What girl?"

"The girl in your painting. Juliette."

"I'm sorry, monsieur, I don't know what you're talking about. I don't have a painting of a girl and I don't know any Juliette."

The Colorman considered him again, tilted his head the other way. Lucien was trying to radiate innocence. He tried to assume the beatific look he'd seen on the Renaissance Virgin Marys in the Louvre, but he only succeeded in looking as if he were being touched inappropriately by the Holy Ghost.

"Two baguettes, then," said the Colorman.

Lucien exhaled with relief, then turned to retrieve the loaves and heard the bell over the door ring. When he turned back with the baguettes in hand, Le Professeur was standing behind the Colorman.

"*Bonjour,* Lucien," said the Professeur.

"*Bonjour,* Professeur," said Lucien. "Welcome home."

The Colorman looked from Lucien to the improbably tall and thin Professeur, then back to Lucien, then blinked.

"Excuse me," said Lucien. "Professeur, this is the Colorman. Monsieur Colorman, this is the Professeur."

The Professeur offered his hand to shake, and the Colorman just looked at it. "Your first name is '*The*'?" He seemed disturbed.

"Émile," said the Professeur. "Professeur Émile Bastard."

"Oh," said the Colorman, taking the Professeur's hand. "The Colorman."

"Charmed," said the Professeur. "You are a wise man, no doubt, having sought out the best baker in Paris."

"The painter?"

"I mean Lucien," said the Professeur.

"I have to go," said the Colorman. He hurried out the door without looking back. His donkey had been tied up outside, a large wooden case strapped to his back. The Colorman untied him and led him across the square.

They watched through the bakery window until he disappeared on the stairs down the butte to Pigalle, then the Professeur looked at Lucien.

"So that was him?"

"Yes."

"What is he doing here?"

"Juliette killed him a week ago."

"Not very thoroughly, evidently."

"I have much to tell you," said Lucien.

"And I you," said the Professeur.

"We'll go across the square to Madame Jacob's, have coffee," said Lucien. "I'll get Régine to watch the front." He peeked his head through the curtain. "Régine, could you watch the counter please, I need to speak with the Professeur."

The baguette hit Lucien square in the forehead and wrapped around his head, crunching in his ear.

"Perhaps *The Circus,* with all the figures off balance, ready to tumble down on each other in the next second, would be his portal back into life." *The Circus*—Georges Seurat, 1891

"Ouch! What—"

"Maman is right," said Régine, regarding the crust. "Perfect. Just double-checking."

GEORGES SEURAT STOOD BEFORE HIS PARTIALLY COMPLETED PAINTING *The Circus,* holding a small round brush loaded with red, trying to ascertain where, exactly, the next small red dot would go. Four identical brushes loaded with different colors poked through the fingers of his left hand, as if he had snatched some great, gangly insect out of the air and its multicolored legs were shot with rigor mortis or surprise. He was making a picture of a bareback rider standing atop a palomino, trying to convey the dynamic movement of the scene while meticulously forming the figures out of one dot of color placed next to a complementing color, laid down in harmony and contrast so that when one stood back, the scene formed for the first time in the mind of the viewer. It was a solid theory, and applying it in his major paintings, *The Bathers* and *A Sunday Afternoon on the Island of La Grande Jatte,* had brought him great success and had made him the unofficial leader of the Neo-Impressionists, but the process was the problem. It was too meticulous. It was too static. It took too damn long to do a painting. In ten years he had completed only seven major paintings; his last one, *The Models,* a scene from an artist's studio, with models undressing, had been panned by critics and rejected by the public as being a picture of daily life with all the life taken out of it. The nude models appeared as cold and sexless as marble pillars. And meanwhile, Degas and Toulouse-Lautrec were splashing their dancers and singers, acrobats and clowns across the public's consciousness with vivid, fluid vigor and movement. Seurat had invented and perfected a technique, pointillism, based on solid color theory, but now he felt imprisoned by it. Sometimes, it turned out, art was *what* you had to say, not *how* you said it.

At only thirty-one, Seurat felt used up, or at least weary of standing still, tired of the intellectual art of theory; he wanted to grasp the visceral, the sensual—grab the movement of life before it got away. Perhaps *The Circus*, with all the figures off balance, ready to tumble down on each other in the next second, would be his portal back into life.

As he placed a precise and tiny dot of red in the clown's hair, there was a knock at the door. Life interrupting art. He wanted to be angry, but in fact he was grateful. Perhaps it would be a delivery of supplies, or better, Signac or Bernard dropping by to see the progress on his painting. So much easier to discuss theory than to apply it.

He opened the door and nearly dropped the brushes, still splayed out of his left hand. It was a young woman, stunning in a satin dress the color of cinnamon, fair skinned with dark, nearly black hair, eyes as blue as sapphires.

"Pardon me, monsieur, but I understood that this is the studio of the painter Seurat. I am a model in need of work."

Seurat stood for an embarrassing moment just looking at her, sketching her in his mind's eye, then she smiled and jolted him out of his imagination. "I'm sorry, mademoiselle, but I have all my studies for the painting I am working on. Perhaps when I begin another—"

"Please, Monsieur Seurat, I am told that you are the greatest painter in Paris, and I am desperate for the work. I will pose nude. I don't mind. I won't get cold or tired."

Seurat forgot completely what he meant to say next. "But, mademoiselle—"

"Oh, I beg your pardon, monsieur," she said, extending her hand. "My name is Dot."

"Come in," said Seurat.

When Lucien and the Professeur arrived at Madame Jacob's *crémerie*, Toulouse-Lautrec was already seated at one of only three tall café tables, eating Camembert spread on bread, drinking espresso with a touch of cream floated over it. Seated with him, still in her overdone theatrical makeup, was a very thin, very tired Jane Avril. Lucien had never seen her in person but recognized her immediately from Henri's drawings and posters.

"Lucien, Professeur, have you met the great, the wonderful, the beautiful Jane Avril? Jane, my friends—"

"*Enchanté*," said the singer. She slid off her stool, steadied herself on the table, then presented an elegantly gloved hand each to Lucien and the Professeur, over which each bowed. She turned back to Henri, lifted his bowler hat, and placed a kiss on his temple. "And now, puppet, since you have someone to look after you, I am going home." She raised an eyebrow to Lucien. "He wouldn't let me go home unless I took him with me. Then what would I do with him?"

Lucien saw her to the door and offered to help her find a cab, but she elected to stumble down the long stairway to Pigalle, saying the brisk morning air might sober her up enough to sleep.

When Lucien joined them at the table, Henri threw a bread crust down on his plate. "I am a traitor, Lucien. I'm ashamed you've found me here eating some stranger's bread. I don't blame you if you abandon me. Everyone does. Carmen. Jane. Everybody."

Lucien signaled to Madame Jacob, who stood among her cheeses, to bring coffee for him and the Professeur and shrugged. He'd seen her at the bakery only an hour ago, so the pleasantries of the day had already been exchanged.

"First, Henri, you *are* eating my bread. Madame Jacob has been serving Lessard bread for fifty years, so you're not a traitor. And Mademoiselle Avril did not abandon you, she simply went home, exhausted, no doubt, after watching you drink all night, and if things had gone differently, and she'd taken you home and taken you to bed, you'd either be passed out or singing annoying sailor songs. Yours is a false melancholy, Monsieur Toulouse-Lautrec."

"Well," said Henri, picking up his bread again. "In that case, I feel better. How are you, Professeur? Anything interesting in Spain?"

"There has been a new cave discovered in the south, at Altamira. The drawings on the walls may be the oldest that have ever been found."

"How can you tell?" asked Lucien.

"Well, the interesting thing about that is my colleague and I have formulated a relative date, only relative, because of the color used in the drawings. It seems there is no blue in any of the drawings that remain."

"I don't understand," said Lucien.

"You see, mineral-based pigments for blue, azurite, copper oxide, and lapis lazuli, were not used until after three thousand B.C., when the Egyptians began to use them. Before that, the blue pigments used in Europe were all organic, like woad, which is made from crushing and fermenting the leaves of the woad shrub. Over the years, the organic pigments deteriorated, molded, were eaten by insects, so only the mineral pigments like clays, chalks, charcoals remain. If there's no blue pigment in the drawing, we can assume that it is at least five thousand years old."

"The Picts of Scotland used woad to paint themselves, didn't they?" asked Henri.

The Professeur seemed surprised at the painter's interjection. "Why yes, yes they did. How did you know that?"

"One of the few truths of history the priests at my school actually taught us."

"That's not true at all," said Lucien. Juliette had just told them about the Picts.

The Professeur drained his espresso and signaled to Madame for another. He seemed very excited now. "That is not all I saw in Spain. I may have some disturbing news about your Colorman. You see, when I was in Madrid, I went to the Prado and looked at their entire collection. It took days. But it was in a painting by Hieronymus Bosch that I saw the figure, amid hundreds of others in *The Garden of Earthly Delights,* a depiction of hell. It was a knotted, apelike figure, with spindly limbs, and he was torturing a young woman with a knife. And his hands and feet were stained with blue."

"But, Professeur," said Toulouse-Lautrec, "I saw the Boschs at the Uffizi in Florence when I went there with my mother as a boy. I remember that they are all filled with twisted, tortured figures. They gave me nightmares."

"True, but there was a plaque depicted in the painting, hung around the figure's neck, and on it was writing in Sumerian cuneiform. As you know, in addition to my other studies, I am an amateur necrolinguist—"

"It means he likes to lick the dead," explained Henri.

"It means he studies dead languages," corrected Lucien.

"Are you sure?"

"Yes," said the Professeur.

"My education is shit," said Henri. "Lying priests."

"Anyway," said the Professeur. "I was able to make out the cuneiform and translate it. The plaque read '*Colorman.*' As long as three hundred years ago, there was someone acting as your Colorman. I think it must have been some kind of warning from Bosch."

"It wasn't *a* Colorman, it was the same Colorman," said Lucien.

"I don't understand," said the Professeur. "Then he would be—"

Lucien held up a hand to stop the Professeur. "I told you, we have much to tell you. There's a reason that I said that Juliette killed a man whom you saw walking by not an hour ago."

Lucien and Henri told the Professeur of the Colorman, the Picts, all that Juliette had told them, all that they had experienced, and when they had finished, finally, and admitted that it was now on them, two painters, to vanquish the Colorman and free the muse, the Professeur said, "By Foucault's dangling pendulum, I have to rethink it all. Science and reason are a sham, the Age of Reason is a ruse, it's been magic and ritual all along. If this is true, can we even trust Descartes? How do we even know that we exist, that we are alive?"

"A question that often plagues me," said Toulouse-Lautrec. "If you'd like to accompany me to rue des Moulins, I know some girls there who, if they cannot convince you that you are alive, will at least help soothe your anxiety about being deceased."

"And now, puppet, since you have someone to look after you, I am going home." *Jane Avril* (poster)—Henri Toulouse-Lautrec, 1893

Twenty-seven

THE CASE OF THE
SMOLDERING SHOES

TWO MEN IN BROAD-BRIMMED HATS, ONE TALL, ONE OF AVERAGE HEIGHT, stood at the taxi stand at the east end of the Cimetière du Montparnasse, looking toward the entrance to the Catacombs across the square. One carried a black ship's signal lantern with a Fresnel lens, which he held by his side as if no one would notice; the taller one had a long canvas quiver slung over his shoulder, from which protruded the wooden legs of an artist's easel. Both wore long coats. Other than the lantern, they were conspicuous only in that they were standing at a taxi stand, at midday, with no intention of taking a taxi, and the shoes of the taller man were smoldering.

"Hey, your shoes are smoking," said the cabbie, who leaned against his hack, chewing an unlit cheroot and scowling. He had already asked them three times if they needed a taxi. They didn't. They were both peeping out from under the brims of their hats, surreptitiously checking on the progress of a little man in a bowler hat who was leading a donkey across the square.

"It is no concern of yours, monsieur," said the tall man.

"I think he's going into the Catacombs," said the shorter one. "This may be it, Henri."

"Are you two detectives?" asked the cabbie. "Because if you are, you are horrible at it. You should read this Englishman Arthur Conan Doyle to see how it is done. The new one is called *The Sign of the Four*. His Sherlock Holmes is very clever. Not like you two."

"The Catacombs?" Henri pulled his pant legs up so that the cuffs hovered above his shoes, showing his gleaming brass ankles. "I'm finally tall and I have to go into the Catacombs, where it will be a disadvantage."

"Perhaps the Professeur can design a new model powered by irony," said Lucien, tilting his head so the brim of his hat lifted to reveal his grin. The Loco-ambulators had allowed them to follow the Colorman at a distance for over a week, without revealing Henri's conspicuous height or limp, but now it seemed the steam stilts were going to become a distinct disadvantage.

"We have a little time." Lucien set the lantern down and crouched by Henri's feet. "We need to let him get ahead of us if we're going to follow him down there. You there, cabbie, help me get his trousers off."

"Messieurs, this is the wrong neighborhood and the wrong time of day for such a request."

"Tell him you're a count, Henri," said Lucien. "That usually works."

Five minutes later Toulouse-Lautrec, with his trousers rolled up and his long coat dragging the ground, led the way across the square. They'd given the cabbie five *francs* to watch the Loco-ambulators and showed him the double-barreled shotgun in the canvas quiver, borrowed from Henri's uncle, to let him know what would happen to him should he decide to abscond with the steam stilts. He, in turn, charged them two *francs* for a guaranteed—more or less—complete map of underground Paris.

Toulouse-Lautrec unfolded the map until he had revealed the seventh level below the city, then looked to Lucien. "It follows the streets as if on the surface."

"Yes, but with fewer cafés, more corpses, and it's dark, of course."

"Oh, well then, we'll just pretend we're visiting London."

The city of Paris had installed gaslights for the first few hundred yards of the Catacombs, as well as a man at the entrance who charged twenty-five *centimes* for the pleasure of looking at the city's bones.

"That shit is morbid, you know that, no?" said the gatekeeper.

"You're the gatekeeper of an ossuary," said Lucien. "You know that, yes?"

"Yes, but I don't go down there."

"Give me my change," said the baker.

"If you see a man with a donkey, tell him I turn the gaslights off at dark and he'll have to find his own way out. And report to me if he's doing anything unsavory down there. He goes down there and stays for hours at a time. It's macabre."

"You know you charge people money to look at human remains, no?" said Lucien.

"Are you going in or not?"

They went down the marble steps into wide tunnels lined with stacked tibiae, fibulae, femurs, ulnae, radii, and skulls. When they reached the iron gate with the sign that said NO VISITORS BEYOND THIS POINT, Lucien knelt down to light the signal lantern.

"We're going in there?" asked Henri, staring past the bars to infinite black.

"Yes," said Lucien.

Henri held the cabbie's map up to the last gas lamp. "Some of these chambers are massive. Surely the Colorman will see our lantern. If he knows he's being followed, he'll never lead us to the paintings."

"That's why the signal lantern. We close it down until we can only just see beyond our feet, so we don't trip. Keep it directed downward."

Lucien held a match to the wick, then, once it was going, adjusted the flame until it was barely visible.

"And how will we know which way he goes?"

"I don't know, Henri. We'll look for his lantern. We'll listen for the donkey. Why would I know?"

"You're the expert. The Rat Catcher."

"I am not the expert. I was seven. I went into the mine only far enough to set my traps, that was all."

"Yet you discovered Berthe Morisot naked and painted blue. If not an expert, you have extraordinary luck."

Lucien picked up the lantern and pushed open the gate. "We should probably stop talking. Sound carries a long way down here."

The arch that contained the iron gate was smaller than the rest of the vault and Lucien had to duck to go through. Henri walked straight through, until the easel he carried on his back caught the archway and nearly knocked him off his feet.

"Perhaps we should leave the easel here, just bring the shotgun."

"Good idea," said Henri. He pulled the shotgun from the canvas sleeve, then set the bag and the easel to the side of the gate in the dark.

"Breech broken," said Lucien, thinking that the next time Henri tripped, the gun might discharge, taking off one of their heads or some other appendage to which they might have a personal attachment.

Henri broke the shotgun's breech and dropped in two shells he'd had in his pocket, then paused.

Lucien played the hairline beam of light up and down his friend's face. "What?"

"We are going into these tunnels to kill a man."

Lucien had tried not to think of the specific act. He'd tried to keep the violence abstract, an idea, or better yet, an act based upon an ideal, the way his father had helped him through dispatching the rats when he was a boy and he'd find a suffering rodent still alive, squirming in the trap. "It is mercy, Lucien. It is to save the people of Paris from starvation, Lucien.

It's to preserve France from the tyranny of the Prussians, Lucien." And one time, when Père Lessard had drunk an extra glass of wine with lunch, "It's a fucking rat, Lucien. It's disgusting and we're going to make it delicious. Now smack it with the mallet, we have pies to make."

Lucien said, "He killed Vincent, he killed Manet, he's keeping Juliette as a slave: he's a fucking rat, Henri. He's disgusting and we're going to make him delicious."

"What?"

"Shhhhh. Look there, it's a light."

After only a minute out of the gaslights their eyes had adjusted to the darkness. In the distance they could see a tiny yellow light bouncing like a moth against a window. Lucien held the signal lantern so Henri could see him hold his finger to his lips for silence, then signal for them to move forward. He pointed the light down, so it barely cast the shadow of their feet. They followed the flame in the distance, Henri walking with a pronounced waddle to cover the heavy steps of his limp and to compensate for not having his walking stick.

At times, the flame would disappear and they found themselves trying to find some speck in the distance, and Henri remembered, as a very small boy, closing his eyes to sleep at night, only to see images on the back of his eyelids, moving like ghosts. Not afterimages, not memories, but what he was actually seeing in the absolute darkness of night and childhood.

As they stepped carefully, quietly, over the even, dusty floors of the underground, those images came to him again. He remembered seeing electric blue moving among the black, and sometimes a face would come at him, not an imagined specter, nothing that he had conjured, but a real figure made of darkness and blue that would charge him from out of the infinite nothing, and he would cry out. That was the first time, he realized, there in the Catacombs, that he had seen Sacré Bleu. Not in a painting, or a church window, or a redhead's scarf, but coming at him, out of the dark. And that was when he realized why he would kill the

Colorman. Not because he was evil, or cruel, or because he kept a beautiful muse as a slave, but because he was frightening. Henri knew then he could, he would, put down the nightmare.

"Can you get us out of here with that map?" Lucien whispered, his lips nearly touching Henri's ear.

"Maybe if we turn the lantern up," Henri whispered back. "The chambers are supposed to be marked for the streets above."

The Colorman's light stopped bouncing for a second and Lucien reached back to stop Henri. He slid the lens of the signal lantern closed. The donkey brayed and with the echo they realized that they were not looking down a long tunnel at the Colorman's light but through a vast, open chamber. Ever so gently, slowly, using his palm to dampen the sound, Henri closed the breech of the shotgun. They froze with the faint click, but what they thought was the Colorman reacting to their presence was, in fact, his playing his lantern over a wall, revealing a heavy brass ring set in the stone.

The Colorman set down his lamp, grasped the ring with both hands, and backed away, pulling what appeared to be a piece of the stone wall with him. The painters scurried forward with the cover of the noise, then paused when the Colorman turned to pick up his lantern. They were barely fifty meters away now; every scrape of the Colorman's foot, every snort of the donkey, sounded as if it were inside their heads.

The Colorman walked out of their sight, into a passageway or a room, perhaps, but the donkey waited by the open portal.

Lucien set the signal lantern on the ground, then leaned in until he felt Henri's hat brim against the bridge of his nose and whispered, "Please, do not shoot me."

He felt his friend shake his head, even heard him smile, something he hadn't thought possible up until then, and they crept forward, shoulder to shoulder. When they were only twenty meters away, Henri paused and cocked one of the hammers of the shotgun. The donkey flinched at the sound of the click.

"Who is that?" said the Colorman. "Who is there?"

He appeared in the doorway, holding his lamp high. "Dwarf! I see you!" He pulled a pistol from his waistband and pointed it toward them. Lucien dived out of the circle of light cast by the lantern as the Colorman fired. The bullet ricocheted off the chamber walls, sounding like an angry hornet. The donkey kicked and bolted into the darkness, leaving a trail of frightened braying that sounded like the perverse laughter of a dying consumptive psychopath. Lucien rolled to his feet to see the flash of the second shot. The report set his ears ringing, and the echo was lost in the high-pitched tone.

"I see you, dwarf!" said the Colorman. He raised the lamp above his head and charged forward, leading with the pistol. He cocked the hammer and aimed, but instead of the sharp crack of the pistol there was the roar of a large-bore shotgun and the Colorman's lamp exploded over his head, showering him and the stone floor behind him with flaming oil. He screamed, hideously, more out of outrage than pain, it seemed, and continued to advance, a walking pillar of flame, and to fire the pistol into the dark until it clicked, empty. Still he stumbled after his attacker into the dark.

"You fucks!" he growled, then he fell on his face and lay there sizzling, the flames jumping up and down his prostrate body—deep-blue flames.

By the light of the burning Colorman, Lucien could see Henri looking down on the corpse, the shotgun breech open, the gun draped over his forearm.

"Henri, are you all right?"

"Yes. Are you hurt?" He didn't look from the Colorman.

"No. He missed."

"At the last second I shot over his head. I was trying to frighten him. I didn't mean to hit him."

"You didn't."

"You won't tell Juliette I was a coward, will you?"

"No, that would be a lie."

"Do you mind if I take a sip of cognac? My nerves are somewhat jangled."

"I'll join you."

"We are medicating," said Toulouse-Lautrec. He pulled the silver flask from his inside pocket, unscrewed the cap, and handed it to his friend, revealing a distinct tremble in his hand. "Not celebrating."

"To life," said Lucien, toasting the rapidly blackening Colorman. He drank and handed the flask back to Henri. "I'd better get our lantern while I can still find it. I don't relish the idea of trying to get out of here with the candles I have in my coat pocket."

When Lucien returned with the lantern, Henri had already gone inside, had lit a candle, and was looking at the first of the paintings that were leaning against the walls in three stacks, sorted by size. Henri was playing the candle up and down a medium-sized portrait of a young boy with dark eyes and a dark shock of hair falling across his forehead.

"Lucien, I think this is a Pissarro. Bring the lantern. Look at it. It looks like Manet's and Cézanne's style rolled into one. I've never seen a Pissarro portrait that looked like this."

"Well he's painted with Cézanne since the sixties. It might be his influence on Cézanne you're seeing." Lucien opened the lens on the signal lantern all the way to fully illuminate the painting.

"But these dark eyes, haunted almost, the hair, this . . ." Henri looked from the painting, to Lucien, back to the painting.

"It's me," said Lucien.

"You? This is one of the paintings that Pissarro remembered painting that no one could remember seeing."

"Yes."

"And you don't remember posing for it?"

"No."

"Well, you were only a boy. Childhood memories blur—"

"No. She said she had only been both the painter and the model twice; once was Berthe Morisot. I am the other. She was me."

Henri stood in front of the largest canvas. The first was a raging seascape, the Sacré Bleu dominating the swamping of a ship.

"Turner," said Henri. "I don't understand. Was she a ship?"

"She doesn't have to be the model, she just has to be the artist's obsession," Lucien said, deadpan, pronouncing a fact, nothing more, a chilly calm coming over him as he was beginning to realize the impact the muse had effected on his life, on so many lives.

Lucien knelt to flip through the stack of smaller paintings. The first a Monet, a field of lupine. The next he didn't recognize, something Flemish, a peasant scene, old. The third was Carmen Gaudin, Henri's Carmen, sitting splay-legged on the floor, the top of her blue dress pulled down, revealing her nude back, hair pinned up, the same red scimitar swoops of fringe across her cheeks, the same pale skin, but unlike every picture he had ever seen of her, she was smiling, looking coquettishly over her shoulder at the painter, looking upward in false modesty. Lucien knew the look. He'd seen it dozens of times on Juliette's face, but only Henri

A moment later, Carmen looked over her shoulder.
La Toilette—Henri Toulouse-Lautrec, 1889

de Toulouse-Lautrec had ever seen it on Carmen Gaudin. He pushed the paintings back in place as if he were slamming the cover of a forbidden book and stepped back.

Toulouse-Lautrec leaned the large Turner forward until he could see the painting behind it, then nearly dropped the Turner and fought to catch it.

"Oh my," he said.

Lucien jumped to his side and gazed at the painting, a nude woman reclining on a divan draped with ultramarine satin.

"She is a large but a very fetching woman. I don't think I would have thought of her as a redhead before, more of a chestnut brunette, but then, her hair is always up in a *chignon* when I see her. With it down, here, where it trails over her hip, yes, she is very fetching indeed."

Lucien set the lantern down at Henri's feet and snatched the lit candle from his hand, splattering wax over the painting. "Burn them," he said, turning and walking out of the room. "Burn them all. Use some of the oil from the lamp to start them."

"I understand your consternation, but it is very well painted," said Henri, who had picked up the lantern and was still studying the nude.

"It's my mother, Henri."

"Look, it's signed. '*L. Lessard.*' "

"Burn it."

"Don't you want to see the others? There may be masterpieces here that no one has ever laid eyes on before."

"Nor will they ever. If we see them we may not be able to do this. Burn them." Lucien stepped out of the chamber and stood in the large vault, where blue flames were still playing across the tarry remains of the Colorman. He shivered.

Henri flipped the Turner back into place in front of the nude of Madame Lessard, then stepped back. "I killed the Colorman, I don't think it's fair that I have to burn the paintings, too. It seems sacrilegious."

"You've always said that you come from a long line of accomplished heretics."

"Good point. Come, hold your candle so I can see. I'm going to have to extinguish the lantern for a bit so I can pour out some oil."

A minute later the small chamber glowed like a glassblower's furnace, the light from the flames licking out into the large vault and dying with the snap of a serpent's tongue. Black smoke moved across the ceiling in inky waves.

Henri read the map by the light from the fire. "If we follow this wall, it will take us to the passage and stairs that lead to the next level."

"We should go, then."

"What about the Colorman's donkey?"

"There's no telling how far he's run, Henri. We've barely enough lamp oil to make it to the surface as it is. Perhaps he'll find his own way out. He's been down here before."

Toulouse-Lautrec folded the map and set out along the wall, using the unloaded shotgun as a crutch and limping badly now that stealth was no longer required.

"Are you in pain?" Lucien asked, holding the lantern high so his friend could see ahead.

"Me? I'm fine. This is nothing compared to killing a man and burning a room full of masterpieces."

"I'm sorry, Henri," Lucien said.

"But even that is nothing compared to the possibility that you may have shagged your mother and killed your father."

"That is *not* what happened."

"Well, then, what happened?"

"I don't know."

"Do you think your mother would pose for me? My interest is only as a painter."

"YOU KILLED MINETTE!"

They were the first words he said to Juliette when they found her waiting at Henri's studio.

"Who?" she said.

"Minette Pissarro. A little girl. I loved her and you killed her."

"It was you or her, Lucien. One of you had to pay. I chose her."

"You said that the Colorman chose."

"Yes, and he wanted you. I talked him out of it."

"You're a monster."

"Well, your mother is a whore."

"Only because you possessed her, too."

"Oh, you know about that?"

"I saw the painting."

"So the Colorman is dead? Really dead? I thought I felt him let go."

"Yes," said Henri. "I shot him. And the paintings are burned. You are free."

"That little bastard, he told me he used the nude of your mother years ago."

"So you killed my father, too?"

"What? Pfft. No. Silly. No, of course not. You know, Lucien, your father was a truly lovely man. He loved painting. Truly lovely."

Henri said, "Since you have been Lucien, and you have been Lucien's mother, then technically, he has slept—"

"My father died in his studio," Lucien said. "And none of his paintings were ever found. Explain that."

"Hey, look at these!"

"That is not going to work," said Lucien.

"What were we talking about?" asked Henri.

"I didn't kill your father, Lucien. It was his heart. He just died. But he died doing something he loved."

"Painting?"

"Sure, let's say painting."

"My sister Régine has gone through life thinking that my father was cheating on my mother."

"When, in fact, he was cheating *with* your mother," said Henri.

"And she thinks she caused the death of my sister Marie. That was you then, wasn't it?"

"Remember how much you like these? Mmmmmm, touch them."

"Button your blouse, Juliette, that is not working."

"But since you're offering," said Henri. "While you two are talking—"

"Oh, all right," Juliette said, turning aside and pulling her blouse closed. "Marie's death was convenient. I didn't cause her to fall off the roof, but when she did, it served the purpose, she became the sacrifice. Poor Père Lessard didn't have to die for the Sacré Bleu. That was that bitch Fate."

"Fate is a person, too?" asked Henri.

"No, that's just an expression. And yes, Lucien, yes, yes, yes your sister's life was the price for the Sacré Bleu. I'm sorry. And I'm not a monster. I love you. I've loved you from the first moment I saw you."

"And you possessed me."

"To know you. No one knows you like I know you, Lucien. I know how much you loved your papa. Really know. I know how Minette's death broke your little heart. I know your passion for painting, like no one else will ever know. I know how it feels to be hit in the head, morning after morning, with a perfect baguette. I was there when you discovered the magic, elastic properties of your willy. I—"

"That's enough."

"You are my *only* and my *ever,* Lucien. I'm free now. I am yours. Your Juliette. We can be together. You can paint."

"And what will you do?" asked Lucien. "Work in the hat shop?"

"No, I have money. I'll model, for *you*. I'll inspire *you*."

"You've given him syphilis, haven't you?" said Toulouse-Lautrec.

"No, I haven't. But it appears Monsieur Lessard needs to consider our good fortune. Dear Henri. Dear, brave Henri, you have some cognac around here, don't you?"

"But of course," said Toulouse-Lautrec.

Twenty-eight

REGARDING MAMAN

LUCIEN WAITED A WEEK AFTER THE COLORMAN WAS DEAD, FOR HIS ANGER to cool, before he was ready to tell Régine that their father had not been a philanderer and that she was not responsible for their sister Marie's death. The trick was how to tell her without revealing the entire bizarre story of Juliette and the Colorman. He'd been faithful to his duties at the bakery, letting his sister sleep late and relieving her at the counter as soon as the baking was done, which went a long way in lightening her disposition.

It was Thursday morning, around ten, when the push of the day was already past, and he heard her singing a sweet song to herself as she swept the crumbs from behind the counter, when he decided to share the news that he thought might relieve her of a lifetime of guilt.

"Régine, Maman is a slut," he said. "I thought you should know."

"I knew it," said an old man who had been sitting at one of the high tables by the window, so still up until that point that he'd become part of the furniture.

"You just mind your own business, Monsieur Founteneau." She turned so abruptly to Lucien that had the broom been her tango partner she would have snapped his neck. "Perhaps in the rear," she growled.

"Oh, I'm sure she likes it that way, too!" said Monsieur Founteneau. "You can tell by the way the slut waves it around."

Lucien stepped gallantly between his sister and the customer. "Monsieur, that is my mother you are talking about."

"Don't blame me, you brought it up," said Monsieur Founteneau.

Régine grabbed Lucien's sleeve and dragged him through the curtain into the kitchen. "Why would you say such a thing? And in front of a customer."

"I'm sorry, I've been waiting to tell you. I don't mean that Maman is a slut, I mean that she is *the* slut."

"She could come down the stairs any second and if she kills you, I'm not going to save you again."

Régine started to walk away. Lucien grabbed her arm and spun her around. "I will tell you, but you must not mention it to Maman."

"That she's a slut?"

"That she was the woman you saw go into Papa's studio all those years ago."

Régine slapped his hand off her arm. "Go away, Lucien. You're being silly."

"Did you really get a good look at her? The woman in the studio with Papa."

"No, you know I didn't. That's why Marie was up on the roof—to look through the skylight. But I know it wasn't Maman. She was away visiting Grandmother."

"No, she wasn't."

"The woman I saw had long red hair. She was wearing a blue dress I'd never seen before. Don't you think I would recognize my own mother? Why are you saying these things, Lucien? I've known about Papa and the slut for—"

"I found Papa's journal. When I was cleaning out the storeroom. He wrote all about Maman coming to him in the studio. Spending days at a time there."

"But she hates painting. She never said a good thing about Papa's painting. Let me see this journal."

Lucien hadn't quite thought this all through. He thought that once he'd told Régine about their mother being the strange "other" woman she'd be so relieved that—well, he hadn't expected to be questioned. "I can't, I burned it."

"Why would you burn it?"

"Because it contained embarrassing secrets about Maman and Papa."

"Which you are telling me now. I'm going to ask Maman about it."

"You can't. She doesn't remember."

"Of course she would remember. Papa died in that studio. Marie died trying to look into that studio. She may not want to, but she'll remember."

"No she won't, because she was taking opium. Lots and lots of opium. Papa wrote about it. He wrote about how she would take opium and come to the studio and they would make love for days and days. But she doesn't remember any of it. There, now you know."

"Maman was taking opium and none of us noticed?"

"Yes. Think about it. All the times we said that Maman was insane. It turns out she wasn't insane at all, she was just a drug fiend."

"And a sex fiend, evidently."

"Papa described it in detail, the disgusting, revolting things they did together. That's what you were hearing the night Marie went out on the roof. That's why I had to burn the journal. To spare your sensibilities, Régine. I did it for you."

"To spare my sensibilities you decided to reveal to me, in the middle of my workday, that our mother is a pervert and a drug fiend and our father not only took advantage of those things but wrote about them, and that is supposed to spare my sensibilities?"

"Because you've felt responsible for keeping the secret of the other woman from Maman all these years, because you felt responsible for Marie. See, none of it is your fault."

"But now, knowing the truth, I have to keep this secret from Maman?"

"It would hurt her feelings."

"She boinked our father to death!"

"Yes, but in a nice way. Really, when you think about it, it's kind of sweet."

"No it's not. It's not sweet at all."

"I think Papa's and Marie's deaths shocked her out of her drug use, so it's all turned out for the best, really."

"No it hasn't."

"You're right, we should murder her in her sleep. Do you think Gilles will help us with the body? She *is* a large woman."

"Lucien, you are the worst liar in the world."

"I'm more visual than verbal, really. The painting and so forth."

She leaned into him and kissed his cheek. "But it's very nice of you to try to make me feel better. I don't know why, but you have a good heart under all those layers of stupidity."

"What is going on here?" Mère Lessard's voice came from the top of the stairs.

Régine pinched Lucien's arm and turned to her mother. "I was just sweeping up and Lucien was telling me how you took opium and shagged Papa to death in his art studio."

Lucien cringed, then bolted through the curtain to the front.

"Hmmpf. He should be so lucky," said Mère Lessard.

Evidently, mothers and daughters had a different relationship than mothers and sons, or else Régine would have been trying to remove a rolling pin from her *derrière* right then.

Well, I tried, thought Lucien.

THAT EVENING, HENRI DE TOULOUSE-LAUTREC DINED AT THE LAPIN AGILE with his friend Oscar, an Irish writer who was in from London. He had not seen Lucien or Juliette since the night after they'd killed the Colorman. In fact, since burning the masterpieces, he couldn't bear to spend time with any of his artist friends, and even the girls in the brothels could not distract him from the wretchedness he had heaped on himself, so he had crawled alone into a very deep bottle and stayed there until Oscar arrived at his apartment on the butte and insisted they do the rounds of the cafés and cabarets.

Oscar, a tall, dark-haired dandy and raconteur, preferred the cafés to the cabarets, so he could spout his practiced witticisms for all to hear, despite his dreadful French. But this would not be the week that Oscar would extend to Paris the reputation he already enjoyed in the English-speaking world as a most vainglorious tosser, for over the first meal Henri could remember eating in a week, he slurred a fantastic story that captivated the Irishman and left him nearly speechless in both languages.

"Surely, you're doing me badly," said Oscar in French. "No one eats such a book."

"Your French is shit, Oscar," said Henri around a bite of bloody steak. "And it is true."

"My French is liquid and fat," Oscar said, meaning to say that his French was fluent and expansive. "Of course it's not true. I don't care a fly. But it makes a delicious book. May I take notes?"

"More wine!" Henri shouted to the bartender. "Yes. Write, write, write, Oscar, it's what men do when they can't make real art."

"Here it is," said Oscar. "This little man never died because of the paintings."

"Yes," said Henri.

And so, for another hour, as he became more drunk and more incoherent, and Oscar Wilde became more drunk, and more incoherent in French, Henri spun the tale of the Colorman and how he had defeated death by using the paintings of masters. By the end of the evening, or what would have been the end for a sane person, the two stumbled out of the Lapin Agile, Oscar bracing himself on Henri's head, and Henri bracing himself on his walking stick, and they paused at the split-rail fence on rue des Saules, realizing with some despair that no taxi was going to come by and they would have to navigate the stairs down the butte to Pigalle to catch a cab or continue their bar crawl, when a woman called out.

"Excuse me," she said. "Excuse me, Monsieur Toulouse-Lautrec?"

They looked to the bare vineyard across the street from the restaurant, and on the bench where once Lucien and Juliette had looked out over Paris, sat a lone figure in the dark.

Hanging on Oscar's lapels for balance, Henri dragged the playwright across the street and leaned in close to the woman's face, which he could now make out by the moonlight and the light spilling from the windows of the Lapin Agile.

"*Bonsoir,* mademoiselle," he said. He grasped the edge of his *pince-nez,* and while swinging from Oscar's lapel, he did a semicircular inspection of the woman's face. "And what brings you to Montmartre this evening?"

"I'm here to see you," she said. "The concierge at your building said I would find you here."

Henri swung in close again, and yes, he could see the light in her eyes, the recognition, the smile that he had missed so. This was *his* Carmen. He let go of Oscar's lapel and fell backward into her lap.

"Oscar Wilde, may I present Carmen Gaudin, my laundress. I'm afraid you will have to continue the adventure on your own."

"*Enchanté,* mademoiselle," said Oscar with a slight bow over Carmen's hand, which Henri tried to lick as it passed his face.

"I will leave you two to your sugary times," the Irishman said, thinking he had said something far more clever and gallant. He stumbled down the butte's stairs to Pigalle and happened into the Moulin Rouge, where he met and became quite fascinated with a young Moroccan man who worked there as a dancer and an acrobat, who taught the Irishman how to light the sugar cube over a glass of absinthe to release the green fairy, among other tricks.

The next morning Oscar awoke to find in his breast pocket a sheaf of notes, written in his own hand, which he had no recollection of having written and which were almost entirely incoherent, except for the repeated concept of a painting whose magical powers kept an old and twisted man eternally vibrant. A concept he would use as a theme for his next novel, which he would call *The Picture of Dorian Gray*.

Back on the bench, across from the Lapin Agile, Carmen ran her hand over Henri's beard and said, "Oh, my sweet count, I have missed you so. Let us go to your flat, or even your studio."

"But my dear," said Henri, on the razor's edge between joy and passing out, "I fear I may not be able to perform."

"I don't care, you can paint, can't you?"

"Of course, if I can draw breath I can paint."

IN THE MONTH THAT FOLLOWED THE COLORMAN'S DEATH, LUCIEN FOUND IT very difficult to paint, despite Juliette's inspiration. For one thing, she was only seeing him every second or third day, and then only for a few hours. And while he had hoped that she would stay with him in his little flat on Montmartre, she insisted that she keep the apartment in the Latin Quarter that she had shared with the Colorman.

"But, *mon chèr*," she'd said, "the rent is paid for months in advance. It would be a shame to waste it. And besides, I am thinking of going to university and the Sorbonne is so close."

"I could stay there, then," he'd argued, but as soon as he'd said it, he knew it wouldn't work. Until his paintings began to sell better, he still needed to be at the bakery at four in the morning. It was an hour's walk from the Latin Quarter to Montmartre, and there was no finding a taxi at that hour. Finally, he relented, and had stayed in with Juliette only on Saturday nights.

He had even suggested that she let him mix up some of the last of the Sacré Bleu that the Colorman had made, use it to shift time so he could paint for weeks on end and still make it back to the bakery to make the dough for the loaves, but she would not hear of it.

"No, *cher*, we cannot use the Bleu. That is all there is left. It would be wrong."

She never told him exactly why it would be wrong but redirected his questions, as she often did, with her physical charms.

So, one afternoon after finishing at the bakery, when Juliette had announced that she would be otherwise engaged and Henri was nowhere to be found, Lucien made his way down the butte to the Maquis to visit Le Professeur, in the hope that a man of science might help make sense of it all.

"My boy, I'm so glad you've come," said the Professeur with enthusiasm he seldom showed for anything that anyone else could understand. "Come in. Come in. I was going to come see you at the bakery. I've just received a telegram from a colleague of mine, Dr. Vanderlinden from Brussels. He's working at a place called Pech Merle, near Albi, and he's just discovered a new series of caves with drawings. I thought you'd want to know."

"Oh, that's terrific," said Lucien, not understanding why he would want to know, but not wanting to be rude.

"You see, from the animal bones they've found among the ashes, they know the caves were used by humans many years before the others we've found."

"Splendid," said Lucien, having no idea whatever why this would be splendid.

"They could have been used ten, twenty thousand years ago. We don't know."

"No?" Lucien was having trouble coming up with falsely enthusiastic things to say, so he was going with false incredulity.

"Yes. And these drawings, older than any we have found, have figures rendered in blue pigment."

"But you said ancient blue pigment didn't last, it—"

"Exactly. I'm leaving in the morning to go test the pigment against the samples we used when I tested the color Toulouse-Lautrec brought to me."

"You think it could be—"

"Yes! Do you want to come with me? The train to Albi leaves from Gare du Nord at eight."

"Absolutely," said Lucien. There had been a lot of interest in primitive art among Paris artists lately, but no artist had seen anything this old, and apparently, no one at all had seen anything this old and blue. And nothing was going well for him in Paris. Why not?

"And Monsieur Toulouse-Lautrec?"

"Henri is from Albi. He'll probably want to join us. I'll find him and meet you here at six thirty."

But Henri was nowhere to be found, and Lucien even ended up leaving a note for Juliette with the concierge at her building.

"Do you want me to give it to her maid?" asked the woman.

"She has a maid?"

"Oh yes, for nearly a month now. The first she's been able to keep. That uncle of hers was—well, monsieur, their last maid shot him, and I don't mind telling you—"

"I know," Lucien interrupted. "No, please, just give it to Juliette, personally. Thank you, Madame."

LUCIEN LEFT A MESSAGE FOR HENRI AT THE MOULIN ROUGE, WHERE LAUTREC could be depended upon to show before anywhere else, and so Lucien boarded the train to Albi with only the Professeur. They were met at the Albi station by Dr. Vanderlinden, a silver-bearded walrus of a man who spoke French with a clipped Dutch accent that accentuated his formal, academic demeanor, despite the fact that he dressed like a mountaineer in canvas and leather, his boots dusty and run over at the heels.

Vanderlinden installed them in a modest inn where he kept his quarters, and in the morning they rode several miles into the hills in a workman's wagon, then hiked two more, on steep forest trails that would not have accommodated a horse, let alone the wagon.

The mouth of the cave at Pech Merle was long and low, as if some giant, clawed creature had worked away the stone while trying to dig out its prey. They had to crawl on their hands and knees for nearly twenty meters before they entered a chamber in which they could even stand. Dr. Vanderlinden had prepared them for the crawl, however; they all wore gloves and had padded their knees with leather backed with wool.

The Belgian had the hardest time making the crawl, but when they stood in the open chamber and turned up their lanterns, it was difficult to tell if his breathlessness was from exertion or excitement.

"So you see, Bastard!"

The chamber they were in was at least six meters tall, and the walls were decorated floor to ceiling with pictures of horses, bison, some sort of antelope, rendered in white and red and brown ochre. Each animal was marked with spots that sometimes extended to the area around them. Lucien was impressed with the skill of the artist, because even on the rough surface there was the hint of perspective, shading on the horses that indicated dimension.

"The examples are better preserved as you go deeper into the cave," said Vanderlinden.

"Why do the spots extend outside of the outlines?" asked Lucien.

"I have a theory about that," said Vanderlinden. "You see, I don't be-

lieve these are actually animals. You see here and there the human figures? Small compared to the animals. No dimension, just shadows, yes?
But the animals are fully formed."

"Hunters?"

"That's just it," said the Belgian. "We've excavated several fire rings in
this cave. From the strata, and the smoke built up on the ceiling, people
lived here on and off for thousands of years, yet there are no large animal
bones to be found in any layer. Many, many examples of small animals,
rabbits, marmots, badgers, even a few human bones, mostly teeth. These
people did not hunt large animals."

"Then?"

"Close your eyes," said Vanderlinden.

Lucien did as he was told.

"What do you see?"

"Nothing. Darkness."

"No, what do you really see? What do you see in the darkness?"

"Circles, like auras, where our lanterns were. Afterimages."

"Exactly!" exclaimed the Belgian, clapping his hands. "These are images that were seen in the dark. In the mind's eye. I believe that these
people were drawing images of animals that they saw in trance. These
are spirit animals, not corporeal animals. That's why the humans are not
fully developed. These drawings are shamanistic. Religious, if you will.
Not narrative. They are not telling a story, they are invoking the gods."

"Interesting," said Professeur Bastard.

"Oh that's just fucking grand," said Lucien. He'd really had enough of
trying to reconcile the spirit world lately and had really hoped for some
hands-on empirical science you could taste.

"I know," said Vanderlinden, missing the sarcasm. "Wait until you
see the rest."

He led them farther into the cave, ducking through very low pas-
sages, following chalk marks at forks he'd obviously left himself from
previous explorations. At one point they had to shimmy through an

opening on their bellies, handing their lanterns ahead of them, but the narrow passage opened into a huge chamber.

"This passage had been blocked by debris for what must have been thousands of years, but one of my students saw a pattern to the stones, larger at the bottom, getting smaller and smaller to the top. They had been placed. This had been purposely walled up. Thank heavens for fresh, young eyes. I'd have never seen it myself."

Vanderlinden played his lantern over the walls.

"These, Bastard, these are the drawings I sent the message about." The drawings higher up on the walls were similar to those outside the chamber, but lower, there was a repeated motif, most of the figures black.

"You can't see anything under this yellow lamplight. Wait, let me light a magnesium light. The small arc light you provided, Bastard. The battery will only work for a few minutes, but you'll see. You can take samples for your analysis."

Vanderlinden took a strange-looking brass lantern from his knapsack, and then a battery about the size of a cantaloupe, but it must have been very heavy by the way the doctor handled it, and Lucien felt guilty for not having helped the older man carry his burden.

"Now, don't look into the light. It will blind you. I'm pointing it away." He attached wires to the leads on the lantern, then turned a small knob at the top of the lamp, which advanced a thin magnesium bar toward an electrode. When the current arced, the cave lit up like bright sunshine, and Lucien could see the size of the chamber. It was larger than the nave at Notre-Dame, and all around it, for about a meter from the floor up the wall, were drawings of human figures, many different human figures: dancing, fighting, hunting, traveling. In every motif, however, two figures were repeated again and again: that of a small, twisted figure, smaller than the others, rendered in brown ochre, holding a black knife; and a tall, slender female figure, rendered in bright, ultramarine blue.

"So you see! The blue is mineral, I'm sure of it," said Vanderlinden. "The blue brushes off quite easily, so it's never been disturbed. I've tested some of it in a flame. It's not copper. Perhaps your liquid chromatography method—"

Professeur Bastard held up his hand to signal for his colleague to pause. "And you believe these drawings are how old?"

"It's only a theory, this chamber has been dry for millennia, but because we had to remove some stalactites and stalagmites on the other side of the constructed barrier, and we have some idea of how long it takes them to grow, given the amount of minerals in the water around here, these could have been painted as long as forty thousand years ago."

Le Professeur looked at Lucien looking at the drawings—the painter's face was contorted in horror.

"Sacré Bleu," he said. "These are *his*. He lives."

Twenty-nine

TWO GRUNTS RISING

Pech Merle, France, 38,000 B.C.

H E WAS BORN A TINY, TWISTED, BROKEN THING AND EVERYONE WAS SUR-
prised that he lived beyond a few hours, but his mother protected
him fiercely, despite his deformities. She was a holy woman who com-
muned with the spirit world and could make the pictures, and so com-
manded respect and fear from the people. As was the calling, the holy
woman had congress with many of the men, so no man had to bear the
shame and weakness of fathering the abomination, and he survived.
Nevertheless, there was seldom a fire circle in which leaving him outside
the cave for the tigers was not discussed. Upon his weaning, the boy was
named Two Grunts and a Shrug, which translated from the language of
the People as Poop on a Stick.

Even up until the time he grew into manhood, Two Grunts survived
in the protection of his mother's bosom, as no children would play with
him, nor, when he came of age, would any girl have him as a mate. So

while other boys were learning to hunt and fight, and girls learning to gather roots and prepare hides, Two Grunts was learning the ways of the shaman, the chants, the dances, and most important, where to find the ochres and earths to prepare the colors for the drawings.

"I'm not going to have to bone all those guys, the way you do, right?" asked Two Grunts of his mother, and in the very asking, which involved no little bit of gyrating and thrusting mime, two women who were watching were frightened by the erratic swinging of Two Grunts's disproportionately large man-tackle, and thus he found his single source of joy in the society of other people: frightening the girls with his penis.

When Two Grunts's mother grew older, she began to incorporate her broken son into the rituals, hoping the People would bestow the same respect and fear, and ultimately care, upon him, but after she died, her ashes had not even cooled before two of the strongest men threw Two Grunts out of the cave to be eaten by tigers, despite his grunts of protest and no little bit of angry willy wagging, which is more or less why they'd chucked him out in the first place. Behind him they threw his skin bag of colors and a long shard of black obsidian, from which he might fashion a weapon or a tool, a particular generosity suggested by a woman named Two Cupped Hands and an Oh-Baby (which translates to Bubble Butt), who, while as frightened of Two Grunts as the rest of the girls, had experienced a pleasant dream involving his dong, and so wasn't entirely sure he didn't have power in the spirit world after all.

Two Grunts found himself wandering the hills in the dark, with no skills to protect himself, except the ability to make fire. He was fairly certain that he was being stalked by a dire wolf, or a saber-tooth, or an enormous dire woodchuck, and for protection he crawled into the hollow stump of a tree that had been struck by lightning, from which all he could see was a small swath of the starry midnight sky. He held the shard of black volcanic glass above his head, and to overcome his fear of whatever might be circling his tree, he chanted all the holy songs that his mother had taught him, calling upon all of the spirit animals to please send him strength, send him power, send him protection, and please, please, please, let the night be over.

And just as he was improvising a chant that more or less translated to, "And fuck you, too, bears! I hope my pointy bones get stuck in your poop chute!" a huge streak of fire lit up the sky and there was an explosion like a dozen thunderbolts hitting the ground at once, the shock wave of which rolled across the land, flattening the forest for a mile around, including knocking over Two Grunts's stump and rolling him out into the open.

He had been rendered temporarily deaf, so he did not hear animals fleeing or the crackling branches of destroyed trees trying to spring back into shape. Stunned, he wandered toward a light he saw in the distance, his addled brain telling him that he would find safety from predators near the fire.

Even as the smoke blew over the flattened forest, he followed the light until he came upon a great crater, the mounded earth at its edges still warm from whatever had struck and burrowed deep under the ground and now glowed dull blue at the center of the crater in a mass the size of a mammoth.

Two Grunts was terrified, but as he backed away on all fours from the edge of the crater his hand fell upon a smooth, cool stone no bigger than his fist. He grabbed it and dropped it into his color pouch, then limped away to the shelter of his hollow tree, picking up a few meteorite-concussed squirrels along the way to have as breakfast.

When dawn broke he climbed from his tree and examined the smooth stone for the first time. It was a brilliant blue, such as he had never seen before, but it tasted like roasted sloth scrotum, which was one of his least-favorite flavors, so he struck it against a black rock jutting from the forest floor and the blue stone broke in two, leaving a trace of blue powder, brilliant in the sun against the black. He tucked the blue stone in his pouch and went about building a fire to roast his squirrels.

The shock wave from the meteor's impact revealed a crack in the earth that Two Grunts first explored looking for grubs, but crawling inside found it led to a large cavern, which was relatively dry. With plenty of food and fuel outside provided by the heavenly destruction, Two Grunts was able to set up a camp inside the cave, where he could keep a fire burning constantly with only the effort of crawling outside and gathering the fallen timber. Soon he was decorating the walls of his cave with pictures of the spirit animals, drawing the story of the fire from the sky that the spirit animals had sent to avenge his mother and provide for him. When it came time to paint the fire in the sky, he pounded the blue stone into powder and made it into paste with urine, then painted the fire, blue and white across the cave walls, huge to show its power. He painted until the blue was gone, then slept under the protecting light of the sky fire, as it had begun to glow, pulse with light in its own right.

On the third night the painting began to fade, and Two Grunts chanted and danced and tried to conjure a vision in the dark, but nothing would come. The painting was pulsing and fading away.

And she arrived.

He had known her as Two Cupped Hands and an Oh-Baby, but she was different now as she crawled into the narrow opening of the cave and stood up. She wasn't afraid of him. She wasn't disgusted. She looked at him with a sparkle in her eye that he had only seen before in the stars of the winter night. She shrugged off the skins she was wearing and stood naked by his fire, and he watched as her skin appeared to become a vivid, powdery blue. Then her eyes rolled back in her head and she fell to the ground and convulsed.

He limped to her and tried to hold her still, afraid she would injure herself on the stone of the fire ring, but his hands came away powdery blue, and even as he wiped the pigment on the skins he wore, on the cave floor, against the cave wall, the color continued to appear on her skin.

Soon she settled, slept, at peace. He touched her and when she didn't protest, as he was sure she would, he touched her some more. He touched her until he was exhausted and covered in the blue. When finally he rolled off of her and looked up at the cavern wall he saw that his painting of the fire in the sky was gone. He heard movement beside him and she was lying on her side looking at him, her eyes and the center of her lips the only parts of her not covered in the powdered blue. She licked the powder off her lips and even her tongue took on a deep blue color.

"Well, this should be fun," she said in their language (a language poor in vocabulary yet rich with gesture), which involved the roll of her eyes, a joyful screech, a pelvic thrust, and a finger pointing into the future.

After another two days together in the cave, they returned together to the camp of the People. He carried his newly found blue color to show them, an offering, so they might take him back, accept him as their shaman. Outside the cave, where the women were scraping the tough skins off of yams, the man who had claimed Two Cupped Hands as his mate crushed the little shaman's skull with a rock and threw his body off a cliff. The girl shook her head, even as the murder happened, their language not having developed the vocabulary to say, "Wow, that was a really bad idea." She would sneak out of the cave when everyone was asleep and find the broken body on the rocks.

At dawn, when Two Grunts returned to the cave of the People, he was accompanied by a great she-bear, whose fur was dusted with blue, and who proceeded to slaughter the entire band, who were ripped from their slumber by the screams of the dying.

Their escape from the cave was blocked by a raging fire Two Grunts had set at the mouth. He moved into their cave, letting the bear drag away the corpses to share with the scavengers of the forest, while he painted his pictures with the blue, over the very sacred pictures drawn by his mother and those who had come before her.

When, at last, the bear went away and the girl he had known as Two Cupped Hands returned, they made the color, and this time she shed a great mound of the blue, produced by the sacrifice and suffering of the People.

Eventually the girl grew sick and died, and when he moved on he was followed by a she-tiger, whose tail was tipped with ultramarine. She accompanied him to the next encampment of people, who were much more respectful of the twisted little man who brought a brilliant blue color for their own shaman-painter. They fed him and cared for him, and gave him his own corner of the cave where he could sleep with his tiger. Their shaman would even paint pictures of the little man and the bluish tiger on the cave walls, but for some reason, none of the paintings survived the ages.

No longer was he Two Grunts and a Shrug, no longer Poop on a Stick; in their more developed language, they would call him the Colorman.

"HE LIVES," SAID CARMEN. SHE DROPPED HER FAN AND LOOKED DIRECTLY AT the painter. She was posing in a Japanese kimono, white silk with a bright blue chrysanthemum pattern, her garish red hair pinned up with black lacquered chopsticks. Henri liked the idea of her shy aspect in the Japanese motif.

"Who lives?" Henri asked, putting up his brush.

"He! He! Who do you think? The Colorman. I can feel him. I have to go." She rustled around his studio, shrugging off the kimono and gathering her clothes from the floor, where they had been thrown in the passion of the night before.

"But, *ma chère*, I watched him burn." Henri was distressed at the idea that the Colorman might be alive, but also that she had broken the illusion they had been sharing. Yes, he knew that she was possessed by the muse, but she was *his* Carmen, shy, sweet, rough at the edges, raw and tired from a life of hard work, and not at all like Lucien's Juliette other than she was a masterful model. "Please, Carmen."

"I have to go," she said. She snatched her bag from the shelf by the door, then stopped and returned to him, looking at the small canvas on which he'd been working. "I'll need this." She took it from him, kissed him on the nose, and bolted out the door.

He wanted to follow her, but he, too, was wearing a silk kimono with a floral pattern, and a wig pinned up with chopsticks. He would need to change before going out into the street and she'd get away, but he had some idea of where she might be going.

Quickly, he gathered his clothes.

MORNING TWILIGHT OVER MONTPARNASSE. THE COLORMAN STUMBLED OUT of the Catacombs a blackened, broken, twisted thing, and while alive, he was not completely recovered from his latest death, and great chips of blackened skin crackled and flaked off him as he limped through the alleys of Paris.

Well, if Bleu was going to keep killing him, he was going to kill her right back. The baker and the dwarf didn't have the stones to follow him to his cache of paintings and attack him—to burn his paintings. They would have required inspiration, and that was her *raison d'être*. She had used them as her weapons.

He would kill her quickly, then slowly and painfully—no, better, he would ravage her Juliette body first, then kill her. Then ruin the body and resurrect her as a ferret. She was strong, but he was stronger. He would do it. Kill her, then ravage her dead body, then call her up, then tell her that he had ravaged her until she screamed with rage, then kill her again and laugh at her when she came back as a ferret. Yes, that's what he would do. But he'd have to make the Sacré Bleu. He needed the Sacré Bleu to resurrect her into a new body, and he needed the Sacré Bleu for himself or he would remain a blackened, crispy thing for some time. The old paintings had protected him, but he'd had to wait, first for a rat to stumble into the tarry puddle of his remains, then for Étienne, lost in the dark, to come to him. It was his faithful steed who had provided the life that had gotten him this far, but without more painting, he couldn't make himself heal any more. It was a good thing he didn't have to take a new body, like Bleu, though. He would have been a rat, or just as bad, Étienne. He had never told the donkey, but he hated that fucking boater hat he had worn. Still, that was a penis that you could frighten some girls with. He sighed a sooty sigh of a dream denied.

As he passed through the Latin Quarter, he found some clothes hanging from a line between buildings. They were far too large, so he rolled the sleeves and trouser cuffs, but they cut the cold somewhat.

For once, the nosy concierge at his building was sleeping, and he had remembered to find his keys in the mess of his charred belongings before making the long crawl out of the underground city. He wasn't even sure how he had found his way. It was as if he had been given new strength from long, long ago.

Where he'd gotten it, of course, was from the intense ultraviolet light bathing his paintings at Pech Merle. Until Dr. Vanderlinden had lit his arc light, those powerful talismans had never seen daylight, never emitted their full power.

"Aha!" he said as he burst through the door. The Juliette doll was standing there in the dark, in her pretty periwinkle dress, doing nothing more than blinking. She turned to look at him but registered no recognition. She blinked. It was wildly unsatisfying. He would have fired his pistol for emphasis, but he had left it in the Catacombs because he had no more bullets for it.

"Aha!" he said again. And again, Juliette blinked.

She had her hands tucked into the small of her back, as if she was about to curtsy to her dance partner before beginning the minuet.

The Colorman limped to her, reached up and grabbed the ruffles on the bodice of her dress and tore it across the front. She blinked.

"I'm going to ravage you, then kill you," he said with a charred leer. "Or vice versa!" He dropped his oversized trousers, then cackled at her.

She blinked.

He sighed. A key was clicking in the door and a redheaded woman burst in.

"Aha!" said the Colorman. "I'm going to ravage and—"

"Where have you been?" said Bleu. "I've been looking all over for you."

"No you haven't."

"Look." She held up the Toulouse-Lautrec painting. "And there's a completed Seurat, too. We need to make the color. I'm feeling weak."

"You got Seurat to finish a painting?"

She gestured to the canvas that was leaning against the wall by the divan. Small for a Seurat, dynamic for a Seurat, but a Seurat nonetheless.

"What were you doing to Juliette?" she asked.

"I was going to kill and ravage her—I mean, you."

"Oh, then proceed," said Carmen. And then Bleu jumped bodies.

"You'll be needing this, Poopstick," said Juliette as the Colorman turned to her.

Her hand came around from behind her back in a great arc, holding the black glass knife. She struck him deep in the side of the neck and his head flopped to one side; on the return arc she struck again and his head plopped off onto the carpet and rolled to the wall with a thump, while his body crumpled into the pile of oversized clothing.

Carmen Gaudin had her hands at her cheeks and was breathing as if she might pass out or explode. Juliette pointed the knife at her. "Don't you scream. Don't you dare fucking scream."

Henri Toulouse-Lautrec stumbled through the door behind Carmen.

"And don't you scream, either."

Henri looked to Carmen, eyes wide to the point of panic, about to hyperventilate, and put his arms around her shoulders. "I presume all this is a bit of a surprise to this Carmen."

"It's not to you?" said Juliette.

"I may be becoming jaded."

"Good, take the head. Get it out of the building." She pulled the Colorman's stolen shirt from the pile and tossed it to Henri. "You can wrap it in this."

The Colorman's body pushed up to its knees and grabbed at the black blade, pulling it out of her hand even as she could feel the edge grinding into his bones, then, quick as a wolf spider, the blackened body scuttled toward its head.

"Too late," said Juliette.

LUCIEN EMERGED FROM THE CAVE BLACKENED AND SMOLDERING AT THE SEAMS but not seriously hurt, although it would be some time before he regrew his eyebrows and the dark shock of hair that normally fell over his eyes. He was dragging a mop stick with the yarn at its head burned to a charcoal nub.

"What have you done?" asked the Professeur.

Lucien smiled weakly, then saw Dr. Vanderlinden coming up the trail fifty meters behind the Professeur, and the painter slumped in shame.

"I'm sorry, Professeur, the cave paintings are no more. They've been burned."

"How? The mineral on stone—"

"Magnesium powder," said Lucien. "There was a large tin of it among the doctor's photographic equipment. I mixed it with turpentine and painted it over the paintings with a mop, then ignited it with the electrode from Vanderlinden's arc light. It was more of an explosion than a fire."

"That *is* why they call it *flash* powder," said the Professeur. "How is your vision? Have you burned your retinas?"

Lucien touched a pair of dark mountaineering goggles slung around his neck. "These were also among the doctor's equipment."

"You've destroyed priceless archaeological artifacts, you know?"

"And I hope that's not all," said Lucien. "I'm sorry. I had to. I love her."

THE COLORMAN SMASHED HIS HEAD DOWN UPON HIS NECK, BUT THE OPERA-tion being somewhat imprecise, he had to hold it in place with one hand while he brandished the knife with the other. The fury had never left his eyes, even when his head had rolled across the room. He turned on Juliette.

"I'd run," said Juliette to Carmen and Henri.

"*En garde!*" said Toulouse-Lautrec, stepping between Carmen and the Colorman and boldly drawing a cordial glass from his walking stick. "Oh balls. Run it is, then."

He turned as the Colorman leapt, knife-first, at Juliette. She was side-stepping, hoping to duck under the blow, perhaps shoulder him through the window, when there was a loud pop in the air and he simply came undone—whatever elements had shaped themselves into the Colorman assumed their original form of salt or stone or metal or gas. The black knife dropped to the rug along with the clothes, among what appeared to be multicolored grains of sand. The watery bits of the Colorman assumed their hydrogen and oxygen forms and dissipated quickly, the increased volume causing everyone's ears to pop for a second.

Juliette stood up from a defensive crouch and poked the toe of her shoe in the small spray of sand that had once comprised the Colorman's head. "Well that's new," she said.

Toulouse-Lautrec had sheathed his cordial glass and was staring at the spot where a second ago an ancient enemy had stood. Carmen was winding up to what looked to be a complete hysterical breakdown, panting, as if gathering her energy for a skull-cracking scream.

Juliette prodded the pile that had been the Colorman's torso with her toe, then stepped back.

"Check his trousers," said Henri.

"Sure, he'd love that," said Juliette, but she prodded the trousers and grinned at Henri.

That's when Carmen began to let loose with her siren wail, her eyes rolled back in her head until there were only the white eyes of a madwoman. She barely got an eighth note of terror out before Bleu jumped back into her.

Carmen's eyes rolled back down, she took a deep breath, then she assumed the same smile that Juliette had worn a second before. "That was new," Carmen said.

"You said that," said Henri. "I mean, she did." He nodded to Juliette, who was now the vacant beautiful doll with the torn dress standing in a pile of sand and laundry.

"That's just it, Henri, it's new." She grabbed him by the ears and kissed him chastely. "Dear, brave Henri, don't you see, nothing is ever new. He's really gone, for good."

"How? He was burned to little more than cinders before. Why is this different?"

"Because I don't feel him."

"But you didn't feel him when we thought he was dead before, then you did."

"But now I feel the presence of another. I can feel my *only*, my *ever*, my Lucien. He saved us, Henri. I don't know what he did, but I can sense him, like he is part of me."

Toulouse-Lautrec looked at her hands, her rough, red laundress's hands, and nodded. "I suppose that Carmen's time modeling for me is finished?"

The redhead cradled his cheek. "She can't be allowed to remember this. It would break her. But she will always know that she is beautiful because you saw the beauty in her. The woman would have never known but for your eye, for your love. Because of you, she will always have that."

"*You* gave her that. *You* are the beauty."

"That's the secret, Henri. I am nothing without materials, skill, imagination, emotions, which you bring, Carmen brings. You obtain beauty. I am nothing but spirit, nothing without the artist." She reached into her—into Carmen's—bag and pulled out an earthenware pot about the size of a pomegranate and worked the wide cork lid off. The Sacré Bleu, the pure powder, was there. She poured a bit, perhaps a *demitasse* spoon's worth, into her palm.

"Give me your hand," she said.

He held out his hand and she rubbed the color over his palm, between their palms, until both of their hands were colored a brilliant blue.

"Carmen is right-handed, right?"

"Yes," said Henri.

With her uncolored hand, she unbuttoned her blouse. "What I just told you, about being nothing without the artist, that's a secret, you know?"

He nodded. "But of course."

"Good, now put your hand, with the blue, on my breast, rub it in as long as you can."

He did as he was told, looking more perplexed than pleased. "As long as I can?"

"I hope there isn't much pain, my dear Henri," she said, and she jumped to Juliette.

Carmen Gaudin became aware of a strange little man in a bowler hat and a *pince-nez* kneading her breast under her blouse with blue powder, and as quickly as she realized it she slapped him in the face, knocking his *pince-nez* completely into the hallway (as the door had been open all this time), sending his hat askew, and leaving a blue handprint from the tip of his beard to his temple. "Monsieur!" she barked, then she pulled her blouse together, stormed out the door, and ran down the stairs.

"But . . ." Henri looked around, perplexed.

"Ah, women," said Juliette with a shrug. "Perhaps you should follow her, or instead, take a taxi to rue des Moulins, where the girls are more predictable. But first the secret."

"What secret?"

"*Exactement,*" said Juliette. "Good night, Monsieur Toulouse-Lautrec. Thank you for seeing me home."

"But of course," said Henri, having no recollection of having seen anyone home, but then, he thought it might be a safe guess that he had been drinking.

Thirty

THE LAST SEURAT

THE MUSE LOUNGED ALONE IN THE PARLOR OF HER FLAT IN THE LATIN Quarter, sipped wine, and gloated over the remains of her enslaver, which were contained in a large glass jar on the coffee table. Occasionally she giggled to herself, unable to contain the rising, ecstatic joy of freedom from the Colorman, whom she'd found was much more appealing as a jar full of multicolored sand.

"Hey, Poopstick, the only way you'll frighten the maid now is if she forgets to bring her broom, *non?*"

She snorted. Perhaps taunting a jar of minerals did not evince the maturity of a creature of her years, but winning felt so good. She might have been a little drunk, too.

She had found, through the millennia, that being the inspiration, passion, and abject lesson in suffering for so many imaginative, whining narcissists made for long periods of suffering and neglect visited back upon her. She loved all of her artists, but after a time, after she'd endured enough sulking, paranoia, withdrawal of affection, moody self-aggrandizement, berating, violence disguised as sex, and beatings, the only way to clear her head was to occasionally murder some sons-a-bitches, with great vigor and violence, and over the years she had performed this catharsis to varying degrees of satisfaction, but nothing had been quite so exhilarating as slaughtering the Colorman. Ultimately. Forever. What a sweet, screaming death-gasm it was, and the only time that destruction had ever felt more arousing than creation. Much of that joy owed to lovely, sweet Lucien, whom she could feel was in the hall outside her flat.

"Where are your eyebrows?" she said when she opened the door. She was naked except for her thigh-high black stockings, but her hair was up in a *chignon,* affixed with chopsticks, a style she had only recently adopted.

Lucien forgot what he was going to say, so he said, "Where are your clothes?"

"I was dusting," she said. Then she threw her arms around his neck and kissed him. "Oh, Lucien, my *only*! My *ever*! You saved me."

"The Colorman came back, then?"

"Yes!" She kissed him quickly, then let him breathe. "But he is no more."

"When I saw the cave paintings at Pech Merle, I thought he might return. They had been sealed in the dark for thousands of years, but when the arc light hit them, I could feel the Sacré Bleu, the power in it."

"Of course you could. They were the source."

"I realized they meant that you were still not free of him, so I destroyed them. I think I'm guilty of a crime against history, or art, or something."

"For saving your beloved? Nonsense."

Footfalls sounded on the steps below. A heavy person trying to be stealthy. The concierge, no doubt.

"Perhaps we should go inside," said Lucien, although he was reluctant to let go of her at this point.

She dragged him into the flat, kicked the door shut, then pushed him back onto the divan. "Oh, *mon amour,*" she said, straddling him.

"Juliette!" He took her by the shoulders and pushed her back to her feet. "Wait."

"Suit yourself," she said. She sat on the other end of the divan and clutched a silk cushion over her breasts as she commenced a tragic pout.

"You said he was dead. You said he was gone forever."

"So?"

"Well he wasn't, was he?"

"It felt as if he was. More than it had before. Longer than before."

"Before? How long have you been trying to kill him?"

"On purpose? Not that long, really. Since the fifteenth century. Of course he'd been mortally wounded many times before then, but that's when I started planning. I couldn't be obvious about it, because ultimately we would have to make the color, and he would control me then. At first it was accidents, then I hired some assassins, but he always came back. I knew he was protected, given power from the Sacré Bleu. That was when it first occurred to me that it wasn't just the raw color but certain paintings. The first time I tried to destroy what I thought was *all* the paintings was in Florence, in 1497. I persuaded poor Botticelli to burn many of his best paintings in Savonarola's Bonfire of the Vanities. Not all, fortunately, since now I know that it wasn't those paintings that protected the Colorman anyway. The cave paintings at Pech Merle were the source of his power, of his becoming the Colorman. They always had been. I know that now. Silly, I suppose, not to have thought of it."

"But how do you know he won't come back again?"

She pointed her toe to the jar on the coffee table. "That's him."

"He was only a gob of burning goo when we left him in the Catacombs."

"I'm going to put a spoonful of him in the Seine every day. He's gone though. I know that because I can feel *you.*"

"You stay on your side of the couch, at least until we sort this out."

She held a finger in the air to mark the moment, then rose and co-quetted across the parlor, where she stopped at the writing desk and opened a leather box, then looked over her shoulder at him and batted her eyelashes.

Lucien really thought he should be angry, or disappointed, but here she was, his ideal, conjured from his very imagination, his Venus, and she loved him and wanted him and was teasing him. "Hey, how did you know it wasn't a stranger in the hall when you opened the door, nude?"

"I could feel you out there," she said, reaching into the box. "I wasn't really dusting. I lied."

She pirouetted, snapping to his eyes as her spot, her arms out to her sides. In her right hand she held a black glass blade shaped like a long, razor-sharp fang. She smiled and approached him, never letting her eyes leave his.

Lucien felt his pulse quicken, leap really, in his neck, but he smiled back. *So this is how it ends.*

"I really thought you'd use syphilis on me," he said.

She stepped around the coffee table, knelt, and presented the knife to him on the flat of her palms. "This is yours," she said. "You use it to make the Sacré Bleu."

"I don't understand."

"Take it!"

He took the knife.

She cradled his cheek. "Those times, before, when I tried to rid myself of the Colorman, I had never thought it through, planned for someone to take his place. You have to make the Sacré Bleu or I will be no more."

"I don't know how."

"I'll teach you."

"You said we have to have a painting."

She held her finger to her lips, then went to the bedroom and re-turned carrying a small canvas, Henri's oil of Carmen in the Japanese kimono.

"But we burned all of the—" He leaned forward, set the black knife on the coffee table, and touched the surface of the painting lightly near the edge. "This is still wet. It's just been painted."

"Yes."

"But that means Carmen—you, were with Henri. That's where you were when I couldn't find you."

"He saved me. Well, I *thought* he saved me. Carmen was something I could give him as a reward. I love him."

"I thought you loved me."

"You are my *only* and my *ever,* but I love him, too. I am your Juliette. No one but you shall ever touch, ever be loved, by Juliette."

"Ever?" he asked.

"Ever and ever," she said.

"If I make the Sacré Bleu, you will have to inspire other painters, to make more paintings. The price always has to be paid; you said that. You'll be with them, in whatever form. And I'll be what—alone?"

"Juliette will be with you, even when I am not, Lucien. You can paint her, watch her dust, whatever you want, and I will return to you. You are unique, Lucien, among all the painters I have known, over thousands of years. I chose you, shaped you to grow into the man who would be my ever when I saw how you loved painting when you were still a little boy."

"Then I knew you, as my—? When you were—?"

"Do you remember when your mother told you that women were wondrous, mysterious, and magical creatures who should be treated not only with respect but with reverence and even awe?"

"That was you?"

Juliette grinned. "Did I lie?"

"You weren't always my mother?"

"To you? Just a few times."

"God, that's a disturbing thought."

Lucien looked at the painting of Carmen—the soul that Henri had captured, the intimacy he'd put on the canvas—then into Juliette's eyes. She had been there present and adoring in Carmen when this was painted. "How will I ever know you're true?"

"You'll know. If you want recipes, bake bread. I love you, Lucien, but I am a muse, you are an artist, I am *not* here to make you comfortable."

He nodded, letting the reality of it wash over him, all of his father's words, all of the words of his masters, Pissarro, Renoir, Monet. All the uncertainty that they accepted, the risks they took, the peace they resolved to never have, all so they could paint, all for art.

He looked at her again, smiling at him adoringly over the beautiful painting his friend had made. He said, "Henri has to be protected. We can't make the Sacré Bleu from Henri's painting if it means he will come to harm."

She sat, still holding the painting, looking over the edge to Carmen's image. "We'll have to leave Paris," she said. "Not forever, but for a long time. Henri must forget our story. If we are here he will remember, eventually, and that can't be. He's already forgotten the Colorman's death, those last sessions with Carmen, but he remembers the rest, about me, us."

"And you'll need the Sacré Bleu to make him forget?"

"Yes. And there is no more."

"Then we have to use his painting, and he'll suffer."

"No, we'll use another painting."

"The *Blue Nude*? My painting? Can I do that? Can I paint the paintings that we make the color from?"

"No. You would waste away. No, your *Blue Nude* has been crated, wrapped in layers and layers of oilskin, and the entrance to the mine sealed by a discreet explosion. To protect you, the way the cave paintings protected the Colorman."

"Why would you do that?"

"Because I love you."

"But if we don't use my painting, and Henri doesn't have to suffer for the ones he's made, how will you—how will we make the Sacré Bleu?"

Juliette handed him the Toulouse-Lautrec, which he leaned face-in against the wall under the window behind him; then he turned back to her.

She reached behind the divan. "Just dusting," she said. Then she looked over her shoulder and grinned. "I jest. *Voilà!*" She pulled up a medium-size canvas with a wild motif of nymphs playing in a meadow, pursued by satyrs, all of it rendered in meticulously placed dots of pure, bright pigment, a dominant blue tint to the air all around the figures.

"What is that?" he asked. He'd never seen something with so much motion and life rendered in the pointillist technique.

"The last Seurat," she said. "Pick up your knife, love. I'll teach you to make the Sacré Bleu."

"I have to say good-bye to my family, and Henri."

"You will, we both will. We have to."

"The bakery. Who will make the bread?"

"Your sister and her husband will take over the bakery. Pick up the knife."

He did, felt the blade vibrating in his hand. "But there's blood on it."

"Well, you want to make an omelet . . ."

THEY MET FOR COFFEE AT THE CAFÉ NOUVELLE ATHÈNES IN PIGALLE, JUST below the butte. Lucien had only just told Henri that he was leaving when Toulouse-Lautrec said, "You know Seurat is dead?"

"No? He's barely older than us. What, thirty-one, thirty-two?"

"Syphilis," said Henri. "You didn't know?"

Lucien shrugged, giving up the ruse. "Yes, I knew. Juliette would like to say good-bye, too, Henri. She's going to meet us at your studio."

"I look forward to it," said Henri.

Later, as they made their way up rue Caulaincourt, Henri limping badly and Lucien walking sideways so he could keep his friend in sight, Lucien told him.

"I probably won't see you again. Juliette says we have to stay away from Paris for a while."

"Lucien, I know you love her, but if you don't mind me saying, I think Juliette is inordinately fond of syphilis."

"What do you mean *you know I love her*? She was Carmen. You love her, too."

"But I have chosen to ignore that."

"You slept with her when she was possessed by a muse who is, as you put it, 'inordinately fond of syphilis,' particularly as a way of dispatching painters."

Henri looked at the cobbles, then bounced his walking stick off its tip and caught it in front of his face as if snatching an idea from the very air.

"I think I should like to paint a clown fucking a bear. To round out my *oeuvre*. You know, they say that Turner left thousands of erotic watercolors and that twat critic Ruskin burned them upon his death to save his reputation. Critics. I'm glad Whistler ruined Ruskin with that lawsuit over his night paintings. Served him right. Can you imagine? Turner erotica? I'm going to buy Whistler a drink the next time he's in Paris."

"So, you're choosing to ignore the whole Juliette-Carmen-syphilis connection?"

"*Exactement.*"

"Well then," said Lucien. "What kind of bear?"

"Brown, I think."

WHEN THEY CAME TO THE STUDIO, JULIETTE WAS WAITING BY THE DOOR, wearing a dark dress, appropriate to winter.

"*Bonjour,* Henri!" She bent and they exchanged kisses on the cheeks.

"*Bonjour,* mademoiselle. Lucien tells me that you're leaving."

"*Oui,* I am sorry to say."

"Where will you go?"

"Spain, I think," she said, shooting a glance at Lucien. "There is a young painter there who needs to start using more blue in his work. Barcelona, I think."

"Ah, well, it will be warm there. You will both be missed."

"As will you, *mon cher.* Shall we go in and say good-bye properly?"

Henri tipped his hat. "Over a cognac, you mean?"

"But of course," she said.

Epilogue in Blue:
Then There Was *Bleu, Cher*

New York, October 2012—The Museum of Modern Art

IT WAS A WEEKDAY AND THE MUSEUM WAS NOT BUSY, WHICH WAS UNUSUAL anytime. A striking, fair-skinned brunette, her hair pinned up with chopsticks, in an elegant suit of ultramarine blue wool and impractically tall shoes, stood in front of *Starry Night,* staring into the white and yellow swirls painted through a night sky of Sacré Bleu. She had staked out a territory directly in front of the painting, about a meter away, making the other museum patrons look around her, or just peek at the painting as they passed by, most thinking she was a self-absorbed model, as there were a lot of those wandering around this neighborhood, and her skirt seemed confidently well fitted about the bottom. She rubbed at a pendant on chain around her neck as she examined the painting.

"This is mine, you know?" she said. "I wouldn't try to take it. I'm not going to take it, but it's mine."

The young man, who sat on a bench nearby, sighed, slightly amused. He was about thirty, and had dark eyes, and a shock of dark brown hair fell across his forehead.

She said, "He painted it at night and had Theo store it in the dark. That's why Poopstick couldn't find it."

"As you've told me," said Lucien. "Don't you have someone you have to be?"

She did. There was a boy in the Bronx who painted subway cars with spray cans, who loved a Latina girl with vibrant blue eyes. She would go to him, enchant him, inspire him, and leave the Juliette doll in an apartment with Lucien to wait. And when the boy finished his work, she and Lucien would go to a tunnel or depot where no one was around, and Lucien would light the fires and chant the strange words, sending her into a trance, then he would scrape the Sacré Bleu from her body, as he had done now for more than a century, as the painting on the train faded away.

"Yes, I do," she said. "Shall we?"

As they walked, she continued to worry the pendant, which looked like a scrap of distressed leather.

"I wish you'd get rid of that thing."

"It's a memento. He gave it to me."

"It's a dried-up old ear."

"Oh, Lucien, I would carry your ear if you gave it to me. Please don't be jealous."

"Never, *chérie*. Never," he said. He took her hand and kissed the tips of her fingers.

Hand in hand, the handsome young couple, the painter and the muse, walked out of the Museum of Modern Art into a soft autumn New York day.

Finis

Afterword:
So, Now You've Ruined Art

I KNOW WHAT YOU'RE THINKING: "WELL THANKS LOADS, CHRIS, NOW you've ruined art for everyone."

You're welcome. It's my pleasure. I simply set out to write a novel about the color blue; I can't remember why now. When you start with a concept that vague, you have to narrow your scope fairly quickly or it will get out of hand, so very early in my research great bits of history had to go by the wayside so I'd have room to make stuff up.

So what I'd be asking right now, if I were you, is what, among this big blue lie, is true? What really happened?

First, I drew the characters' personalities mostly from accounts written by people who knew them, many of the accounts of the Impressionists coming from Jean Renoir's biography of Pierre-Auguste Renoir, *Renoir, My Father*. Jean Renoir had been wounded in World War I and had come home to Paris to recover in his father's apartment, where the artist recalled his life to his son in an interestingly sanitized version. Jean Renoir talks in his book about "this little girl, Margot," whom his father had such an affection for, and who died, and how he must find out more about her. Margot was no little girl, as one can see from the paintings in which she appears— his major paintings from the 1870s to the 1880s, *Moulin de la Galette* and *Déjeuner des Canotiers* (*Luncheon of the Boating Party*), as well as other portraits, although Margot (Marguerite Legrand) isn't actually the girl in the painting *The Swing*. I chose that figure for the character because of the vivid ultramarine bows on her dress. It was clear from the accounts of his friends that Renoir was in love with Margot, and when she died (Dr. Gachet did come from Auvers to treat her), the painter became despondent and went off wandering for a couple of years, only to return to Paris to marry Aline Charigot, who was "his ideal." It's no accident that Renoir's girls all seem to have a similar look to their faces. He chose them by his ideal. He is quoted in his son's book: "You need only find your ideal, then marry her, and you can love them all." After which he says, "But never trust a man who is not moved by the sight of a pretty breast."

My portrayal of Les Professeurs is inspired by another character written about in Renoir's biography. Renoir writes of a retired academic who lived in the Maquis, wore a medal given to him by the state, and tried to train rats and mice to perform the chariot-racing scenes from the novel *Ben-Hur*. The novel was not published until 1880, and Renoir's account refers to the 1890s, when Renoir had moved back to Montmartre with his wife and family, but I have placed Le Professeur's rat races in 1870 to coincide with the Franco-Prussian War.

Letters were less helpful than you might think for revealing the artists' personalities. Most letters of the period are formal and seem at odds with the accounts of the artists who wrote them. Cézanne's letters reveal a thoughtful, educated man, almost painfully polite, while all accounts of him from his fellow painters speak to his need to portray himself as the country bumpkin, uncouth, uncultured, with no manners, slurping his soup and wearing his garish red belt to mark that he was a Provençal. One suspects he played the role to the expectation of the Parisians. While the letters between Vincent van Gogh and his brother Theo reveal the deep, analytical approach Vincent took to painting, a very calculated method to what seems to be madness on the canvas, they do reveal much of the pain that Vincent was experiencing and trying to work through while painting away from Paris.

There's absolutely nothing in the letters of Henri Toulouse-Lautrec to indicate the debauched lifestyle he was leading in Paris. He was the earnest and dutiful son or grandson, always writing home with news of how hard he was working, how his health was progressing, and when he might next visit. Yet, in Paris he was the very model of the *bon vivant*: there are photos of him clowning, dressed as a geisha, a choirboy, a samurai, displaying his paintings in his studio with a completely nude prostitute named Mireille (who really was his favorite, and probably because she was, indeed, shorter than he). He *did* live in brothels for weeks at a time, and he was an installation in the dance halls and cabarets of Montmartre and Pigalle, including the infamous Moulin Rouge. The account of his challenging someone to a duel over the offender's criticism of Vincent van Gogh's painting is true and was recounted by several friends who were present. He *did* study with Vincent at Cormon's studio, along with Émile Bernard, and they all idolized the Impressionists. Jean Renoir's biography of his father speaks of Toulouse-Lautrec with great affection. It was Jean Renoir's nanny and his father's model, Gabrielle, who always referred to Lautrec as "the little gentleman."

What doesn't appear in any context I could find is the depressed, heartbroken victim portrayed in John Huston's 1952 film *Moulin Rouge*. Henri Toulouse-Lautrec *did* drink to excess and would die at thirty-six from complications from alcoholism, but it appears that he drank not because he was depressed or self-pitying, but because he really liked being drunk. I suppose it's a minor miracle that he didn't die of syphilis, given his social regimen.

Speaking of which, Manet, Seurat, Theo van Gogh, and Gauguin all really did die of syphilis as described, although none of their wives appeared to have contracted the disease and all lived into old age. It was Johanna van Gogh, Theo's wife, who promoted, defended, and stridently protected Vincent's paintings and she is probably responsible for us having ever heard of the painter, although it appears that she and Vincent did not get along well while he was alive.

While most of the scenes in *Sacré Bleu* are from my imagination, including all between Lucien and Henri, many scenes were inspired by real events. Monet really did go to Gare Saint-Lazare, announce himself as "the painter Monet," and convince the station manager to direct all of the engines to fire up and release the steam so he could paint it. And he really did paint his wife, Camille, on her deathbed to capture the particular shade of blue she was turning. Even today, if you go to Giverny and the laboratory of light that Monet built there, you will see the dark carp, hiding under the water lilies, almost invisible but for the light line that is his dorsal fin. Monet and his student friends Renoir and Bazille *did* go to the Salon des Refusés and saw Manet's *Déjeuner sur l'herbe,* and while Manet himself never counted himself as one of the Impressionists, they acknowledge him as "their source." Monet and his friends went to great lengths after Manet's death to get the French state to buy *Déjeuner sur l'herbe* and *Olympia* and install them in the Louvre.

While Berthe Morisot was an accomplished painter, one of the original group of the Impressionists, and she did marry Manet's brother Eugène, there is no evidence that Manet had anything but the most proper relationship with her, and that affair is entirely of my invention. Neither is there any evidence that Manet had an affair with the model Victorine Meurent, who posed for his most famous paintings. There is a terrific confrontation scene between Madame Manet and Victorine in the short story "Olympia's Look" from Susan Vreeland's collection *Life Studies,* which I would recommend, as I would her excellent novels portraying the lives of artists, if you're interested in more accurate biographical fiction.

Whistler and Manet did know each other, were friends in fact, and while both showed at the famous *Salon des Refusés,* described in chapter 5, Whistler didn't attend the Salon in person; he sent his painting, *The White Girl,* later retitled *Symphony in White Number 1.* Whistler was in Biarritz at the time, recovering from lead poisoning from painting *The White Girl,* and really was nearly drowned while making a painting called *The Blue Wave,* when he was swept out to sea by a rogue wave and was saved by fishermen.

Whistler did have a redheaded Irish mistress named Joanna Hiffernan, whom he hid from his stern mother when she visited London. He really did throw his brother-in-law through a restaurant window when he criticized Jo, and Whistler was said to have gone quite mad for a time when he was with Jo. Joanna really did run off with Whistler's friend Courbet and posed for some of the most notorious and lewd pictures that anyone had ever painted at the time. Courbet would, indeed, die in exile and poverty in Switzerland, of alcoholism. Whistler did, for a time, only paint at night, and it was his libel lawsuit against the critic John Ruskin, who equated one of the nocturnes with "flinging a pot of paint in the public's face," that eventually destroyed the famous critic. It was not the damages, which were only a farthing (one quarter penny), but the expense and effort of defending the suit that put him over the edge. Ruskin died a few weeks after the trial was completed.

There was no Boulangerie Lessard on Montmartre, nor a Père Lessard, baker, but there was a real baker, named Muyen, who had a shop on rue Voltaire near the École des Beaux-Arts, who did, indeed, hang the work of the Impressionists and bought their paintings to keep them alive. When Paris was besieged during the Franco-Prussian War, Muyen made country *pâtés* from rat meat to feed his customers. He even raffled off one of Pissarro's paintings as I wrote in chapter 3, and the girl who won the painting was supposed to have actually asked if she could have a sticky bun instead.

Speaking of Pissarro, when one reads any accounts of the Impressionist and post-Impressionist periods in art, he will find no more glowing reviews than those for Pissarro. Less well-known, even today, than the other Impressionists, and less successful in his time, he was teacher, friend, and mentor to nearly every one. He painted alongside Cézanne, Gauguin, Monet, Renoir, Sisley, and probably a dozen others. The oldest of the group, he remained open always to learning new techniques and was the only one of the original Impressionists who would follow Seurat into pointillism and the techniques of optical painting, even though Seurat was young enough to be his son.

THE ENTIRE TIME FRAME OF *SACRÉ BLEU* WAS CONSTRUCTED AROUND THAT July afternoon in 1890 when Vincent shot himself because of a fact I stumbled across very early in my research. Vincent van Gogh *did* shoot himself in that field in Auvers where three roads converge—shot himself in the chest—then walked a mile cross-country to Dr. Gachet's house seeking treatment. Vincent and Theo are buried beside each other within sight of that field in Auvers. I have stood in that spot, and walked from there to the doctor's house, which is a museum now, and I thought, *What kind of painter does that? Who tries to kill himself by shooting himself in the chest, then walks a mile to seek medical attention?* It made no sense at all. Even when you read Vincent's letters, look at his last paintings—*The Church at Auvers, Wheat Field with Crows, Portrait of Adeline Ravoux* (the innkeeper's daughter from chapter 1), *Portrait of Doctor Gachet*—you realize that this is a fellow at the height of his powers, and apparently getting better. His death was both a mystery and a tragedy, a resignation, and yet, there's the evidence of a great passion for excellence that only the artist himself could define, and pursuing that passion seems to have been the basis of much of his self-torment. What is the standard when you are doing something that's never been done? What kind of muse inspires that? Exactly.

WHEN YOU START TO WRITE ABOUT ART AND PARIS IN THE 1890S, THE POS-sibilities absolutely explode. During the time frame of Lucien's story, between 1863 and 1891, nearly everyone who was anyone was in Paris, and not just Paris, but on Montmartre. Mark Twain, Claude Debussy, Erik Satie, Jules Verne, Oscar Wilde, Charles Baudelaire, Émile Zola, John Singer Sargent, and on, and on, and on. It would take a hundred books to tell the stories of the painters alone, so deciding what and whom to leave out became a bigger challenge than writing a novel about the color blue.

Where, you ask, is Degas? Gustave Caillebotte? Mary Cassatt? Alfred Sisley? Why so little on Cézanne? Truth be told, in the case of Cézanne, it was geography—he didn't like Paris, and for most of the time frame of the story, he was in Aix, in Provence, or in one of the villages outside Paris, painting with Pissarro. Cassatt was a passionate collector and an accomplished painter, but like Berthe Morisot, Eva Gonzalès, and the other women Impressionists, she was confined to the world allowed to a woman at the time, which is reflected in her paintings of children and home life; convention did not allow her to travel in the *demimonde* in which *Sacré Bleu* takes place. Caillebotte was also an accomplished painter, but as a member of a banking family, it was his collecting and patronage, which kept Renoir, Monet, and Cézanne alive to paint on, that became his greatest contribution to the group. He also (like Frédéric Bazille) died young, and I sensed he was never really part of the Montmartre community. As for Degas, well, Degas was unpleasant. I started my engagement with art knowing absolutely nothing about the artists, just looking at the pictures in museums—the biographies of the artists didn't much matter to me. I like Degas' paintings and sculptures, I have since I studied photography in college, but now, as a storyteller, considering him as a potential character, it seemed as if he was a miserable, unlikable guy, and I didn't want to have to portray that. So he doesn't get a part in my book. See, if you hadn't been a jerk, you'd have had a speaking part, Degas, but no. And as much as I'd have liked to explore the whole Art Nouveau movement that started in Paris in the 1890s, and with which Toulouse-Lautrec was involved, well, that's another story.

As far as the history and mystical properties of ultramarine pigment, some details are based in truth, most are just constructed for the story.

The pigment *was*, for a long time, more valuable than gold, and during that time, to commission a painting that used it was a sign of status for the patron and his family. The two Michelangelo paintings Lucien and Juliette see in London, *The Entombment* and what is called *The Manchester Madonna*, are unfinished, the blue parts remain unpainted, and both hang in the National Gallery in London to this day, but it's likely that they remain unfinished because the painter was unable to obtain the ultramarine he needed and moved on to other commissions, or the patron refused to pay the high price of the color. The physics of light and color were as close to factual as I could convey within my understanding, but to be honest, I'm still a bit fuzzy on the whole refraction, absorption, and scattering aspects of how color is produced and perceived, so it's not your fault if you're a bit confused as well.

Penultimately, a word on the Impressionists.

There is a tendency, I've found, among academics and art enthusiasts, to dismiss the Impressionists, with their fields of flowers and their pink-cheeked girls, as insignificant, pablum for the masses, and once you've seen your thousandth tote bag sporting Monet's lilies, it's understandable. Among museums, the Impressionists represent a cash cow, because any show that features them will pack the museum for weeks, even months, while it runs, and so they are often regarded with a restrained resentment, if not for the painters, for the masses who come to see their work. Out of the context of their own time, the Impressionists just seem to be producing "pretty pictures." Yet, Impressionism represented a quantum leap in painting and ultimately art in general. They came from all walks of life, from all economic strata, and as above, had wildly different ideas about both society and art, but what they all had in common, the single element that united them beyond a rebellion against tradition, was their love of painting. Whether it was the invention of photography, the middle class that rose up because of the Industrial Revolution, or simply because paint became available in tin tubes, thus freeing the painter to leave the studio and paint the world, time and events conspired for the

Impressionists—their technique as well as their philosophy of capturing the moment—to rise. The conditions, the context were there, but the engine of the revolution, I think, can be traced to a group of people who chose, over their own economic and social interests, to pursue an idea. There's courage in those paintings of placid ponds and pink-faced little girls, a courage that went forth to inspire the next generation, Toulouse-Lautrec, van Gogh, Gauguin, and so on into Matisse and Picasso, and thus modern art through the twentieth century. Amid my dark little fairy tale of the color blue, I hope that came through.

Samuel Johnson said, "A man will turn over half a library to make a book," but there are damn few books an author will uncover during research that actually make for decent further reading. Here are a few:

If you're interested in the rise of Impressionism, try *The Private Lives of the Impressionists* by Sue Roe, HarperCollins, 2006. For more on Henri Toulouse-Lautrec, the Taschen biography *Toulouse-Lautrec* by Gilles Néret, edited by Ingo F. Walther, is a terrific collection of paintings and photographs in the context of a very readable biography. For further reading on colors and their source, *Color* by Victoria Finlay, Random House, 2002, is the story of one woman's adventure in traveling the world to the sources of the great natural pigments, in the process imparting interesting history and anecdote to bring the science and geography of color to life. Likewise, Philip Ball's *Bright Earth,* University of Chicago Press, 2001, is also an exploration of the history and science of color, written in lyrical prose that explores the role of color as it applies to art history as well.

Acknowledgments

MY THANKS TO THE FOLLOWING PEOPLE WHO HELPED IN THE RE-search and production of *Sacré Bleu:* Charlee Rodgers for ar-ranging travel and logistics in Paris, London, and Italy, where it turns out they keep a lot of the art discussed in this book. My friend and agent, Nicholas Ellison, for his advice on Paris and France in general, as well as handling the dirty business of the book business. Maxime Lachaud, for help with French idiom, and for calling the Toulouse-Lautrec Museum in Albi for me when I needed to know what to call stuff. My editor, Jen-nifer Brehl, for, as usual, her clean hands and patience in putting this blue beast together. Also, my thanks to Chelsea Lindman, Sarah Dickman, Lynn Grady, Ben Bruton, Liate Stehlik, Emily Krump, and Michael Mor-rison. I have no idea what any of them do, but I'm pretty sure it has a lot to do with my books.

SAN FRANCISCO, APRIL 2011

About the author

About the book

Insights,
Interviews
& More . . .

Read on

Meet Christopher Moore

Garry Kravit

CHRISTOPHER MOORE is the author of twelve previous novels including *Lamb*, *A Dirty Job*, and *Fool*. He invites readers to email him at theauthorguy@gmail.com. You can follow him on Twitter @theauthorguy or on Facebook at facebook.com/theauthorguy.

For more information on the story behind *Sacré Bleu*, the author's research, the Impressionists, and the color blue, please visit SacreBleu.me; check it out.

Questions for Discussion

1. Do you think that Vincent van Gogh was simply insane and that is why he committed suicide, or was there more to this story, as *Sacré Bleu* suggests?

2. In the beginning of *Sacré Bleu* it says that many people in Paris were beginning to argue that painting was just color, nothing more. What does this mean? Do you think that was the case in 1890? Is that the case now?

3. The artists in *Sacré Bleu*, especially Toulouse-Lautrec, indulged in drugs, alcohol, and prostitutes. Is there something about their artistic natures that makes them more susceptible to these vices or is it simply human nature? How do these vices empower Juliette and the Colorman?

4. Mère Lessard/Bleu tells Lucien that women are wondrous, mysterious, and magical creatures who should be treated not only with respect but with reverence and awe. The artists especially see these qualities in their muses. What similar qualities do the women—Carmen, Juliette, Vuvuzela, et al.—possess that the artists find particularly inspiring? Is it simply that these women are beautiful, or is there something more? What do you think makes ▶

a person or place inspiring? What inspires you?

5. At what point did you realize that the Colorman was more than the crass little man he appears to be? Do you ever feel sorry for him in *Sacré Bleu*?

6. Why do you think Regine doesn't believe Lucien when he tells her that her mother is the "other woman" who killed their father and sister? How well do we know our family members? Is it ever better not to know everything about someone you are related to?

7. Christopher Moore's novels are known for their outlandish, bawdy characters. Is there one character in *Sacré Bleu* who stood out for you among the rest? Why? Are these characters more surprising because many of them are based on historical figures?

8. *Sacré Bleu* does not include paintings from all of the major Impressionists, nor do all of the Impressionists appear. Are there any paintings or artists you wished had been included? Did you come across a new image or an artist in *Sacré Bleu* that you particularly resonated with?

9. Did *Sacré Bleu* ruin art for you, as the epilogue suggests it might? ∽

Read More
Christopher Moore

THE GRIFF: A GRAPHIC NOVEL
(WITH IAN CORSON)

The always outrageous Christopher Moore joins forces with award-winning screenwriter and director Ian Corson to bring you *The Griff*. An absurdly entertaining graphic novel about alien invasion, *The Griff* is vintage Chris Moore . . . with pictures! Get ready for thrills, chills, and a chain-smoking professional squirrel, in this high-octane tale of the infestation of Earth by extraterrestrial interlopers and the motley crew of humans who save the world . . . sort of.

BITE ME: A LOVE STORY

The city of San Francisco is being stalked by a huge shaved vampyre cat named Chet, and only I, Abby Normal, and my manga-haired love monkey stand between the ravenous monster and a bloody massacre of the general public.

Whoa. And this is a *love* story?

Yup. 'Cept there's no whining. But there is everybody's favorite undead couple, Tommy and Jody, who've just escaped from imprisonment in a bronze statue. And now that they're out, they've joined forces with Abby, her boyfriend Steve, the frozen-turkey-bowling Safeway crew, the Emperor of San Francisco and his trusty dogs Lazarus and Bummer, gay Goth guy Jared, and SF's finest Cavuto and Rivera to hunt big cat and save the city. Really.

FOOL

Verily speaks Christopher Moore, much-beloved scrivener and peerless literary jester, who hath writteneth much that is of grand wit and belly-busting mirth. In *Fool* he takes on no less than the legendary Bard himself (with the utmost humility and respect) in a twisted and insanely funny tale of a moronic monarch and his deceitful daughters—a rousing story of plots, subplots, counterplots, betrayals, war, revenge, bared bosoms, unbridled lust . . . and a ghost (there's always a bloody ghost), as seen through the eyes of a man wearing a codpiece and bells on his head.

YOU SUCK: A LOVE STORY

"You bitch, you killed me. You suck!"

Just ask C. Thomas Flood. Waking up after a fantastic night unlike anything he's ever experienced, he discovers that his girlfriend, Jody, is a vampire. And surprise! Now he's one, too.

For some couples, the whole biting-and-blood thing would have been a deal breaker. But Tommy and Jody are in love, and they vow to work through their issues.

But word has it that the vampire who initially nibbled on Jody wasn't supposed to be recruiting. Even worse, Tommy's erstwhile turkey-bowling pals are out to get him, at the urging of a blue-dyed Las Vegas call girl named (duh) Blue.

And that *really* sucks.

A DIRTY JOB

Charlie Asher is a pretty normal guy with a normal life, married to a bright and pretty woman who actually loves him for his normalcy. They're even about to have their first child. Yes, Charlie's doing okay—until people start dropping dead around him, and everywhere he goes a dark presence whispers to him from under the streets. Charlie Asher, it seems, has been recruited for a new position: as Death.

It's a dirty job. But, hey! Somebody's gotta do it.

THE STUPIDEST ANGEL: A HEARTWARMING TALE OF CHRISTMAS TERROR

'Twas the night (okay, more like the week) before Christmas, and all through the tiny community of Pine Cove, California, people are busy buying, wrapping, packing, and generally getting into the holiday spirit.

But not everybody is feeling the joy. Little Joshua Barker is in desperate need of a holiday miracle. No, he's not on his deathbed; no, his dog hasn't run away from home. But Josh is sure that he saw Santa take a shovel to the head, and now the seven-year-old has only one prayer: Please, Santa, come back from the dead.

But hold on! There's an angel waiting in the wings. (Wings, get it?) It's none other than the Archangel Raziel come to Earth seeking a small child with a wish that needs granting. Unfortunately, our angel's not sporting the brightest halo in the bunch, and before you can say "Kris Kringle," he's botched his sacred mission and sent the residents of Pine Cove headlong into Christmas chaos, culminating in the most hilarious and horrifying holiday party the town has ever seen.

Read More Christopher Moore *(continued)*

FLUKE: OR, I KNOW WHY THE WINGED WHALE SINGS

Just why do humpback whales sing? That's the question that has marine behavioral biologist Nate Quinn and his crew poking, charting, recording, and photographing very big, wet, gray marine mammals. Until the extraordinary day when a whale lifts its tail into the air to display a cryptic message spelled out in foot-high letters: Bite me.

Trouble is, Nate's beginning to wonder if he hasn't spent just a little too much time in the sun. 'Cause no one else on his team saw a thing—not his longtime partner, Clay Demodocus; not their saucy young research assistant; not even the spliff-puffing white-boy Rastaman Kona (né Preston Applebaum). But later, when a roll of film returns from the lab missing the crucial tail shot—and his research facility is trashed—Nate realizes something very fishy indeed is going on.

By turns witty, irreverent, fascinating, puzzling, and surprising, *Fluke* is Christopher Moore at his outrageous best.

LAMB: THE GOSPEL ACCORDING TO BIFF, CHRIST'S CHILDHOOD PAL

The birth of Jesus has been well chronicled, as have his glorious teachings, acts, and divine sacrifice after his thirtieth birthday. But no one knows about the early life of the Son of God, the missing years—except Biff, the Messiah's best bud, who has been resurrected to tell the story in the divinely hilarious yet heartfelt work "reminiscent of Vonnegut and Douglas Adams" (*Philadelphia Inquirer*).

Truthfully, the story Biff has to tell is a miraculous one, filled with remarkable journeys, magic, healings, kung fu, corpse reanimations, demons, and hot babes. Even the considerable wiles and devotion of the Savior's pal may not be enough to divert Joshua from his tragic destiny. But there's no one who loves Josh more—except maybe "Maggie," Mary of Magdala—and Biff isn't about to let his extraordinary pal suffer and ascend without a fight.

THE LUST LIZARD OF MELANCHOLY COVE

The town psychiatrist has decided to switch everybody in Pine Cove, California, from their normal antidepressants to placebos, so naturally—well, to be accurate, artificially—business is booming at the local blues bar. Trouble is, those lonely slide-guitar notes have also attracted a colossal sea beast named Steve with, shall we say, a thing for explosive oil tanker trucks. Suddenly, morose Pine Cove turns libidinous and is hit by a mysterious crime wave, and a beleaguered constable has to fight off his own gonzo appetites to find out what's wrong and what, if anything, to do about it.

Take a wonderfully crazed excursion into the demented heart of a tropical paradise—a world of cargo cults, cannibals, mad scientists, ninjas, and talking fruit bats. Our bumbling hero is Tucker Case, a hopeless geek trapped in a cool guy's body, who makes a living as a pilot for the Mary Jean Cosmetics Corporation. But when he demolishes his boss's pink plane during a drunken airborne liaison, Tuck must run for his life from Mary Jean's goons. Now there's only one employment opportunity left for him: piloting shady secret missions for an unscrupulous medical missionary and a sexy blond high priestess on the remotest of Micronesian hells. Here is a brazen, ingenious, irreverent, and wickedly funny novel from a modern master of the outrageous.

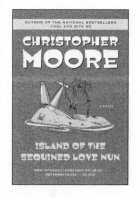

BLOODSUCKING FIENDS

Jody never asked to become a vampyre. But when she wakes up under an alley Dumpster with a badly burned arm, an aching neck, superhuman strength, and a distinctly Nosferatuan thirst, she realizes the decision has been made for her.

Making the transition from the nine-to-five grind to an eternity of nocturnal prowlings is going to take some doing, however, and that's where C Thomas Flood fits in. A would-be Kerouac from Incontinence, Indiana, Tommy, (to his friends) is biding his time night-clerking and frozen-turkey bowling in a San Francisco Safeway. But all that changes when a beautiful undead redhead walks through the door . . . and proceeds to rock Tommy's life—and afterlife—in ways he never imagined possible.

COYOTE BLUE

Sam Hunter has spent twenty years escaping his past. Now it has caught up to him in the weirdest of all possible ways.

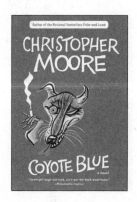

As a boy growing up in Montana, he was Samson Hunts Alone—until a deadly misunderstanding with the law forced him to flee the Crow reservation at age fifteen. Today he is a successful Santa Barbara insurance salesman with a Mercedes, a condo, and a hollow, invented life. Then one day, shortly after his thirty-fifth birthday, destiny offers Samuel Hunter the dangerous gift of love in the exquisite form of Calliope Kincaid—and a curse in the unheralded appearance of an ancient Indian god by the name of Coyote. Coyote, the trickster, has arrived to transform tranquility into chaos, to reawaken the mystical storyteller within Sam . . . and to seriously screw up his existence in the process.

Read More Christopher Moore *(continued)*

PRACTICAL DEMONKEEPING

In Christopher Moore's ingenious debut novel, we meet one of the most memorably mismatched pairs in the annals of literature. The good-looking one is one-hundred-year-old ex-seminarian and "roads" scholar Travis O'Hearn. The green one is Catch, a demon with a nasty habit of eating most of the people he meets. Behind the fake Tudor façade of Pine Cove, California, Catch sees a four-star buffet. Travis, on the other hand, thinks he sees a way of ridding himself of his toothy traveling companion. The winos, neo-pagans, and deadbeat Lotharios of Pine Cove, meanwhile, have other ideas. And none of them is quite prepared when all hell breaks loose.

Don't miss the next book by your favorite author. Sign up now for AuthorTracker by visiting www.AuthorTracker.com.